PIRATE:
BUCCANEER

TIM SEVERIN, explorer, filmmaker and lecturer,
has retraced the storied journeys of Saint Brendan the
Navigator, Sindbad the Sailor, Jason and the Argonauts, Ulysses,
Genghis Khan and Robinson Crusoe. His books about these
expeditions are classics of exploration and travel.

He made his historical fiction debut with the hugely successful
Viking series, followed by the Pirate and Saxon series.

Visit Tim's website to find out more
about his books and expeditions:
www.timseverin.net

Follow Tim on Facebook:
Facebook.com/TimSeverinAuthor

TIM SEVERIN

PIRATE

VOLUME TWO
BUCCANEER

PAN BOOKS

First published 2008 by Macmillan

This edition published 2015 by Pan Books
an imprint of Pan Macmillan, a division of Macmillan Publishers Limited
Pan Macmillan, 20 New Wharf Road, London N1 9RR
Basingstoke and Oxford
Associated companies throughout the world
www.panmacmillan.com

ISBN 978-1-4472-7745-3

1 3 5 7 9 8 6 4 2

A CIP catalogue record for this book is available from the British Library.

Map artwork by Neil Gower
Typeset by Ellipsis Digital Limited, Glasgow
Printed and bound by CPI Group (UK) Ltd, Croydon, CR0 4YY

Visit *www.panmacmillan.com* to read more about all our books
and to buy them. You will also find features, author interviews and
news of any author events, and you can sign up for e-newsletters
so that you're always first to hear about our new releases.

In 1679 the Caribbean was a dangerous and lawless sea. Jamaica, Hispaniola and the arc of islands known as the 'Caribees' were variously claimed by rival nations — notably France and England. The opposite shore, the 'Main' or continental coast, was jealously guarded by Spain as the vulnerable frontier of her vast land empire in the Americas. Smuggling was rife. For years the island governments had made up for a lack of men and ships by deploying irregular local forces, which operated as little more than licensed brigands. They had acquired a taste for plunder, and — though officially the region was now at peace — these soldiers and sailors of fortune were prepared to attack any easy and lucrative target.

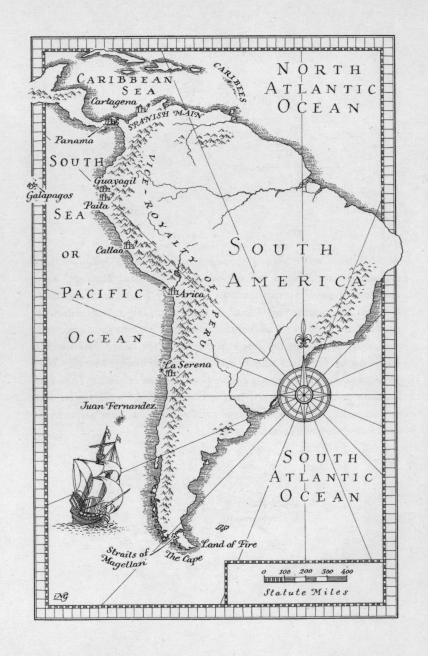

NORTH ATLANTIC OCEAN

CARIBBEAN SEA

CARIBBEES

Cartagena

SPANISH MAIN

Panama

SOUTH

Galapagos

Guayaqil

Paita

SEA

Callao

OR

VICE-ROYALTY OF PERU

PACIFIC

Arica

OCEAN

SOUTH AMERICA

La Serena

Juan Fernandez

SOUTH ATLANTIC OCEAN

Land of Fire

Straits of Magellan

The Cape

NG

0 100 200 300 400

Statute Miles

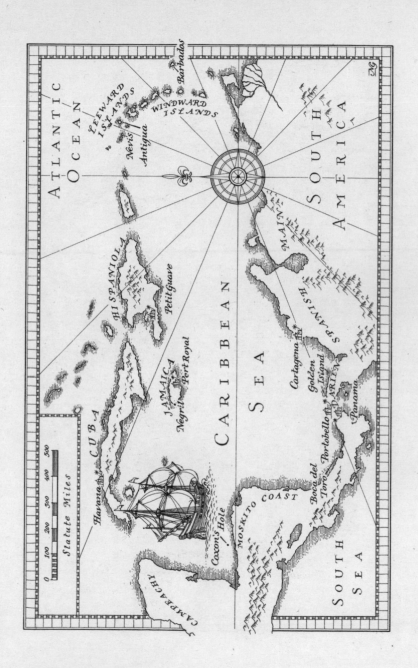

ONE

HECTOR LYNCH leaned back and braced himself against the sloop's mast. It was hard to hold the little telescope steady against the rhythmic rolling of the Caribbean swells, and the image in the lens was blurred and wavering. He was trying to identify the flag at the stern of a vessel which had appeared on the horizon at first light, and was now some three miles to windward. But the wind was blowing the stranger's flag sideways, directly towards him, so that it was difficult to see against the bright sunshine sparkling off the waves on a late-December morning. Hector thought he saw a flicker of blue and white and some sort of cross, but he could not be sure.

'What do you make of her?' he asked Dan, offering the spyglass to his companion. He had first met Dan on the Barbary coast two years earlier when both had been incarcerated in the slave barracks of Algiers, and Hector had developed a profound respect for Dan's common sense. The two men were much the same age – Hector was a few months short of his twentieth birthday – and they had formed a close friendship.

'No way of telling,' said Dan, ignoring the telescope. A Miskito Indian from the coast of Central America he, like many of his countrymen, had remarkably keen eyesight. 'She has the legs of us. She could be French or English, or maybe from the English colonies to the north. We're too far from the Main for her to be a Spaniard. Perhaps Benjamin can say.'

Hector turned to the third member of their small crew. Benjamin was a Laptot, a freed black slave who had worked in the ports of the West African coast before volunteering to join their vessel for the voyage across the Atlantic and into the Caribbean.

'Any suggestions?' he asked.

Benjamin only shook his head. Hector was unsure what to do. His companions had chosen him to command their little vessel, but this was his first major ocean voyage. Two months ago they had acquired their ship when they had found her stranded halfway up a West African river, her captain and officers dead of fever, and manned only by Benjamin and another Laptot. According to the ship's papers she was the *L'Arc-de-Ciel*, registered in La Rochelle, and the broad empty shelves lining her hold indicated that she was a small slave ship which had not yet taken on her human cargo.

Hector wiped the telescope's lens with a strip of clean cotton rag torn from his shirt, and was about to take another look at the stranger's flag, when there was the sound of a cannon shot. The noise carried clearly downwind, and he saw a black puff of gun smoke from the sloop's deck.

'That's to attract our attention. They want to talk with us,' said Benjamin.

Hector stared again at the sloop. It was obvious that she was closing rapidly, and he could see some sort of activity on her stern deck. A small group of men had clustered there.

'We should show them a flag,' Benjamin suggested.

Hector hurried down to the dead captain's cabin. He knew there was a canvas bag tucked away discreetly in a locker behind the bunk. Pulling open the bag, he tipped out its contents on the cabin floor. There were some items of dirty linen and, beneath them, several large rectangles of coloured cloth.

One had a red cross stitched on a white ground, which he recognised as the flag worn by the English ships that had occasionally visited the little Irish fishing port where he had spent his summers as a child. Another was a blue flag with a white cross. In the centre of the cross was a shield bearing three golden fleurs-de-lys. That flag too he recognised. It had flown on the merchant ships of France when he and Dan had been prisoner-oarsmen at the royal galley base in Marseilles. The third flag he did not know. It also displayed a red cross on a white background, but this time the arms of the cross ran diagonally to each corner of the flag, and the edges of the arms of the cross were deliberately ragged. They looked like branches cut from a shrub after the shoots had been trimmed away. It seemed that the deceased captain of *L'Arc-de-Ciel* had been prepared to fly whichever nation's flag suited the occasion.

Hector returned on deck, all three flags under his arm in an untidy bundle. 'Well, which one is it to be?' he asked. Again he glanced across at the unknown vessel. In the short interval he had been below decks it had come much closer. Well within cannon shot.

'Why not try King Louis's rag,' proposed Jacques Bourdon. In his mid-thirties Jacques was an ex-galerien, a thief condemned to the oar for life by a French court and who had 'GAL' branded on his cheek to prove it. He, together with the second Laptot, made up their five-man crew. 'That way, our colours will agree with our ship's papers,' he added, shading his eyes to scrutinise the approaching sloop. 'Besides . . . if you look there, she's flying the French flag as well.'

Hector and his companions waited for the stranger to come closer. They could see someone at her rail waving his arms. He was pointing at their sails and gesturing that they should be lowered. Too late, Hector felt a prickle of suspicion.

'Dan,' he asked quietly, 'any chance that we can get away from her?'

'No chance at all,' Dan answered without hesitation. 'She's a ketch and carries more sail than us. Best heave to and see what they want.'

A moment later Bourdon was helping the two Laptots loose the sheets and lower the sails so that *L'Arc-de-Ciel* gradually slowed to a halt, and lay gently rocking on the sea.

The approaching ketch altered course to come alongside. There were eight cannon on her single deck. Then, without warning, the little group on her stern deck parted to reveal someone hauling briskly on a halyard. A ball of cloth was being pulled aloft. A puff of wind caught it and the folds of cloth shook out, revealing a new flag. It carried no marks, but was a plain red sheet.

Jacques Bourdon swore. 'Shit! The jolie rouge. We should have guessed.'

Startled, Hector looked at him. 'The jolie rouge,' Bourdon grunted. 'The flag of the flibustiers, how do you call them – privateers? It's their mark. I shared a Paris prison cell with one of them once, and a right stinking bastard he was. Smelled worse than the rest of us gaolbirds all put together. When I complained, he told me that in the Caribees he had once gone two years without a proper wash. Claimed to have dressed in a suit of untreated cattle skins.'

'You mean he was a buccaneer,' Dan corrected him. The Miskito seemed unworried by the sight of the red flag.

'Are they dangerous?' Hector wanted to know.

'Depends what sort of mood they're in,' replied Dan quietly. 'They'll be interested in our cargo, if there's anything they can steal and sell. They'll not harm us if we cooperate.'

There was a clatter and slap of canvas as the strangers' vessel came up into the wind. Her helmsman must have carried out the manoeuvre many times and was obviously an expert for he deftly laid the ketch alongside the smaller *L'Arc-de-Ciel*. Hector counted at least forty men aboard, an uncouth assembly of all ages and shapes, most of them heavily bearded and deeply tanned. Many were bare-chested and wore only loose cotton drawers. But others had chosen a ragbag of clothes that ranged from soiled lawn shirts and canvas breeches to seaman's smocks and broadcloth coats with wide skirts and braided cuffs. A few, like Jacques's former cell mate, were dressed in jerkins and leggings of untanned cattle skin. Those who were not bare-headed displayed an equally wide range of hats. There were brightly coloured head cloths, sailor's bonnets, tricornes, leather skull caps, and broad-brimmed hats of a vaguely military style. One man was even sporting a fur hat despite the blazing heat. A few hefted long muskets which, Hector was relieved to observe, were not being pointed at *L'Arc-de-Ciel*, nor were the deck guns manned. Dan had been right: the buccaneers were not unduly aggressive towards a ship's crew that obeyed their instructions. For the present the mob of ill-assorted strangers were doing no more than lining the rail of their vessel and looking appraisingly at *L'Arc-de-Ciel*.

The slightest thump as the hulls of the two vessels touched, and a moment later half a dozen of the buccaneers dropped down on *L'Arc-de-Ciel*'s deck. Two of them carried wide-mouthed blunderbusses. The last man to come aboard seemed to be their leader. Of middle age, he was short and plump, his close-cropped reddish hair turning grey, and he was dressed more formally than the others in buff-coloured breeches and stockings, with a purple waistcoat worn over a grubby white shirt. Unlike his fellows who preferred knives and cutlasses, he had a rapier hanging from a shabby baldrick. He was also the only boarder wearing shoes. The heels clumped on the wooden deck as he strode purposefully to where Dan and Hector were standing. 'Summon your captain,' he announced. 'Tell him that Captain John Coxon wishes to speak with him.'

Closer up, Captain Coxon's face, which at first sight had seemed chubby and genial, had a hard set to it. He bit off his words when he spoke and the corners of his mouth turned down, producing a slight sneer. Hector judged that Captain Coxon was not a man to be trifled with.

'I am acting as the captain,' he replied.

Coxon glanced at the young man in surprise. 'What happened to your predecessor?' he demanded bluntly.

'I believe he died of fever.'

'When and where was that?'

'About three months ago, maybe more. On the river Wadnil, in West Africa.'

'I know where the Wadnil is,' Coxon snapped irritably. 'Have you any proof, and who brought this ship across? Who's your navigator?'

'I did the navigating,' Hector answered quietly.

Again the look of surprise, followed by a disbelieving twist of the mouth.

'I need to see your ship's papers.'

'They're in the captain's cabin.'

Coxon nodded to one of his men who promptly disappeared below deck. As he waited, the captain slipped his hand inside his shirt front and scratched at his chest. He seemed to be suffering from some sort of skin irritation. Hector noticed several angry red blotches on the buccaneer captain's neck, just above the shirt collar. Coxon gazed around at *L'Arc-de-Ciel* and her depleted crew. 'Is this all your men?' he demanded. 'What happened to the others?'

'There are no others,' Hector replied. 'We had to sail shorthanded, just the five of us. It was enough. The weather was kind.'

Coxon's man came out from the cabin door. He was holding a sheaf of documents and the roll of charts that Hector had found aboard when he, Dan and Bourdon had first set foot on *L'Arc-de-Ciel*. Coxon took the papers and stood silently for a few moments as he read through them while absent-mindedly scratching the back of his neck. Abruptly he looked up at

Hector, then thrust one of the charts towards him. 'If you're a navigator, then tell me where we are.'

Hector looked down at the chart. It was poorly drawn, and its scale was inadequate. The entire Caribbean was shown on a single sheet and there were several gaps or smudges on the surrounding coastline. He placed his finger about two-thirds across the parchment, and said, 'About here. At noon yesterday I calculated our latitude by backstaff, but I am unsure of our westing. Twelve days ago we saw a high island to the north of us, which I took to be one of the windward Caribees. Since then we could have run perhaps a thousand miles.'

Coxon stared at him bleakly. 'And why would you want to go due west?'

'To try to reach the Miskito coast. That is where we are headed. Dan here is from that country, and wishes to get home.'

The buccaneer captain, after a brief glance towards Dan, looked thoughtful. 'What about your cargo?'

'There is no cargo. We came aboard the ship before she had loaded.'

Coxon gave another jerk of his head, and two of his crew opened up a hatch and clambered down into the hold. Moments later, they reappeared and one of them said 'Nothing. She's empty.'

Hector sensed the captain's disappointment. Coxon's mood was changing. He was becoming annoyed. Abruptly he took a step towards Jacques Bourdon who was loitering near the mast. 'You there with the brand on your cheek!' Coxon snapped. 'You've been in the King's galleys, haven't you? What was your crime?'

'Being caught,' Jacques replied sourly.

'You're French, aren't you?' A ghost of a smile passed across Coxon's face.

'From Paris.'

Coxon turned back towards Hector and Dan. He still had the sheaf of papers in his hand.

'I'm seizing this ship,' he announced. 'On suspicion that the vessel has been stolen from her rightful owners, and that the crew has murdered her captain and officers.'

'That's absurd,' Hector burst out. 'The captain and his officers were all dead by the time we came aboard.'

'You have nothing to prove it. No certificate of death, no documents for transfer of ownership.' It was evident that Coxon was grimly satisfied with himself.

'How could we have obtained such papers?' Hector was getting more angry by the minute. 'The bodies would have been put overboard to try to stop the contagion, and there were no authorities to go to. As I said, the vessel was halfway up an African river, and there were only native chiefs in the region.'

'Then you should have stopped at the first trading post on the coast, sought out the authorities, and registered the events,' countered Coxon. 'Instead you set sail directly across to the Caribees. It is my duty to regularise the matter.'

'You have no authority to take this ship,' Hector insisted.

Coxon treated him to a thin smile. 'Yes I do. I have the authority of the Governor of Petit Guave, whose commission I carry on behalf of the kingdom of France. This vessel is French. There is a branded convict aboard, a subject of the French king. The ship's papers are not in order, and there is no proof of how the captain died. He could have been killed, and the cargo sold off.'

'So what do you intend to do?' Hector asked, choking down his anger. He should have realised that from the start Coxon had been trying to find an excuse to seize the vessel. Coxon and his men were nothing more than licensed sea brigands.

'This vessel and those found on her will be taken to Petit Guave by a prize crew. There the vessel will be sold and you and your crew will be tried for murder and piracy. If found guilty the court will decide your punishment.'

Unexpectedly, Dan spoke up, his voice grave. 'If you or

your court mistreat us, you will have to answer to my people. My father is one of the old men council of the Miskito.'

Dan's words seemed to have carried some weight because Coxon paused for a moment before replying. 'If it is true that your father is of the Miskito council then the court will take that into account. The authorities in Petit Guave would not wish to anger the Miskito. As for the rest of you, you will stand trial.'

Coxon again slipped his hand inside his shirt front and scratched at his chest. Hector wondered if the itching was what made the man so irritable. 'I need to know your name,' the buccaneer said to Hector.

'My name is Hector Lynch.' The hand stopped scratching. Then Coxon said slowly, 'Any relation to Sir Thomas Lynch?'

There was a wariness in the man's tone. His question hung in the air. Hector had no idea who Sir Thomas Lynch was, but clearly he was someone well known to Coxon. Hector also had the distinct impression that Sir Thomas Lynch was a person whom the captain respected, perhaps even feared. Alert to the subtle change in the buccaneer's manner, Hector seized the opportunity.

'Sir Thomas Lynch is my uncle,' he said unblushingly. Then, to increase the effect of the lie, he added, 'It was why I agreed with my companions that we sail for the Caribbean without delay. After we had brought Dan to the Miskito coast, I intended to find Sir Thomas.'

For an alarming moment Hector thought that he had gone too far, that he should have kept the lie simple. Coxon was staring at him with narrowed eyes. 'Sir Thomas is not in the Caribees at this time. His estates are being managed by his family. You didn't know?'

Hector recovered himself. 'I was in Africa for some months and out of touch. I received little news from home.'

Coxon pursed his lips as he thought over Hector's statement.

Whatever Sir Thomas Lynch meant to the buccaneer, the young man could see that it was enough to make their captor reconsider his plans.

'Then I will make sure that you are united with your family,' the buccaneer said at last. 'Your companions will stay aboard this ship while she is taken to Petit Guave, and I will send a note to the authorities there that they are associates of Sir Thomas's nephew. It may stand in their favour. Meanwhile you can accompany me to Jamaica – I was already on my way there.'

Hector's mind raced as he searched Coxon's statement for clues as to the identity of his supposed uncle. Sir Thomas Lynch had estates on Jamaica, therefore he must be a man of substance. It was reasonable to guess that he was a wealthy planter, a man who had friends in government. The opulence and political power of the West Indian plantation owners was well known. Yet at the same time Hector sensed something disquieting in Coxon's manner. There was a hint that whatever the buccaneer captain was proposing was not entirely to Hector's advantage.

Belatedly it occurred to Hector that he should put in a good word for the Laptots who had proved their worth on the trans-Atlantic voyage.

'If anyone is to be put on trial in Petit Guave, captain,' he told Coxon, 'it should not be either Benjamin here, nor his companion. They stayed with the ship even when their previous captain had died of fever. They are loyal men.'

Coxon had resumed his scratching. He was raking the back of his neck with his nails. 'Mr Lynch, you need have no worries on that score,' he said. 'They will never be put on trial.'

'What will happen to them?'

Coxon brought his hand away from his collar, inspected the fingernails for traces of whatever had been causing the irritation, and wriggled his shoulder slightly to relieve the pressure of the shirt on his skin.

'As soon as they are brought to Petit Guave, they will be sold. You say they are loyal. That should make them excellent slaves.'

He looked straight at Hector as if to challenge the young man into raising an objection. 'I believe your uncle employs more than sixty Africans on his own Jamaican plantations. I am sure he would approve.'

At a loss for words, Hector could only stare back, trying to gauge the buccaneer's temper. What he saw discouraged hope. Captain Coxon's eyes reminded him of a reptile. They protruded slightly and the expression in them was utterly pitiless. Despite the balmy sunshine, Hector felt a chill seeping deep within him. He was not to allow himself to be deceived by the pleasantness of his surroundings, with the warm tropical breeze ruffling the brilliant sea, and the soft murmuring sound as the two ships were gently moving against one another, hull to hull. He and his companions had arrived where self-interest was sustained by cruelty and violence.

TWO

COXON's tatterdemalion company wasted little time in securing their prize. Within half an hour *L'Arc-de-Ciel* had been cast off and was bound for Petit Guave. Hector was left on the deck of the buccaneers' ketch wondering if he would ever see Dan, Jacques and the others again. As he watched the little sloop grow smaller in the distance, Hector was uncomfortably aware of Coxon standing not ten feet away and observing him closely.

'Your shipmates should reach Petit Guave in less than three days from now,' the buccaneer captain observed. 'If the authorities there believe their story, they'll have nothing to worry about. If not . . .' He gave a mirthless laugh.

Hector knew that Coxon was goading him, trying to get a reaction.

'Unusual, isn't it . . .' the captain went on and there was a hint of malice in his voice, 'that Sir Thomas Lynch's nephew should associate himself with a branded convict? How does that come about?'

'We were both shipwrecked on the Barbary coast, and had to team up if we were to save ourselves and get clear,' explained Hector. He tried to make his answer sound casual and unconcerned, though he was wracking his brains to think how he could learn more about his supposed relative, Sir Thomas

Lynch, without arousing Coxon's suspicion. Should the buccaneer discover he had been hoodwinked, any hope of reuniting
with his friends would be lost. It was best to turn the questioning back on his captor.

'You say you are bound for Jamaica. How long before we
get there?'

Coxon was not to be put off. 'You know nothing of the
island? Didn't your uncle speak of it?'

'I saw little of him when I was growing up. He was away
much of the time, tending to his estate' – that at least was a
safe guess.

'And where did your spend you childhood?' Coxon was
probing again.

Fortunately the interrogation was interrupted by a shout
from one of the lookouts at the masthead. He had seen another
sail on the horizon. Immediately, Coxon broke off his questioning and began bawling orders at his crew to set more sail and
take up the chase.

*

AMID ALL the activity Hector sauntered over to the freshwater
butt placed at the foot of the mainmast. It was only a few hours
to sunset yet the day was still uncomfortably hot, and a pretence
of thirst was an opportunity to move out of Coxon's earshot.

'What's Jamaica like?' he asked a sailor who was drinking
from the wooden dipper.

'Not what it was,' replied the man. He was a rough-looking
individual. The hand which held the pannikin lacked the top
joints of three fingers, and his nose had been badly broken and
set crooked. He smelled of stale sweat. 'Used to be a grog
shop at every corner, and harlots on parade in every street.
They'd stroll up and down in their petticoats and red caps, as
bold as you like, ready for all kinds of fun. And no questions
asked about where you got your silver.' The man belched, wiped
the back of his hand across his mouth, and handed Hector the

dipper. 'That changed when our Henry got his knighthood. Things went quiet, but it's all still there if you know what to look for, and hold your tongue afterwards.' He gave Hector a sly look. 'I reckon that even though he's Sir Henry now, he still looks after his own. His sort will never be satisfied, however much he's got.'

Another titled Jamaican, and a rich one, Hector thought to himself. He wondered who this Sir Henry might be, and if he had any dealings with his 'uncle'. He took a sip from the pannikin.

'Wouldn't mind getting a taste of those harlots myself,' he observed, hoping to strike a comradely note. 'We were more than six weeks at sea from Africa.'

'No whoring this cruise,' answered the sailor. 'Port Royal is where the strumpets wag their tails, and the captain stays clear of that port unless he's invited in. Nowadays he carries a Frenchy's commission.'

'From Petit Guave?'

'The deputy governor there gives them out already signed and the names left blank. You fill in what you want and then go a-hunting, just as long as you let him have a tenth of any takings. Used to be much the same in Jamaica until that bastard Lynch started interfering.'

Before Hector could ask what he meant, he heard Coxon's steps on the deck behind him, and the captain's voice snapped.

'Enough of that! You're speaking to Governor Lynch's nephew. He'll not wish to hear your opinions!'

The sailor glared at Hector. 'Nephew to Lynch, are you! If I'd known, I'd have pissed in the dipper before you drank from it,' and with that he turned and stalked away.

✳

HECTOR BROODED on the sailor's information throughout the two days and nights it took to reach Jamaica. The pursuit of the distant sail had been abandoned when it became clear that there was no hope of catching the prey. Each night the young man bedded down on a coil of rope near the sloop's bows, and by day he was left alone. Any buccaneer who came his way either ignored him or gave him a black look so he presumed that his alleged relationship to Lynch had become common knowledge. Coxon paid him no attention. When dawn broke on the third morning he was feeling stiff and tired and concerned for his own fate as he got to his feet and looked out over the bowsprit towards their landfall.

Straight ahead, Jamaica rose from the sea, high and rugged, the first rays of the sun striking patterns of vivid green and dark shadow across the folds and spurs of a mountain range which reared up a few miles inland. The ketch was heading into a sheltered bay where the land sloped down more gently to a beach of grey sand. There was no sign of a harbour though beyond the strand was a cluster of pale dots which Hector presumed were the roofs of huts or small houses. Otherwise the place was deserted. There was not even a fishing boat to be seen. Captain Coxon had made a discreet arrival.

Within moments of her anchor splashing into water so clear that the rippled sand of the sea floor could be seen four fathoms down, Coxon and Hector were being rowed ashore in the ship's cockboat. 'I'll be back in less than two days,' the buccaneer captain told the boat crew as they hauled up on the beach. 'No one to stray out of sight of the ship. Stay close at hand and be ready to set sail as soon as I return.' He turned to Hector. 'You come with me. It's a four-hour walk. And you can make yourself useful.' He removed the heavy coat he was wearing, and handed it to the younger man to carry. Hector was surprised to see the curls of a wig sticking out of one of its pockets. Underneath his coat Coxon was wearing an embroidered linen shirt with a ruffled front and lace at the cuffs. His stockings and breeches were clean and brushed and of fine quality, and he had changed into a new pair of shoes with silver buckles. Hector wondered at the reason for such elegant clothes.

'Where are we going?' he asked.

'To Llanrumney,' was the brusque reply.

Not daring to ask an explanation, Hector followed the buccaneer captain as he set off. After so many days at sea since leaving Africa, the ground tilted and swayed beneath the young man's feet, and until he found his land legs it was difficult to keep up with Coxon's brisk pace. At the back of the beach they skirted around a small hamlet of five or six wooden huts thatched with plantain leaves and occupied by families of blacks, usually a woman with several children. There were no menfolk to be seen and no one paid them a second glance. They came upon the start of a footpath which led inland, and very soon the hollow, open sounds of the sea had been replaced by the buzzing and chirping of the insects and birds in the dense vegetation on either side of the trail. The air was hot and humid, and in less than a mile Coxon's fine shirt was sticking to his back with sweat. At first the track kept to the bank of a small river but then it branched off to the left where the river was joined by a tributary stream, and here Hector saw his first native birds, a small flock of bright green parrots with yellow beaks which flew away with quick wing beats, chattering and scolding the intruders.

Coxon stopped to take a rest. 'When was the last time you saw your uncle?' he asked.

Hector thought quickly. 'Not since I was a boy. Sir Thomas is my father's oldest brother. My father, Stephen Lynch, died when I was sixteen and afterwards my mother moved away and kept in touch only with an occasional letter.' At least part of that statement was true, he thought to himself. Hector's father, of minor Anglo-Irish gentry, had died while Hector was in his teens, and his mother, originally from Galicia in Spain, could well have returned to her own people.

He did not know what had happened to her since he had been locked away on the Barbary coast. But one thing was sure: his father had never referred to anyone called Sir Thomas Lynch, and he was certain that Sir Thomas was nothing whatever to do with his family.

'Rumour has it that Sir Thomas is seeking to be reappointed as governor. Do you know anything about that?' said Coxon. He had begun scratching again, this time at his waistband.

'I haven't heard. I've been away from home too long to keep up with family news,' Hector reminded him.

'Well, even if he was already back on the island you wouldn't find him at Llanrumney . . .' — again the strange name. 'He and Sir Henry never saw eye to eye on anything.'

Hector seized his opportunity to learn more. 'Sir Henry . . . ? Whom do you mean?'

Coxon gave him a sharp glance. There was mistrust in his look. 'You've not heard of Sir Henry Morgan?'

Hector did not answer.

'I was with him when he captured Panama in seventy-one. We needed nearly two hundred mules to carry away what we took,' Coxon said. He sounded boastful. 'Panama silver bought him Llanrumney, though he fell out with your uncle who accused him of false accounting of the spoils. Had him sent as a prisoner for trial in England, but the old fox had powerful friends in London, and he's back here now as lieutenant governor.'

The buccaneer captain stooped down and removed a shoe. There was a patch of blood on the heel of his stocking. A blister must have burst.

'So it will be in your best interests to be discreet until we know his mood and what is our own situation,' he added darkly.

It was another several hours of hot and weary walking before Coxon announced that they were almost at their destination. By then the captain was limping badly, and they were making frequent stops so that he could attend to his oozing blisters. A journey he had predicted would last four hours had taken nearly six, and it was almost nightfall before they finally emerged from a patch of woodland and into an area of cultivation. The native vegetation had been cleared back here and, in its place, field after field had been laid out and thickly sewn with tall green plants like giant stalks of grass. It was Hector's first sight of a sugar plantation.

'There's Llanrumney,' said Coxon, nodding towards a substantial one-storey building situated on the far slope so that it looked out over the cane fields. Off to one side were various large sheds and outbuildings which Hector took to be workshops for the estate. 'Named it after his home place in Wales.'

They found their way along a cart track cut through the cane fields, seeing no one until they were close to the house. Coxon seemed cautious, almost furtive, as though he wished to conceal his arrival. Eventually a white man, apparently a servant for he was dressed in a simple livery of a red jacket and white pantaloons, stopped them. He looked at them doubtfully, the buccaneer captain in his sweat-stained garments, Hector barefoot and wearing the same loose cotton shirt and trousers he had worn aboard ship. 'Do you have invitations?' he asked.

'Tell your master that Captain John Coxon wishes to speak with him privately,' the buccaneer told him curtly.

'Privately will not be possible,' answered the servant, hesitantly. 'Today's his day for Christmas entertainment.'

'I have come a long way to see your master,' snapped Coxon. 'I'm an acquaintance of long standing. I need no invitation.'

The servant quailed before the testy edge to his visitor's voice. 'Sir Henry's guests have already arrived and they are in the main reception room. If you would wish to refresh yourself before meeting them, please follow me.'

Hector had been standing with the captain's coat over his arm. It was evident that he was thought to be some sort of attendant and was not included in the invitation into the house. 'I'll be introducing my companion to Sir Henry,' Coxon announced firmly.

The servant's glance took in Hector's workaday costume. 'Then if you'll allow, I'll have him given something more suitable to wear. Sir Henry's gathering includes many of the most important men on the island, and their ladies.'

They followed the man to a side entrance of the main building. Tethered in front of its long sheltered porch were a dozen or more horses, and off to one side stood a couple of light, two-wheeled open carriages.

The servant showed Coxon into a side room, telling him that water and towels would be brought. Then he led Hector to the rear of the building and into the servants' quarters.

'I took you for an indentured man like myself,' he apologised.

'What's that?'

The servant, evidently an under-steward, had opened a cupboard and was sorting through some clothing. He found a pair of breeches and turned to face Hector.

'Indentured?' he said, sounding surprised. 'It means pledged to serve your master in return for the cost of your passage out from England and your upkeep while you're here.'

'For how long?'

'I signed for ten years, and still have seven years left. Here, try these breeches on. They are about the right size.'

As Hector pulled on the garment, the under-steward managed to find a short waistcoat and a clean lawn shirt with a frilled neck and wristbands. 'Here, put these on too,' he said, 'and this broad leather belt. It'll hide any gaps. And here's a pair of shoes that should fit, and stockings too.' He stood back and looked Hector over. 'Not bad,' he commented.

'Whom do these clothes belong to?' Hector asked.

'A young fellow came out here from England a couple of years back. Was intending to become an overseer, but he caught a flux and died.' The servant gathered up Hector's old clothes and tossed them into a corner. 'Forgot to ask your name,' he said.

'Lynch, Hector Lynch.'

'No relation to Sir Thomas are you?'

Hector decided it was wiser to be vague. 'Not as far as I am aware.'

'Just as well. Sir Henry can't abide Sir Thomas . . . or his family for that matter.'

Hector saw his chance to learn more. 'Does Sir Thomas have a large family?'

'Big enough. Most of them live down near Port Royal. That's where they have their other properties.' He paused, and his next words came as a shock. 'But this being so near Christmas, Sir Henry has invited a few of them this evening. They came by carriage, a full day's journey. And one of them is quite a beauty.'

Hector could think of no escape as he was led back to where Coxon was waiting. The buccaneer captain had cleaned himself up and put on his wig. He looked more of a gentleman and less of a brigand. Taking Hector by the elbow, he led him aside and whispered harshly. 'Once we step into that room, you are to hold your tongue until I've found out Sir Henry's temper.'

The under-steward brought them before a pair of tall double doors. A buzz of conversation could be heard coming from the other side, and the strains of music, a couple of violins and a virginal by the sounds. As the servant was about to pull open both doors, Coxon stopped him. 'I can manage that myself,' he said. The buccaneer captain eased open one door and quietly stepped inside, pulling Hector behind him.

The room was thronged with guests. They were mostly men, but there was also a scattering of women, many using fans to lessen the stifling atmosphere. Scores of candles were adding to the lingering heat of the day, and although the windows stood open, the room was uncomfortably warm. Hector, who had seen the lavishly decorated salons of wealthy Barbary merchants, was surprised by how plainly this reception room was furnished. Although it was some thirty paces long, its plaster walls were bare except for one or two indifferent paintings, and there were no carpets to cover the hardwood floor. The room had a raw, unfinished look as though the owner, having constructed it, had no further interest in making it comfortable or attractive. Then he saw the sideboard. It must have been forty feet in length. It was covered from end to end with refreshments for the guests. There were heaps of oranges, pomegranates, limes, grapes and several varieties of luscious-looking fruit unknown to Hector, as well as massed arrangements of coloured jellies and sugar cakes, rank upon rank of wine bottles, and several large basins of some sort of punch. But it was not the array of exotic food which caught his eye. Every one of the platters, salvers and bowls holding the food and drink, as well as the ladles, tongs and serving implements beside them, appeared to be of solid silver, and if they were not of silver, they were made of gold. It was a breathtakingly vulgar display of bullion.

No one in the gossiping throng had noticed their entrance. Hector felt Coxon's hand on his elbow. 'Stay here until I come to fetch you, and remember what I said . . . not a word to anyone until I have spoken with Sir Henry.' Hector watched the captain make his way discreetly through the assembly of guests. He was heading towards a group of men in the centre of the gathering. They were standing talking to one another, and it was evident from the space that had been left clear around them, the richness of their dress and their self-confident manner that they were the host and his chief guests. Among them was a tall, thin man with a sallow, almost sickly complexion, dressed in a plum-coloured velvet gown with gold trimming and a full-bottomed wig. He was talking to a fat, red-faced colleague in vaguely military attire who had several decorations pinned to his chest and wore a broad sash of blue silk. All the men in the group were holding glasses, and from their manner Hector guessed they had been drinking heavily. As he watched, Coxon reached the little group and, sidling round until he was next to the taller man, whispered something in his ear. His listener turned and, on seeing Coxon, an expression of irritation crossed his face. He was either annoyed at being interrupted or angered by the sight of Coxon. But the buccaneer stood his ground, and was explaining something, speaking rapidly, making some sort of point. When he stopped, the tall man nodded, turned and looked in Hector's direction. It was clear that whatever Coxon had been saying, it concerned Hector.

Coxon pushed his way back to where Hector waited. The buccaneer was flushed and excited, perspiring heavily under his wig, the sore patches on his neck prominent against the paler skin. 'Sir Henry will see you,' he said. 'Look smart now and follow me.' He turned and began to lead Hector into the centre of the room.

By now the little exchange had attracted the attention of several guests. Curious glances followed the newcomers' progress, and a path opened up for them as they walked forward. Hector felt himself light-headed as well as awkward in his borrowed clothes. With chilling certainty he knew that his deception was about to be exposed.

By the time the two men had reached the centre of the room, the babble of conversation was lessening. A hush had spread among the nearest spectators. The late arrival of two unfamiliar faces must have been some sort of diversion, for people were craning their necks to see what was happening. Coxon came to a halt before the taller man, bowed, and announced with a flourish:

'Sir Henry, allow me to introduce to you a young man that I took from a merchant ship recently. The vessel was stolen from its rightful owners and was in the hands of the thieves.

This is the young man's first visit to our island, but he comes with excellent connections. May I introduce Hector Lynch, nephew to our esteemed former governor Sir Thomas Lynch who, no doubt, will be in your debt for the rescue.'

The tall man in the plum-coloured coat turned to face Hector, who found himself looking into the pale eyes of Sir Henry Morgan, lieutenant governor of Jamaica.

'Lynch, did you say?' Sir Henry's voice was surprisingly thin and high pitched. He spoke with a slight slur, and Hector realised that the lieutenant governor was tipsy. He also looked very unhealthy. The whites of his eyes had a yellowish tinge, and though he must have been in his late forties, he did not carry his years well. Everything about him was gaunt – his face, shoulders and legs, yet his belly was bloated and jutted out unnaturally, straining the lower buttons of his coat. Hector wondered if Morgan was suffering from some sort of dropsy, or perhaps the effects of regular heavy drinking. But the eyes that looked him over were bright with intelligence, and speculative.

'Byndloss, did you hear that?' Morgan was speaking to his military-looking colleague, evidently a drinking companion to judge by the familiar tone. 'This young fellow is Sir Thomas's nephew. We must make him welcome to Llanrumney.'

'Didn't know Sir Thomas had any more nephews,' grunted Byndloss rudely. He too was drunk. His complexion was on its way to matching his red uniform jacket. Hector sensed a stir of unease from Coxon beside him.

'A junior branch of the family,' the buccaneer captain explained swiftly. His tone was obsequious. 'His father, Stephen, is the youngest of Sir Thomas's brothers.'

'Then how come he's not been out to visit us before? Some Lynches must think themselves too grand for us?' observed Byndloss petulantly. He took another drink from his glass, spilling a few drops down his chin.

'Don't be so prickly,' Sir Henry Morgan chided his friend.

'This is the Christmas season, a time to put aside our differences, and of course for families to get together.' Turning to Hector, who had still not said a word, he added in that high voice, 'Your family will be delighted by your arrival. I am pleased that it should have taken place under my roof.' From his greater height he looked out over his guests, and called out, 'Robert Lynch, where are you? Come and meet your cousin Hector!'

Hector could only stand helplessly, paralysed by the certain knowledge that his deception was about to be exposed in public.

There was a stir at the back of the gathering and a young man shouldered his way forward through the crowd of onlookers. Hector saw that Robert Lynch was about his own age, a round-headed, pleasant-looking fellow dressed fashionably in a brocade vest tied with a buckled girdle. His freckles and round grey-blue eyes gave him a remarkably boyish look.

'My cousin Hector, did you say?' Robert Lynch sounded eager, yet puzzled.

He stepped into the circle surrounding his host, and looked closely at Hector. He seemed baffled.

'Yes, yes. Your uncle Stephen's son . . . he landed unexpectedly just this morning, with Captain Coxon.' Morgan answered, and turning to Hector asked, 'Where did you say you are from?'

For the first time at that gathering, Hector spoke. His false identity was about to be exposed, and he knew he could no longer maintain the deception. 'There's a misunderstanding . . .' he croaked. His throat was dry from nerves.

Morgan checked, his eyes narrowed and he was about to speak, when Robert Lynch announced in astonishment, 'But I don't have an uncle. Two aunts, yes, but no Uncle Stephen. No one ever said anything about a cousin Hector.'

For a long, unpleasant moment, Sir Henry Morgan said nothing. He stared at Hector, then switched his gaze to Coxon, who was rooted to the spot. Hector and all those in earshot tensed, awaiting an outburst of rage. Instead Morgan let loose a sudden, ringing neigh of laughter. 'Captain Coxon, you've been taken in! You've swallowed the gudgeon, every last morsel. Sir Thomas's nephew indeed!' Beside him, Byndloss let out a guffaw and, waving his glass, added, 'Are you sure that he's not Sir Thomas's son and heir?'

A wave of sycophantic laughter washed around them as the crowd of onlookers joined in the mirth.

Coxon flushed crimson with embarrassment. He clenched his hands by his side and swung to glare straight at Hector. For an instant the young man thought that the buccaneer, his face working with anger, was about to strike him, but Coxon only snarled, 'You will regret this, you little swine!' and turned on his heel. Then he stalked out of the room, followed by the hoots of laughter, and someone calling out over the heads of the crowd, 'He's *Sir* Hector, you know.'

Like a good host, Morgan turned back to his friends who were still smirking at Coxon's humiliation, and they took up their former conversation. Pointedly, Hector was ignored. Awkwardly he stood there in his borrowed clothes, uncertain what he should do next. He feared to follow Coxon in case the buccaneer captain might be waiting for him outside the door.

While he stood there hesitating, a sharp rap on his elbow made him jump, and a female voice said playfully, 'I would very much like to meet my new cousin.' He turned to find himself looking into the mischievous smile of a young woman in a light evening cloak of turquoise satin. She was a couple of inches shorter than himself, and no more than seventeen years old. Yet the shape of her body was accentuated by a tight bodice whose low neckline was only partially covered by a lace-trimmed gorget to reveal the curves of full womanhood. Involuntarily Hector found himself reflecting that women ripened in the Jamaican climate as early and seductively as the island's exotic fruit. Her dark brown hair was arranged so that it tumbled down to her shoulders, but she had left a fringe of curls to frame the wide-set blue eyes which now regarded him with such amusement. In her hand was the fan which she had used to attract his attention. 'I am Susanna Lynch, Robert's sister,' she told him in a light, attractive voice. 'It's not often that a relation appears from nowhere.'

Hector found himself blushing. 'I'm sorry,' he began, 'I meant no disrespect. Lynch truly is my family name. The deception was forced upon me to protect myself and my friends . . .'

She interrupted him with a quick grimace. 'I don't doubt it. Captain Coxon has a reputation as a ruthless man, always eager to advance himself. In him you have made a dangerous enemy. Someone you had best avoid in future.'

'I know almost nothing about him,' Hector confessed.

'He's a ruffian. He used to consort with Henry Morgan in the days when harrying the Spanish was permitted. But that's against government policy now, largely thanks to the efforts of our "uncle".' Here she smiled teasingly. 'Men like Coxon still hang around on the fringes, waiting to snap up anything that has been overlooked. There are plenty who would help him.'

'I gather that sometimes includes Sir Henry.'

She gave him a sharp glance. 'You are quick on the uptake. I heard Morgan say that you only landed this morning in Jamaica, yet you've already sniffed out a few truths.'

'Someone told me that Sir Henry Morgan's preferences still incline towards his former buccaneering friends.'

'Indeed they do,' Susanna said casually. Hector had to admire the young woman's self-confidence, for she did not bother to drop her voice. 'Henry Morgan is still as gold-hungry as ever. But he is now on the governing council and a very powerful man. He's someone else you should be wary of.'

With every moment Hector found himself appreciating much more than Susanna Lynch's self-confidence. The way she stood before him, with her eyes boldly seeking his, left no doubt that she was deliberately calling for his attention. She was a very alluring young lady, and knew it. With a pang, Hector realised that he had never before had an opportunity to engage closely with a young woman so obviously on display. He realised that he was succumbing to her good looks and, without wishing to, falling under the spell of her provocation.

'Then I'm at a loss as to what I should do next,' he admitted. 'I feel stranded. I don't know anyone in Jamaica.'

She gave him a calculating look, though there was softness in it. 'No one at all?'

'My friends were despatched to the French colony at Petit Guave, and I need to try to join them.'

'One thing is for certain. You should get away from Llanrumney as soon as possible. You'll get no sympathy in this place.' She thought for a moment, then treated him to a quick smile which made his heart race. 'Tomorrow Robert and I return home – we live on the opposite side of the island, near Spanish Town, not far from Port Royal. You can travel with us, and from there continue to Port Royal itself. That's the best place to find news of your friends, or even a ship that will take you to rejoin them.'

THREE

✳

THAT NIGHT Hector found it almost impossible to get to sleep. The friendly under-steward arranged a cot for him in the servants' quarters, but keen yearnings for Susanna Lynch kept the young man awake for several hours, and when he opened his eyes soon after dawn, her image was the first thing in his mind. Dressing hurriedly, he went to find someone who might be able to tell him where she could be found. To his delight the under-steward told him that the carriage belonging to Susanna Lynch was already prepared. She and her brother Robert were to set out for home shortly, and word had been sent that Hector was to travel with them.

'Will they breakfast with Sir Henry first?' he asked, impatient for his first sight of Susanna that day. The indentured man gave a world-weary laugh. .

'Sir Henry and his cronies were up drinking until well past midnight. My master will not be out of his bed much before noon.'

'What about Captain Coxon? Where's he?' Hector asked. He had a sudden, vivid recollection of the furious expression on the buccaneer's face as he had left the party.

'Disappeared last night, after you made such a fool of him. I suppose he went back to his ship with his tail between his legs.' The servant grinned. 'He's an arrogant blackguard. Likes to let everyone know what a hard man he is. Can't say I would want to be in your shoes if he ever gets his hands on you.'

'Someone else said much the same to me last night,' admitted Hector, 'and talking about shoes, shouldn't I be returning these borrowed clothes to you?'

'You can keep them.'

'Won't your master find out?'

'I doubt it. The rum has been rotting his brain for a long time now. When he was campaigning against the Spaniards some years back, he and his friends blew themselves up. They were sitting carousing in the wardroom of a King's ship, and some drunken fool dropped his lighted pipe into a scatter of loose gunpowder on the floor. The explosion split the vessel into matchwood. Sir Henry was only saved because he was sitting at the far side of the table.'

Thanking the man for his kindness, Hector made his way outside to find that one of the carriages he had seen the previous evening was already standing before the front door of the main house. 'Is this the Lynches' carriage?' he asked the driver who, by the look of him, was another indentured servant. But before the man could answer, Susanna and her brother stepped out on the porch. Suddenly Hector felt his stomach go hollow. Susanna had chosen to wear a loose gown of fine cotton, dark pink, with short sleeves. It was open at the front to reveal a bodice laced with ribbon, and her grey skirt was looped up at one side to show a matching satin petticoat. Her hair was held back by a ribbon embroidered with roses. She looked ravishing.

Her brother greeted Hector cheerfully. 'You caused quite a stir yesterday evening! I'm told that the fellow you discomforted is an utter scoundrel, and well deserved to be put in his place. Always creeping about and trying to ingratiate himself. My sister tells me that your family name really is Lynch.'

'It's a happy coincidence which I was obliged to turn in my favour.'

'Well, no harm done. Susanna tells me that you will travel with us, so I've arranged an extra horse for you.'

To his chagrin Hector saw that a groom had appeared from behind the house, leading two saddle horses. But Susanna came to his rescue. 'Robert, you are not to deprive me of Mr Lynch's company. It will make the journey pass more agreeably if he joins me in the carriage, at least for the first few hours.'

'As you please, Susanna. His horse can be attached to the carriage until needed,' answered her brother meekly, and Hector could see that Robert usually gave way to his sister. Susanna Lynch climbed into the carriage and took her seat. 'Come, sit beside me, Hector. After all, we are cousins,' she said invitingly, and gave a throaty chuckle which sent Hector's mind reeling.

The road was very bad, little more than a dirt track which, after passing a neighbouring plantation, climbed inland by a series of tight curves on to a spur ridge covered with dense forest. On either side grew immense trees, mostly mahogany and cedar, smothered with rope-like lianas and other climbing plants. Some showed the pale flowers of convolvuli, others hung from the branches in shaggy grey beards. Here and there was the bright crimson or yellow blossom of an orchid. A profusion of ferns and canes sprouted between the massive tree trunks, forming impenetrable thickets of greenery above which hovered butterflies of extraordinary shapes and colours, dark blue, lemon yellow and black. In the background was the constant chatter and calls of unseen birds, ranging from a flute-like whistle to the harsh cawing of crows. All this Hector barely noticed. For him the first few hours of the journey passed in a daze. He was acutely aware of the nearness of Susanna, her warmth and softness, and the jolting of the carriage which occasionally brought her knee in contact with his, a contact which, if he was not mistaken, she occasionally allowed to linger. Her brother rode on ahead so they were left alone to their conversation, ignored by the driver seated on the box in front of them.

In this heady atmosphere Hector found himself pouring out his life story, telling his companion about his days in Barbary, the time he had spent as a prisoner of the Turks, his escape, and how he came to be aboard *L'Arc-de-Ciel*.

It was as they crossed the watershed and began to descend the farther slope and the forest began to thin out in more open woodland that he finally thought to ask her, 'Why did Captain Coxon bring me to Llanrumney?'

Susanna replied without hesitation. 'Knowing Coxon's reputation, I would say that he was trying to curry favour with Henry Morgan. As you already know, Sir Henry is at odds with my uncle who is expected to return here for a second term as governor. Morgan is always looking for ways to gain advantage over Sir Thomas, whom he sees as his rival. The fact that a nephew of Sir Thomas was found aboard a stolen ship could have been useful in his power struggle. Coxon would have been keen to deliver you into Henry Morgan's hands so that it could be shown that the Lynch family stooped to robbery on the high seas.'

'But Coxon had no proof of that,' Hector objected.

'If the French at Petit Guave decide that your friends stole *L'Arc-de-Ciel*, then you too would be guilty of piracy, and Morgan could have you hanged. That would be a neat twist and give Morgan a great deal of satisfaction because it was Sir Thomas who brought in the death penalty for buccaneering. He said it was little better than piracy. Then again, perhaps Morgan would have you thrown in prison and held, to be used as a pawn when Sir Thomas returns.'

Hector shook his head in bewilderment. 'But it is Coxon who acts the pirate, not me.'

Susanna gave a snort of derision. 'The truth is of no consequence. What matters is the way the wind is blowing, who has the most power on this island, the most influence back in London, or the most money to lay out in bribes.'

She broke off her explanation as her brother Robert

appeared alongside the carriage and reined in his horse. He was looking worried. 'Listen!' he said, 'I think I hear noises in the woods, somewhere over to the left.'

Moments later came the sound of a gunshot, followed by whoops and shouts, and then the baying of dogs. The carriage driver hastily reached under his seat and produced a blunderbuss even as Robert pulled a pistol out of his saddlebag and began to load it. 'Hector,' he said urgently, 'I think you had better get up on your horse in case we have to defend ourselves. There's a sword in my luggage. I trust you know how to use it.'

'What's the trouble?' Hector asked as he began to search for the weapon.

'No one lives in these woods,' came the reply. 'I fear we might have run into a roving gang of maroons.'

'Who are they?'

'Runaway slaves.'

Hector paused as the shouts came again, very much louder and closer. Now there was also the noise of bodies crashing through the undergrowth. Unsheathing the sword that he found, Hector unfastened his horse from the carriage and swung up into the saddle. The disturbance seemed to be coming from behind the carriage, and he turned his horse to face back down the track. A minute later several black shapes burst out of the undergrowth and raced across the path before vanishing into the thickets on the opposite side. They were pigs, wild ones, led by a massive boar, its jaws flecked with foam. The boar smashed a gap through the undergrowth, and behind him scampered at least a dozen piglets, small dark hairy creatures, which disappeared equally suddenly from view. Then came an interval when the track was empty until, equally abruptly, a human figure sprang out onto the path. He was a tall, black man with long matted hair down to his shoulders. Barefoot and naked to the waist, his only garment was a pair of tattered loose pantaloons. In one hand he held a hunting spear, and there was a heavy cutlass hanging from a strap over his shoulder.

He was some thirty yards away. He checked his stride and turned to face Hector. For a moment he paused, seeing the young man, sword in hand, the carriage behind him with its driver and the seated woman, a second rider armed with a pistol. There was no fear, only calculation in the black man's expression. Behind him half a dozen hunting dogs appeared on the track, running nose down and following the scent of the wild pigs. They also crossed the path and disappeared on the far side. But the black man stayed where he was, eyeing the travellers. Hector felt a cold spike of fear as a second, then a third black man appeared from the bushes. They too were armed. One of them held a musket. All three stood still, sizing up the travellers. Hector tightened his grip on the sword, the hilt now slippery with his sweat. Beneath him the horse, alarmed by the dogs and the wild-looking strangers, began to fidget nervously. Hector feared that the animal might rear up. If he was thrown to the ground, the hunters might take their chance to attack. He was also very conscious of Susanna in the carriage just behind him. She must be looking back, seeing the danger and aware that only he stood between her and the runaway slaves. For what seemed like an age, both sides regarded one another in total silence. Then a sudden burst of barking deep within the undergrowth broke the tension. The hunting dogs must have cornered their prey because the sound rose to an excited crescendo. The nearest black man turned and, raising his spear, waved his comrades onward towards the sound of the hunting pack. As suddenly as they had arrived, all three hunters vanished into the undergrowth.

Hector found himself in a cold sweat of relief as he looked back at Susanna. She was slightly pale but otherwise remarkably calm. Her brother seemed to be the more shocked. 'I never thought there were maroons in this area,' he said, and he sounded contrite. 'If I had known, I would have arranged an escort, or made sure we had travelled in greater company for safety. They were hunting well outside their usual territory.'

'Those men looked savage,' Hector commented.

'That's how they got their name,' Robert explained. 'The Spaniards called them *cimarron*, meaning wild or untamed. The first maroons were slaves whom the Spanish left behind on the island when the English took Jamaica from Spain. Now the maroons have gone native. They've established themselves in the roughest parts of the country, in areas too difficult for them to be rooted out.'

'Mr Lynch was telling me that his best friend is also a native, a Miskito,' Susanna intervened.

'Oh, the Miskito are very different,' her brother replied. 'They are good allies to the English and the French, or so I'm told. Besides, they are not found in Jamaica. They live on the mainland, and they hate the Spanish.'

'Mr Lynch's mother is Spanish,' warned Susanna.

'I'm sorry,' Robert replied, blushing. 'Nothing I say seems to strike the right note.'

'I've never heard of the maroons before,' Hector hastened to assure him. 'They seem to live in much the same way as the first buccaneers . . . by hunting wild animals.'

'That's true,' said Robert. 'Indeed my uncle told me that the buccaneers are named after the boucans, the racks on which they grill the flesh of the beasts they kill. It's a French word, the same which the Spanish call a barbacoa or barbecue.'

'I'm sure Mr Lynch finds all this fascinating,' said his sister. 'But don't you think we should be getting on our way. If we stand here talking long enough, the maroons may return and find us here.'

'Yes, yes. Of course,' her brother replied. And then to Hector's chagrin he added, 'Just in case we do encounter any further trouble, perhaps it would be best if he kept my sword for the moment and stayed on horseback.'

✳

THE LITTLE GROUP travelled on and as if to make up for his lapse of judgement, Robert made a point of riding beside Hector. He chatted with the young Irishman in his friendly manner, explaining to him the more interesting features of the countryside as gradually the land began to slope downward and became more open until eventually they were riding through open savannah. He pointed out wild cattle grazing among the low bushes, and spoke enthusiastically about the fertility of the soil. 'What you do is purchase one hundred acres of prime Jamaican land and invest just four hundred pounds in half a dozen slaves and spades and tools. You have your slaves clear the ground, then plant and cultivate cocoa, and in the fourth year the crop will give you back your original investment. After that, if you are shrewd and your slaves have also set cassava and maize and built their own huts, you have no further expenses. Year after year your cocoa will bring in four hundred pounds back and maybe more. Everything is pure profit.'

But Hector could think only about Susanna riding in the carriage so close to him, and he found it difficult to pay attention to her brother and his business talk. He forced himself not to glance around to look at her, for fear of seeming foolishly besotted. Luckily Robert did not seem to notice his listener's preoccupation and prattled on until, from behind, Susanna called out.

'Robert, do stop talking about money and point out that bird to Mr Lynch. There, over to your left beside the bush with orange flowers. He will not have seen anything like it before.'

Indeed, at first sight, Hector thought that Susanna was mistaken. A large brown and grey butterfly was feeding on the blossoms, moving from one flower to the next. Then Hector saw that it was not a butterfly but a tiny bird, just over an inch long, which was hovering in position, its wings a blur. Turning aside he rode closer, and the bird suddenly rose from the bush and came towards him. For several seconds the tiny creature hovered close beside his head, and he distinctly heard the sound of its wings, a delicate hur! hur! hur!

'Your first hummingbird, Mr Lynch!' called out Susanna.

'It is indeed a remarkable creature. It makes a sound like a miniature spinning wheel,' Hector agreed, able at last to turn and look directly at her.

'You have the soul of an artist, Mr Lynch,' she said, with a smile of delight which made him dizzy. 'Wait until you've seen its cousin. The one they call a streamer. It flies in the same way and has two long velvet black tail feathers which dangle in the air, and you can hear them fluttering. When the sunlight strikes its breast, the feathers flash emerald, then olive or deepest black as the creature turns.'

Hector was tongue-tied. He wanted desperately to say something gallant to this divine creature, to continue the conversation, but he could find no words. The way he looked at her, though, could have left no doubt about the way he felt.

It was some hours later, as the sun was nearing the horizon, that he heard a sound he recognised. It was a long-drawn-out call like a distant trumpet and he had heard it before, on the coast of Africa, and knew it to be someone blowing a call on a conch shell. 'Are we so close to the sea?' he asked Robert.

'No,' the young man replied. 'It's one of our farm workers calling in the hogs. They feed by day in the savannah, but come back to the sty at night when they hear that call. They are unexpectedly intelligent animals. That sound also means that this is where we turn off for Spanish Town.'

He reached out to offer Hector a handshake of farewell.

'The road to Port Royal is straight ahead. It's no more than a couple of hours' walk to the ferry. If you hurry, you should be able to get there while it is still daylight. I wish you well.'

With sudden dismay, Hector realised that his journey beside Susanna was at an end. Crestfallen, he swung himself out of the saddle of his borrowed horse, and handed the reins to Robert.

'Thank you for allowing me to accompany you this far,' he said.

'No, it is I who have to thank you,' Robert replied. 'Your presence helped deter the maroons from attacking us. If we had been fewer, we might have become their prey.'

Walking stiffly across to the carriage, Hector stood beside its door and looked up into Susanna's blue eyes. Once again, he did not know what to say. He did not dare to take her hand, and she did not offer it. Instead she gave him a demure smile, less coquettish now, more serious. 'Goodbye, Hector,' she said. 'I hope you find your friends and, after that, perhaps your path will lead you back to Jamaica so we will meet again. I feel there is more that we have in common than just our names.' With that the carriage moved away, leaving Hector standing in the red dirt road, and hoping fervently he had been more than a day's amusement for the first girl he had ever fallen in love with.

FOUR

PORT ROYAL had more taverns than Hector imagined possible in such a small area. He counted eighteen of them in the ten minutes it took him to walk from one end of the town to the other. They ranged from The Feathers, a grimy-looking ale-house close by the fish market, to the new-built Three Mariners where he turned back, realising that he had reached the town limits. Retracing his steps along the main waterfront, Thames Street, he found himself skirting around stove-in barrels, broken handcarts, discarded sacking, and several drunks lying snoring in the rubbish or slumped against the doors of the warehouses which lined one side of the street. The wharves across the road were built on pilings because Port Royal perched on the tip of a sand spit and land was very scarce. Every berth was occupied. Vessels were loading cargoes of tobacco, hides and skins, indigo and ebony, and above all sugar whose earthy, sickly sweet smell Hector was beginning to recognise. Whenever he met a longshoreman or a half-sober sailor he asked if any of the vessels might be bound for Petit Guave, but he was always disappointed. Often his request was ignored, or the hurried reply was accompanied by an oath. It seemed that Port Royal was a place where most inhabitants were too busy making money or spending it in debauchery for them to give a civil response.

The town was also astonishingly expensive. He had arrived there at dawn on the morning after saying goodbye to Susanna and her brother, and the ferryman had demanded six pence to bring him from the mainland. It was no more than a two-mile trip across the anchorage, and Hector had been obliged to spend half the night on the beach until the night breeze was favourable. He had no money for the fare so he had sold his coat to the ferryman for a few coins. Now, looking for something to eat for his breakfast, Hector turned into one of the taverns – it was the Cat and Fiddle – and was taken aback by the price of a meal. 'Just a drink of water will suffice,' he said.

'You can have beer, Madeira wine, punch, brandy, or rap,' the man replied.

'What's rap?'

'Good strong drink made from molasses,' came the reply, and when he insisted that water was enough, he was advised to stick with beer. 'Nobody drinks water here,' observed the potman. 'The local water gives you the gripes. The only drinkable stuff has to be brought in barrels from the mainland so you'll still have to pay: a penny a jug.'

Hungry and thirsty, Hector abandoned the tavern and went back out into the street where a frowzy strumpet flaunted herself from an upper window and beckoned to him. When he shook his head, she spat over the balcony. It was not ten in the morning yet, but the day was already hot and sticky, and he had not the least idea what he should do, or where he should stay. He had resolved to remain in Port Royal until he could find passage to catch up with Dan and Jacques, but first he had to find some sort of employment and a roof above his head.

He cut through a narrow laneway and emerged on the high street. The close-packed houses were substantial, brick built and two or three stories high. Most had shops or offices on the ground floor, and living accommodation above them. Shoulder to shoulder with alehouses and brothels were the premises of tradesmen – cordwainers with their shop windows full of shoes, tailors displaying rolls of cloth, two or three furniture makers, a hatter and a pipemaker as well as three gunsmiths. Their businesses seemed to be flourishing. He passed a vegetable market at the central crossroads and reached the end of the street. Here the early-morning meat market was already closing down because the slabs of hog flesh and beef on display would soon begin to stink. Large, black flies were settling on the blood-encrusted tables, and he was puzzled to see two men lugging between them what looked like a heavy shallow cauldron. On closer inspection it turned out to be an unsold turtle, upside down and still alive. Curious to see what they would do with it, he watched them carry the animal to a short ramp leading down to the water's edge. There they placed it in a fenced holding pen half in and half out of the water, a turtle crawl where the creature could drag itself into the shallows, to await the next day's sales.

At the end of the high street, he was close back where he had started, for he recognised the bulk of the fort which guarded the anchorage. Turning left, he entered a thoroughfare that looked more respectable, though the roadway was still nothing more than an expanse of hard packed sand. He noted the door plaques of several doctors, then a goldsmith's shop, securely shuttered. Next to an apothecary's hung a trade sign which raised his hope: it depicted a pair of mapmaker's compasses and a pencil stub. The proprietor's name was written underneath in black letters on a scroll: Robert Snead.

Hector pushed open the door and stepped inside.

He found himself in a low-ceilinged room, furnished sparsely with a large table, half a dozen plain wooden chairs and a desk. In the light of an open window an older man was seated at the desk. He was wearing a shabby wig and a rumpled gown of brown linen. His head was bent over his work as he scratched away with a quill pen. On hearing his visitor enter, he looked up and Hector saw that the man had thick spectacles balanced on a nose that showed a drunkard's broken veins.

'Can I help you?' the man asked. He removed the spectacles and rubbed a hand across his eyes. They were bloodshot.

'I would like to speak with Mr Snead,' Hector said.

'I am Robert Snead. Are you looking for a design or practical advice?' The man's near-sighted gaze took in Hector's clothing which, now that he had sold his jacket, was not as respectable as it had seemed earlier.

'I hope to find employment, sir,' Hector answered. 'My name is Hector Lynch. I have worked with maps and charts, and have a fair hand.'

Robert Snead looked uneasy. 'I am an architect and surveyor, not a mapmaker.' He shifted uncomfortably in his chair. 'Anyone who makes maps and charts, or sells them, needs to have a licence.'

'I did not know,' Hector apologised. 'I saw the sign outside and thought it was for a mapmaker.'

'We use many of the same tools of trade,' Snead admitted. He gave Hector a shrewd glance. 'Is it true that you can work with charts?'

'Yes, sir. I have worked with coastal maps, harbour plans, and the like.' Hector thought it politic not to mention that his work had been for a Turkish admiral in Barbary.

Snead thought for a moment. Then, sliding a sheet of paper and a pen across the desk towards him, he said, 'Show me what you can do. Draw me an anchorage protected by a reef, showing the depths and marking the best place where a vessel might lie.'

Hector did as he was asked, and after Snead had inspected the little drawing, he rose from his chair and said cautiously, 'Well ... there may be something for you to do after all, for a few days at least. If you will follow me.' He led Hector up a flight of stairs at the back of his shop and brought him into the room directly above. Its balcony looked out over the street. Here too was a broad table, apparently used for entertaining as it was set with pewter plates and mugs and there were several chairs and a bench beside it. Snead pushed aside the tableware to leave a clear space, and crossing to a chest standing in one corner lifted the lid and took out several sheets of parchment. He laid them on the table and began to leaf through them. 'These are for the conveyancing lawyers and landowners,' the architect explained. The top sheets were surveyor's plans of what seemed to be plantations, and it was evident that an important part of the architect's job was to make drawings that established the boundaries of newly cleared estates. These sheets Snead laid aside until he came to what was obviously a sea chart concealed among the other papers. The chart was in some detail for it extended across two sheets of parchment. Snead took just one of the pages and spread it out on the table. 'Can you make a fair copy of that?' he asked, peering over his spectacles, and carefully turning the second sheet face down.

Hector glanced down at the map. It was a navigation chart. It showed a length of coastline, various off-shore islands and a number of landmarks which would be useful to anyone navigating along the coast. He had no idea what coast it displayed.

'Yes,' he replied. 'That should not be difficult.'

'How long would it take you?'

'Two days, perhaps less.'

'Then you've got yourself ten days' work if the first copy is to my satisfaction. I'll want five copies made and I'll pay two pounds for each, plus a bonus if they are ready by next Wednesday.' He paused, and gave Hector a sly look. 'But you don't leave this house, and you don't speak to anyone about the work. I'll arrange for my housekeeper to prepare your meals, and you can sleep in a spare room in the garret. Do you understand?'

'Yes, of course,' said Hector. He was scarcely able to believe his good fortune. On his first morning in Port Royal he had found both employment and accommodation. With the pay he could resume his search for a ship that would take him to Petit Guave.

'Good,' said Snead, 'then you can begin work as soon as you have gone to collect your things.'

'I have nothing to collect,' Hector admitted.

Snead looked him up and down, a gleam of understanding in his eyes.

'Runaway, are you? Well, that's no concern of mine,' he said with obvious satisfaction, 'but if you breathe a word to anyone about your work, I'll see to it that your master learns exactly where you are to be found.' He nodded towards the pile of surveys. 'Most of the big landowners and the wealthy merchants come to seek my services, and I can soon find out who is missing an indentured man.'

✳

BEFORE THE DAY was out, Hector had discovered that Snead was not as fierce as he at first made out. The architect had scarcely left the young man to his work in the upper room when he came back up the stairs and announced that he was closing his shop and would be back in half an hour. If Hector needed additional supplies of paper, pens and ink, he would find them in the downstairs office. A moment later the young man heard the front door close, and glancing out of the window he saw Snead walking off down the street, then turn into a nearby alehouse. When Snead came back rather more than an hour later, Hector concluded that his employer was drunk. He heard him knock over a chair as he fumbled his way back to his desk. By then Hector had identified the region shown by the chart he was copying.

It was a map of the Caribbean shores of Central America. He remembered the general outline of the coast from the smaller scale chart that he had used aboard *L'Arc-de-Ciel*. Now he was being asked to copy out a larger and much more accurate version which covered the northern half of that coast. He guessed that the second sheet, the one that Snead had hidden from him, showed the southern portion. Clearly someone had recently sailed along the coast and made numerous observations. The sheet in front of him was covered with handwritten notes to help a navigator recognise his landfall, then track his progress, avoiding reefs and other outlying dangers, select from a number of different harbours and anchorages, and find watering places. Whoever had written these notes had not ventured more than a few miles inland because the interior of the countryside was left blank.

The map seemed harmless and it was puzzling that Snead was being so secretive about it. Hector supposed that even if the architect was caught dealing in maps without a licence, he would receive only a minor penalty. Yet more mysterious was the fact that he needed five copies.

As Hector began work, Susanna's image kept appearing in his thoughts. He saw her walking in the garden of her father's plantation house, or as he had last seen her, seated in a carriage and smiling at him gravely. From time to time he put aside his drawing materials and gazed sightlessly out of the window, dreaming of what it must be like to hold her in his arms. Once or twice he even dared to wonder whether she too was thinking about him.

His reverie was broken by the sound of Snead's footsteps on the stair. With a start Hector realised that it was late in the day. When the architect entered the room, he glanced over the part-finished copy that Hector had been working on, and appeared to be satisfied with what he saw, for he sat down heavily on the bench at the end of the table and announced that it was time for Hector to stop work. 'So you say your name is Lynch,' he observed, picking up the quill pen that Hector had been using. 'Not a convincing nom de plume.' He waved the feather in the air, smirking owlishly at his pun. 'I would have thought you could have come up with something more original.'

Hector realised that Snead was convinced that he was sheltering a fugitive indentured man, also that the architect was very tipsy. He smelled the rum on his new employer's breath.

'Lynch is my real name, sir,' Hector protested.

Snead seemed not to hear him. He gave a drunken hiccup and stared at Hector. 'You can't be a Lynch. You don't look like one.'

Hector saw his opportunity. 'You know the Lynches, sir?' he asked.

'Who doesn't? Richest family on the island. I've done surveys for three of their plantations. They must own at least thirty thousand acres.'

'Have you met Robert Lynch or his sister?' Hector was desperate to glean a few more details about Susanna.

'Young Robert? He came to the office a few times when I was doing drawings for their new townhouse here in Port Royal. And a very elegant structure it is, if I do say so myself,' Snead hiccuped.

'And what about his sister?'

'You mean Susanna? I think that's her name. Quite a catch, that one. I doubt there's anyone on the island who would be a match for her. She'll probably find her husband in London next time she goes there. Pretty girl but said to be headstrong.'

Snead swivelled round on the bench to face the door. Raising his voice, he shouted for food to be brought. A voice answered from somewhere deep within the house, and a little while later an elderly woman, whom Hector presumed to be Snead's housekeeper, appeared with a tray of food which she placed on the table.

'Come on. You share this with me,' said the architect, waving to a seat near him as he began to ladle soup into his mouth. Hector came to the conclusion that the architect was a lonely man and eager for company.

✻

IT WAS MID-MORNING on the following day that Hector received an unwelcome jolt of recognition. He had slept the night in a small room on the topmost floor of Snead's premises, and next morning with the tropical sunlight flooding his work table from the open window, he had made good progress with copying the first chart. He was at the stage when he had drawn the coastline and all its islands and reefs, and begun to write in their names, consulting the handwritten notes from the original. He was labelling the anchorages and harbours when he saw that one of the anchorages was marked 'Captain Coxon's Hole'. He checked the handwritten notes again, and there was no mistake. A small natural harbour on one of the islands had been named after the buccaneer. Hector could see that it made an ideal refuge. The island lay far enough off the mainland to be rarely visited, and the anchorage was very discreet. It was concealed behind a reef, and protected by a low ridge of hills. So when Snead came to check on his employee's progress just before his noontime visit to the tavern, Hector casually asked how Coxon's Hole had got its name. The reaction he received was a surprise.

'It's named after a friend of mine,' Snead announced and he sounded proud of the association. 'He used to have a house here in Port Royal. Knows that coast as well as anyone. Discovered that anchorage and been using it on and off ever since.'

Hector puzzled over the architect's answer all that afternoon, and when Snead was in a particularly good mood at supper, he asked the architect when he had last seen his friend. 'Not for the past couple of years but – who knows – he could turn up at any time.'

Hector noted how Snead had cast a quick glance towards the finished chart still lying on the end of the table. Alarmed, Hector risked a further question.

'Is Captain Coxon a good customer then?'

His enquiry was met with a suspicious stare. Then Snead must have decided that he could trust his new assistant. Rising from his chair he took the second page of the chart from the chest and laid it beside the one that Hector had just completed. As Hector had suspected, the two maps covered almost the entire Caribbean coast of Central America. Waving his hand over the maps, Snead exclaimed, 'There you have it! The key to the South Sea!' Then he sat back down heavily in his usual place and picked up his tankard.

'The South Sea?' Hector asked. 'But that's on the far side of the isthmus. Is that not another word for the Pacific?'

'You misunderstand me,' Snead declared, waving at the map again. 'Here we have the gateway. The riches lie beyond. We are opening the way for our clients.'

'And will we also provide them with charts of the South Sea?' Hector enquired.

Snead looked at him in drunken astonishment.

'Charts of the South Sea!' he exclaimed. 'You speak of Golconda and the Valley of Diamonds! If I had such charts, either I could command a king's ransom or both of us would find ourselves victims of a Spanish stiletto.'

'For what reason?'

'How else do the Spaniards sail up and down the coast of Peru, and safely bring back the silver from their mines and the other products of their possessions in South America, if they did not have such maps? But they are state secrets. Men would murder for them. That is why men talk of the South Sea Adventure.'

Abruptly the architect must have realised that he had said too much for he quickly swept up both charts, rose to his feet and walked unsteadily across the room to put them back in the chest. Then, mumbling a farewell, he set out for his evening's drinking in the tavern.

✳

NEXT MORNING Snead had still not appeared in his shop when Hector heard a knock on the door to the street. Opening it, he found a middle-aged, weather-beaten man dressed in a sea captain's coat that looked the worse for wear. 'I wish to speak with Robert Snead,' the visitor asked.

'I'm afraid he is not available,' Hector said. 'Perhaps I can help.'

The man stepped inside, and closed the door behind him. He looked carefully at Hector, then said, 'I've come for a chart.'

'I'm afraid that Mr Snead is an architect . . .' Hector began, but his response was brushed aside.

'I know all about that,' the man replied, 'but I've bought maps from him before. The name is Gutteridge, Captain Gutteridge.'

'Then perhaps you will wait here, and I will consult Mr Snead,' Hector answered. Leaving Gutteridge in the shop he hurried up to the architect's bedchamber. He found Snead still in bed, huddled under a quilt and dressed in his nightclothes. He was looking liverish and the room stank of liquor.

'There's a Captain Gutteridge in the shop,' Hector began. 'He's come for a map. I told him that you do not deal with maps. But he says he's bought them from you before.'

Snead gave a groan. 'And never paid me for them either,' he said sourly. 'Go back down, and tell Captain Gutteridge that he won't get any more charts until he's settled his account.'

On his way back to the shop, Hector found that the captain had followed him up the stairs and was now standing in the room where Hector worked, looking down at the chart being copied.

'That . . .' said Gutteridge, tapping the chart with a blunt forefinger, 'will do me very well.'

'I'm afraid it is not for sale. It's a special order.'

'I suppose it must be for that lot who are assembling off Negril.'

'I have no idea. They are for Mr Snead's private clients.'

Gutteridge noticed the stain of ink on Hector's fingers. 'Are you his draughtsman?' he asked, and when Hector nodded, he gave the young man a sideways look and said, 'How about letting me have a copy, on the side. I'd make it worth your while.'

'That's not possible, I'm afraid. And Mr Snead asked that you settle your account.'

Gutteridge shrugged. He seemed unperturbed. 'Then I'll do without. A pity. I wish you good day.' He descended the stairs but on reaching the ground floor, he turned and made one last appeal to Hector. 'If you change your mind,' he said, 'you'll find my ship, the *Jamaica Merchant*, at the quay at Thames Street. She'll be there for three days at most, then I sail for Campeachy to load logwood.'

Hector hesitated for a moment before asking, 'By any chance will you be calling at Petit Guave on your way?'

Gutteridge fingered the lapel of his shabby coat. 'I'm thinking of it. French brandy is popular with the Bay Men.' Then he walked across the shop and let himself out into the street.

The moment Gutteridge left, Hector hurried back to his work table. He still had two more charts to prepare and it was only three days before they must be ready. If he could finish them in time and get his pay from Snead, he might be able to purchase a passage aboard the *Jamaica Merchant* and find his way to Petit Guave to rejoin Jacques and Dan. Glancing out of the window as he picked up his pen, he watched Gutteridge walking away down the street. As the sea captain passed the door to Snead's favourite tavern Hector saw a figure which he recognised. Loitering on the doorstep of the grog shop was the sailor he had met on Coxon's ship, the man with the broken nose and missing fingers.

'I'll want you to be on hand next Wednesday when my clients come to collect their charts,' said Snead who had finally come into the room behind him. The architect was unshaven and pale. 'There may be last minute changes to be made. I trust you will have all five copies ready.'

'Yes, of course,' said Hector. He tried to sound confident, but it was on the tip of his tongue to ask if Captain Coxon was one of the clients and likely to collect his chart in person. He was fearful of meeting the buccaneer again. If he and Coxon came face to face, it could only turn out badly. Coxon was certain to take revenge for his humiliation, and at least one of his men was in town to help him do so. Hector imagined he would be lucky if he escaped with nothing more than a severe beating, but it could be much worse. From the little he had seen of Port Royal, it was a lawless seaport where corpses were regularly found floating in the harbour.

✳

WHEN WEDNESDAY came, Hector was in an agony of antici-pation. By ten o'clock in the morning he had completed the fifth copy of the chart, though the ink was still wet and he had to go down to Snead's desk to take a pouncet box of sand to sprinkle over the parchment. 'When will your clients arrive?' he asked the architect.

'We gather in the tavern this evening,' Snead told him. 'As soon as everyone is present, I will bring them across to inspect the work.'

The architect had dressed more carefully than usual and was shaved though he had nicked his chin with the razor in several places, and there were flecks of dried blood on his neckcloth. Hector wondered how much longer the architect would be able to do his own drawings now that his hand shook so badly. If the evening passed off well and Coxon did not appear, perhaps it was the moment to ask for permanent employment as a draughtsman. If Snead took him on permanently, it would mean that he could stay on in Port Royal and perhaps meet Susanna again. Increasingly Hector was aware that his attraction to the young woman was in conflict with his loyalty towards Dan, Jacques and his former shipmates. He could still accept Gutteridge's offer and sail for Petit Guave and there rejoin his friends. But he would have to hurry. The *Jamaica Merchant* was due to sail next day. Unable to make up his mind what he should do, he told himself that the events of the evening would decide the matter for him.

At sunset just before Snead left for his meeting in the tavern, he told Hector to prepare the upper room. He was to have all five copies of the chart set out on the table for inspection, and make sure that wine and grog were to hand. Then he was to go up to his own room in the garret and be ready if Snead called him. If summoned, he was not to speak to anyone, and he was to forget the faces of those in the room. Hector, still hoping that his fears of meeting Coxon were unfounded, made sure everything was ready but instead of withdrawing to the garret he stationed himself at the upper window. From there he could at least see who would be coming to collect the charts, and if necessary he could make his escape.

The street outside was as busy as usual in the cool of the evening. Clumps of drunken sailors stumbled and lurched from one alehouse and grog shop to the next, working whores paraded enticingly or disappeared up sidestreets and into doorways with their customers, several gaunt beggars importuned for alms, and – just once – a small patrol of militiamen straggled past, their uniforms ill-fitting and shabby. It was ten o'clock before he saw the door of the tavern open, the light spilling out, and a group of half a dozen men emerge. He recognised Snead at once, for the architect's walk was familiar. There was enough of a moon to cast shadows, and as the little group began to walk towards the shop they passed into a pool of darkness. A few moments later Snead's clients were at the door. Hector stood very still, listening. He had left the window open, and the sounds of the visitors came up to him clearly. He heard Snead, tipsy as usual, fumbling at the lock. The architect was apologising to his guests.

'Hurry up, man,' said a voice. 'I don't wish to be kept standing in the street for all to see.'

Hector knew Coxon's voice at once. The buccaneer's harsh bullying tone was unmistakable. The door opened, and Hector heard the men walk towards the stairs. Footsteps sounded on the boards.

Hector quietly tiptoed across to the table, gathered up one set of the charts, folded it in a neat square, and stuffed it into his shirt front. Stepping out onto the balcony, he swung a leg over the rail, and climbed over until he could let himself hang, his arms at full stretch. Then he let go. He had expected to land on the hard packed sand of the street. But as he dropped, his feet touched something soft, there was a grunt of surprise, and Hector sprawled sideways. As he struck the ground, he realised that he had not seen the man who was standing in the shadow of the doorway. Someone had been left as a lookout, and he was as startled as Hector.

Hector sprang to his feet as the stranger recovered and with a grunt of anger reached out to grab him. The young man ducked and twisted to one side, and sprinted away up the street. He expected to hear the sounds of running feet behind him as the lookout gave chase. But there was nothing. Hector could only imagine that the sentinel had gone inside to report on the incident and ask instructions. Hector forced himself to slow down to a walk. Earlier that afternoon he had consulted a town plan that Snead had made for the town commissioners. The drawing showed the haphazard pattern of Port Royal's roads and alleyways, and Hector had picked out a discreet route that would bring him to the quayside on Thames Street. There he would search for the *Jamaica Merchant* and offer his services to Captain Gutteridge. But he had not calculated on colliding with one of Coxon's men. He was certain that the lookout was from the buccaneer's crew, most likely the man with the broken nose.

Hector shivered slightly as he tried to anticipate how the buccaneers would hunt him. Port Royal was such a small place that, without shelter, he would soon be found. He wondered just how many of the citizens, besides Snead, were friends with Captain Coxon and would be pleased to join the pursuit. If Snead were to mention that his assistant had been speaking with Captain Gutteridge earlier, the buccaneer would quickly guess where his quarry was heading. The young man was uncomfortably aware that, if he was to escape Coxon, he would have to move very quickly but also in an unexpected direction.

Making up his mind, Hector walked rapidly in the direction of Thames Street and turned up a narrow alleyway, Sea Lane, which brought him out on the waterfront. Away to his right stretched the line of ships tied to the wharves, their masts and spars and rigging making a black tracery against the night sky. His difficulty was that he did not know which of the vessels was the *Jamaica Merchant*. The most likely candidate was a small sloop almost at the farthest end of the wharf. But there was no one he could ask for information, and he did not want to draw attention to himself by rousing a night watchman and asking for directions.

For several moments he stood motionless, wondering what he should do. He had paused in the shelter of a warehouse doorway, and as he looked along the quay, two men appeared not fifty yards from him. They ran out from a laneway and turned to look in his direction. Hector shrank back farther into the shadow and when he peered out again, he saw that the men had decided to go in the opposite direction. They were proceeding briskly along the waterfront, looking into every side road, clearly searching for someone. At the farthest end of the quay, they halted. They appeared to confer together, and then one of them walked away and out of sight. His companion stayed where he was. There was enough moonlight to show that the figure had seated himself on a pile of lumber at a position where he could scan the waterfront.

Hector tried to think of a way of getting past the lookout. He toyed with the idea of mingling with a gang of sailors returning to their ship, but then rejected the scheme. There was no guarantee that such a group would show up or welcome him in their company. Nor that they would be returning to the *Jamaica Merchant*. Or he could wait until Coxon's watchman – there was little doubt that the lookout was one of Coxon's crew – grew inattentive or was withdrawn from his post. But that might not happen and Hector was still faced with the problem of identifying the *Jamaica Merchant*.

Then he remembered the turtle crawl.

He slipped quietly out of the warehouse doorway and darted back into Sea Lane. Keeping to the shadows he retraced his steps until he reached the high street. There he turned to his right until he came to the empty stalls and tables of the meat market. It would be another two or three hours before the butchers and meat sellers arrived to prepare their booths. Finding his way to the ramp, Hector climbed over the low palisaded fence which surrounded the turtle pen. Removing his shoes and stockings, he walked barefoot down the slope until he felt the sea water on his feet. Treading carefully, he continued forward down the slope. He was in the shallows now, the water up to his knees. He put each foot down gently and slowly, anxious not to make any splashes. Suddenly his foot touched a hard round surface, which moved sluggishly to one side. He had trodden on a resting turtle. Cautiously he pushed forward with his leg until he found a gap between the animal and its neighbour. There must have been at least a dozen large turtles lying in the shallows, close-packed like flat boulders. Most of the creatures ignored him, but one of them rose up with a swirling surge that almost knocked him off his feet. Then he had reached the far end of the turtle pen, where the water was now up to mid-thigh. Floating, half submerged at the far end of the turtle pen was a small dugout canoe. He had noticed it on his previous visit, and supposed that the turtle men used it to bring their catch closer to the ramp, loading the captive turtles on the canoe rather than dragging them through the water.

Carefully Hector lifted one end of the canoe and placed it on the fence. Here the wooden palings projected less than two or three inches above the water. Slowly Hector eased the little canoe out over the fence, sliding it carefully across the obstruction. As soon as the canoe was on the seaward side, Hector clambered over the fence, and hauled himself aboard, straddling the dugout. He paused for a moment to check that the charts in his shirt were still dry, and then he lay back and pulled his legs inboard. The canoe was very small, barely longer than his own body and it fitted him like a narrow coffin. But that suited his plan.

He lay face up, the bilge water soaking into the back of his clothes. Dipping his hands into the warm water of the harbour on either side of his little vessel, he began to paddle gently. Barely moving, the dugout drifted forward, and Hector gently steered it towards the town quays.

He kept close to the shore where the looming bulk of the fort threw a dark shadow. Only someone standing right at the edge of the parapet and looking directly downward would have seen him. There was no warning shout, and as soon as he reached the wharves themselves, he pushed himself in amongst the wooden piles, sliding the little dugout into the space beneath the decking. Twice he thought that his progress was blocked by a cross brace, but he managed to find a way around. The fetid air under the quay stank of ordure, and he heard the rustle and squeak of rats. As he progressed, Hector counted the number of ships' hulls he passed. The first one was obviously a ship of war, probably the frigate on the Jamaica station, for he heard the stamp and call of a sentry answering the officer of the watch. Then there were two more hulls, large merchant ships, too substantial to belong to Gutteridge who had said the *Jamaica Merchant* was his own vessel and Gutteridge was not a wealthy man. Hector eased past the next five hulls until he came to the last in line, the modest vessel he suspected being the *Jamaica Merchant*. The stem post was worn and chewed, and there was a patched area where the hull had been poorly mended.

Gently Hector eased the little canoe from under the wharf and around the rudder of the sloop. He could hear the gentle slap of wavelets against the timber. With one hand he fended off the hull as he paddled forward until he had brought the canoe to the farther side of the sloop, away from the dock. He sat up carefully and placed a hand in a scupper hole. Silently he blessed the fact that the little sloop was so small that it lay low in the water. Then, taking a deep breath, he stood up in the bottom of the canoe, feeling it tilt alarmingly beneath him. He reached up with his right hand and laid hold of the capping rail. Then he pulled himself aboard. As his foot left the canoe, he gave a gentle kick and it floated away out of sight. With luck it would not be found until much later, and such a worthless craft might not even be worth reporting.

There was no one on deck as he began to worm his way cautiously aft. If the little sloop was anything like *L'Arc-de-Ciel* this was where he would find the captain's cabin. He still had no idea whether he was aboard the *Jamaica Merchant* or another vessel but now there was no turning back. When he came to the cabin door, he crouched down. Judging that it was another three or four hours until daybreak, he did not wish to alarm whoever was asleep inside. So he waited.

As the time passed, he became aware of soft snoring from within the cabin. That was reassuring. Sometimes a ship captain would choose to spend his nights ashore rather than on his vessel, but Hector had an idea that Captain Gutteridge, if he did not pay his bills, was not welcome in the local boarding houses. The young man squeezed himself more tightly into a corner behind a pile of sacks, hoping that he was not discovered by a sailor before he had a chance to speak with the captain.

The sky began to lighten, and he heard the sounds of the port awakening. There was the cry of gulls, the hawking and spitting of a longshoreman arriving for work, the mutter of voices as dockers began to assemble. He felt, rather than saw, Coxon's watcher still on the quay, not ten yards away, still scanning the length of the wharves, waiting for him.

The snores behind the cabin door changed in pitch. They stopped, then started again, and Hector heard the sleeper turn over in his bunk. He was nearly awake. Softly Hector tapped on the door. The snores continued. The young man tapped again, and this time the snoring ceased altogether. A short while later he heard the sound of bare feet as someone came to the door, paused, and opened it cautiously. In the half light Hector was relieved to see that it was indeed Captain Gutteridge. He held a cudgel in his hand.

'May I come in? I have your chart,' Hector said, speaking in scarcely above a whisper.

Gutteridge looked down at him, and there was a flash of recognition in his eyes. He drew back the door, and Hector slipped inside. The captain closed the door behind him.

Inside the small cabin it was stuffy and airless. It smelled of unwashed clothes, and Gutteridge himself was dishevelled.

'Here, I have your chart for you,' Hector repeated, bringing out the charts from his shirt. 'But Mr Snead will not be pleased.'

Gutteridge reached for the folded sheets, opened them, and gave the maps a quick glance. He looked up, a look of satisfaction on his face. 'Serve the greedy sot right,' he said. 'What do you want in return? We never agreed a price.'

'Mr Snead has men searching for me.'

Gutteridge gave him a penetrating look. 'Mr Snead ... or Mr Snead's friends?' he said grimly. 'The word's out that there's an assembly off Negril. Several hard cases are recruiting for some sort of mischief. One of my own men ran off yesterday to volunteer.'

'So you'll be needing a replacement,' said Hector.

'Yes, but I wouldn't want to make enemies of that lot.'

'No one need know. You could conceal me aboard until your ship sails. Then I can make myself useful until we reach Petit Guave. That would be a fair price for the map.'

Gutteridge nodded. 'All right. We have a bargain.' He reached down and pulled at a trap door in the cabin floor. 'This leads down to the aft hold. You can stay down there.' He reached for an earthenware jug standing on the floor beside his bunk. 'Take this water with you. It'll be enough until I can get you some food later in the day.'

Hector sat down on the edge of the open hatch, his legs dangling into the dark space below. He looked up at Gutteridge. 'And when do you expect to reach Petit Guave?' he asked.

Gutteridge avoided his eyes and did not answer.

'You said you were stopping there, to take on brandy,' Hector reminded him.

Gutteridge was shamefaced. 'No, I did not say that. I said only that I was thinking of stopping there on the way to Campeachy.'

'But I have friends in Petit Guave ... a Miskito and a Frenchman. This is why I want to join you.'

Gutteridge continued to look evasive. 'Maybe on the return trip . . .' he said lamely. 'And if we bring back a good load of logwood, I'll cut you in for five per cent of the profit.'

He gave Hector a gentle push with his foot, and the young man dropped down into the darkness, suddenly aware that he was unlikely to see either Susanna or Dan and his friends until his voyage to Campeachy was over.

FIVE

'CHRISTMAS,' said Captain Gutteridge cheerfully, 'is the best season to take up logwood.' He was leaning over the rail as his vessel edged slowly along a low swampy coast. Beyond the swamp a cloudless sky came down to the horizon in a pale harshness that made Hector's eyes ache. The land was so flat that all he could see was the endless dark green barrier of mangroves on their tangled mud-coloured roots and the feathery top of an occasional palm tree. It had taken less than ten days to sail from Port Royal to the Campeachey coast, and Gutteridge was in good humour. 'You'll be back in Jamaica before you know it,' he was saying. With Hector's stolen chart in hand, he was carefully tracking their progress. 'Logwood fetches a hundred pounds a ton on the London market, and with your share of the profit you can begin to make your fortune.'

Everyone in the Caribees, Hector thought to himself, was ready with advice on how to make vast great riches. Earlier it had been Robert Lynch, now it was the threadbare captain of a worn-out trading sloop. He no longer resented Gutteridge for his dishonesty over the mythical trip to Petit Guave. It was three weeks since Hector had last seen Dan, Jacques and the two Laptots, and he had accepted that whatever had happened to them in the French colony it was too late for him to make a difference. As for his yearning to see Susanna again, perhaps the captain was right. The niece of Sir Thomas Lynch would be more impressed with a rich suitor than a penniless admirer. Maybe a lucrative trip to the Campeachy coast would be his first step on the road to making a fortune.

He turned his attention back to the shoreline. 'The logwood cutters call themselves Bay Men and they live scattered all along the coast,' Gutteridge told him. 'Maybe five or six of them live together in a shared camp. They could be anywhere, so we cruise quietly along the shore until they spot us and make a signal. Then we drop anchor and they'll come out to trade. They'll exchange their stock of logwood for the goods we bring. Our profit is rarely less than five hundred per cent.'

'How do we know what they want?'

The captain smiled. 'They always want the same thing.'

'But wouldn't they get a better price if they brought their logwood to Jamaica themselves?'

'They can't. Too many of them are wanted by the authorities. They'd be arrested the moment they set foot ashore. Many of them are ex-buccaneers who failed to come in and surrender when there was an amnesty. The rest are knaves and ruffians. They like the independent life, though I can't say I envy them.'

Now Gutteridge was staring fixedly at a stretch of mangrove. 'Is that smoke?' he asked. 'Or are my eyes playing tricks?'

Hector looked carefully. A light grey haze was rising from the greenery. It might be smoke or a patch of late-morning mist that had not yet cleared. 'They hide themselves like fugitives. Surely the authorities would not send ships here to arrest them,' he said.

'It's the Spanish they are afraid of,' Gutteridge explained. 'The Spaniards claim all of Campeachy as their territory and regard the Bay Men as trespassers who steal the timber. If the

Spanish patrols catch the loggers, they are carried off to the cities where they are thrown into prison or auctioned off as slaves.'

He was shading his eyes with his hands and staring long and hard. He gave a grunt of satisfaction. 'Yes, that's smoke all right. We stop here.'

He despatched Hector with a sailor into the ship's hold with orders to bring up a barrel of rum. Stooping under the deck beams, Hector noted that the cargo space was three-quarters empty. In one corner were stacked a few rolls of cloth. Elsewhere were several cases of hammers, axes, cutlasses, wedges, crowbars. Against a bulkhead several more chests contained blocks of refined sugar. But the bulk of the sloop's cargo was three dozen barrels and casks of varying sizes, ranging from a little eighteen-gallon rundlet to a massive puncheon. He checked their contents. Perhaps a quarter of them were kegs of gunpowder, the rest held rum, great quantities of it. With the help of his companion, Hector rolled a rum barrel to the companionway, and rigged a block and tackle to raise the cask on deck. There a rough table had already been made by laying planks across yet more barrels, and was set with loaves of ship's bread, ham and salted beef.

'Here they come now in that pirogue,' said Gutteridge, looking towards the shore. A large dugout canoe was already halfway out to the ship, paddled by three men. It was difficult to see much of the men because all were wearing hats with extravagantly broad, drooping brims which completely shaded their faces.

The captain himself went to the ship's rail, ready to hand his visitors up on deck. 'Greetings, my friends, greetings! Welcome to my ship!' he called out jovially. Hector could see that the newcomers were heavily armed. Each man had his musket, and there were pistols tucked in their belts. One of them paused his stroke for a moment, waved his paddle in the air, and let out a great whoop of elation.

Moments later their canoe was alongside, and the three logwood cutters were climbing over the rail. Gutteridge was slapping them on the back and gesturing towards the table of food and the keg of rum. Hector had never seen such uncouth characters. Their tangled hair hung down to their shoulders, and their beards were matted and unwashed. Every garment was filthy and reeking of sweat. Two of them had facial wounds – one had a scar that ran from his ear down the side of his neck, and another was lacking an eye. The third man in the group seemed to be their leader and was a colossus. He stood nearly six and a half feet, with heavily muscled shoulders and arms, and the knuckles on his enormous hands were callused. His face looked as if it had been struck a dozen times for there was a tracery of fine scars across his forehead and cheeks, and his nose had been flattened by a cruel blow. All three men carried themselves with a swaggering menace as they set foot on deck and looked around. Most striking of all was the colour of their skin. Their hands and faces were a strange dark red as though they had been roasted on a spit or were suffering from some strange disfiguring disease.

To Hector's astonishment, Gutteridge continued as if he was greeting long-lost bosom friends. 'Come! Be seated! You are most welcome. This is the festive season!' He was ushering the new arrivals to the empty kegs which served as seats beside the rough table, and already had begun to pour neat rum into pewter mugs which he handed to his guests. With barely a word said between them, the loggers swilled down their first drinks and held out their tankards for more. The giant reached out for a loaf of bread. He tore it in half, and then began softening it by splashing rum on the crust. He crammed the soggy mass into his mouth.

'Hector!' called the captain. 'Take the top off that barrel. We must not stint our guests.'

As Hector was prising open the barrel, a musket shot rang out just behind him, and he almost dropped the chisel. He turned to find one of the logwood cutters had loosed off a shot into the air. 'Bravo!' cried Gutteridge, not in the least taken aback. He poured the man another drink, and then took a swig from his own tankard. 'Here's to Kill-devil! There's plenty more where it came from.' Then he ordered the ship's cannon, a miserable little six-pounder, to be loaded and primed. With a theatrical gesture, he brought a lighted match to the touch hole, and the resulting explosion caused a flock of pelicans to flap up from the mangrove swamps and fly away in fear.

The headlong carousal lasted all afternoon, and by sunset the three logwood cutters were incapable of getting to their feet. One had fallen from his seat and was sprawled on deck, and the others were head down on the table, snoring. Gutteridge himself was little better. He tried to make his way to his cabin, but staggered so drunkenly that Hector feared his captain would blunder over the ship's side. He put an arm round Gutteridge's shoulders, and steered him back to his cabin where the man toppled face down onto his bunk.

Next morning, to Hector's awe, the Bay Men were calling for more rum to wash down their breakfast. They had iron constitutions because they seemed no worse for their debauch, and to all appearances were ready to carry on drinking for the rest of the day. Gutteridge was looking bilious as he appeared shakily from his cabin and finally managed to steer the conversation around to the question of trade. Did the Bay Men have any stocks of logwood ready for sale? He was told that the three men cut their timber individually, but pooled production. They were willing to exchange their timber for barrels of rum and additional supplies, but would need a few days to bring all their logs to a central stockpile close to a landing place.

'Hector,' said Gutteridge, 'perhaps you would oblige me by going ashore with our friends. They can show you how much logwood they have ready, and how much more is yet to be got together. Then we can calculate a fair price. Meanwhile I'll take the sloop farther up the coast and locate other suppliers.

I should be gone two or three days, at most a week. When I return we will commence loading.'

Hector was eager to go ashore and see the countryside, but before he clambered down into the pirogue, Gutteridge found an excuse to take him aside and speak to him privately. 'Be certain to put some mark on the existing stocks, something to show that we have a claim to it,' he said. 'The Bay Men can be fickle. With you on hand, they will not sell to the next ship that turns up. But I also want you to check on the logs they have on offer. There's something I must show you.'

He led Hector to a cubbyhole beneath the poop deck, and pulled out a billet of wood about three feet long. The timber was close-grained and the darkest red, almost black. 'This is what cost me the profits of my last voyage,' the captain said, handing the sample to Hector to inspect. 'That's logwood. Some people call it bloodwood because if you chop it into shavings and steep it in water, the stew looks like blood. Dyers add it in their vats for colouring cloth. They pay a handsome price, but only for the best quality. What do you make of it?'

Hector hefted the billet in his hands. It was very heavy and seemed flawless. It gave off a very faint odour, like the smell of violets. 'Here, let me show you,' said Gutteridge, taking it back from him. He struck the length of timber fiercely against a bulkhead, and the end section of the billet flew off. The exposed interior was hollow, rotted through. The cavity had been packed with dirt as a makeweight. 'More than half my last cargo was like that,' Gutteridge said. 'Useless, though I had paid top price. The loggers had already sold all their good stock, and they then spent weeks preparing the dross. They had covered the ends of all the rotten billets with plugs of decent wood, disguising the rubbish. It was cleverly done, and I was taken in. That's how I lost my capital.'

Shortly afterwards Hector rode thoughtfully ashore in the pirogue with the three Bay Men. By an unspoken agreement it seemed that he was assigned to accompany the giant whose name was Jezreel. But beyond that he knew nothing. Jezreel only grunted, 'Get a hat and bring some cloth' and had then fallen silent. Hector presumed that their solitary life made the Bay Men taciturn. None of them had said a word of thanks when Gutteridge handed each of them a sack stuffed with provisions and several bottles of rum to take back ashore.

His companions steered the pirogue into a gap in the mangroves, and a little way inside beached the vessel on a patch of hard sand. From there a narrow path threaded its way through a dreary wasteland of swamp. Within a few paces Hector felt a fierce stab of pain on the back of his neck as if a hot ember had landed on his skin. It was a biting insect and he slapped it away. Seconds later there were three or four more stings as he was attacked by swarms of mosquitoes. He squirmed in discomfort, for the insects were gorging on every exposed part of his body, even biting through his clothing. He stooped and splashed water from a puddle onto his face and bathed his arms. But the respite was only temporary. He could feel the insects settling on his face, and his eyelids were already beginning to puff up with the effect of their bites. He wondered how his companions put up with such an onslaught for they seemed untroubled.

When they reached a place where the path divided, the other Bay Men turned aside, leaving the giant Jezreel to stride forward, his sack of food and drink over his shoulder as if it was empty. Hector trotted behind him, still frantically sweeping aside the insects. A few minutes of hard walking brought them to where the mangroves gave way to more open, marshy scrubland. Here sloughs and ponds of stagnant water were linked by a great network of shallow creeks and channels. Marsh birds – herons, egrets, curlews and plovers – stalked the soggy ground, feeding on insects and small fish. Hector wondered how anyone could live in such watery surroundings, yet Jezreel waded through the obstacles without breaking stride. Soon they came to Jezreel's camp. It was no more than a huddle of simple open-sided huts, their roofs thickly thatched with palm leaves. In every hut were platforms raised on stakes at least three feet above the ground. One of the platforms appeared to be Jezreel's sleeping place, another was his living quarters. A few yards away his cooking place was yet another elevated platform, this time covered with earth.

'The flooding must be very bad,' observed Hector who had quickly understood the reason for this arrangement. Jezreel made no reply but took down a cloth bundle hanging from the thatch and tossed it across to Hector. 'Spread that. It helps against the insects.' Unwrapping the cloth, Hector found it contained a slimy yellow lump of rancid animal fat. Gingerly he began to smear it across his face and neck. The suet smelled and felt foul but seemed to discourage the worst of the insect attacks. Now he appreciated why the logwood cutters seldom removed their broad-brimmed hats. Their headgear prevented the mosquitoes tangling and biting in their hair. 'Make yourself a pavilion over there,' continued the Bay Man indicating one of the shelters. Hector saw that he was to rig up a canopy, using the cloth he had brought from the ship. It would keep away the insects from his bed.

'Know how to shoot?' asked Jezreel. Clearly he was someone who wasted few words.

Hector nodded.

'We'll get in some fresh meat for your captain when he returns.'

The big man reached up and tugged a musket from where it had been stored within the thatch, and handed it to the young man. From a hanging satchel he produced half a dozen charges of gunpowder wrapped in paper, a small powder horn, and a bag of bullets. Checking over the gun, Hector saw that it was an old-fashioned matchlock. To fire it, he would need to load, then add powder to the priming pan and keep the fuse lit until he was ready to pull the trigger. He thought to himself that a flintlock would have been much easier to use in such wet conditions, and could only suppose that Jezreel had been unable to obtain modern weapons.

He followed the giant out of the camp, and was led at the same brisk pace deeper into the swampy savannah. The ground was moist and soggy with a thin layer of rotting leaves covering yellow clay. From time to time they passed scatterings of pale wood chips on the ground. 'Logwood,' explained the big man, and seeing that Hector was puzzled, he added. 'Only the dark heartwood is taken. You must trim away the rest. The sap rind is near white or yellow.'

They walked on in silence.

Eventually they came to the margins of a wide, shallow lagoon. Here and there were low islands covered with grass and small thickets of brushwood. Hauled up on the shore was a small dugout canoe, evidently kept by Jezreel for his hunting trips. The boat was little larger than the one Hector had used in his escape from Port Royal. There were two paddles wedged under the thwarts.

＊

THEY WADED OUT into the shallows, pushing the little craft ahead of them and holding their muskets high. Jezreel gestured for Hector to climb in and take a seat in the bow, then the big man took up his position in the stern and soon they were moving forward across the mere. From where he was sitting, Hector felt the canoe surge forward each time Jezreel took a stroke. By comparison his own efforts felt feeble. Neither of them said a word.

After some fifteen minutes Jezreel abruptly stopped paddling, and Hector followed suit. The canoe glided forward as Hector felt a tap on his shoulder, and the giant's hand appeared in the corner of his vision. Jezreel was pointing away into the distance. On the shore of an island and difficult to see against the background vegetation stood half a dozen wild cattle. They were smaller than the domestic cows that Hector had known at home in Ireland, dark brown in colour, almost black, and armed with long curving horns. Three of them were standing up to their hocks, feeding on lilies. The others were on the shore, grazing.

Behind him there was the sound of flint on steel. A moment later his companion passed him a length of glowing slow match. Hector fixed it in the jaws of his musket's firing lock. Very gently, they stalked the wild cattle, closing the gap without being observed. From time to time one of the animals would raise its head from feeding, and scan for danger.

Hector calculated that they had got within a very long musket shot when, unexpectedly, there came the thump of a distant explosion. For a moment he thought that Gutteridge's sloop had returned and was firing a signal gun. But the sound had come, not from the sea behind them, but somewhere over to his left, from the savannah.

Whatever the source of the detonation, it had stampeded the wild cattle. Tails held high in panic, they abandoned their island and dashed deeper into the lake, then began swimming away. All that was visible was a line of horned heads disappearing in the distance.

Hector was about to turn and speak to Jezreel when the big man's voice said 'Hold still!' and the muzzle of a musket slid past beside his right cheek. The barrel was placed on his shoulder. He froze in position, all thought of paddling gone. Instead he gripped the sides of the canoe, scarcely breathing. He heard Jezreel behind him shifting his stance, and felt the musket barrel on his shoulder move a fraction. There was a whiff of slow match. The next moment there was the flat explosive crack of the weapon firing. The sound was so close to Hector's face that it made his head ring, and left him half deaf. His eyes watered with the cloud of gun smoke, and for a moment his vision was obscured. When the gun smoke blew away, he looked forward to where the cattle had been swimming. To his amazement one of the animals had swerved aside.

The creature was already dropping back, separating from its fellows. Jezreel's marksmanship was far out of the ordinary. To have hit his target from such a distance while seated in an unstable canoe was a remarkable feat. Even Dan, whom Hector considered the best marksman he knew, would have found it difficult to achieve such accuracy.

Already Jezreel was back at work, driving the canoe forward with huge paddle strokes. Hastily Hector joined his effort, for the wild cow was still able to flounder through the water and had turned directly for shore. Moments later it was in the shallows, and with great thrashing leaps was plunging towards safety, blood streaming from its neck and staining the water a frothy red.

The two hunters reached their prey while the animal was still hock deep on the shelving edge of the lake. It was a young bull, wounded and very angry. It turned to face its tormentors, snorting with pain and rage, and lowered its vicious horns.

Hector put down his paddle. The bull was perhaps fifteen yards away, still at a safe distance. The young man poured priming powder into the pan of his musket, blew gently on the burning matchcord to make it glow, raised his musket, and pulled the trigger. At that range it was impossible to miss. The ball struck the bull in the chest and he saw the animal stagger with the impact. But the animal was young and strong, and did not drop. It still stood on the same spot, menacing and dangerous. Hector expected his companion to hold back, until the two men had reloaded, then finish off their prey. Instead Jezreel drove the canoe into the shallows, and leaping out into the water began to wade towards the wild bull. To Hector's alarm he saw that the logwood cutter was empty-handed. There was a long hunting knife in Jezreel's belt but it stayed in its sheath. The young man watched him advance until, at the last moment, the bull lowered its head and charged. The attack could have been mortal. But Jezreel stood his ground, and in one sure movement leaned down and seized the creature's horns before the animal could lift its head and impale him. As Hector watched, the big man twisted and, using his great strength, threw the bull off its feet. In a welter of foam and muddy water, the beast fell on its side, the logwood cutter dropped one knee on the animal's neck, then forced its head under water. For several moments there was a succession of desperate heaves as the trapped animal attempted to escape. Then gradually its struggles eased and, after one last shudder, it ceased to move.

Jezreel held the drowned creature's head submerged a full minute to make sure that it was really dead. Then he rose to his feet and called to Hector. 'Pull the canoe up on land, then come and give me a hand to butcher the beast. We'll take what we can carry, and they can have the rest.'

Following his companion's glance, Hector saw the snouts of two large alligators gliding across the water towards them.

'You'll see plenty of others,' explained his companion. 'Mostly the caymans stay their distance. But if they are hungry or in a bad humour, just occasionally they will run at you and take you down.'

Working quickly, they began to butcher the wild bull into quarters. Here, too, Jezreel was an adept. The blade of his hunting knife sliced through skin and flesh, skilfully working around the bones and severing the sinews, until the slabs of fresh meat had been separated from the carcass. They dropped them into the canoe, and pushed off, heading back towards their camp. Looking over his shoulder, Hector saw the caymans crawling up the slope. As he watched, they began to snap and chew at the bloody carcass, like huge olive brown lizards attacking a lump of raw flesh.

When they arrived at their original departure point, Jezreel secured the canoe. Then he leaned over and picked up a great slab of raw beef from the bilges. With his knife he cut a long slit in its centre. 'Stand closer,' he demanded, 'and take off your hat.' Hector did as he was told, and before he could react, his companion held up the meat, and slipped it over the young man's head so the beef hung like a tabard, front and back, the blood soaking through his shirt. 'Best way to fetch it to camp,' said Jezreel. 'Leaves your hands free so you can carry a musket. If it's too heavy, I'll trim off a portion and lighten the load.' He carved slits in two more of the meaty parcels, and with a double load draped over his own massive shoulders, started walking back along the track.

As they trudged back along the path, Hector asked about the explosion that had scared the cattle. 'At first I thought it was Captain Gutteridge signalling his return. But the sound came from the savannah. It wasn't Spaniards was it?'

Jezreel shook his head. 'If it had been Spaniards, we would have made ourselves scarce. That was one of our companions preparing logwood.'

'But it sounded like a cannon shot.'

'Most of the logwood is small stuff, easy to handle. From time to time you fell a big tree, maybe six feet around, and the wood is so tough that it's impossible to split into smaller pieces. So you blow it apart with a charge of gunpowder, shrewdly placed.'

'The captain asked me to make a list of all the logwood ready to load. Can we do that tomorrow?' asked Hector. But the giant did not reply. He was looking away to the north where a thick bank of cloud had formed. It lay in the lower sky as a heavy black line, its upper edge as clean and sharp as if trimmed with a scythe. It looked motionless, yet unnatural and menacing.

'Tomorrow may prove difficult,' Jezreel said.

✳

THE CLOUD BANK was still there at dawn. It had neither dispersed nor come any closer. 'What does it signify?' Hector asked. He and Jezreel were eating a breakfast of fresh beef strips cooked on the barbacoa.

'The sailors call it a North Bank. It could be a sign that the weather is changing.'

Hector looked up at the sky. Apart from the strange black North Bank, there was not a cloud in the sky. There was only the same baking haze that he had seen every day since his arrival on the Campeachy coast. He detected just the faintest breath of a breeze, barely enough to disturb the plume of smoke rising from their cooking fire.

'What makes you say that?' he enquired.

Jezreel pointed with his chin towards dozens of man of war birds that were circling over the area where the hunt had taken place. The fork-tailed sea birds were dipping down in spirals, then rising up, clearly disturbed, and constantly uttering their shrill high-pitched cries. 'They don't come inland unless they know something is going to happen. And these last two days I've noticed something odd about the tides. There's been almost no flood, only ebb. The water has been retreating as if the sea is gathering its strength.' He rose from his seat and added, 'If we are checking on the logwood stocks, we better hurry.'

As it turned out, the logwood cutters still had much work to do. Their caches of timber were widely scattered, and they had yet to carry them to the landing place on the creek. Jezreel was more advanced in this work than his companions because he had the strength of two men. Transporting the billets of wood was as much drudgery as cutting the timber in the first place. The men worked like pack animals, stooped under immense loads which Hector calculated at two hundred pounds a time, and staggering through the swamps. He wondered why the Bay Men did not make rafts of the timber and float them along the many backwaters, but realised the reason when one of the logs slipped from Jezreel's load. The dense timber sank like a rock.

An hour before sunset the wind, which had continued faint all day, moved into the north and began to strengthen. The increase was steady, rather than dramatic, but continued through the night. At first Hector, dozing on his platform, was aware only that the sides of his cloth pavilion were stirring and lifting in the breeze. But within an hour the folds of cloth were flapping and billowing, and he got up and took down the cloth because it was evident that no insects would be flying in such conditions. He enjoyed the respite for a short while, listening to the rushing of the wind as it swept through the mangroves. But soon the wind was plucking at the thatch of his shelter and he found it difficult to get to sleep. He lay there, thinking of Susanna and wondering whether he would be able to see her again after Gutteridge had loaded the logwood and brought him back to Jamaica. Maybe he would have earned enough money from the logwood sale to invest in a commercial enterprise and start to make the fortune that would impress the young woman into accepting him as a formal suitor. Riches, by all accounts, were swiftly gained in the Caribees.

Eventually he did fall into a deep sleep, only to be woken shortly before daybreak by a rattling noise. The wind was so strong that the fiercer gusts were shaking the entire fabric of his shelter. Unable to rest, Hector swung his legs over the side of his sleeping platform, and stood up. To his shock, he found that he was standing in six inches of water.

As the light rapidly strengthened, he saw that the entire camp site was under water. In places it was submerged to a depth of at least a foot. The flood was flowing inland like a vast river. He dipped a finger into the water and sucked on it. He tasted salt. The sea was invading the land.

Splashing his way out of the hut, he found Jezreel assembling a bundle of his possessions, his guns and powder, a coil of rope, a water bottle, a hatchet, food. 'Here, take these, you may need them later,' he said to Hector, handing him a spare water bottle, a cutlass and a gun. 'What's happening?' enquired Hector. He had to raise his voice for the sound of the wind had now risen to a steady roar. 'It's a North,' shouted the giant. 'December and January is their time and this looks to be a bad one.'

The big man looked round to make sure that he had everything he needed, then led Hector inland towards a swell of rising ground. As they waded through the water, the young man observed that the water level was constantly rising. It was now halfway up the supports of his sleeping platform.

'How much higher will it flood?' he shouted.

Jezreel shrugged. 'No way of telling. Depends how long the gale blows.'

They reached the knoll. Here stood a single enormous tree, fifteen or twenty feet around its base. Lightning must have struck it, for all but a handful of the upper branches were shorn away, and those which survived bore no leaves. Jczreel went to its farther side. There the lightning had left a jagged open gash which extended almost down to the ground. Jezreel swung his hatchet and began to widen the crevice, enough to jam in hand or foot. 'You better climb up first. You are more nimble,' he advised Hector. 'Take the rope and get as high as you can. At least up to the first large branches. Once you're there, lower the rope to me and we'll haul up our gear.'

Half an hour later they were both seated some twenty feet above the ground, each astride a thick branch. 'Might as well make ourselves secure,' said Jezreel, passing him the end of their rope. 'If the wind gets stronger we'll be blown off like rotten plums.'

Fastened in place with a rope around his waist, Hector watched the floodwaters rising. It was an extraordinary sight. A great swirling, rippling brown mass of water was sliding inland, carrying everything before it. Branches, leaves, all sorts of clutter were being swept along. Bushes disappeared. The corpse of a wild pig floated by. What made the scene all the more remarkable was that the sky still remained bright and sunny, except for the ominous bank of cloud which lay heavily on the horizon. 'Will rain come?' Hector asked his companion.

'No, a North is not like a hurricane,' answered Jezreel. 'Everyone knows of the hurricane and the downpours it brings.

But a North stays steady as long as that black cloud is there, and without any rain. But it can be just as fatal if you are on a lee shore.'

By mid afternoon the wind had risen to gale force and was threatening to pluck Hector from his perch. He felt the great dead tree vibrating in the blasts, and wondered if its dead roots would hold. If the tree were toppled, he could not see how they would survive.

'What about the others?' he shouted above the clamour of the wind.

'They'll do the same as us, if they can find a refuge high enough,' Jezreel called back. 'But it's the end of my stay here.'

'What do you mean?' shouted Hector.

'Nothing will remain after this flood,' answered the big man. 'All our stock of logwood is being washed away. Some may stay in place, but the rest will shift and be buried in the mud. It will take weeks to salvage it, and even then it will be almost impossible to bring it to the landing place. A North rarely lasts more than a day or two, but it will be weeks before the flood waters recede far enough for us to begin any recovery. Besides, all our food stores will have been destroyed, and the gunpowder soaked and ruined.'

Glumly Hector looked down at the swirling water. His mind was on Gutteridge and his sloop. Unless the captain had found a truly secure anchorage there was little chance that his vessel would survive.

That evening they ate a meal of cold meat washed down with gulps of water. From time to time they shifted position by a few inches, cautiously easing the discomfort of their perch because the gale still raged. Occasionally a bird flashed past them, swept helplessly downwind.

The gale began to slacken about the time the stars came out and, looking north, Hector saw that the long black cloud had gone. 'That means the North is finished,' Jezreel told him.

They dozed fitfully and at sunrise looked out on a scene of

devastation. The flood water extended as far as the eye could see. Here and there the tops of small trees were still visible, but their branches had been stripped of foliage. The only movement was the small, reluctant swirls and eddies in the brown flood which told that the water had reached its peak and was slowly beginning to recede.

'It'll be some hours yet before we can descend,' Jezreel warned. He leaned his head back against the tree trunk, and there was a companionable silence between them.

'Tell me,' said Hector, 'how did you finish up here of all places?'

Jezreel waited several moments before answering. 'Those scars on my face are the mark of my former profession. Did you ever hear of Nat Hall, the "Sussex Gladiator"?'

When Hector did not reply, he continued. 'You might have done if you had lived in London and visited Clare Market or Hockley in the Hole. It was there I fought trials of skill, gave exhibitions, taught classes too. The singlestick was my favourite, though I was handy enough with the backsword.'

'I've seen prize fights at home,' said Hector. 'But that was with fists, between farmers at the country fairs.'

'You are talking about trials of manhood,' the big man corrected him. He stretched out his hands to show the callused knuckles. 'That's what fistics leave you with, and maybe a flattened nose and mis-shapen ears. Trials of skill are different. They're done with weapons. My nose was shaped by a blow from a singlestick, and the same caused my scars. Had I received a slash from a backsword that would have left no ear at all.'

'It must take courage to follow such a dangerous profession,' commented Hector.

Jezreel shook his head. 'I drifted into it. I was always very big for my age, and strong too. By the time I was fourteen, I was taking wagers on feats of strength – breaking thick ropes, pulling saplings up by their roots, lifting heavy stones, that sort of thing. Eventually I found my way to London where a showman promised me that I would be the new English Samson in his theatre. But I was never quite good enough, and he was a cheat.'

Jezreel leaned over from his branch and spat down into the flood water. He waited for a moment, watching the blob of spittle float on the surface. Slowly it drifted seawards. 'On the ebb,' he commented as he settled back against the tree trunk, and continued with his tale. 'I was always quick, as much as I was strong. Have you ever seen hot work at the singlestick?' he asked.

'Never. Is it some sort of cudgel?'

Jezreel made a grimace of distaste. 'That's what some people call it, but gives the wrong idea. Imagine a short sword, but with a blade of ash, and a basket handle. Two men stand face to face, no more than a yard apart, easy striking distance. They hold their weapons high and make lightning cuts and slashes at one another. Each blocks the other's blow and strikes back in an instant. The target is any part of the body above the waist. The feet must stay on the ground, not moving.'

Jezreel's right hand was above his head now and, with bent wrist, he was whipping an imaginary blade through the air, down and sideways, slashing and parrying. For a moment Hector feared that the big man would lose his balance on the branch and tumble into the flood.

'How is the winner decided?' he asked.

'Whoever first suffers a broken head is the loser. To win you must draw blood with a blow to the head, hence my scars.'

'But that doesn't explain why you are here now.'

The prize fighter waited a long time before he continued. 'Like I told you, singlestick was my favourite, but I was handy with the short sword too. It's the same style and technique but with a sharp metal blade, and when you fight for big money, the crowd wants to see the blood flow freely.'

Hector sensed that the big man was finding it difficult to speak of his past.

'I was matched against a good man, a champion. The purse was very big and I knew that I was outclassed. He need not have cheated. He cut me across the back of my leg, tried to hamstring me, and in my anger and pain I lashed out with a lucky stroke. It split his skull.'

'But it was an accident.'

'He had a patron, a powerful man who lost both his wager and his investment. I was warned that I would be tried for murder, so I fled.' Jezreel gave a bitter smile. 'One thing, though, all that exercise with singlestick or backsword will have its uses.'

'I don't grasp your meaning,' said Hector.

'This cursed flood has put an end to my hopes of making a living out of logwood. I expect my comrades will go back to what they did before – buccaneering. I think I'll join them.'

When eventually Jezreel judged it was safe to descend from their perch, Hector accompanied the prize fighter as they waded waist deep through the retreating flood water. They found their camp was wrecked. The huts still stood, though skewed and made lopsided by the current, but all their contents were either washed away or ruined. There was nothing to salvage. They made their way to the landing place among the mangroves and were relieved that the pirogue was undamaged though they had to extract it from the upper branches of a mangrove thicket where it had lodged. Just when they had succeeded in relaunching the pirogue, the two other Bay Men straggled in. They too had shifted for themselves and managed to climb out of harm's way.

'What do we do now?' asked the man with the scarred face whom Jezreel called Otway.

'Best try to link up with Captain Gutteridge . . . if his ship still floats,' answered Jezreel. The little group stacked their last remaining possessions into the pirogue, then paddled out from among the mangroves, and along the coast in the direction they had last seen the sloop. They had not gone more than five miles when they saw in the distance a sight which confirmed Jezreel's fears. Cast up a hundred yards into the coastal swamp was the dark outline of a ship. It was Gutteridge's sloop. She lay on her side. A shattered stump showed where the mainmast had once stood. The spar itself lay across the deck in a tangled web of rigging. The mainsail was draped over the bow like a winding sheet.

'Poor sods,' breathed Otway. 'She must have driven ashore in the gale. I doubt there were any survivors.'

They paddled their pirogue closer, looking for any signs of life. Jezreel fired his musket as a signal. But there was no response, no answering shot, no call. The big man reloaded and fired again in the air – still there was nothing. The shattered hulk was abandoned, dark, and silent.

SIX

THE NORTH's baleful effect was detected far to the south. In Dan's homeland on the Miskito coast his people saw the tide recede beyond its normal range, then flood in with unusual strength, and they knew that it signified a great, distant upheaval. The flotsam washed ashore was still being gathered by children from the Miskito villages when Dan came home a fortnight later. He recounted how he and Jacques had been taken by Coxon's buccaneers and sent aboard *L'Arc-de-Ciel* to Petit Guave. The French settlement had been abuzz with preparations for a freebooting raid on the Spanish Main, and the governor, Monsieur de Pouncay, was absent. Rather than wait for his return to decide if their prisoners were guilty of piracy, Captain Coxon's prize crew saw their chance of easy plunder. They volunteered to join the French expedition, freed their prisoners, and recruited Dan to pilot them to the Miskito coast for it was from there that the French proposed to march on the Spanish settlements in the interior. Jacques was happy to join them as he had encountered several former acquaintances from the Paris gaols among the freebooters. But when the French expedition disembarked, Jacques had changed his mind, preferring to stay behind on the beach and watch out for any Spanish patrol ships and wait for Dan to return from a visit to his Miskito family.

'Weren't they happy to see you again?' asked Jacques. He had been surprised to see Dan reappear after less than a week. Dan looked up from where he was kneeling on the sand, about to butcher a turtle for their midday meal.

'Of course. They wanted to hear about all the places I had seen during my travels.'

'And didn't they expect you to stay at home?'

'That's not our custom,' the Miskito replied. 'Our young men are encouraged to join the foreign raiding parties who come to our coast. They get well rewarded as scouts and hunters.'

He turned the turtle on its back and tickled it under the chin with the point of his cutlass. The creature extended its neck, and with a lightning stroke he chopped down with his blade. The head spun away, the beaked jaws still snapping and narrowly missing Jacques who jumped aside.

'How are you going to get into the shell?' the Frenchman asked.

'It's easy. You slip the tip of your cutlass into this slot where the upper and lower shells meet. Then carefully slice sideways, following right around the joint. If you try to cut anywhere else, you'll find it impossible.'

Jacques rubbed the galerien's brand on his check as he watched his companion. Within moments the Miskito had prised apart the turtle, opening it like a clam shell.

'Why, the gut's like the intestines of a cow,' the Frenchman noted in surprise.

'I suppose that's because the turtles also feed on grass.'

'But they are sea creatures.'

'If it's calm tomorrow,' answered the Miskito, 'I'll take you out in a canoe to where you can see four fathoms down. You'll see grass growing on the sea floor. That's the turtle's food.'

He turned back to his work and pointed out two discoloured patches of flesh in the body of the turtle, close to the muscles of the front flippers. 'You must cut those out,' he said. 'If you don't, the flesh will have a bad taste when cooked.'

'Just leave the cooking to me,' said Jacques impatiently. He was of the opinion that the Miskito showed a great lack of imagination by only grilling or boiling turtle meat. He had already suggested to Dan that a sauce of lemon juice, pimento and pepper would enhance the flavour.

'As you wish,' said Dan equably. 'For frying the meat, use that yellowish fat on the inside of the lower shell. But please leave me the greenish fat of the upper shell.'

'Is it poisonous?' asked Jacques who felt that perhaps he was too hasty in his culinary plans.

'Not at all. I'll set the shell upright in the sand after we've got all the meat out of it. When the sun has softened the green fat, you can scrape it off and eat it raw. It's delicious.'

A halloo attracted their attention. A hundred yards offshore a dugout canoe was passing down the coast under a small triangular sail. Its occupant was standing up and waving to them. Immediately Dan got to his feet and waved back, beckoning the newcomer to come to land. 'That's Jon, one of my cousins,' the Miskito explained. 'He's been away on a fishing trip.'

Dan hurried down the slope of the beach to greet his relative, and to Jacques's astonishment, as the newcomer stepped out of his canoe Dan fell flat on his face on the sand. For a moment Jacques thought that his friend had tripped. But then the Miskito got to his feet, and his cousin also dropped prone in front of Dan, and lay spreadeagle and face down for the space of a few heartbeats, then stood up again. Next the two men threw their arms around one another and hugged tightly, each with his face pressed against the other's neck. Jacques, who had walked towards them, distinctly heard both men snuffling loudly and with gusto. His puzzlement must have shown, for when Dan introduced the Frenchman, he added, 'Don't look so surprised. That's our way of greeting someone we are fond of and have not seen for a long time. We call it *kia walaia*. It means "to smell, to understand".'

The two Miskito exchanged news and when Dan turned back to Jacques, he was looking thoughtful. 'Jon has been fishing to the north. He heard rumours of a party of white men travelling along the coast in pirogues. Three boatloads of them. They are coming this way, but very slowly, for they are weak and sickly. Also he says that a Spanish patrol ship was seen five days ago.'

Dan asked his cousin a few more questions, then added, 'My guess is that the men in the pirogues are English or French. If so, they should be warned about the Spanish patrol ship. Jon is willing to lend me his canoe if I want to go there to find out more. I could be back inside three days if this wind holds.' Dan seemed eager to make the trip.

Jacques considered for a moment before replying. 'All right then. I'll wait here for you.'

'In the meantime you can try out your turtle recipe on my cousin,' said Dan cheerfully.

＊

THE UNIDENTIFIED travellers were much closer than expected. Before noon on the second day Dan glimpsed the three pirogues. They were beached inside a river mouth less than thirty miles from where he had left Jacques. Cautiously Dan steered across the sandbar at the river mouth, keeping close under the bank so that the canoe's sail brushed the overhanging branches of the mangroves which stretched away in an unbroken wall on both sides of the estuary. When he reached the travellers' camp, the first person he saw was Hector. Moments later the two friends were greeting one another with astonished delight.

'How on earth did you get here?' the Miskito exclaimed as Hector helped him haul his canoe up on the muddy bank. 'I thought you were in Jamaica.'

'I managed to get away and join the Bay Men,' Hector explained. 'But we were flooded out by a bad storm, and had to abandon the site. Coming down the coast we met up with these other logwood cutters. They had all suffered the same misfortune. We joined forces, keeping the largest of our boats. But it's been a difficult journey. We've been living on wild fruit and an occasional seabird we shot.'

Dan could see that the survivors were in a bad way. There were about twenty men in the party and they looked emaciated. One man was shivering with fever. 'There's a Spanish cruiser in the area. You know what will happen if they catch the Bay Men,' he warned Hector.

'But they've resolved to go no further until they've filled their bellies. That's why they decided to stop here in the estuary. They intend to go inland and hunt wild cattle or pigs, if they can find them.'

Dan shook his head. 'That's foolish. The Spaniards could be here by then. I'll fetch meat for them.'

'Jezreel!' Hector called out, 'I want you to meet a good friend of mine. This is Dan. He was with me in Barbary.'

The prize fighter's glance took in the Miskito's long black hair and the narrow face with its high cheekbones and dark, sunken eyes like polished pebbles. 'Did I hear you say that you can get food for us?'

Hector glanced into the Miskito's canoe. 'You haven't even brought a musket with you.'

'I won't need one. This is my cousin's canoe and he left his fishing gear in it. But you'll have to help me.'

Mystified, Hector was about to step into the bow of the canoe when Dan stopped him. 'No, your place is in the stern,' he said. 'I'll tell you what to do.'

Under Dan's instructions, Hector hoisted the little sail and together the two men rode the river current out across the bar and to the sea. Instead of heading out to the fishing grounds as Hector had expected, Dan told him to steer close along the shore. 'Stay in the shallows, close to the mangroves,' he instructed.

Occasionally Dan rose to his feet and stood in the bow, silently scanning the surface of the water. Every time he did this, Hector feared that the canoe would capsize through his own lack of skill as steersman. But Dan shifted his weight to counteract any clumsiness and, sensing his friend's uneasiness, would soon sit down again.

'What are we looking for?' Hector asked his friend. He spoke in a whisper for it seemed to him that Dan was listening as well as watching for his mysterious prey.

An hour passed, and then another, and still Dan had not found what he was searching for. Then, suddenly, he held up his hand in warning. His gaze was fixed on something in the water, not fifty yards away and close to the edge of the mangroves. He reached down into the bottom of the canoe, not taking his eyes off what he had seen, and eased out from the bilge a straight staff about eight or nine feet long. With his free hand Dan groped between his feet and produced what appeared to be an oversized weaver's bobbin wrapped around with several fathoms of cord. The free end of the cord was lashed to a barbed metal spike as long as his forearm. Carefully Dan pushed the shank of the spike into a socket in one end of the staff. Then he unwound enough cord until he could slip the bobbin over the butt of the pole. Now he rose to his feet and stood in the canoe, the harpoon in his hand. Using it as a pointer, he showed Hector the direction that he should steer.

Hector squinted against the glare of the late-afternoon sunlight as he tried to make out the target. But there was nothing unusual. The water was green-grey and opaque, cloudy with particles of vegetable matter. He thought he saw a slight ripple, but could not be sure. The canoe slipped forward silently.

Ahead of him Dan had moved into the classic posture of a man about to throw a javelin: his left arm pointed forward, his right arm bent. The hand which held the harpoon shaft at its balance point was close beside his ear. He stood poised, ready.

Hector heard a faint breath, the puffing sound of lungs expelling air. He leaned sideways, trying to see around Dan, hoping to identify the source of the sound. His sudden movement upset the balance of the boat even as Dan threw.

The harpoon soared through the air. But as it left Dan's hand, Hector knew that he had spoiled his friend's aim. He saw Dan twist his body, swivelling to keep the direction of his throw. 'I'm sorry, Dan,' he blurted, apologising for his clumsiness.

His words were lost in the explosive upheaval at the spot where the harpoon had struck the water. The metal spike and the first two feet of shaft plunged out of view. A second later the surface of the sea rose up in a great, roiling mass. A large grey-brown shape surged upwards, water sluicing off a rounded back. Hardly had this shape appeared than it sank downwards almost as quickly, returning into the murky water, and the sea was closing over it in a small whirlpool. The entire length of the harpoon vanished, dragged downward.

The Miskito spun round, plucked the canoe's short mast out of its place and hastily wrapped the sail around the spar. Dropping the untidy bundle on the thwarts he picked up a paddle, knelt in the bottom of the canoe, and began to paddle with all his strength. 'Over there!' he shouted back at Hector who was trying to follow his friend's example. Looking forward, Hector saw that the harpoon's shaft had risen back to the surface, and was floating free a few yards ahead of them. Leaning forward as the canoe came level with the pole, Dan retrieved it. Both the metal spike and the wooden spool were gone. With a clatter Dan flung the shaft into the bottom of the canoe and was already scanning the surface of the water again. He gave a grunt of satisfaction and pointed. A little way ahead floated the wooden spool. It was spinning rapidly in the water, the coils of line unreeling and making the spool bob and twist as if it had a life of its own. The line was being stripped from the reel at a great pace.

'Come on!' urged Dan. 'We must get that too!' He was digging furiously at the water with his paddle. They reached the gyrating spool when only a few turns of the line remained. Dan dropped his paddle and threw himself forward to grab the bobbin. In one swift movement he had hoisted it inboard and jammed the spool under a thwart as he called, 'Hang on, Hector!'

An instant later Hector felt himself flung backward, the thwart striking him painfully in the small of the back as the canoe suddenly shot forward. The line had snapped taut, droplets of water squeezing from the fibres. It had become a tow rope linked to an unseen and powerful underwater force. The canoe swayed from side to side as it tore onward, lurching wildly. The pull of the line was both forward and down, and for a terrifying moment Hector thought that the entire canoe would be dragged underwater as the bow dipped and the water rose to barely an inch below the rim of the dugout.

For three or four minutes the mad, careering rush went on. In the bow Dan anxiously watched the line where it was pulled taut across the edge of the canoe. Hector was sure that the cord was too thin to resist the strain. He wondered what would happen if it snapped suddenly.

Then, without warning, the water ahead of the canoe again burst into swirling turbulence. The grey-brown shape emerged in a welter of foam, and this time Hector distinctly heard the air rushing out of animal lungs. 'Palpa!' shouted Dan in triumph. 'A big one.'

It took a full hour before the harpooned creature was exhausted and by that time the canoe had been dragged far along the coast. Gradually, the intervals between each surfacing of their prey grew shorter as the animal came up for air more frequently. With each appearance Hector could see more of it. At first it reminded him of a small whale, then of one of the seals he had seen when they hauled themselves out on the rocks off his native Ireland. But this animal was much larger than any seal he had known, seven or eight feet long, and far stouter. When it turned its head to look back at the hunters, he saw long pendulous lips, piggy eyes and a sprouting of whiskers.

Finally the creature gave up the struggle. It no longer had the strength to dive. It lay wallowing on the surface, close enough for Dan to pull in on the line and haul the canoe right alongside. From his cousin's fishing gear he produced a second harpoon head, shorter and more stubby this time, and fitted it to the staff. He chose his moment and stabbed down several times. A stain of blood spread in the water. There were a few last convulsive heaves. Then the creature lay still. 'Palpa. Your sailors call it sea cow,' said Dan with evident satisfaction. 'And a good fat one too. There will be enough meat to feed everyone.'

'What does it taste like?' asked Hector looking at the bloated shape. He recalled an old sailor's yarn that claimed such creatures were mermaids because they suckled their young at their breasts. But this animal looked more like an overgrown and bloated seal with a drooping pug face.

'Some say it tastes like young cow. Others that it is like the finest pork.' Dan was lashing the carcass alongside the canoe. 'It'll be a slow journey back to camp. One of us can sleep while the other steers.'

Hector was still conscious that not everything had gone to plan. The hunt had taken far longer than it should. 'I'm sorry that I spoiled your aim, Dan.'

His friend gave a dismissive shrug. 'You did well. It takes years to learn how to strike palpa properly. If my striking iron had been better placed, the palpa would have died more quickly. What matters is that the creature did not escape, and we have the meat we promised.'

*

IT TOOK THE entire night, and more, to sail back to where they had started. The drag of the dead sea cow slowed the canoe to less than walking pace, and the sun was well above the horizon by the time they approached the river mouth. It was promising to be another very humid and hazy day. They were keeping close to the green wall of mangroves along the shoreline to escape the worst effect of the ebbing tide when they heard the distant thud of an explosion.

'What's that!' Hector blurted, sitting up in alarm. He and Dan had changed positions in the canoe, and he had been dozing in the bow as his friend steered the craft.

'It sounded like a cannon shot,' said Dan.

'But the Bay Men have only got muskets.'

Again there came the thump of a distant explosion, followed by another. This time there was no doubt. It was cannon fire.

'Dan, I think we had better leave the sea cow where we can collect it later, and go ahead to see what's happening.'

Dan brought the canoe to the edge of the mangroves. He untied the carcass of the sea cow and fastened it securely to a lattice of roots. 'It should be safe here if the tide does not wash it away,' he said.

Warily the two men edged their little vessel forward until they reached the point where they had a clear view of the river mouth.

A two-masted brigantine was sailing slowly across the estuary, but making no attempt to enter the river. The large ensign flying from her stern was clearly visible, three bands of red, white and gold and in the centre some sort of crest. As they watched, the vessel came within a pistol shot of the far bank and began to turn. A few minutes later she had taken up her new course and was retracing her path across the mouth of the river. Hector was reminded of a terrier that has cornered a rat in a hole and is pacing up and down excitedly, waiting to finish off the prey.

'It's the Spanish patrol ship you were warned about,' he said.

There was a cloud of black smoke and the sound of a single cannon. He could not see where the shot landed, but clearly it was aimed towards the three pirogues still lying beached on the river bank.

'That's to make it clear who has the upper hand,' commented Dan. 'With six cannon a side and maybe forty men aboard, the Spaniards have got it all worked out.' He was backing water, forcing the canoe into the fringe of mangroves.

'What are they waiting for?' Hector asked.

'For the tide to turn. See that line of broken water on the bar at the river entrance. The river current and ebbing tide are too strong for the brigantine to make any headway upriver. Besides, the pilot will be cautious. He's waiting for the flood tide, and when he's sure there's enough water to carry him in over the bar, he'll take the ship upriver and blast the pirogues to pieces.'

Hector examined the Spanish guardship now heading directly towards where he and Dan lay hidden. Doubtless every pair of eyes on board the patrol vessel was looking towards the pirogues in the river. Still, he felt vulnerable and exposed.

He was about to say that a single hit from a cannonball would shatter a pirogue when he felt the canoe tilt underneath him. He grabbed for the rim of the little craft, but it was too late. Water was pouring in over the gunwale. Looking back over his shoulder he saw Dan was leaning sideways, pressing down at an angle, deliberately flooding the canoe. As the water rose within the hull, the canoe began to sink, settling on an even keel until it was awash and almost nothing showed above the surface. Hector slid out into the water. He found that he could stand, though his feet were sinking several inches into silt. By bending his knees slightly, only his head remained above water. 'No point in making ourselves obvious,' explained

Dan calmly. 'Miskito fishermen do likewise whenever they see a strange ship approaching.'

Now the brigantine was nearing the limit of her present course. Hector could see the sailors preparing to haul in on the sheets and braces. Men armed with muskets were clustered along the rail, looking into the river mouth and pointing at the beached pirogues. He heard a shouted command from the sailing master, and again the brigantine began to turn, this time presenting stern and rudder towards him. The guardship was close enough now for him to see that the crest on her ensign was a black eagle, wings spread under a royal crown.

'Is there anything we can do?' he asked Dan.

There was a long silence, and then the Miskito said, 'Hector, do you think you can reach the Bay Men's camp without being seen from that ship? It'll be hard going.'

Hector looked at the distance he would have to cover. It was almost a mile.

'You won't be able to push through the mangroves. They grow together too thickly,' Dan warned. 'You'll have to work your way along the edge of the mangroves, staying in the shallows.'

'I believe I can manage,' Hector answered him.

'Tell the Bay Men to be ready to break out an hour after low water. At that time their pirogues will be able to get over the bar, but the Spaniards will not yet have enough depth to enter the river.'

'And what are you going to do?'

'I'll stay here with the canoe and deal with the guard ship.'

Hector tried to read his friend's expression. 'Is this another of those Miskito skills, like killing sea cows and sinking canoes?'

'Sort of . . . but the Bay Men can make it easier for me. Tell them to gather up all the dead branches and fallen tree trunks and other lumber they can find, and launch them into the river while the tide is still on the ebb. They might even cut down a few trees and float them too.' He gave a thin smile. 'But make sure they are floaters, not sinkers like their logwood.'

'Anything else?'

'You'll have to hurry. There's not more than three hours of ebb left. When I see trees and other trash floating downriver, I'll know that you've managed to reach the camp. As soon as I make my move, you must get the Bay Men to start downriver in the pirogues.'

'How will I know when that is?'

'Find a place from where you can keep an eye on me here. My plan, if it is going to work, will be obvious. Now go.'

Hector turned to leave. The water was pleasantly warm, but rotting vegetation had coloured it a deep brown so it was impossible to see where he was putting his feet. Within a few paces he understood Dan's warning that progress would be difficult. The mangroves spread their roots sideways underwater, and he found himself tripping and stumbling over their new shoots as he half-swam, half waded towards his destination. Soft slime underfoot made it difficult to take a firm step, and often he sank ankle deep into the mud. When he tried to withdraw his foot, the ooze clung to him, holding him back. To keep his balance, he grasped at the mangroves and found that their bark was scaly and ridged. Soon his palms were raw and painful. He tried to stay hidden within the overhang of the mangroves, but there were sections where their matted roots made an impenetrable barrier and he was forced to swim along their outer edge, holding his breath and ducking down to avoid being seen from the Spanish patrol ship. As he floundered on, his breaths came in gasps and he had an unwelcome memory of the final moments of the hunted sea cow.

It was difficult to judge his progress. On his right the wall of mangroves seemed endless, a barrier of fleshy green waxy leaves at head level, their tangle of black and grey roots beside his shoulder. Small crabs scuttled away in fright, disappearing downwards into the water. Black and orange insects crawled upward in rapid jerks. Once he glimpsed the hurried sideways undulations of a snake swimming deeper into shelter. A little farther on he disturbed a colony of egrets and he feared they had betrayed his position as they flapped up into the sky like scraps of white paper.

The biting insects again found him a juicy victim, settling on his face the moment his head appeared above the surface, some delivering a jab as painful as a wasp sting. But his worst torment were the shellfish. Viciously sharp-edged, they clung in great clusters to the roots of the mangroves. Whenever he brushed against them, they lacerated his skin. Soon he was bleeding from dozens of slashes and cuts, and he wondered if blood in the water would attract caymans. He knew that the reptiles lived in the mangroves, and Jezreel had mentioned that he had occasionally encountered pythons in the swamps.

At length he crossed a shallow patch where finally he trod on firm sand instead of ooze, and guessed it was where the sandbar joined the river bank. Then gaps began to appear in the wall of mangroves, and finally he arrived at an opening where he could stagger up the bank and push his way through the undergrowth.

A warning shout stopped him. One of the Bay Men was facing him, musket levelled. It was a logcutter named Johnson who had joined the refugee flotilla as it followed the coast.

'It's me. Hector Lynch. I'm here with Jezreel,' he explained. He was dripping blood, exhausted and covered in slime.

Johnson lowered his gun. 'Didn't expect to see you here again. Where's that Indian friend of yours?'

'He's back beyond the sandbar, waiting. He can help us get clear.'

His statement was met with a look of disbelief. 'That I doubt,' said the Bay Man but he led Hector to where the remainder of the group were gathered in a fold of ground, safe from a stray cannonball. They had abandoned their hunting trip and were discussing what they should do.

'Lynch says that there's a way we can get clear,' said Johnson by way of introduction.

'Let's hear it then.' The speaker was an older man with a mouthful of badly rotted teeth and dressed in a tattered smock. Like his colleagues', his hair hung down to his shoulders in a greasy, matted tangle.

Hector raised his voice. 'Dan – that's my Miskito friend – says that we must be ready to break out an hour after the tide turns.'

'That's nonsense,' someone shouted from the back of the group. 'Our best chance is to wait until dark. Then make a run for it in the boats.'

'Dark will be too late,' Hector answered him. 'Well before sunset the tide will have risen far enough for the Spaniards to sail in. Their cannon will smash our boats to pieces.'

Jezreel came to his support. The big man was standing a little to one side of the gathering. 'If we make a dash for it soon after the tide turns, we do stand a chance because we'll be able to pick our course. Our pirogues will have room to manoeuvre while the Spanish ship is still confined to the deeper water. If we can get around the patrol ship, we can outpace her in the open sea.'

His intervention was met with a murmur of approval from several of the Bay Men and someone called out, 'Better than waiting here to be killed or captured by the Dons. I don't fancy being hauled off to a Havana gaol.'

'There's more!' Hector called out. 'Dan has asked that while we are waiting for the tide to turn, we dump as much trash as possible into the river – dead trees, branches, that sort of thing.'

'Does he think that the Spanish ship will get tangled up in all the driftwood?' This sally brought mocking laughter from the audience.

Again Jezreel came to his rescue. 'All of us know that the Miskito have no love for the Spaniards. I, for one, will do what

Dan asks.' He left the group and began to make his way along the river bank. About a dozen men followed him, and soon they were manhandling fallen trees and dead branches down the river bank and shoving them into the river. Hector watched the flotsam drift away and turn slowly in the current as it was carried seaward.

The other Bay Men showed no interest in helping. Several sat down on the ground and lit their tobacco pipes. Hector walked over to the older man who had been sceptical. 'If you won't help Jezreel and the others, you can at least make sure that everyone is ready to embark the pirogues the moment I give the word. I must go back to where I can keep an eye on the patrol ship, and see what my friend is doing.'

The Bay Man regarded him quizzically for several moments, then nodded. 'All right then. My mates and I will stand by.'

＊

HECTOR FOUND a vantage point on the river bank where he could keep watch on the Spanish guard ship and also see where Dan was hidden. The brigantine was still patrolling back and forth, following the same track each time as if there was a furrow in the water. He wondered why the captain did not anchor and wait for the tide to turn, and could only suppose that the Spanish commander wanted to be ready in case the Bay Men made a sudden sally.

He shifted his gaze to where he knew Dan lay concealed with his sunken canoe, but could see nothing except the green border of the mangrove swamp. Dotted about the estuary were the black shapes of the timber that Jezreel and his companions had thrown into the river. A few pieces had grounded in the shallows and lay stranded, but most of them had already been carried out over the bar. Several were already out beyond the Spanish guardship.

He concentrated on the area of broken water where the

river ran out over the sandbar. The wavelets were much smaller than earlier. The tide was definitely on the turn. Soon it would be making up the channel.

Hector looked back in Dan's direction. Still there was nothing to see, only the scatter of flotsam and the Spanish vessel. Each sector of its patrol was taking about twenty minutes. He estimated that when the vessel had turned one more time, the moment would come for the Bay Men to break out from the trap.

He sucked at an open cut on his thumb. The blood was attracting more insects. Then something caught his eye. A chunk of flotsam, a log perhaps, seemed out of place. It lay among the other floating debris, part-way between the Spanish ship and the shore. He looked harder, shading his eyes. Unlike the rest of the flotsam which was nearly stationary, the log was moving slowly. Then Hector realised that it was not a log, but the hull of the upturned hunting canoe. Dan was swimming beside it, quietly pushing it forward. He was headed towards the place where the brigantine was bound to turn.

Hector ran back to where the Bay Men were waiting. 'It's time to go!' he shouted.

They gathered round their pirogues and began to manhandle them into the river. Hector joined Jezreel who was already stepping the mast on their own pirogue. In less than five minutes, the three boats were dropping downriver, their sails filling as they headed towards the sea.

The Spaniards had seen them move. The brigantine opened a ragged fire but the range was too great for accuracy, and the shots splashed harmlessly into the water. Hector counted six guns, all on her port side, and knew that there would be a brief respite while the gunners reloaded.

'Steer for the left-hand edge of the channel,' he said to Otway who was at the pirogue's helm. It was important to lure the brigantine in the direction where Dan lay waiting. A rapid clatter of wavelets slapping against the hull told that the pirogue was now crossing the bar. The water was less than three feet deep, and there was a brief scraping sound as the bottom of the pirogue touched the sand. Hector felt the hull shiver beneath his feet. But the boat's progress was scarcely checked. Now they were in deeper water, and picking up speed as the sail filled in a strengthening breeze.

Two hundred yards ahead the Spanish patrol ship had reached the end of her track and begun to turn. Her port guns had not yet been reloaded. Hector could imagine the gun crews crossing the deck to help their comrades prepare the starboard battery for the killer blow. They would be checking that each gun was properly charged, its shot wadded firmly home, priming powder in place, match burning. All they then had to do was wait until the brigantine came round on her new course and steadied. Then they would make the final adjustment to bring their guns to bear. By that time the pirogues would be within point blank range.

'We're done for,' muttered Johnson, 'but we'll not go without a fight.' He was checking his musket, waiting for the Spanish ship to come within range.

Hector's gaze searched the water beside the patrol ship. He could no longer see the dark shape that was Dan and the upturned canoe. Perhaps the Spanish vessel had run him down.

Then, unexpectedly, the brigantine appeared to falter. Halfway through her turn, she hung in one position, her bow directly downwind, her stern towards the pirogues and unable to bring any of her cannon to bear. There was confusion visible on her deck. Sailors were climbing into the rigging, trying to readjust the sails. Others were scurrying along the deck, apparently without purpose.

'Their helmsman's a right blunderer,' said Otway who was steering the pirogue. 'He's lost control of the ship.'

'Head directly for the brigantine,' yelled Hector. 'There's a man in the water. We have to pick him up.'

Otway hesitated and Jezreel gave him a great shove which

sent him flying. Seizing the tiller the big man set the pirogue's course towards Dan's head which had bobbed to the surface. Hector looked round to see what was happening with the other two pirogues. Both had set extra sails and were increasing speed. They were drawing away. Soon they would be past the Spanish patrol vessel, and out of danger.

There was a ragged volley from the Spaniards, musketry not cannon. Some of the musket balls whizzed overhead, but others puckered the water around the swimmer. The Spaniards had seen Dan. He ducked down, making a more difficult target.

'Now that's a foolish thing to do. Let's see how far he gets,' said Johnson. On the stern of the brigantine half a dozen sailors were clustered at the rail, an officer with them. A rope had been lowered, and one man was climbing over, ready to descend. The Bay Man slid the ramrod back into its place beneath the long barrel of his gun, crouched down in the pirogue, and held steady. There was a second's pause before he pulled the trigger. The noise of the shot was followed immediately by the sight of the sailor losing his hold and tumbling down into the water.

Hector pushed past to where he could look forward, directly down into the sea. He heard a musket ball thump into the woodwork beside him, and more shots from the Bay Men. Less than ten yards away, Dan's head had reappeared, the long black hair sleek and wet. He was grinning. Hector gestured to Jezreel at the helm, pointing out the new course. A moment later, Dan's hand reached up and in one smooth movement the Miskito wriggled aboard.

'What did you use?' asked Hector.

'My cousin's striking iron,' his friend replied. 'I slipped it between the rudder and the stern post when the steering was hard over. It'll have driven in even further when the rudder was centred. They'll not get it free until they have a man down who can hack it out with a chisel. Until then their rudder's jammed.'

Hector was aware that the sound of the Spaniards' musketry

was growing more distant. Jezreel had turned the pirogue so the boat was running directly away from the brigantine, presenting the smallest target. Looking astern, he could see the patrol ship was still crippled, driving helplessly downwind. By the time she was under control again, it would be dark and the three pirogues would have made their escape. Several of the Bay Men were already on their feet, waving their hats at the enemy and jeering. One man turned his back and dropped his pantaloons in derision.

'The Bay Men have agreed to go farther south,' Hector explained to his Miskito friend. 'There are former buccaneers among them who claim to know the hidden places on the coast where their old comrades-in-arms gather. They plan to rejoin them, finding safety in numbers now that there's a Spanish warship on the prowl.'

'Then they'll have to go hungry for a while. We can't go back to collect the sea cow. But it means we can pick up Jacques on our way,' said Dan.

He settled himself more comfortably against a thwart, and Hector found himself contemplating how the unselfish comradeship of men like Dan and Jacques contrasted with the cold-hearted, self-serving avarice of men like Captain Coxon.

SEVEN

JACQUES HAD at last been able to try out his pimento sauce. It was something he had wanted to do ever since he first tasted one of the dark brown berries. The flavour had intrigued him, a peppery mix of clove and nutmeg with a hint of cinnamon. He had bought a handful of pimentos in the spice market at Petit Guave and kept them safe and dry in a cartridge box. Now he crushed his hoard and sprinkled the fragments into the cavity of a large fish Dan had gutted for their supper. Adding coconut milk and salt, the ex-galerien had wrapped the fish in leaves and buried it in a pit of charcoal coals to bake for three hours. Finally, he watched as Hector, Dan and Jezreel sampled the result.

'What do you think of the gravy?' he enquired proudly. He had carefully poured off the juices into an empty coconut shell and was dipping each piece of fish into the sauce before handing out the food.

'I would have added some ginger,' said Jezreel, pursing his lips and adopting a solemn expression.

For an instant the Frenchman took the suggestion seriously. Then he realised that the prize fighter was poking fun at him. 'Being English, you'd put in sugar and oats and make a porridge of it,' he retorted.

'That's if I were Scots, not English. You'll have to learn the difference, Jacques.' The big man licked his fingers. 'But this will do for a start. Some day I will have to show you how to make a decent pudding. Only the English know how to make puddings.'

The banter between the former prize fighter and the ex-galerien had begun within moments of their first meeting when the three pirogues had collected Jacques from the beach where Dan had left him. Then they had continued along the coast to a sheltered inlet which, according to Otway, was a favourite careenage for buccaneer ships. 'It's known as Bennett's Cove,' he had explained. 'If we wait here, there's a good chance that a buccaneer vessel will show up, and we can volunteer for her crew.' Hector thought again of the Coxon's Hole on the chart he'd copied for Snead in Port Royal, but said nothing. His previous encounter with buccaneers had left him wary of joining their company. Anyone associated too closely with them might finish up condemned for piracy and dangling on the end of a hangman's rope.

Fortunately the past two weeks had brought a change in the weather, with day after day of blue skies and brilliant sunshine tempered by a sea breeze which kept off the midges and mosquitoes. So the friends were lounging contentedly on the beach while the rest of their party was some distance away, close to the three pirogues drawn up on the strand.

Jezreel finished eating and lay back on the sand, stretching out his massive frame. 'This is the life. Can you imagine what conditions are like back home? March gales most likely, and rain. Can't say I feel like going back there for a while, even if the logwood cutting didn't work out.'

'Only a dolt would think of making his fortune by chopping wood,' Jacques observed. 'Anyone with brains would let others do the work, then relieve them of their profits.'

'You talk like a thief.'

'I only took what others were too stupid to keep safe,' said Jacques smugly.

Jezreel looked over at Hector, eyebrows raised. 'He was a pickpocket in Paris,' the young man explained. 'Until he got caught and sent to the galleys. That was where we met.'

'Nimble fingers make light work,' announced Jacques lazily. He extended one arm up in the air, and closed his fist. When he opened it, there was a pebble held between forefinger and thumb. Closing his fist, he opened it again, and his hand was empty.

'Saw plenty of tricks like that when I was in the fight game,' grunted Jezreel. 'The booths were full of mountebanks and charlatans. Many pretended they were from foreign lands. You would have done well with that foreign accent of yours.'

'Given an audience, I wouldn't even have needed to speak,' rejoined Jacques.

'No wonder it's called dumb show.'

Jacques shied the pebble at Jezreel who caught it deftly and, in the same movement, threw it back. The stone bounced off the Frenchman's hat, dislodging a small black object which fell to the sand.

'Watch what you're doing! I don't want to smell like a logwood cutter,' said Jacques and was about to tuck the item back into the hatband.

'What have you got there?'

Jacques passed the object across to his new friend who looked at it, puzzled. It was the size and shape of a large black bean, slightly shrivelled.

'Why would you want to wear a dried dog turd in your hat?' Jezreel asked.

'Smell it.'

'You must be joking!'

'No, go on.'

Jezreel held it up to his nose and sniffed. It had a definite musky smell.

'What is it?'

'A cayman's cod. I bought it in the market the same time I

got the pimentos you've just been enjoying.' Jacques took back the object. 'It's a gland. Crocodiles and caymans have them in their crotch and armpit, and they give off a pleasant smell. Better than a reeking blood-soaked smock.'

'Well, thank god you didn't put it in the sauce as well.'

Their exchange was brought to an end by a shout from Otway. He was at the back of the beach where the rise of the dunes gave him a vantage point. 'Ship! Standing in,' he called.

Everyone got hurriedly to their feet and gazed out to sea. The sun was behind them so they could easily make out the pale flash of the sails. To Hector's inexperienced eye the vessel looked very much like the Spanish guard ship, for she had two masts and was a similar size. He felt a twinge of fear that the Bay Men had been caught off guard once again. He doubted that they would be able to escape a second time. But Otway was jubilant.

'That's Captain Harris's ship, I'm sure. I served on her once. We're in luck. Peter Harris is as bold a commander as you could wish.'

He was proved right when the newcomer dropped anchor and sent her boats ashore, towing a string of empty barrels. Captain Harris had called at Bennett's Cove to take on fresh water.

'The ship is headed south to Golden Island,' announced Otway who had found former shipmates among the watering party. 'There's to be a gathering of the companies there. But no one seems to know the full details. It's to be decided by a council.'

'Will Captain Harris take on any new men?' asked Hector.

'That's for the ship's crew to decide.' Seeing Hector's look of incomprehension, Otway added, 'Among buccaneers everything is decided by vote. Even the captain is chosen by election.'

'It makes sense, Hector,' said Jacques. 'No one gets any pay. They work for their share of plunder. The larger the crew, the smaller the share-out.'

Otway had an embarrassed look on his face. 'Of course I've said that we all want to join. But the ship is already over-crowded with more than a hundred men aboard, and they are reluctant to add any more.' He was avoiding looking at the others. 'I am known to them already, so the crew is willing to add me to their number, together with my partner over there.' He nodded towards the one-eyed Bay Man who had worked with him at logwood cutting. '. . . and naturally they'll take Dan aboard if he is willing.'

'Why naturally?' asked Hector. He was not sure whether he wanted to join such suspect company but it rankled that they were being so choosy.

'The buccaneers always need strikers,' Dan explained. 'They are not fishermen and they don't have time to go ashore and hunt. They rely on Miskito strikers to get fish and turtle for them, otherwise they would go hungry.' He turned to Otway. 'Tell your friends that I'll not join unless my three friends here come with me.'

Otway went off to consult with the watering party, and returned with the news that if Dan would bring Jacques, Jezreel and Hector out to the ship, they could make their case to the assembled crew.

✳

WHEN THE LITTLE group came aboard with the last of the full water barrels, they found the crew already gathered in the waist of the ship and looking on with interest. Standing in the front rank was a vigorous-looking clean-shaven man, wearing a cocked hat trimmed with green ribbon. Hector presumed he was Captain Harris, though he took no part in the proceedings. The spokesman for the buccaneer company was a bald seaman with a gravelly voice hoarse from years of shouting.

'That'll be the quartermaster,' muttered Jacques. 'He's as important as the captain. Divides the plunder and looks to the running of the ship. Issues arms and all the rest.'

It was the quartermaster who opened the meeting. Addressing the assembly he announced, 'The Miskito tells me that he will only come with us as a striker if we take on his companions. What do you say?'

'How about the Miskito himself. Is he worth it?' called a voice.

'Judging by the number of turtle shells on the beach, he is,' answered someone who must have been ashore with the watering party.

'That big man looks right for us,' observed another. 'But he could be a clumsy slug with that antique gun of his.'

Jezreel was still carrying his old-fashioned matchlock musket.

The quartermaster turned to Jezreel. 'Your gun might be good enough for hunting cattle, but on this ship we don't use firelocks. By the time you've reloaded and fiddled with the match, your enemy will be on you.'

'Then I would use this,' announced Jezreel sliding the ramrod out from under his musket's barrel. He pointed it at the watching crowd. 'Any of you fellows willing to run at me with your cutlasses? Point or edge, it will not matter.'

The quartermaster beckoned to two crew men who stepped forward and drew their cutlasses. But, aware that their comrades were looking on, their charge was half-hearted. Jezreel merely stepped to one side and dodged them.

'Is that the best you can do?' he asked, goading them.

Now his two attackers were genuinely annoyed. Their resentment showed in the angry slashes they launched at their opponent. One man aimed for the giant's head, the other for his knees. But neither blow landed. The rod in Jezreel's hand darted out, faster than anyone could follow, and both his attackers dropped their weapons, cursing. Each was holding his hand where the ramrod had flicked across their knuckles.

'Stage fighter!' cried someone from the back of the crowd. 'I seen that trick done before.'

'Very likely,' called out Jezreel. 'Would anyone else like to try their luck? I'll face three of you at a time, if you wish.'

There were no takers, and the quartermaster intervened. 'We'll put it to the vote. All who wish to accept this man into our company raise your hands. Any objector speak up.' There was a silent show of hands.

'Who joins with you as your mate?' asked the quartermaster.

'Both my friends,' Jezreel answered placidly, sliding the ramrod back in place.

'Only one companion, that's the custom,' insisted the quartermaster. He was frowning now.

'How about that fellow with a brand on his cheek,' suggested an onlooker. 'He looks as if he can handle trouble.'

'Can either of you read or write?' The unexpected question came from a grey-haired man soberly dressed in a dark suit who was standing next to the captain.

Before Hector could answer, Jacques spoke up. 'Not as well as my friend here. He makes maps and navigates, and speaks Latin and Spanish and talks to me in French.'

'I don't want an interpreter. I require an assistant. Someone who's more adept than just a loblolly boy,' said the grey-haired man. From the way he chose his words it was clear that he was well educated.

'That's settled then,' said the quartermaster. He was anxious to close the meeting. 'We take on the big man and his French friend at full share. The other one, if he shows he's any use, can be signed on as mate to our surgeon. His share can be agreed later.'

As the meeting broke up, the grey-haired surgeon walked over to Hector and, after asking his name, enquired, 'Have you any medical experience?'

'None, I'm afraid.'

'No matter. You will learn as we go along. I am Smeeton, Basil Smeeton, and I had a medical practice in Port Royal before coming along on this adventure. Where did you get your Latin?'

'With the friars in Ireland where I grew up.'

'Good enough to converse in that tongue?'

'I think so.'

'Sometimes when discussing a patient's details,' said Smeeton meaningfully, 'it is better that the patient himself is kept in the dark.'

'I understand. But you mentioned a loblolly boy.'

'Surgeon's helper. Changes dressings and feeds gruel to the bedridden. I'm expecting more than that from you.'

Surgeon Smeeton's urbane manner was at such odds with the rough company aboard a buccaneer ship that Hector wondered why he was there. As if reading his thoughts, Smeeton went on, 'Where we are going – which, incidentally, is a land called Darien on the Main – I expect we will be meeting peoples and races whose practice of medicine is very different from ours. Much may be learned from them, perhaps in surgery but more likely in the use of plants and herbs. It is a subject which interests me greatly. I hope you'll be able to help me with my enquiries.'

'I will do my best,' Hector promised.

'There should be plenty of time for research as we won't be the only medical team with the expedition. Every crew like ours recruits at least one surgeon to sail with them, sometimes two or three. You might say that they enjoy the best medical services that their plunder – or prize as they prefer to call it – can buy.' He gave a wry smile. 'They even take out insurance against injury.'

'How can that be?' asked Hector. He did not think that Captain Harris's crew looked wealthy enough to afford medical care.

'If a man gets permanently disabled during the cruise, he receives a special bonus at the end when the quartermaster divides up the prize – this much for a lost eye, more for a limb that has to be amputated, or a hand blown off, and so on. The rates are all agreed at the start when the crew sign their mutual agreement. Very enlightened.'

By now Jacques had reappeared, a brand new musket in his hands. He was looking pleased with himself. 'How about this! Latest model flint lock issued by the quartermaster. Gave one to Jezreel as well.' He pulled back the cock and squeezed the trigger. A shower of sparks fell from the striking plate. 'No more fiddling around and keeping slow match dry in the rain.' He turned the gun over to show Hector the gunsmith's mark. 'What's more, it's French-made. Look, MAGASIN/ ROYAL. God only knows how it got here from King Louis's armoury.'

Hector took him aside and said in a low voice. 'Are you sure that you want to join up with this crew?'

'Too late. Jezreel and I have already signed articles. We are promised one full share of any loot after the investors have been repaid. You'll be able to put in for your own share as soon as you've proved your worth. Why, you may even get a surgeon's share and a half, and that's as much as the gunner and the carpenter.'

'What about the Bay Men who are being left behind?'

'Oh, they'll be picked up by other ships passing this way,' Jacques said casually.

'But from what the surgeon just told me, we will be away for some time and I had been hoping to get back to Jamaica.'

'But you only recently left there . . .' began Jacques. He paused and gave Hector a shrewd glance. '. . . any special reason?'

When Hector did not reply, the Frenchman rolled his eyes and said, 'Don't tell me! It's a woman.'

Hector felt himself starting to blush.

'Who is she then?' Bourdon asked, smirking.

'Just someone I met.'

'Just met! And you were hardly there any time at all. She must be exceptional.'

'She is.' Hector was increasingly tongue-tied, and fortunately Jacques detected his embarrassment.

'All right then. I won't say any more. But don't be too surprised if she breaks your heart.'

*

THE SURGEON wasted no time introducing Hector to his new duties. As soon as the ship had set sail, he led Hector to where a sailor was sitting in a quiet corner of the deck, with a bandage round his leg.

'Did you ever see a Fiery Serpent?' Smeeton asked.

'No, I don't think so.'

'Then I'll show you one.' Addressing the sailor, he said, 'Now, Arthur. Time to take a pull.'

The sailor carefully unwrapped the bandage and Hector saw that it covered a small stick attached to his leg by a thin brown thread.

'Watch carefully, Hector. I want you to do this job in future.' The surgeon took the stick between finger and thumb and rotated it very, very gently, winding in the thread. Looking closely, Hector saw that he was pulling the thread out of the flesh of the leg. 'That's your living Fiery Serpent. Getting it out hurts like the devil,' announced the surgeon. 'Strain gently, just enough to ease it out, an inch or two at a time, morning and evening. Pull too hard, and the creature will snap, and disappear back inside the flesh. Then you get an infection.' Turning to the sailor, he said. 'You may put back the bandage. Tomorrow my assistant will take a turn or two.'

As they walked away, Hector asked, 'What length will the serpent be?'

'Two feet would be normal,' replied the surgeon. 'Of course it is no serpent at all, but a flesh-eating worm. It causes a burning sensation as it is drawn out, hence the name.'

'And how does the victim acquire such a parasite?'

Smeeton shrugged. 'We have no idea. That is the sort of knowledge we may gain from enquiry among the native peoples. Right now you can put your Latin to use by helping me arrange the contents of my medicine chest. I threw it together in a hurry when leaving Port Royal and it is still in disorder.'

He brought Hector to a small cabin under the foredeck. 'As surgeon,' he said, pulling out a leather chest from where it had been wedged in a corner, 'I have the privilege of a cabin to myself, because it can also be rigged as a sick bay. Everyone else, even our captain and the quartermaster, has no right to any special accommodation. At night everyone lies down and sleeps wherever he wishes on the ship, on the plank as they say.'

He undid a strap and threw back the lid of the medicine chest. Inside was a jumble of phials and jars, small wooden containers, packets wrapped in paper and cloth, and objects which looked like dried plants, as well as an array of metal implements which reminded Hector of a carpenter's tool kit.

'Before we sailed, I was provided with one hundred pieces of eight from the common purse to stock it with what I considered might be needed.'

Smeeton reached in and picked out what looked like a pair of tongs with rounded tips. He snapped the jaws together with a clacking sound. 'The speculum ani,' he announced, 'useful for dilating the fleshy lips of a wound when extracting a bullet. In fact it is designed for dilating the arse gut.' He gave Hector an amused glance. 'You might think that a surgeon's work on such a venture as ours would be concerned mostly with the effects of battle, but it is not.'

He waved the speculum in the air to emphasise the point. 'The chief ailments which afflict the sailor are concerned with his digestion – constipation and the flux. For the former we can administer a syrup of cassia pods or licorice juice at one end or, if there is a stoppage, we may dilate the fundament with this implement and extract the offending blockage at the other end. That will provide comfort and remedy.'

Casually he tossed the speculum back into the medicine chest where it fell with a metallic clatter among the other instruments. 'Over the next few days,' he went on, 'I want you to clean and oil all these instruments, sharpen them as needed, and wrap them in well-greased cloth. They must not be allowed to rust.'

Looking into the chest, Hector noted wicked-looking saws and chisels, clamps and drills, pincers and nippers of different shapes and with strangely shaped jaws, even an ebony mallet.

Smeeton pulled a small cloth-bound notebook from his pocket. 'This is something else you will need. I want you to write a list of all the plasters, unguents, chemical oils, syrups, electuaries, pastilles and simples that you find, together with their quantities. I will advise you what each is suitable for so that you may make your own directory.'

＊

HECTOR HAD GOT as far as listing that a plaster of sweet clover would, in Smeeton's words, 'dispel windiness', when their ship reached Golden Island. Six other vessels were already waiting at the rendezvous, a small bay facing directly across to the mainland little more than a mile away. The anchorage was ideal for their clandestine purpose. From seaward it was completely hidden behind the island's rocky peak with its cover of thick scrub and stands of ceiba trees, while a narrow fringe of beach provided level ground for a camp. Numbers of men could be seen moving about under the coconut palms, and a row of cooking tents had been set up on the beach.

'This is almost as large an undertaking as when Morgan sacked Panama. The size of that raid is famous among my people,' commented Dan looking out over the assembled shipping.

'Surely the Spaniards will have taken precautions against another attack,' said Hector. Standing on deck beside the Miskito, he had been thinking about Susanna yet again and wondering if any of the buccaneer ships might later be returning to Jamaica. If so, he would try to persuade his friends to go back there with him.

'The thirst for gold is a great lure,' replied the Miskito. He pointed to a canoe which had just entered the bay and was working its way between the anchored ships, heading towards the beach. 'I'd say those fellows may have something to do with what happens.'

'Do you know who they are?' asked Hector. The dozen or so occupants of the canoe were too dark-skinned to be Europeans. One of them was wearing on his head what looked like a metal bowl.

'They are Kuna, the people who live over there in the mountains.' Dan gestured towards the mainland where ranges of forest-clad hills rose in rank after rank, wreathed with grey wisps of low cloud. On Golden Island the weather was as brilliant and sunny as when they had joined the ship. By contrast the mainland gave the impression of being gloomily drenched in drizzle and mist.

'Hector Lynch,' said a voice behind them. Startled, they turned to find Captain Harris had come on deck. 'Your companion, the Frenchman, said that you speak Spanish.'

'That's true. My mother is Spanish.'

'I need you to accompany me ashore. The captains are holding a council with the Indian chiefs. No one among us speaks the Kuna tongue, but the Indians have lived alongside the Spaniards long enough for them to have a knowledge of their language.'

'I will do my best.'

Harris led the way to a rope ladder, and soon Hector was being ferried ashore with his captain. As he passed through the buccaneer flotilla, Hector could see that Harris's vessel was the largest in the company. The next in size was an eight-gun sloop which seemed vaguely familiar, while the smallest was a pinnace so tiny that it carried no cannon at all. Whatever the buccaneers had in mind, Hector concluded, it depended on their strength in numbers of men, not the firepower of their vessels.

He followed Harris up the beach. Standing in a group beside the path were the Indians who had just arrived by canoe. The Kuna were not as tall as the Miskito, the only natives of the Caribbean he had met so far, but they were well set up and sturdy, with dark brownish-yellow skin and straight black hair. Their faces were dominated by strong noses from which deep furrows extended down to the corners of their mouths, giving them a solemn and severe expression. The leader appeared to be the man who wore the metal bowl on his head which proved to be a vintage Spanish helmet made of polished brass. Like most of his fellows, he was stark naked except for a funnel-shaped penis cover of gold fastened by a string around his waist. From his nose dangled a crescent-shaped plate of gold. Yet the Indian who most attracted Hector's attention was the only Kuna who covered his body. He was wrapped in a blanket from his ankles to his neck. All of his visible skin – his arms and feet, and face – was a ghostly unnatural white and disfigured with red blotches and bites. When he turned to look at Hector, his eyes were half closed, the lids fluttered, and specks of blood were seeping from cracked lips.

Harris politely doffed his hat as he walked past the Kuna, and Hector followed him into the little clearing in the coconut grove where the other buccaneer leaders were already assembled. Hector counted seven captains, together with their aides, and they were standing in small groups, talking together. One of the captains, who was facing away, reached up and scratched the back of his neck. All at once, Hector knew why the eight-gun sloop in the bay had seemed familiar. It was the vessel which had intercepted *L'Arc-de-Ciel*. Even as the realisation dawned, John Coxon turned to greet Peter Harris and his eye fell on Hector. The quick flush of anger which discoloured his features left no doubt that he recognised the young man.

'Captain Harris, it would have been better if you had been with us earlier,' Coxon grated. 'We have been in consultation with the Kuna for these past five days, and are ready to make a decision.'

'I bring the largest company so it was only right that you should wait,' retorted Harris, and Hector detected a simmering rivalry between the two men.

'Let's get down to business,' said another of the captains soothingly. A man of medium height, his round soft face had the down-turned fleshy mouth and protruding lips of a carp. Obviously unwell, he was leaning on a stick and sweating heavily as he looked round the gathering with watery pale blue eyes. Hector thought he detected a whiff of manipulation, of fraudulence.

'That's right, Captain Sharpe. We must not keep our Kuna friends waiting,' agreed Coxon. He crossed to where some benches had been set out under the trees, and beckoned the Kuna to be seated. The pale man in the blanket did not come forward but moved to stand in a patch of deep shade.

As the meeting proceeded, Hector was able to put names to the other buccaneer captains. Two of them, Alleston and Macket, seemed to be lesser figures, for they said little. A third man, Edmund Cook, was a puzzle. For a seagoing man he dressed very fastidiously. He wore a deep, curving lace collar over a loose mauve tunic and had tied a bunch of ribbons to one shoulder. By contrast Captain Sawkins, seated next to him, cared nothing for his appearance. His unshaven cheeks were stubbled and grimy, and he was obviously someone who preferred action to words. He kept glancing impatiently from one speaker to the next, and fiddling with the handle of the dagger in his belt. When Coxon and Harris bickered, as they did constantly, Sawkins tended to side with Harris.

Only two of the Kuna spoke Spanish, and their strong

accents were difficult to follow. With each sentence, their gold nose plates bobbed up and down on their upper lips and distorted the words. Occasionally when no one could understand anything, the speaker would lift up the plate with one hand and address his listeners from under it. Hector was able to gather that the Kuna were confirming an offer of guides and porters to the buccaneers if they would launch a raid against a Spanish mining settlement in the interior. It was clear that the Kuna loathed the Spaniards. According to the Indians, the Spanish miners used gangs of slaves to wash gold dust from the rivers, then brought their production to a town called Santa Maria. Every four months the collected gold was taken on to the city of Panama, and the next shipment was due to be sent out soon.

'Let's not waste any more time.' It was Captain Sawkins who spoke. He looked as though he wanted to spring to his feet and rush into action immediately, sword in hand. 'Every day we spend here increases the chance that the gold will slip through our fingers.'

'What about our ships? Who's to guard them while the men are away?' asked Macket cautiously.

'I suggest that you and Captain Alleston stay here with a detachment,' proposed Coxon. 'The final division of the booty will only be made when we return, and your men will receive full shares.'

A fit of coughing made him look towards Captain Sharpe. 'Do you feel well enough to accompany us?' he asked.

'Of course I do. I'll not miss a chance like this,' answered the ill-looking buccaneer.

'Then it's decided,' concluded Coxon. 'We set out for Santa Maria in, say, three days' time. We march in ships' companies but all under one single commander.'

'And who is that commander to be?' asked Harris ironically. Hector suspected that the decision had already been taken before their arrival.

'Captain Coxon would be the most suited to lead us,' explained Sharpe. 'After all, he was with Morgan at Panama. He is the most experienced.'

Coxon was looking smug. He had slipped his hand inside his shirt front and was scratching contentedly. Hector recognised the gesture.

Then Coxon turned to the Kuna and, deliberately ignoring Hector as the interpreter, he spoke in broken Spanish of their decision. The Kuna looked pleased, and rose to return to their canoe.

'I wonder where they get the gold to make those nose plates of theirs?' muttered a sailor standing next to Hector. The voice was familiar and Hector glanced around to find that the speaker was one of Coxon's men, the sailor with the missing fingers. 'Didn't expect to see you here.' said the sailor recognising him in return. 'Just remember who is in command of this expedition,' and he gave an evil smile.

*

HOWEVER MUCH Hector disliked and mistrusted Coxon, he had to admit that the buccaneer captain knew his business. Before the meeting closed, Coxon gave strict orders that no vessel was to sail from Golden Island for fear that news of the raid might get out. Then the next day every man on the expedition was issued with lead for bullets and twenty pounds of powder from the common stock. In addition, the camp cooks were put to baking buns of unleavened bread, four to a man, as marching rations.

'If this is all we get to eat, we'll soon be asking Hector for those cassia pods he's got in his knapsack,' said Jacques looking dubiously at the food. 'No wonder they're called doughboys.'

He, Jezreel and Hector were on the landing beach in the early dawn of the third day after the conference. Half the expedition had already disembarked, and Dan had gone ahead to scout.

'Don't look so miserable,' he said to Hector who was feeling dispirited that he could not yet return to Jamaica. 'Imagine coming back to your lady with your pockets full of gold dust.'

'As a surgeon's assistant you are not supposed to be involved in any fighting,' Jezreel added. 'Just make sure that the medicine chest stays with the column. A supply of medicines is the next best thing to a keg of rum to keep up the men's morale.'

Dan was coming towards them, accompanied by one of the Kuna guides. 'Hector, can you translate? This man has something to say but I can't follow his Spanish.'

Hector listened to the guide, then explained. 'Everyone is to stay on the footpath. He says the spirits of the forest must be respected. If they are disturbed or angered, they will cause harm.' He shifted the knapsack on his shoulders. It contained a basic medical kit that Smeeton had picked out for him. The surgeon himself had still not landed, and the main medicine chest lay on the ground, awkward and heavy.

'Here, I'll take that,' said Jezreel, lifting the chest on his shoulder. 'That's Harris's green flag up ahead.'

It was another sign of Coxon's competence, Hector thought to himself. The buccaneer captain had given instructions that after landing every man was to muster to his own captain's flag and follow it as the column moved inland. It should mean that the unruly and ill-disciplined buccaneers kept some sort of order on their march and did not degenerate into a chaotic mob. Captain Sawkins and Captain Cook, Hector now saw, had both chosen to display red banners with yellow stripes, but luckily Cook had distinguished his flag by adding the outline of a hand holding a sword.

Captain Sharpe's troop was beginning to move off behind their red flag hung with green and white ribbons. They had been chosen to lead the march and behind them the column slowly got into motion, more than 300 men slipping and stumbling along the shingle beach until they reached a river mouth. Here the Kuna guides turned inland, leading the men through an abandoned plantain grove and then into the forest itself where the trees formed a canopy overhead, blocking out the sunlight. The ground underfoot was soggy with dead leaves and forest mould, the air heavy and damp. The only sounds were the low voices of the men, an occasional burst of laughter, or someone hawking and spitting. The ground sloped upward, the path twisting to avoid places where the trees grew so close together as to be impassable, their trunks wet and glistening. Occasionally the walkers came to a small stream which they splashed across. Those who were already thirsty in the muggy heat, used their hats to scoop up water and drank.

In the early afternoon they halted. The Kuna had already prepared bivouacs for them, small huts with cane walls and thatched roofs built in another abandoned plantain patch. Several buccaneers preferred to go to sleep outside on the open ground, but the Kuna became agitated. The travellers must stay indoors, they insisted. Anyone who slept on the ground risked being bitten by venomous snakes. Hector wondered if this was merely an excuse to prevent the men from straying, but suddenly there was a shout of alarm, followed by some sort of commotion. He saw a cutlass rising and falling. Smeeton, who had joined the column belatedly, hurried off towards the spot, and Hector followed him, curious to see what all the fuss was about. He found a shaken-looking buccaneer holding up the headless corpse of a snake on the tip of his cutlass. The snake was at least four feet long, mottled brown and green. Smeeton found the severed head, picked it up and cautiously prised open the jaws. The poison fangs were unmistakable. 'A true viper, and with a bite almost certainly mortal. Excellent,' the surgeon enthused. He turned over the diamond-shaped head to inspect a yellow patch on the throat, and asked the buccaneer if he could also keep the dead body. Then he stepped behind Hector and the young man felt the flap of his knapsack open. There came the sensation of the dead snake being slid inside. Hector's skin crawled.

'The first reward of our venture,' announced Smeeton from somewhere behind him. 'Cut up into small morsels, it will make an essential ingredient in our Theraci Londini, vulgarly known as London Treacle.'

'What's that for?' asked Hector, uncomfortably aware of the coils of the dead snake pressing against his back. The dead animal was remarkably heavy.

'A sovereign cure for the plague. Snake fragments steeped in a variety of herbs. Perhaps the Kuna will have their own recipe. Fiery Serpent one day, true viper another.' He gave a satisfied chuckle.

*

Next morning Smeeton was eager to track down a Kuna doctor and begin asking about native medicines. Leaving the expedition to trudge deeper into the cordillera, he and Hector were taken by one of the Kuna guides to a nearby village. Away from the hubbub and disturbance of the column, Hector could hear the sounds of the forest. There were the chattering and cooing of birds, the sudden clatter of wings and sometimes a glimpse of red and vivid green or bright blue and yellow as the birds flew to a safe distance, occasionally settling again on an overhanging branch like an exotic blossom. Close at hand came a succession of bold hooting sounds. Minutes later, a troop of black monkeys came swarming through the treetops. They were foraging for wild fruit and, to Hector's astonishment, deliberately pelted the travellers with the skins and stones left over from their meal. One self-confident male scampered until he was directly over them and purposefully urinated to show his disdain, the liquid pattering down on the forest floor.

The cane-and-thatch houses of the Kuna village were scattered across a spur of high ground, each house approached through its own plantain grove. The centre of the settlement was a longhouse as massive and lofty as the largest barn that Hector had ever seen. Like the other Kuna buildings, it had no upper floor, and its vast roof was held up on immensely thick wooden pillars. In the half-light of the windowless interior the two visitors were introduced to the village doctor. He and half a dozen village elders were waiting for them, reclining in hammocks suspended between the columns.

The village doctor had a lined, intelligent face with dark hooded eyes, and could have been anything between fifty and seventy years old. Luckily, he also spoke Spanish.

'How much time has your friend got?' he asked Hector when the young man explained that Smeeton was a surgeon and hoping to learn from the Kuna doctors.

'We must rejoin our companions later in the day,' said Hector.

The Kuna looked amused. 'For five years I was an assistant to my father. Next I was sent to study with one of my father's friends. I stayed with him for another twelve years. Only then could I begin to look after my patients.'

'My colleague just wants to learn about what plants can heal, and how to employ them. I can take notes and, if it is permitted, take away a few samples.'

The Kuna made a restraining gesture. 'Then he should talk with an ina duled. He is the one who prepares medicines. I am an igar wisid, a knower of chants. Medicine by itself does not cure. True health is to be found through the spirit world.'

Smeeton looked disappointed when Hector translated, and asked, 'Perhaps the knower of chants has some patients at this time that I could see?'

The igar wisid swung down from his hammock. 'Come with me.'

He led his visitors a short distance out of the village to a small hut isolated in a clearing. The building seemed to be on fire, for a haze of smoke was seeping out through the thatch. The Kuna pushed open the low door and ducked inside. Hector stooped to follow him and found himself choking for breath. The interior of the hut was so thick with smoke that his eyes watered and he could scarcely see. A man lay motionless in a hammock strung across the small room. Beneath the hammock stood an array of dolls, dozens of them. Some were no more than six inches high; others three or four times that size. Nearly all were human figures. They were carved from wood, and some appeared to be very ancient for they had lost all shape and were stained black with age. The Kuna doctor crouched down and began rearranging them, crooning to himself. 'Ask what he is doing,' said Smeeton.

'These are nuchunga,' said the knower of chants. 'They represent the hidden spirits which always surround us. They can help restore the patient's soul. The patient is sick because his soul has been attacked. With my song lines I try to summon the assistance of the nuchunga.'

'Let's get out into the fresh air,' coughed the surgeon after some minutes of listening to the Kuna's chanting.

As they made their way back to the village with the igar wisid, Hector asked about the pale-skinned Kuna he had seen at the council meeting on Golden Island. Was he suffering from some sort of sickness?

For several paces, the igar wisid said nothing. When he spoke, he sounded reluctant to talk about the subject.

'He is one of the children of the moon. They are born among us, and never change their colour. Their skins remain white, and their hair stays pale. They are only happy in the darkness. Then they skip and sing. Their eyes can see in the dark, and they shun the light. It is our custom that they only marry among themselves.'

'He had many sores as well as bites from insects. Are you able to help such problems with your chants?' Asking the question, Hector felt a little ashamed. He was thinking not so much of Smeeton's researches, but his own torments from biting insects. He was hoping that the Kuna had something to treat the stings and pain.

'The great Mother and Father created these children of the

moon and they will always be as they are. Chants would have no effect on their condition. Poultices made from forest plants offer a little relief to their suffering.'

They arrived back at the Kuna village and, out of courtesy to the village elders, spent some time in the longhouse, answering their questions. The Kuna wanted to know the number of buccaneers, where they were from, and what they intended. Hector had the impression that the Kuna were pleased to see anyone who would harry the Spaniards but suspicious that the foreigners might wish to stay. It was as Smeeton and Hector were leaving the village to rejoin their colleagues that the igar wisid quietly came up to Hector and placed a small packet in his hand. It was a leaf folded over and tied with a length of plant fibre. 'You asked about the poultices prepared for the children of the moon,' he said. 'I have been able to find this for you. It is some of the ointment used in those poultices and has been given to me by one of the children of the moon. I hope you will find it useful.'

'What does it contain?'

The Kuna gave an apologetic shrug. 'I know only that it contains the seed of a certain fruit whose name has no translation. The seed is hard and black, about the size of a child's fist, and the ina duled grinds it into powder which he then mixes into a paste with other herbs. The paste also cures ulcers and other sores of the skin.'

Hector unslung his knapsack and as he was stowing away the packet, Smeeton asked, 'What's that you've got there?'

'Some sort of skin ointment,' Hector explained.

'Let's hope it's effective. It's not much to show for our enquiries.'

But Hector did not reply. He was noticing that what he had thought was a small dark mound of dirt beside the path had uncoiled itself and was slithering off into the undergrowth.

EIGHT

WHITE SPLINTERS of snapped branches, churned-up mud and scrapes where the moss had been knocked off rocks told them when they had rejoined the main trail. Shortly afterwards they met a buccaneer returning back down the path. He was soaked with sweat and in a bad temper. 'Shit-awful country,' he growled, eyeing them morosely. 'I've had enough of clambering through this stinking forest. I'm going back to the boats.'

'How far ahead is the column?' Smeeton asked.

'Over the next crest,' came the surly answer. 'A company of idiots, if you ask me. Some of them are cracking open the rocks and searching for gold. If anything glitters or sparkles they think they've discovered the mother lode.' He gave a derisive snort. 'Fool's gold, more likely.' He took off his hat and wiped the sweat from the browband before heading on towards the sea.

'A very republican rule, as I mentioned,' said Smeeton coolly, 'a buccaneer can abandon a project with the agreement of his fellows, and he will not be treated as a deserter as would be the case if he was a military man. Admittedly, it is unusual to see a single buccaneer turn back. Normally they fall away in groups.'

They reached the buccaneer camp just before dusk and

found the expedition in a sour mood. The exhausted men were lying on the ground or seated in small groups around sputtering camp fires. Everything was already damp, and to make matters worse a brief shower of rain was followed by a fine drizzling mist that soaked through their clothes. In the grey evening light Hector tracked down his friends and found Dan skinning the carcasses of several small animals about the size of hares that he had hunted. Jezreel and Jacques were looking on critically.

'How do you propose cooking them?' Jezreel was asking the Frenchman.

'To my way of thinking they have the head of a rabbit, the ears of a rat, and hair like a pig. So I can broil, fry or bake them depending on your choice,' Jacques replied, a hint of sarcasm in his voice. He sounded weary.

'Just as long as you don't bring out the flavour of rat,' observed Jezreel. Turning to Hector he said, 'The captain was looking for you earlier.'

The young Irishman was surprised. 'Captain Harris?'

'Yes, he wanted you to attend another council with the other captains and a couple of the Kuna chiefs. But I said that you had gone off with our surgeon.'

'Did the council meet?'

'It was a bad-tempered affair with a lot of shouting. I listened on the fringes. Everyone is grumbling and complaining. It seems that no one expected this journey to be such hard going. Coxon was particularly angry. He feels his leadership is being called into question. He and Harris were at one another's throats. Your name came up. Coxon called you a little whoreson – that was the exact phrase he used – and asked Harris why he had brought you along to the last council meeting. Harris replied that it was none of Coxon's business and he did not trust the interpreter that Coxon had provided.'

'Was anything decided?'

'Sawkins is elected to command the forlorn. He's to choose

eighty of our best men to lead the attack when we come into contact with the enemy.'

'Well, at least they got the right man. Sawkins has a reputation as a fire-eater, always ready to lead the charge.'

'Perhaps too much so,' said Jezreel with a slight frown. 'In the ring I learned it's seldom a good idea to rush in. Better to bide your time until you see the right opening. Then strike.'

At that instant there was a shockingly loud explosion very close by. Everyone sprang to their feet and looked in the direction of the noise. A small group of buccaneers had been seated around a camp fire, now one of them was clutching his face and crying out in pain. He seemed unable to get to his feet.

'What in the devil's name was that?' asked Jacques, bewildered. But Hector had grabbed his knapsack of medicines and was already running towards the scene. 'Bring the medicine chest,' he called back over his shoulder, 'and find Smeeton. There are people hurt.'

He arrived at the spot to find the buccaneer was badly burned. His thigh had been torn open by the blast. Hector knelt beside the victim. 'Lie still,' he said. 'A surgeon will be here soon, and we must clean the wound.'

The man was gritting his teeth in pain and staring down at the damaged leg. 'Stupid, stupid, stupid bastard,' he repeated savagely.

Hector gently eased back the shredded clothing. Underneath were patches of charred and blistered skin. 'What happened?'

'It's this rain. Gets into the gunpowder, and makes it useless. Gabriel who has the wits of wooden block was trying to dry out his powder. Spread it on a dish and held it over the fire. Too close, and the whole lot blew up.'

'Hector, I'll take over now.' It was Smeeton. The surgeon had arrived with Jezreel carrying the medicine chest. 'Get someone to fetch a basin of water, and I'd be obliged if you would pass me a pair of small tongs from the chest. Search this man's pack and see if there's anything in it which can be used for bandages.'

For several minutes the surgeon cleaned and probed with his forceps, removing traces of cloth and dead skin. The surface of the thigh was pitted with several irregular wounds, the largest two or three inches across. The skin around them was a dead white or a flaring angry red.

'This is going to take a very long time to heal,' commented Smeeton. With a start Hector realised that the surgeon was speaking to him in Latin.

'Will he lose the leg?' asked Hector, also in Latin. He had a nightmare vision of having to use the saws and clamps he had cleaned and sharpened.

'Only if there is an infection. No bones are broken.'

'What are you two gabbling about!' An angry shout ended their discussion. Coxon was standing over them, his face working with anger. 'God's Bones! Can't you talk in English. What's the matter with this wretch?'

Smeeton rose to his feet, wiping his hands on a cloth. 'He's badly injured in the thigh by an explosion of gunpowder. From now on he'll have to be carried in a litter.'

'I'll not have the column slowed down by invalids,' Coxon snapped. 'If tomorrow morning he cannot get on his feet, we leave him here. He's wasted enough gunpowder as it is.' The buccaneer captain's glance fell on Hector who had remained kneeling beside the injured man. 'You again,' he barked. 'A pity you weren't standing closer to the blast,' and he turned on his heel and strode away across the soggy ground.

'Not much sympathy there,' sighed Smeeton. 'Hector, look in the medicine chest for a jar of basilicon, and add hyperium and aloe if they are readily to hand. You should know where to find them.'

Hector did as he was asked and watched the surgeon spread the salve on the open wounds.

'Best keep your leg covered with a cloth to prevent insects feasting on the sores,' Smeeton told his patient. 'Tomorrow we will decide what is to be done.'

*

NEXT MORNING the injured man could barely hobble, even with a crutch cut for him. So while the column were breakfasting on the last of their doughboys, mildewed and mushy with damp, Smeeton asked Hector to prepare a good quantity of the healing salve. 'We'll leave it with him, and he can attend to his own wound. In a day or so he should be able to begin making his way back to the ships by slow stages. I doubt that he will have the strength to catch up with us.'

That day's march, it turned out, would have been impossible for the invalid. The Kuna guides led the column up the steep side of a mountain. In places the narrow path skirted the edge of ravines and was only wide enough for one man at a time. Here each buccaneer had to hold on to the vegetation to prevent himself slipping over the edge. It was small consolation that the Kuna guides told them that they were now crossing the watershed, and that the next stream they reached flowed towards the South Sea. When they descended the far slope, it was to find that the trail often used the stream bed itself. They had to wade knee-deep in the water, avoiding sink holes and hidden snags.

Eventually, and after another two days of this tortuous progress, the stream grew wide and deep enough for the Kuna to provide a number of small dugout canoes to carry them. But there were only enough boats for half the expedition, and the remainder of the column still had to march along the slippery, overgrown banks. The men who thought themselves lucky to be in the canoes quickly found that their optimism was misplaced. Dozens of fallen trees lay across the stream, and there were so many shallows and rapids that much of each day was spent manhandling the craft over the obstacles. Hector found himself treating numerous sprains and cuts and gashes, and the contents of the medicine chest were rapidly depleted.

Only after a full week of this wearisome marching and canoeing did the Kuna guides finally announce that the buccaneers were close to their target. The town of Santa Maria was less than two miles downriver. That night the tired expedition made camp on a spit of land, and ate cold food for fear that the smoke from their cooking fires would alert the Spanish garrison.

*

HECTOR AWOKE to the sound of a distant musket shot and the staccato beat of a drum. For a moment he lay with his eyes closed. He was aware that he was lying on the ground and that a sharp lump of stone was pressing into his hip but he was hoping to steal a few more moments of sleep. Then he heard the drum again. It was sounding an urgent tattoo. He rolled over and sat up. It was daybreak and he was in a small makeshift shelter made of leafy branches of the sort that the Kuna had taught the buccaneers to construct during their long march over the mountains. Beside him Jacques was still snoring softly, but Jezreel had heard the sounds. The prize fighter was propped up on one elbow and wide awake.

'Last time I heard that noise I was still in the fight game,' observed Jezreel. 'We had a drummer who walked up and down the streets, rattling away and announcing when the next bout would take place. I'd say that this time it means that the good citizens of Santa Maria have learned we are here, and they're getting ready to greet us.'

'Do you know where Dan has got to?' asked Hector. He had not seen the Miskito since the previous evening when Dan had gone off to talk with the other strikers.

'He's probably still with his chums.'

'Get up! On your feet! Time to move!' There were shouts outside, and Hector recognised the hoarse voice of Harris's quartermaster.

He followed Jezreel out of the low doorway to find that the buccaneer camp was stirring. Men were emerging from their shelters, rubbing the sleep from their eyes, and looking around for their comrades or heading off into the bushes to relieve themselves.

'Muster to your companies! ' The yelling was insistent.

Captain Sawkins came loping towards them. He was wearing a bright yellow sash that made him look very dashing. 'You and you,' he said briskly, pointing to Jezreel and to Jacques who had just appeared. 'I want both of you in the forlorn. Attend to my flag.' He hurried on, selecting other men for the initial attack.

Left to himself, Hector looked around trying to find Smeeton. A little distance away the surgeon was talking to Harris and the other captains. He went towards them.

'Hector,' said the surgeon catching sight of him. 'Take your knapsack and go forward with Captain Harris and deal with any minor injuries on the battlefield itself. Leave the medicine chest here. I will set up a medical station where the worse injuries can be brought back for treatment. Hurry now.'

Hector found himself following Harris and the other captains through the woodland in the direction of where the drum had sounded. The ground rose steadily and they had to push their way through dense undergrowth, unable to see more than a few yards ahead. Their Kuna guides were nowhere to be seen, and it took nearly half an hour to arrive at a vantage point on a low ridge. From there they had a clear view of their objective, the gold-rich town of Santa Maria they had struggled so hard to reach.

Their first impression came as a shock. They were expecting a substantial colonial town with stone-built ramparts and paved streets, red-tiled roofs and a market square, perhaps even with a fort and cannon to guard its treasures. Instead the scene was of a haphazard scatter of thatched buildings which amounted to little more than an overgrown village built on open land sloping gently down to the river. There was no defensive wall, no gate, not even a watchtower. But for the Spanish flag hanging limp from its pole, the place might even have been mistaken for a large Kuna settlement. In addition the town looked deserted.

'Is that really Santa Maria?' said Harris wonderingly as he stepped back into the fringe of the woodland so as not to be seen from the town.

'Must be. There's a Spaniard scuttling for cover,' observed Captain Sharpe. A figure dressed in an old-fashioned breastplate and helmet had run out from one of the thatched houses and was heading towards a crude stockade built a little way to one side of the settlement.

'That's their only defence,' stated Harris, narrowing his eyes as he gazed down towards the Spanish position. 'The palisade can't be more than twelve feet high, and it's only made of wood posts. That may be enough to defend against a Kuna attack using bows and arrows, but nothing to stop a force of musketeers. The Spanish garrison must be holed up inside, and scared out of their wits.'

'That's no reason for us to be reckless,' said a harsh voice from behind him. Coxon had joined them. He was accompanied by a spear-carrying Kuna. It was the Indian who had been wearing the brass helmet at the original conference on Golden Island, though now he had put aside his shining headgear. 'We will wait for our Kuna allies. They are bringing up two hundred of their warriors in support.'

Coxon was making it clear that he was in command of the attack. 'I have given orders for Captain Sawkins to muster the forlorn in the cane brakes by the river.'

'Surely we should attack at once.' Harris spoke sharply, showing his frustration. 'The Spaniards may have sent for reinforcements. We need to take the place before they get here.'

'No! If we play our cards right, we might be able to get the Spaniards to hand over what we want – the gold and valuables – without a fight.'

'And how would you propose doing that?' Harris demanded. His tone was mocking.

'We pretend that we are a far larger force than is the case, and propose to the Spaniards that they withdraw from Santa Maria unharmed, provided they leave behind the treasury and any gold dust recently brought in.'

'What makes you think that they will accept?'

'It's worth a try,' Coxon answered, and a sly expression passed across his face. 'Besides, if we begin a parley, it will distract the Spaniards from launching a sortie and discovering our true strength.'

Harris looked sceptical. 'There's no sign that the Spaniards are going to leave the shelter of that stockade.' As if to support his words, a ragged volley of musket fire came from the Spanish position. Puffs of smoke burst out from the loopholes cut in the stockade. The defenders must have glimpsed Sawkins' assault party forming up in the cane brakes because the shots were aimed towards the river. There was no sign of the Kuna auxiliaries.

'That makes my point for me,' said Coxon caustically. 'If the Spaniards are concerned for their own skins, they will agree to abandon their position. We will offer them full honours. We have nothing to lose.' He glanced at Hector, a calculating gleam in his eye.

'And, Captain Harris, you have provided exactly the right person to carry our message to the Spaniards. This young man, as you have assured me so often, speaks excellent Spanish. He can take our offer to the stockade under a flag of truce, and we will wait here for the answer. Captain Sawkins will await my signal before he launches the first attack.'

When Harris did not reply, Coxon took his silence as assent. Addressing Hector, the buccaneer said, 'Lynch, you are to approach the stockade carrying a flag of truce. There you will ask to speak to the Spanish commander. Inform him that we are in overwhelming strength – tell him, we are over one thousand muskets. He's no way of knowing our true numbers – and, to avoid unnecessary bloodshed, we are willing to allow him and his garrison to withdraw peacefully. Our only condition is that all valuables are left within the town. If he agrees to these terms, his men will be permitted to retain their weapons and leave with full honours, colours flying and drums beating. Do you understand your instructions?'

'Yes,' replied Hector. He was relieved that Coxon seemed no longer to resent his presence, but a little puzzled by his abrupt change of manner. Coxon now appeared to place his trust in him.

'Good. Put down your knapsack, and use your shirt as a white flag. You'll need some sort of staff.' Coxon glanced at the spear that his Kuna companion was carrying. 'That spear will do. Ask for the loan of it.'

In slow careful Spanish Hector explained to the Kuna what was proposed. The man looked baffled. 'But we have to kill the Spaniards,' he said.

'Get on with it,' snapped Coxon. 'We haven't got all day to stand talking.'

Hector repeated his request, and reluctantly the Kuna handed over his lance. The young man tied his shirt to the shaft and was about to step out into the open when Coxon caught him by the elbow. 'Don't go too fast! Walk slowly. Remember we are also giving Captain Sawkins time for his forlorn to take up position.'

Hector stepped from cover and immediately attracted several musket shots from the palisade. But the range, some four hundred yards, was too great for accurate shooting and he did not even know where the shots went.

Anxiously he held the lance higher and waved it from side to side so that the white cloth could be seen clearly. The musketry ceased.

Hector walked slowly forward. A hard knot of fear formed in his stomach and within a few paces the staff was slippery with sweat from his hands. He took deep slow breaths to calm himself, and concentrated on keeping the white flag visible. After about fifty yards he stole a quick glance to his right, hoping to see where Jezreel and Jacques were with Sawkins' assault group. But a fold of ground obscured his view. He hoisted the white flag still higher and decided that he would keep his gaze fixed unwaveringly on the wooden palisade as if this focus would somehow make them respect his flag of truce.

The ground between the palisade and the edge of the woods where he had emerged was rough pasture dotted with low scrubby bushes. He guessed that the original woodland had been cut back by the Spaniards to give a clear field of fire from the stockade, but over the years this precaution had been neglected. The bushes and long grass had been allowed to grow back so that he was obliged to pick his route carefully, making sure to stay within full view of the stockade. From time to time briars and thorns snagged his breeches, and he wondered what would happen if he put his foot into a hole, tripped, and fell. Would the Spanish musketeers think it was a trick, and shoot? There was no doubt that their marksmen were on edge and that they kept their sights trained on him as he moved closer.

An insect landed on his shirtless shoulder, and a second later he felt the burning pain of a bite. He clenched his teeth and restrained himself from slapping away the insect. He needed both hands to hold the white flag high and steady.

Perhaps three or four minutes had passed since he had left Coxon and the other captains, and still there had been no response from the Spanish stockade. No musket fire, no movement. Everything was quiet. He began to breathe a little more easily. He became conscious of the warmth of the morning sun on his skin, a faint smell of something sweet – rotting fruit on the ground under the bushes perhaps – and a black shape circling in the sky high above the stockade, a bird of prey.

Steadily he paced onward.

He had covered perhaps half the distance to the stockade safely when, without warning, there was a sudden fusillade of shots, followed by a fierce, defiant yell. Shocked, he faltered in his stride, scarcely believing that the Spaniards had ignored his flag of truce. But there was no gun smoke billowing from the palisade, and in the same instant he realised that the gunfire had not come from the Spaniards, but from behind him. It was Sawkins and the forlorn who had begun shooting.

Seconds later came the counter-fire from the stockade, an irregular succession of shots as the defenders responded. This time he clearly heard the hum of musket balls whizzing past him. Some of the Spanish marksmen were taking him as their target where he stood exposed on the open ground. A musket ball slashed through a nearby bush, followed by the noise of the cut twigs pattering to the ground. Another musket ball hummed past his head.

Appalled, he threw away the staff and flag and flung himself to the ground, seeking cover. As he lay there, face down to the earth, he heard another volley of musketry from behind him and then a second cheer.

He lay still, not daring to move. For a moment he considered jumping to his feet and running back towards the woods, but dismissed the idea as suicidal. He was certain to be cut down by the Spanish marksmen.

Another cheer, and this time much closer. There was a tearing and crashing, and the thump of running feet. Cautiously he looked up and to his right. Some forty yards away was Sawkins, instantly identifiable in his bright yellow sash. He was bounding forward through the long grass, whooping and shouting and charging straight at the stockade, musket in one hand and cutlass in the other. Close behind him a score of heavily armed buccaneers was running full pelt towards the Spanish defences. As Hector watched, one of the buccaneers dropped to one knee, took aim with his musket and fired at the palisade. A second later he was back on his feet and careering onward, ready to use his musket as a club.

Within a few moments the first of the forlorn had reached the stockade. Someone must have found a chink between the wooden posts because two or three of the attackers were levering away with some sort of crowbar. A second later a small section of the palisade collapsed, leaving a small gap.

Now the buccaneers were tearing at the opening, making it wider. Later arrivals were thrusting their musket barrels through the loopholes and shooting in at the defenders. In the general mayhem there seemed to be little or no resistance from the Spanish garrison.

Shakily Hector started to get up. 'What the devil are you doing here?' said someone with a French accent. It was Jacques, musket in hand. He was clearly shocked at the sight of Hector rising from the ground.

'I was on my way to parley, carrying a white flag, when you attacked,' blurted Hector. He was still appalled by his narrow escape.

'We didn't see you,' said Jacques. 'You could have got yourself gunned down and that for nothing.'

'But I was on my way to offer the garrison safe conduct if they surrendered the town gold.'

'Christ! What imbecile came up with that idea?'

'Captain Coxon sent me.'

'Coxon? But he must have known that Captain Sawkins' idea of a battle is to charge straight at the enemy. That's why Sawkins was given the forlorn.'

'But Coxon had ordered Sawkins to await his signal before launching an attack.'

'Did he?' Jacques looked incredulous. 'That's the first I've heard of it. Sawkins didn't mention it to myself nor Jezreel or any of the others. He brought us up through cane brakes, and as soon as we had a clear sight of the Spanish position, gave the order to fire and charge.'

'Coxon claimed that the parley would also give the forlorn more time to get into position and prevent the Spaniards from learning our strength.'

Jacques grimaced with disgust. 'Now you may have the truth of it. A white flag can be a ruse. But it was crazy of you to volunteer to carry it.'

'I didn't volunteer,' confessed Hector. 'Coxon ordered me to do it, and I thought it was a genuine parley.'

Jacques gave him a searching look. 'Hector, I would say that Captain Coxon very nearly arranged your death.'

❋

BY NOW the fight at the palisade was over, and the Spanish garrison had surrendered. The battle had lasted barely twenty minutes, and the buccaneers had complete mastery of the stockade and the town itself. Hector went forward with Jacques to where the Spanish prisoners were being herded together. They were a sorry-looking lot, men of all ages from teenage lads to greybeards. Some of their weapons were arquebuses so obsolete that they required props on which to support the clumsy barrels.

'No wonder their rate of fire was so dismal,' commented Jacques. 'It must have taken ages to reload. How could anyone ever think that they were capable of defending this place?'

'Perhaps it was not worth defending,' said Hector. He had seen the disappointed expressions on the faces of buccaneers returning from investigating the settlement. They had with them a frightened Spaniard dressed in the clothes of a clerk.

'What a dump!' exclaimed one of the buccaneers. 'Nothing of value. Just miserable houses and wretched people.

'Didn't you find any gold?' asked Jacques hopefully.

The man laughed bitterly. 'There's a town treasury all right. We kicked in the door. But it was empty. This fellow was hiding nearby. He's some sort of a bookkeeper.'

'Perhaps you'll let me question him,' Hector suggested.

'Go ahead. He's in a complete funk. Thinks we'll hand him over to the Kuna.'

The Spaniard was more than eager to answer any question that Hector put to him. The townsfolk of Santa Maria had known for days that the buccaneers were approaching, so the governor had arranged a fleet of boats to evacuate as many of the women and children as possible. The treasury had been emptied out, three hundred weight of gold put aboard a small sloop and sent by river to the capital in Panama. Finally the governor, his deputy, the local dignitaries and the priests had also left. All that remained in Santa Maria were townsfolk who were too poor or insignificant to get away.

'So that's it then,' exclaimed Jacques. 'We've come all this way, done all the marching and wading through rivers and lying on hard ground and eating vile food, only to find that the cupboard is bare.' He gave a snort of disgust.

At this point Captain Sawkins walked up to them. His yellow sash was speckled with flecks of gunpowder, and there was a sword cut in the shoulder of his buff coat. 'What have you managed to find out from this Spaniard?' he asked.

Hector told him about the Spanish withdrawal, and immediately Sawkins was eager to set off in pursuit. 'If we hurry we might catch up with that boat carrying the gold dust. There's a pirogue the Spaniards left behind which we can use.'

He crooked a finger at Hector. 'You come along, and bring that Spaniard with you. He'll be able to identify the boat for us.'

'I am assistant to Surgeon Smeeton. He's waiting for me at the camp,' Hector reminded him. 'I'll need to inform him where I'm going.'

'Then do so, and while you're about it, bring some more medicines with you. We may have some fighting to do.' Sawkins glanced at Jezreel and Jacques. 'You two are still members of the forlorn. You also come with me. Be ready to set off downriver in an hour.'

＊

HECTOR RAN back to where he had left his knapsack, stopping to pick up the abandoned spear and put on his shirt. When he got back to the camp, it was to find the bald quartermaster from Harris's ship seated on a log, his head bowed. Smeeton was standing over him and sewing a flap of skin back onto the quartermaster's scalp.

'Hector, there you are,' said the surgeon as casually as if he was in his consulting rooms in Port Royal. 'A minor head wound, and you see the advantages of hair loss. No need to shave the hair away before deploying needle and thread.'

His stitching finished, the surgeon wrapped a bandage around the wound, and the quartermaster got up and walked away.

'Captain Sawkins has asked me to accompany him downriver, in pursuit of the Spanish treasure,' said Hector.

'Then by all means go,' answered Smeeton. 'There's precious little medical work for you here. We lost just two dead in the entire action, and half a dozen wounded, so there's hardly enough work to go around. The other companies have brought along at least a couple of surgeons apiece. In fact we seem to have so many medical men on this expedition that I'm thinking of returning to the ships, accompanying the walking wounded. Now that we've crossed the isthmus I don't expect to add much to my pharmacopoeia.'

'Is it all right if I take some medicines with me?' Hector asked. 'Captain Sawkins requested I do so.'

Smeeton smiled indulgently. 'But of course. It'll be a chance to use those notes you made while sorting through the medicine chest.'

Hector opened the chest and looked inside. The salves and ointments used up during the march across the isthmus had been replaced by Smeeton's collection of items he thought might possess curative powers – dead snakes, odd-shaped roots, dried leaves, strips of bark, seeds, coloured earth, monkey dung, even the skull of a creature·like a dwarf elephant that Dan and other Miskito strikers had found feeding beside the river. The animal's flesh had provided fresh meat for three dozen hungry buccaneers. The surgeon had kept the cranium.

Then his eye fell on the packet that the Kuna medicine man had given him. It was the ointment made for the children of the moon as a poultice for their skin sores. He took the packet from the chest, consulted his notes and found a jar labelled 'Cantharides'. Turning his back so Smeeton could not see what he was doing, the young man carefully untied the leaf wrapper of the Kuna medication. Inside was a blob of pale waxy ointment about the size of his fist. Spreading the leaf on the ground, Hector carefully tipped out several spoonfuls of yellowish-brown powder from Smeeton's ·medicine jar and, using a twig, stirred the powder into the Kuna salve. Then he wrapped up the packet once again, and returned both it and the jar to the chest.

He finished loading his knapsack with medicines, and said goodbye to Smeeton. As he turned to leave, he said casually, 'Have you had a chance to try out the Kuna skin ointment yet?'

'No,' replied the surgeon. 'It would be interesting to do so.'

'Captain Coxon was asking if you had anything to relieve the rash on his skin. The past few days in the jungle have made the itching much worse.'

'So I noticed,' said Smeeton. 'I shall suggest that he tries the ointment. It can do no harm.'

As he headed off to where Jezreel and Jacques would be waiting, Hector was smiling to himself. It was the quartermaster's bald head which had reminded him of Smeeton's store of cantharides powder. Smeeton had cited it as another example – like snake venom – of a poison that could have beneficial properties. Cantharides powder was made from the powdered wings of a beetle and very popular with the buccaneers as an aphrodisiac. More prosaically, Smeeton had said, the powder applied very sparingly to the skin would encourage hair to grow. However, if used in quantity, it brought on violent itching, caused a burning rash, and raised a mass of painful blisters.

NINE

A HUNDRED MILES away in the city of New Panama, the governor, His Excellency Don Alonso Mercado de Villacorta, was shocked by the fall of Santa Maria. The news was brought to the city by stunned refugees who described how the Kuna, given the chance, had massacred the Spanish settlers once they had been disarmed by the buccaneers.

'This has all the potential to turn into a disaster,' he said in his characteristically despondent tone to the emergency meeting he had called in his office. 'A gang of pirates is now on the loose in the South Sea. It is exactly what I and others have been warning the authorities about for years. But no one took a scrap of notice. What are we to do?'

He looked round the conference table. His glance swept past the city councillors and church dignitaries, barely paused on the two colonels who commanded his cavalry and infantry, and came to rest on Don Jacinto de Barahona, the officer in charge of the Pacific naval squadron.

Barahona was thinking to himself that the governor was being unduly negative.

'We go on the offensive,' he said firmly. 'Stamp out the threat immediately. If we don't, other pirates will follow the route they have found over the isthmus. We risk being overwhelmed.'

'But we don't know where to find the pirates, nor their number,' objected the governor. He had a habit of tugging at his right ear lobe when he was worried. 'They could be anywhere. The coast is a maze of islands and inlets. Our forces could search for weeks and not discover them. Meanwhile the city would be left without protection.'

'Could we not ask the Indians to keep a look out on our behalf?' The suggestion came from the bishop. He was newly arrived from Old Spain, and had yet to learn that the Indians were not the devout and loyal Christians he had been led to expect.

'The Indians!' exclaimed the cavalry colonel, his mouth turned down in a grimace. 'It was the Indians who showed the pirates their trail over the mountains.'

'There's no need to go searching for the pirates. They will come to us,' said a quiet, firm voice. The speaker was Capitan del Navio, Francisco de Peralta. His swarthy tan and the maze of lines and wrinkles on his face were the legacy of a lifetime sailing the Pacific Ocean. For thirty years Don Francisco had worn a furrow in the sea between Panama and the southern ports of the viceroyalty of Peru. There was hardly a vessel which he had not commanded, navigated or escorted – galleons with cargoes of bullion, tubby urcas loaded with merchandise, fast pataches carrying official correspondence, even a pasaca-ballo, a flat-bottomed horse ferry, out of which he had once disembarked a troop of cavalry to fight the Aurocanos in Chile. Now, as Capitan del Navio, his ship was a barca longa, an armed brigantine, anchored off Panama City.

'The pirates have succeeded in crossing the mountains, but they find themselves in a quandary,' Peralta went on. 'They must have boats if they are to reach and attack Panama. To march overland along the coast is too slow and too hazardous. The only craft available to them will be small dugout canoes made by the Indians, and perhaps a piragua or two. This makes them vulnerable.'

Barahona had grasped the point Peralta was making. 'We must shut down the sea lanes. None of our vessels are to sail from any port. All those currently at sea will be ordered into harbour,' he said.

'But surely we should send out boats to warn our coastal settlements that the pirates are on the prowl,' protested the bishop. He was feeling piqued that his earlier suggestion had been dismissed out of hand.

'No. The pirates might capture our vessels and turn them against us.'

'What naval forces do we have to defend us if the pirates do get this far?' The governor put the question directly to Barahona though he already knew the answer. It was better that the civilians and the Churchmen were made aware just how acute the danger was.

'There are five merchant ships currently at anchor. One of them, *La Santissima Trinidad*, is a large galleon, but currently she is fitted out as a merchant vessel so has no armament. Then there are the three small warships of the South Sea squadron.' Barahona was careful to describe the colonial navy as an armadilla, a squadron. Its official title might be far grander as an Armada or Fleet, but the merchants of Peru and Panama had been stingy about paying the situados, the special taxes which were meant to fund the colony's defences. So now the royal vessels were few in number, undersize and decrepit. The warships at his disposal were barca longas like Peralta's, a two-masted craft equipped with a dozen cannon.

'Surely that should be sufficient to deal with a handful of pirates in canoes,' sniffed the cavalry colonel.

'Our main problem is not in ships, but in men,' retorted Barahona crisply. As always the land soldiers overlooked the fact that sailors took far longer to train than infantrymen.

'We have enough competent seamen to man just one of the warships. They are mostly Biscayners, so they are prime seamen and excellent at their job. But the other two vessels will be relying on locally raised crews.' Barahona's eyes flicked towards Peralta and the officer seated next to him, Capitan Diego de Carabaxal. The latter was a competent seaman but Barahona was not sure that Carabaxal would have the necessary courage when it came to a fight. 'Both those vessels are short-handed. So I propose stripping the merchant ships of their sailors and redistributing their men to the warships.'

'Is that wise? Without crews they cannot save themselves,' objected one of the councillors. From the note of alarm in the man's voice Peralta suspected that he was part-owner of one of the merchant ships and dismayed at the threat to his investment.

'If any merchant ship is about to fall into the hands of the pirates, it will be scuttled or burned on my orders.' Barahona had the satisfaction of seeing the councillor go pale at the prospect.

'Then it's decided,' announced the governor. 'The armadilla will put itself in a state of readiness to intercept and destroy the pirates while they are still in small boats. The land forces are to concentrate in the city and look to the defences should the pirates succeed in coming ashore.'

The bishop closed the meeting with a prayer for salvation, beseeching the Almighty to thwart the evil designs of the heathen sea robbers, and Francisco de Peralta left the governor's office. He had only a short walk to where his ship's cockboat was waiting. As he crossed the main square of New Panama, he remembered what it had been like the last time the pirates had attacked. Henry Morgan, the great pirate, had marched across the isthmus with 1,200 men. A garrison of four regiments of foot and two squadrons of horse had failed to stop a ragtag force so poorly supplied that the bandits had been obliged to eat their leather satchels during their advance. The entire city, seven thousand households, had panicked. People ran about, frantically hiding their valuables down wells and cisterns or in holes in walls. Then they fled into the countryside, trying to escape before the city was invested.

Peralta had received orders to warp his ship up to the quays. There he had taken on an astonishing variety of refugees and their baggage – nuns and priests, high-born ladies with their children and servants, senior government officials. They had brought the contents of the city treasury, boxes of official deeds and documents, sacks stuffed with church plate, paintings, sacred relics hastily wrapped in altar cloths, chests of privately owned jewellery, gold, pearls, all manner of portable wealth. The value of the cargo rushed aboard his vessel that day had exceeded all that was left behind in the city for the pirates to plunder. In vain he had warned that his vessel was not fit for sea. Its sole defence was seven cannon and a dozen muskets, and her sails had been condemned and taken ashore. No one listened. Everyone begged him to leave port at once and save them and their goods.

What followed had seemed like a miracle. His grossly overloaded vessel had cast off, and his crew had spread a set of topsails, the only canvas they still had on board. It was barely enough to push the vessel through the water. Half-sailing, half-drifting on the current, his ship had limped away from the city, and Peralta had spent the next forty-eight hours waiting for the pirates to commandeer local boats, catch up and take their plunder. A score of pirates in a piragua would have been enough. But it never happened. The enemy failed to appear, and for years he had wondered why. Eventually he had learned that the pirates had got drunk. They had wasted so much time on shore, guzzling captured wine, that when they emerged from their stupor Peralta and his precious cargo had drifted away over the horizon.

Don Francisco allowed himself a wry grin at the memory. The ladrones del mar, the sea thieves as he thought of them, were courageous and unpredictable. But they had two weaknesses: a love of strong drink and a tendency to quarrel among themselves. Given enough time, they usually fell into disarray and returned from where they had come.

The Spanish captain reached the little creek where his cockboat was waiting for him. Every member of its crew was a black man because Don Francisco preferred to work with negroes. Most were freed slaves and he found them loyal and less likely to desert in search of better pay in the merchant marine. Now they would have half an hour of steady rowing to bring him to his ship. After Morgan had sacked Panama, the city had been rebuilt in a safer location and the planners of New Panama had been so fearful of an attack from the sea that they had picked an easily defended promontory with shoal water all around it. This meant that the merchant ships and the armadilla were obliged to anchor well away from the shore and had no protection from the city's gun batteries. Don Francisco's earlier moment of cheerfulness subsided into a mood of resignation. Whatever happened in the next few days, he and the two other captains would be on their own. There would be no assistance from the landsmen.

He turned to look back over his shoulder as the cockboat pulled out of the creek. He had a clear view down the coast in the direction from which the pirates would come, and towards the ruins of the city that Morgan had sacked and burned. Most of the buildings had been of fine cedar wood, with beautiful carved balconies. All that had gone up in flames. Only the stone-built structures had survived, and one of them still rose above its neighbours. It was the old cathedral, still in use because its replacement in New Panama had not yet been consecrated. But Morgan's pirates had not got away with everything. Hearing that an attack was imminent, the priests had cleverly camouflaged the cathedral's beautiful altar piece, a soaring masterwork of carved wood smothered in gold leaf. They had painted it black, and the pirates had been duped. They ransacked the cathedral but failed to see the deception. The altar piece remained, and the citizens of New Panama still worshipped before it. As he settled back in his place in the stern of the boat, Don Peralta wondered if he too would be able to use deception to hoodwink the new invaders.

✳

HECTOR WAS thankful that he had been selected for Captain Sawkins' vanguard. It put him well out of reach of Coxon. The buccaneer had tried using the Kuna balm spiked with the Spanish Fly, and the last time Hector had seen him, Coxon's face and neck had been disfigured with a great throbbing rash, a seeping expanse like a grotesque birthmark which was giving Coxon agony. Clearly, Hector felt that it was small retribution for what had happened on the ridge before Santa Maria.

'You were set up,' Jezreel had confirmed when Hector told him what had happened during the attack. 'We could not see you and your flag of truce from the cane brakes where the forlorn assembled. Yet you must have been visible to Coxon up on the ridge. He must have enjoyed watching you walk trustingly towards the Spanish guns.'

'And Coxon himself took care to stay out of harm's way,' the big man added. 'He waited until Santa Maria had fallen before he came down from the ridge. Some are saying that our commander lacks courage.'

Now Coxon was somewhere far behind Sawkins and in the early light of dawn the forlorn was advancing on Panama in boats provided by the Kuna – two large piraguas and five small canoes. Jezreel, Dan and Jacques had been assigned to a piragua while Hector had been provided with a musket and ammunition and put with five other men in one of the little dugouts.

Hector put down his paddle and leaned forward to check the lashings that held his musket to the side of the canoe. Dan had advised him to make sure that the knots were tight, the muzzle stoppered, and the lock well wrapped in waxed cloth so that it stayed dry. Also that his cartridge box was fastened somewhere safe, and well sealed with grease, so he didn't lose the gun or wet the ammunition if there was a capsize.

It had been good advice. The canoe had not tipped over but the four days since leaving Santa Maria had brought frequent cloudbursts, heavy and unpredictable, which had drenched his clothes and knapsack and ruined Hector's last remaining store of food. Only his medical notebook had stayed dry. He had put it inside a watertight tube he had made from the hollow stem of a giant cane, sealing the cut end with a soft wooden plug driven in tight.

Hector picked up his paddle and resumed the stroke. Conversation was limited to talking to the man directly in front or behind. Seated just ahead of him was a weatherbeaten buccaneer by the name of John Watling. His scars and gruff manner of speech with its occasional military jargon marked him as a veteran soldier.

'I'm told that Sawkins can't abide oaths and profanity.' Hector said.

'Doesn't like gaming either. Says it's sinful and I agree with him,' Watling replied over his shoulder. 'If he finds a pack of cards or a set of dice, he throws them in the sea. He makes his people observe the Sabbath too.'

'Yet he doesn't hesitate to plunder fellow Christians.'

'Course not. They're Papists, aren't they? He sees them as fair game and it doesn't matter if we don't have a Jamaica commission.'

The mention of Jamaica made Hector think of Susanna yet again.

'I'm hoping to get back to Jamaica soon. Left a girl there,' he said casually though full of pride. It was an exaggeration but it gave him some small throb of satisfaction to pretend that Susanna was in his life.

'Then you better hope that our venture on Panama turns out to be more profitable than Santa Maria. No one's going to be welcome back in Jamaica without a deal of plunder in his purse.'

'That won't make any difference to my girl,' Hector boasted.

'She'll have no say in it,' said Watling curtly. 'We've left a right bad taste behind us in Port Royal. Our captains told the authorities that they were going to cut logwood in Campeachy. Even got government licences to do so. But the moment they cleared the land, they headed for the Main and began this mischief.'

'I can't see how that will affect me when I get back to Port Royal. I joined up later.'

'It'll make no difference,' grunted Watling. He paused his paddling to take up a wooden scoop lying at his feet and bail out a quantity of bilgewater. 'There's meant to be a truce between England and Spain, and I wouldn't be surprised if we've been disowned.'

'Disowned?'

'Put beyond the law.' Watling made it sound very casual. 'If we come back with our pockets full of treasure, it will all be forgotten. Just like Drake back in the time of Queen Bess. The Spaniards still call him the Great Pirate, but the English think he is a national hero and he was knighted by the Queen.' He half-turned to face back at Hector. 'So if you come home in a ship with sails of silk, then you'll be a hero too. If not . . .' – he made a gesture of rope being placed around his neck, and pulled upward – 'We'll be choked off. All of us that are caught . . .'

Watling's blunt prediction filled Hector with foreboding. It was too late to leave the expedition before it reached Panama, even if he was prepared to abandon Dan and his other friends. No longer did he have the excuse that he was only serving as a medical orderly in the campaign. Captain Sawkins had insisted that he carried the musket if he was to travel with the forlorn. The more he thought about his predicament, the more Hector was undecided whether he preferred the attack on Panama to fail so that the expedition would disband, or for the assault to succeed so that he could return to Jamaica and buy himself out of trouble.

There was a long silence, broken only when Watling commented, 'Nice to think it's St George's Day. A good omen!'

But Hector did not answer. He had counted a total of seventy-six men in Sawkins' tiny flotilla. That seemed far too few to assault a major Spanish stronghold. The rest of the buccaneer expedition was lagging far behind, and he doubted that fire-eating Sawkins would wait for them to catch up. Somewhere over to his left were Dan, Jezreel and Jacques in their piragua, but it was too far away to see which one it was. On his right and visible on the low shoreline against the sunrise was the stump of a tower which one of his companions, a man who had marched with Morgan, said was the Cathedral of Old Panama. The vanguard must be getting very close to its target.

'Three sail and bearing directly down for us!' exclaimed Watling as the sun finally dispelled the last of the dawn haze.

Hector craned to one side to look forward over the seaman's shoulder. About two miles distant were three sailing ships. They were heading straight for the buccaneer canoes which were advancing in no sort of formation.

'Warships by the look of them, barca longas,' said Watling, 'and in a hurry to engage us.'

There was a halloo from the nearest canoe about eighty yards away to their right. It was Sawkins himself. Typically his boat had outstripped the rest, and was several lengths in advance of the company. The captain was standing up in his canoe, waving his hat and gesturing that Watling's canoe should turn directly towards the enemy.

'Not much else we can do,' muttered Watling darkly. 'The Spaniards have the advantage of us. The wind is right behind them, and they can pick their prey.' But he appeared remarkably composed as he bent forward and began to unfasten his musket.

Only when he had checked and loaded the weapon did he look up again. By then it was clear to Hector that the leading Spanish vessel was shaping course to pass through the gap between Sawkins' canoe and the one in which he now sat. It would allow the Spanish vessel to use her gun batteries on both sides.

'Any good with a musket?' Watling asked Hector.

'I haven't had much practice recently.'

'Better if you act as my loader then,' suggested the seaman. 'Get your own gun ready, and hand it to me when I've fired mine. Then take my gun and set it up again. If we're quick about it, I should be able to get off at least three shots, maybe more.'

While Hector prepared his own musket, Watling sat quietly, his gun held across his lap, until the leading Spanish ship was almost within range.

'Stand by to receive cannon fire,' he said softly.

A moment later there was a loud bang and a billow of smoke from the deck of the Spanish vessel. The air was filled with the whistle of flying metal, and the surface of the sea a good thirty yards ahead of the canoe spouted small jets of foam.

'Scrubby shooting at this range,' said Watling dryly.

Again the bang of a cannon. This time the Spanish ship was firing in the opposite direction, towards Sawkins' canoe. Hector could not see where the shot fell.

'They'll do better next time,' said Watling, and he crouched down in the canoe. Hastily Hector followed his example, kneeling in the bilge and bending as low as possible. Nevertheless he felt very vulnerable. Behind him the other men were also ducking down.

Another shot from a cannon, and the sound of metal hurtling through the air. It was much closer this time. There was a sudden drone as something skimmed off the surface of the sea. The Spaniards must have loaded their guns with small shot. Watling let out a grunt as he shifted position. Now he was half-reclining in the bottom of the canoe, the barrel of his musket resting on the gunnel, and taking aim towards the Spanish ship. Hector felt the canoe rock slightly from side to side as the buccaneers behind him also took up their firing positions. 'Steady!' came a warning voice. It was the man farthest in the bow. 'Let me take the first shot.'

There was the sound of a musket firing, the familiar smell of gunpowder, and a slight tremor down the length of the canoe. Hector raised his head and squinted towards the Spanish ship. He could see men on deck and in the lower rigging and the steersman at the helm. Next to him was a man dressed in a long dark coat with slashes of silver braid. He must be the captain. A group of four Spanish sailors were gathered near the rail and, almost too late, Hector realised that they were a gun crew preparing to fire. He ducked down as their cannon spurted a stab of flame, and something smartly rapped the hull of the canoe. From behind him came an oath.

One of Watling's bare feet was pushing against his shoulder as the sailor braced himself and took aim. The crack of his musket was followed by a snort of satisfaction. Then Watling was passing back his musket and beckoning for Hector to hand him his own gun. Another wriggle as the sailor adjusted his firing position, and fired a second shot. Hector had to half-kneel in order to reload the empty gun. His head and body were now well above the level of the canoe's rim. He prised open the waxed lid of his cartouche box and pulled out a charge of powder in its paper wrapping. Tearing off the end of the cartouche with his teeth, he carefully tipped the powder into the musket barrel. Wrapping a strip of paper around a musket ball to make it a tight fit, he tamped it firmly down the barrel with the ramrod. Then, turning the musket on its side, he checked that the pin hole leading to the chamber was clear before he reached for his powder horn and poured a pinch of gunpowder into the firing pan and closed its cover. He was concentrating so closely on his work that he scarcely noticed the sound of the third cannon shot from the Spanish vessel.

Their aim must have been poor for he was only conscious of Watling urging him to hurry. 'Quick! Their helm is exposed.' Hector passed the reloaded musket forward, and this time Watling sat up on his thwart and faced over the stern of the canoe to take his aim. His musket barrel was beside the young man's face as he pulled the trigger. Hector was half-deafened by the explosion. But Watling was grinning with triumph. 'Two out of three,' he exulted, baring his teeth.

The men behind Hector had also been firing, though how many shots they had got off he could not tell. When he next looked towards the Spanish vessel, the barca longa had passed through the gap between the two canoes and was now down-wind. It would take some time for her crew to turn the ship and bring her back into action. For the moment the danger from that direction was over.

A low groan dispelled his sense of relief. The man seated directly behind him in the canoe was holding his shoulder. Blood was staining his shirt. 'Here, let me look at that,' said Hector, and was about to climb back over the thwart with his medical knapsack when he was stopped by a sharp order from Watling. 'Leave that for later,' the sailor snapped. 'Here comes the next one.'

Hector glanced up to see a second Spanish warship steering for the same gap between his own canoe and Sawkins' boat. A broad white, gold and red pennant flying from the warship's masthead indicated that this must be the command vessel in the Spanish squadron.

Watling was speaking to him again, his voice urgent. 'Reload your own musket, and this time use it yourself. We'll not have much support from our captain from now.' A hurried glance towards Sawkins' canoe showed that only three members of its crew were visible in their normal places. Their companions must have been killed or wounded.

There was a nudge in his back. 'Here, take my gun as well!' The buccaneer with the bloody shoulder seated behind him was thrusting forward his musket for Hector to use. 'Aim for the helm, always for the helm,' the man advised, his face screwed up in pain.

This time Hector knew what to expect. Copying Watling's example he lay in the bottom of the canoe and rested the barrel of his gun on the rim of the hull. He drew back the hammer and waited patiently. The oncoming Spanish warship was following exactly the same track as its escort. Again the sounds of cannon, the clouds of black smoke, and this time the sharper reports of muskets as the Spaniards on deck opened fire on the small low-lying canoes.

Hector was no longer conscious of where the bullets went. His world narrowed to a single image – the figure of the man steering the Spanish vessel. He focused along the sights of his musket and carefully swivelled the muzzle to follow his target. He was faintly aware of the motion of the canoe on the slight swell, the hull rolling a few inches, just enough to make the target rise and fall in his aim. The motion was regular enough for him to calculate when the moment was right. He took a long slow breath and held it, waited for the uproll and then gently squeezed the trigger.

He ignored the recoil of the butt against his shoulder as he watched, never taking his eye off the figure of the helmsman. The man spun round and dropped.

'Thought you said you were out of practice! My turn now,' crowed Watling who had observed his shot. Within moments another man had appeared at the helm of the Spanish vessel, a replacement steersman, and he was taking control. Watling hunched over his own weapon and took aim. He fired, and there was a brief moment when it seemed that he had missed his mark. The new helmsman was still upright, unharmed. Then, slowly and inexplicably, the warship began to turn sideways, losing speed.

'Christ, what luck!' exclaimed the wounded buccaneer from

behind Hector. The man must have had keen eyesight for he added, 'The main brace is shot through. The mainsail is loose.'

Sure enough, with canvas flapping, the warship was losing all forward motion and veering to one side. The deck guns could no longer be brought to bear on the canoes. The Spanish vessel was crippled.

'There's her commander now!' shouted Watling gleefully. A tall, thin man had climbed up on the rail. He wore a plumed hat and a broad red sash, and there was the glint of gold brocade on the sleeves of his coat. Regardless of his personal safety, he was holding on to the rigging with one hand and with the other frantically waving a white handkerchief over his head. For a moment Hector thought it was a flag of truce and the Spanish officer wanted to parlay or even surrender. But then the young man realised that the Spaniard was not facing the canoes, but looking towards the first barca longa which had led the attack. That vessel was still a quarter of a mile downwind and trying clumsily to work back to return to the fray. The Spanish commander was urgently beckoning to his escort to come to the rescue.

'Too good a chance to miss. Here, give me that spare musket,' gloated Watling. Hector handed him the gun from the wounded sailor, and once again Watling took slow, deliberate aim and fired. The impact of the bullet knocked the Spanish officer backwards off the rail on which he was standing. The white handkerchief fell from his hand and fluttered down into the sea.

'Now we've got 'em!' exulted Watling. 'Come on lads, close the gap.' He picked up his paddle and began to drive the canoe through the water.

The loss of their commander had utterly demoralised the Spanish crew. Dismayed by the accuracy of the buccaneer's musketry, they abandoned their deck cannon, knowing they were dangerously exposed when they stood to load their big guns. Now, instead of standing at the rail or climbing into the rigging to shoot at their attackers, the crew of the warship ducked down and hid out of sight behind the bulwarks, and only occasionally raised their heads to take aim and fire. They had lost the will to fight.

A rousing cheer to his left told Hector that one of the piraguas had at last arrived in support. With sixteen men on board, the piragua rowed straight towards the disabled Spanish warship and, closing to within point blank range, opened up a deadly fusillade of musketry on their victims. One by one the hapless Spanish crewmen were picked off if they showed themselves.

Watling was pointing back towards the first Spanish warship. 'Seems he's seen enough,' he said. That vessel was altering course, withdrawing from the battle and abandoning her consort.

Above the noise of the cheering from the musketeers in the piragua came anxious shouts from the stricken warship. The crew was appealing for quarter. A hand holding a scrap of white cloth appeared above the bulwarks and began to wave the symbol to and fro in surrender. The musket fire from the piragua gradually lessened and finally ceased altogether.

'Sawkins well deserves his victory,' said Hector. He could scarcely believe that a handful of buccaneers had managed to overcome the larger, more powerful vessel so swiftly.

'Our captain's already shifted aboard the other piragua,' Watling told him, nodding towards the south. A quarter of a mile away the second piragua lay alongside the third of the Spanish warships. There was fierce hand-to-hand fighting on deck and, as he watched, Hector saw that the boarding party of buccaneers was being driven back to their own vessel. Only then did he realise that Dan, Jacques and Jezreel must now be fighting alongside Sawkins in his latest suicidal endeavour.

TEN

Capitan Francisco de Peralta had willingly followed his squadron commander in setting sail to intercept and engage the enemy's motley flotilla as soon as it was sighted. He watched Diego de Carabaxal's barca longa make for the gap between the two canoes farthest to the left of the pirate's ragged line, and had entirely approved of this bold response to the pirate threat. Carabaxal's cannon should make short work of the lightly built canoes and piraguas. But when Capitan Barahona chose to follow in exactly the same track, Don Francisco hesitated. It was a mistake, he thought, for two warships to deal with a pair of canoes while ignoring the rest of the pirate flotilla. So Peralta had decided to seek out his own target: he would engage the largest of their vessels, a piragua that had fallen behind and, under oars, was struggling to keep up.

The Spanish captain looked up at the cloudless sky. He would have welcomed a change in the weather, but there was no sign of it. The breeze was so gentle that it raised barely a ripple on the indigo-blue sea. The calm conditions would suit the pirate musketeers. They would be firing from a more stable platform than if there was a choppy seaway to contend with. Peralta held a profound respect for the enemy musketry. He recalled the shock of Morgan's raid when its victims discovered that the invaders carried firearms of the very latest model. With their modern guns the pirates had outranged the defenders of Panama, firing two or three shots for every one their opponents had been able to return from their obsolete firelocks and arquebuses. The defenders' superiority in numbers had counted for little.

So now Don Peralta decided to get as close as possible to the piragua and fire into her with light swivel guns loaded with small shot. Once he had decimated her musketeers, he would despatch a boarding party to over-run the survivors.

'Mount our patareros,' he told Estevan Madriga, his negro contremaestre. 'And make sure that the gun crews have all they need. Ammunition and plenty of powder charges close to hand . . . and a tub of water for them to slake their thirst. This could prove to be hot work.'

Peralta had total confidence in his contremaestre. Madriga had served with him for more than fifteen years, and there was a bond of mutual trust between them. The Spanish captain only wished that his crew had done more practice with the swivel guns. The penny pinching of the colonial administration meant that any gun drill had been rare. The contadores, the bookkeepers, condemned it as a waste of expensive gunpowder.

Peralta chewed his lip in frustration. His ship, *Santa Catalina*, was lagging behind her consorts, easing along at less than walking pace. That too was partly the fault of the bureaucracy. The barca longa's bottom was foul with weeds because the ship had been kept lying at anchor off Panama for more than a month while he waited for permission to take her out of service and careen.

Estevan returned to report that the ship's four patareros had been brought up from the hold. The guns were being checked and loaded and placed on their bronze swivel mounts. With a patarero on each quarter and two in the bows, they gave a field of fire all round the vessel. Unfortunately a shortage of muskets meant that less than half the crew could be issued with firearms. The others would have to make do with pikes and cutlasses. It was all part of the same pattern, thought Don Francisco sourly. He had asked the royal stores for an additional four patareros and, though the guns had been promised, they had never been delivered. Insufficient gunpowder, too few weapons, bad pay – his barca longa was a miniature of the entire viceroyalty of Peru. Brave men were trying to operate a structure that was falling to bits through neglect and parsimony.

He turned to check what was happening with the other vessels in the squadron. Carabaxal had already passed through the pirate line and was manoeuvring his ship to come back upwind. He appeared to have done little damage to the enemy because the two canoes nearest to him were still afloat. Hopefully, Capitan Barahona would be more successful.

A shout from the foredeck brought his attention back to his own plan of attack. A lookout was reporting that the three remaining pirate canoes were altering course. They were converging on his own barca longa. 'Our target remains that big piragua,' Peralta confirmed. 'No one is to open fire until we are in easy range.' He was worried about the patareros. Mounted on the ship's rail the swivel guns looked menacing enough and, if properly handled, were capable of doing great damage. But the patareros had only ever been fired with blank charges to blast out honour salutes for visiting dignitaries or to celebrate the holy days of mother Church. It was typical of the contadores that they had allowed him gunpowder for ceremonials and to flatter grandees, but not for target practice. Outward display came cheaper and pleased the crowds.

Peralta calculated that another ten minutes of *Santa Catalina*'s sluggish advance should bring the enemy within range. He made a tour of his ship, stopping for a brief word of encouragement with as many of his men as possible. He paid special attention to the gunners, two men to a gun. 'I'm counting on you,' he told them quietly. 'Don't believe the old yarn that the foreign pirates are devils from hell. As you can see, they're men, and a scruffy lot at that.'

As Don Francisco returned to his position by the helm, he eyed the gap between his barca longa and the piragua. It was still too far to open fire with any certainty of success. The swivel guns let loose a cruel hail of scatter shot, but their range was limited. The breeze, though very light, was still holding steady from the west.

He came to a decision. 'Contremaestre! We steer to pass to windward of the piragua. I want all four patareros moved to the starboard side.' The guns were light enough to be picked up by their crews and carried across the deck. Alternative mounts were already fixed at several points on the ship's rail. By shifting the swivel guns so that all four of them fired from the starboard rail, he was creating a ready-made broadside.

The last of his gun crews were still heaving their weapon up onto its Y-shaped mount when the first musket shot rang out from the piragua. Don Francisco had expected the pirates to be good marksmen, but the range and accuracy of that first shot startled him. From a distance of 300 paces the musket bullet struck the ship's rail close to the patarero and sent up a shower of splinters. One fragment embedded itself deep in the chest of one of his gunners. The man gave a sudden, surprised cough and fell back on the deck. A comrade immediately took his place, but Peralta noted the looks of fright that passed across the faces of all those who stood nearby.

'Open fire now you have your target,' he called out as if nothing had happened. It was better that the gun crews went into action now, even if the range was long. Gun handling would distract them, and the patareros were simple enough to use. The gunner only had to find his target *por el raso de los metales*, 'by the line of metals', squinting along the crude sights on the barrel and tell his companion when to apply a lighted match to the touch hole.

There was a loud hollow thud like the sound of a slack drum skin hit hard. It was the characteristic noise of a patarero. Don Francisco watched a pattern of small white splashes flower in the sea well short of the piragua. The barca longa was still out of range.

He took a few slow steps along the deck, turned and walked back, careful to keep in full view of the pirates, and of his men. He wanted his crew to see that this was a time to be calm.

Now the musketeers in the piragua were opening up a steady fusillade. They went about their business coolly. Their shots were irregularly spaced so it was clear that they were taking their time to aim accurately. Don Francisco heard several musket balls whizz overhead. A couple of small holes appeared in the courses, the lower sails. Four more of his men were hit by splinters.

At last *Santa Catalina* was in range. A forward patarero fired, and this time the splashes of small shot were all around the piragua. He heard distant cries of pain. The three remaining swivel guns belched their loads of scatter shot. Two of them were poorly aimed, and did little damage. But the fourth gun scored a direct hit, and he saw several of the pirates slump forward.

'Well done!' he shouted as the gunners began to reload. The patareros were of a basic design, loaded by the muzzle, not in the breech. To recharge the weapons, it was safer and easier if they were lifted off their mounts and placed on the deck. There the men sponged out the hot barrel, loaded in a charge of gunpowder and a wad, and finally a canvas bag packed with small shot and broken metal fragments. Minutes later the patarero should be back in place on the rail, and the gunner firing again.

Peralta had to admire the pirates' courage. They did not flinch under the bursts of scatter shot but changed their methods. Only a handful of their men in the bow were still shooting, the rest were straining at the oars, rowing the piragua forwards, roaring and chanting their defiance. They were desperate to close and board.

Let them come, Peralta thought. He had enough men to deal with the onslaught.

A cry from behind him made him spin around. His second mate was running towards the far rail. A hand had appeared at deck level. Someone had climbed up the side of the ship away from the battle. The mate stamped hard on the hand and it withdrew.

Peralta drew a pistol from his belt and hurried to join his officer. Looking over the rail he found himself staring straight down into one of the pirate canoes. It had succeeded in sneaking up, unnoticed, to the stern of the barca longa. There were six men in the canoe, and at least one of them was wounded for he was leaking blood. The faces of the others were turned towards him. Don Francisco thrust his pistol over the rail and fired downwards. It was impossible to miss. The pirate in the centre of the canoe fell back, half in and half out of the canoe.

His second mate was waving a cutlass and screaming curses. Peralta realised that the man had no musket. 'Here, take this,' he shouted, pulling a second pistol from his waistband, and handing it to the man. 'Keep them off.'

He turned and ran back across the deck. He was needed there to direct the patareros. To his dismay he found that the piragua was now far closer than he had expected. Only a gap of a few yards separated the two vessels. A moment later they touched sides and a score of the enemy were clambering on his deck, yelling and whooping like fiends.

Peralta drew his sword, a rapier given him when he first received his commission, and the next instant found himself fending off a haggard, ginger-haired man who rushed at him hefting a boarding axe. Don Francisco felt a heavy jolt as the axe struck his rapier blade. Fortunately it was a glancing blow, otherwise the steel would have shattered. The axe head slid as far as the rapier's hilt and turned aside harmlessly. Peralta took his chance to run his assailant through the shoulder with the point. More and more pirates were climbing aboard, and there was chaos across the entire width of the deck. Buccaneers and his black crew men surged together in hand-to-hand combat. There was an occasional pistol shot, but most of the fight was waged with cutlasses and daggers, cudgels, muskets used as clubs, short pikes and fists. One of his own men was swinging a capstan bar, using it to batter and smash at his opponents. Peralta caught a glimpse of a giant buccaneer who was wreaking havoc with a weapon that the Spanish captain had never encountered before. It was a stubby sword scarcely longer than a cutlass and not as broad in the blade. The giant was wielding it with extraordinary agility, slashing and cutting almost too fast to follow, and he was driving back anyone who challenged him. As the captain watched, the giant cut down two of *Santa Catalina*'s crew.

'Come on! We are more than they are!' he yelled, and flung himself into the thick of the fight. He was conscious of someone at his left shoulder. It was Estevan and he was fighting grimly, protecting his captain's vulnerable side. Peralta shouted again, urging on his crew, and he felt a thrill of pride as they responded with a concerted charge. A score of them began to force the boarders back towards their own vessel. 'Well done! Well done!' he screamed, smashing his sword hilt into a sweating pirate face. His crewmen pressed forward. Now they had the initiative. The pirates were in retreat. Don Francisco was panting with effort. His foot skidded and he almost fell. The deck was slippery with blood. But it did not matter. Already the first of the pirates were jumping back into their piragua; their comrades were fighting a rearguard action. In another few moments the deck of his barca longa would be cleared. Now was the time to smash the enemy into oblivion.

Don Francisco grabbed his contremaestre by the shoulder. 'We must get to the forward patarero, Estevan!' he bellowed in the man's ear. 'Load it with the heaviest shot you can find.

Shoot down into that damned piragua, and send her to the bottom.' Estevan had never failed him in all those years they had served together on the royal ships. He always knew exactly what he was doing. Now he and Don Francisco sprinted forward to the bow, hurdling two badly wounded men sprawled on the deck. As Estevan ran, he was calling out to two of his own men to help him with the patarero.

The four of them reached the swivel gun where it sat on its mounting on the rail. Its muzzle was pointing skyward, left at that angle after the last time it had been fired. Peralta watched Estevan grab the breech and swing the weapon level so that two assistants could take their positions. One man stood at each side of the gun and clasped the barrel. At a command from the contremaestre, all three men heaved the patarero off its mount, then gently laid the weapon on deck ready to reload.

Peralta gave a smile of relief. Now the gun crew was behind the ship's rail, out of sight of the pirates in the piragua. Jeers, confused shouting, and the occasional report of a musket told him that his crew were managing to keep the pirates at bay, preventing them from climbing back aboard the barca longa. In another minute or two, the patarero would be reloaded, hoisted back into position, and then he and Estevan would tilt the gun so that it pointed directly down into the piragua. A single shot at such close range would be devastating. It would rip the bottom out of the pirate's craft, and that would be the end of the fight.

Perhaps it was an ember still smouldering inside the bronze barrel of the patarero which caused the disaster. Or maybe metal struck on metal and produced an unlucky spark, or the inexperienced gun crew bungled their work. Whatever the reason, there was a tremendous explosion on the foredeck. A dozen powder charges ignited simultaneously. Sections of planking flew into the air. Two of the gun crew were blown to pieces, and a blast of heat struck Peralta in the face. He threw up his hands to protect himself from the sheet of flame which followed, and felt a searing pain. Deafened by the clap of sound, he was thrown bodily over the ship's rail and into the sea.

*

HECTOR AND his comrades in their canoe were only fifty paces away when the thunderclap of the explosion occurred. Something terrible had taken place on the barca longa's deck.

'Man in the water!' Hector shouted. He could see the head of someone swimming.

'Let him drown. He's just a Spaniard,' said a voice.

'No! He could be from our boarding party,' Hector insisted, thinking that perhaps it was Jacques or Jezreel who had been in the piragua. He started paddling. Ahead of him, John Watling followed his example. From the Spanish vessel there was no sound at all. Hector supposed that everyone aboard was too shocked and stunned to continue fighting.

When the canoe reached the swimmer, he proved to be an older man with short, nearly white hair. By his dark complexion it was evident that he was a Spaniard. He was supporting the unconscious body of a black man, holding his head above the sea. The negro was horribly wounded. His skin was lacerated and torn, his face a mask of blood.

'Here, grab on and let us help you,' Hector called out in Spanish as he reached down to take hold of the unconscious figure. The swimmer gave a nod of thanks, and the black man was lifted carefully into the canoe. 'You too,' Hector added, holding out his hand. 'Come aboard. You are our prisoner now.'

The stranger clambered into the canoe, and there was something about his manner which indicated that he was an officer.

'My name is Hector Lynch. I'm not a surgeon, but I have a few medicines with me which may help your friend here.'

'I will be grateful for that,' answered the stranger. 'Allow me to introduce myself. I am Capitan Francisco de Peralta, commander of the *Santa Catalina* that you and your colleagues have assaulted. The wounded man is my quartermaster, Estevan.'

'What do we do now? The black man needs proper medical attention,' Hector asked, addressing his colleagues.

'We could bring Peralta to his ship, and get him to call on the crew to surrender,' suggested Watling. He spoke enough Spanish to have followed Hector's conversation with their prisoner.

Cautiously they began to paddle their canoe towards the barca longa. One or two men could be seen moving about on deck of the stricken Spanish warship. There was a thin flicker of flame along the lower edge of the mainsail which had been set alight in the explosion. Someone was attempting to put out the fire, throwing water from a bucket. There was no sign of anyone from the boarding party from the piragua which was still on the opposite side of the Spanish vessel and out of sight.

The canoe had covered less than half the distance when there was a second explosion, even more thunderous than the first. This time it came from the stern of the *Santa Catalina* and was so powerful that it snapped the mainmast and sent it crashing over the side, trailing tattered sails and rigging. A black cloud of smoke rose in the air. Soon afterwards came the sounds of wailing and screams of pain.

Peralta went pale. 'God help my crew. They did not deserve that,' he muttered.

When Hector and the others reached the barca longa, they found carnage everywhere – broad streaks of blood on the deck, broken and shattered gear, scorched planking, the smell of burning. Only about a quarter of the crew seemed still alive, and the survivors were either badly wounded or in a state of shock. Peralta was grim-faced, appalled by the destruction.

Hector and Watling helped the capitan hoist the still unconscious black man aboard and lay him on deck, and Hector knelt beside the injured contremaestre, trying to remember how surgeon Smeeton had treated gunpowder burns.

'Any idea who's the senior Spanish survivor?' someone asked. Hector looked up. It was Sawkins. Miraculously the hot-headed buccaneer captain was still alive though there was a bloody bandage round his head, and his buff coat was smudged with gunpowder. He must have boarded from the piragua.

'This is Captain Francisco Peralta. He's the commander,' Hector answered.

'Ask him about those other ships. We need to know how they are manned and armed,' said Sawkins briskly. He was his usual terrier-like self, eager for action and gazing towards the four vessels which could be seen at anchor in the roadstead off Panama. Hector marvelled at the man's unquenchable energy.

The Spanish captain hesitated for a moment before replying. 'You'll find four hundred well-armed men aboard those ships.'

On the deck beside Peralta the black man stirred and opened his eyes. They were filled with pain. It was clear that he was mortally wounded.

'There's no one over there. Everyone already volunteered for this fight,' Estevan wheezed.

Peralta started to contradict him, but Sawkins cut him short. 'I accept the word of a dying man, captain. You have fought well, and there is no disgrace. What we need now is a hospital ship.'

The contremaestre had spoken the truth. There was not a soul on the anchored vessels when the buccaneers reached them, though someone had attempted to scuttle the largest of them, the galleon *La Santissima Trinidad*. A fire of rags and wood shavings had been deliberately set in her forecastle and several planks punctured with an axe. But the blaze had not yet taken hold and was quickly extinguished, and a carpenter was able to seal the leak. Then the wounded, both buccaneers and their enemies, were laid out on the galleon's broad deck to receive attention.

'I doubt that our Captain Harris will live. He was shot through both legs while trying to climb up onto Peralta's ship,' said Jacques. He was watching Hector stitch up a deep gash in the shoulder of a buccaneer.

'Does that mean our company has to elect a new captain?' asked his friend. He had watched surgeon Smeeton use sewing quill and thread to close a wound and was imitating his technique.

'As soon as our wounded are sufficiently recovered, there'll have to be a council of the entire expedition to decide what to do next,' answered the Frenchman. 'Already some of the men are demanding to return to Golden Island. Others are saying that we haven't gained sufficient plunder yet, and they would prefer to continue with the expedition.'

'How will you vote?'

Jacques spread out his hands in a gesture of resignation. 'It doesn't make much difference to me. On the whole I'd vote to go back, but it will depend on who is elected as our new commander.'

Hector turned his attention to the next patient. It was Capitan Peralta, whose burned hands and forehead needed treatment.

'I'm sorry that so many of your crew were killed. They fought very bravely,' he said to the Spaniard. Fewer than one in four of *Santa Catalina*'s crew had survived the carnage.

'Never in my life have I seen such accurate musketry nor met such audacity,' answered the captain coolly. 'I thank God that the people of Panama are safe behind their walls.'

'So you don't think that the city will fall?'

'Last year the city councillors sent the royal exchequer an invoice for the cost of building their new city rampart. They asked to be reimbursed. The response they got from Spain was a question: had they built the wall of gold or silver?' The veteran Spanish commander gave a mirthless smile. 'I assure you it was made of great stone blocks, each weighing several tons.'

Hector reached for a pot of ointment and began to spread salve on the man's wounds.

'How is it that you speak such good Spanish?' Peralta enquired.

'My mother was from Galicia.'

'And what brought you here with this pack of thieves? You don't seem to be naturally one of their kind.'

'I was trying to avoid one of these thieves, as you call them, and yet I now find myself under his command,' answered Hector. He did not want to go into details.

'Then I advise you to get away from them as quickly as you can. When you or any of your colleagues fall into the hands of the authorities here – which will surely happen – you will be executed as pirates. There will be no mercy.'

'I have every intention of leaving this expedition. And I hope I will be able to persuade my friends to go with me,' Hector assured him.

'The quality of his friends often defines a man, though friendship sometimes brings sorrow in its wake,' said the Spaniard, and it was clear that Peralta was thinking of his contremaestre. Estevan had died of his burns.

'What do you think will happen to you now?' Hector asked.

The Spaniard tilted back his head so that Hector could smear the ointment on the forehead where the fire had burned away the hairline, leaving white patches on the skin.

'I expect your colleagues will demand a ransom for me,' he said. 'But whether the authorities will pay is another matter. After all, I no longer have a ship to command.'

'There will be other ships.'

Peralta gave the young man a shrewd look. 'If you are

trying to extract information from me about the strength of the South Sea Fleet, you will not succeed.'

Hector blushed. 'I had not intended to pry. Perhaps your original vessel will be repaired one day.'

The Spanish captain softened his tone. 'It is clear that you are not experienced in the ways of piracy. Your colleagues will not leave a single vessel afloat that they don't need for themselves.'

Seeing that Hector looked puzzled, Peralta continued. 'They fear retribution for their crimes. As soon as your band of thieves moves on, the authorities will commandeer and arm every available vessel and use them to hunt down your gang of sea bandits.'

As if to confirm the Spaniard's prediction, Captain Coxon was heard shouting orders. He was despatching a party of men to the other anchored vessels. They were to return aboard Peralta's fire-damaged barca longa and complete what the explosions had failed to do.

*

IT WAS ANOTHER five days before the wounded were well enough to attend a general council of the expedition. It was held on the deck of *La Santissima Trinidad*, the men massed in the waist of the galleon, their leaders on the quarterdeck. Coxon, Sawkins, Cook and Sharpe were there. Only Harris was missing as he had died of his wounds. Hector, watching from where he stood with his friends beside the rail, could detect a change in Coxon. Now that his rival Harris was gone, the buccaneer captain appeared even more arrogant and self-confident than at Golden Island, and his harsh voice carried clearly over the assembly.

'We have now been three weeks on this Adventure and I have always counselled caution . . .' he began.

'Caution! Some might call it craven,' someone shouted. Coxon coloured with anger. The flush spread unevenly across his face, leaving darker and lighter patches, and Hector was pleased to see that the effect of the spiked ointment had not yet fully worn off.

'At our outset we agreed to take the gold mines at Santa Maria,' Coxon continued.

'And small prize it brought us,' shouted the heckler, but Coxon ignored him this time.

'We have defeated the enemy in open battle, but our position is exposed and difficult. Our supplies are perilously low. We are in unfamiliar territory, and the enemy will regain their strength and may sever our line of retreat.'

'I dislike the man, but he's right,' muttered Jezreel standing beside Hector. 'We are badly overstretched.'

Coxon was speaking again. 'I therefore think it prudent that we return to our ships waiting for us at Golden Island. Once in the Caribbean we can resume our cruising for purchase.'

'What does Captain Sawkins say?' called out a voice. Sawkins' rampaging courage during the battle off Panama had made him immensely popular.

Sawkins stepped up to the low rail which divided the quarterdeck from the waist of the ship and cleared his throat. As usual he spoke bluntly.

'I propose we continue with the Adventure,' he said firmly. 'The walls of Panama are too strong for us, but there are towns all along the coast which do not yet know we are here in the South Sea. If we act boldly, we can take such places by surprise. We might even find their quays heaped with silver bars ready for shipment.'

His words met with a low rumble of enthusiasm from several in his audience though the majority looked towards Coxon again, waiting for his rejoinder.

'A wise man knows when to retreat, taking his spoils with him,' Coxon declared.

'Half a hat full of pesos!' scoffed Sawkins. He was bright-eyed with enthusiasm. 'We can get twenty times as much if we have the courage to stay in the South Sea. I propose that we sail south and plunder as we go until we reach the land's end. There we round the Cape, and sail home, our pockets full.'

Captain Coxon looked openly scornful. 'Anyone who believes that claim is putting his head into a Spanish noose.'

'Do your people always quarrel so openly?' said someone quietly in Spanish at Hector's elbow. It was Captain Peralta who had edged his way into the assembly and was listening to the argument.

'Can you understand what they are saying?' whispered Hector.

'Only a little. But the anger in their voices is evident.'

Hector was about to ask Dan whether he wanted to return to Golden Island when a loud husky voice rang out. It was the bald quartermaster who had served under Captain Harris. 'There's no point in putting this to a vote,' he shouted, and he marched up the companionway to the quarterdeck where he turned to face the crowd. 'Those who want to go back to Golden Island under Captain Coxon's command, make your way to the starboard rail,' he bawled. 'Those who prefer to stay in the South Sea and serve under Captain Sawkins assemble on the port side.'

There was a low murmuring of discussion among the men, and a general movement as the buccaneers began to separate into two groups. Hector noted that the numbers were broadly equal, though perhaps a small majority had elected to travel back with Coxon. He looked enquiringly at Dan. As usual the Miskito had said little and was standing quietly watching what was going on.

'Dan, I'm for going back to the Caribbean. What do you want to do?' Hector said. He had never mentioned Susanna to Dan, and now he was uneasy that he was not telling his friend the true reason for his decision. To his relief, Dan merely shrugged and said, 'I would like to see more of the South Sea.

Few of my people have ever been there. But I will go along with whatever you, Jacques and Jezreel decide.'

There was another shout from the quartermaster. 'Make up your minds and cut the chatter!'

Glancing round, Hector realised that he and his three friends were almost the last people standing in the middle of the deck, still undecided.

'Come on, Jezreel! Come with us!' shouted someone from starboard side where Coxon's volunteers were clustered. During the hand-to-hand fighting on the deck of Peralta's ship, Jezreel's great height and his obvious fighting skill had made him a favourite with the buccaneers.

'Best take your winnings when you're still on your feet, and not try another bout with a fresh opponent. You'll likely finish up with a broken face as well as an empty purse. That's something else I learned in the fight game,' muttered Jezreel. He strolled across to join the group.

'Hey Frenchy! You too! We need someone to show us how to roast monkey so it tastes like beef!' called another of Coxon's group. Jacques, too, was popular with the men. Jacques grinned broadly and set off, following Jezreel.

Hector was overcome with relief. Without special pleading his friends had chosen the course of action that he had wanted for them. He touched Dan on the arm. 'Come on, Dan. Let's join them.' Then he too started across the deck.

He had not gone more than a couple of paces when Coxon's voice rang out. 'I am not having that wretch in my company!'

Hector glanced up. Coxon was standing at the quarterdeck rail and pointing directly at him, his face working with anger. 'He's not to be trusted!' the buccaneer captain announced. 'He's a Spanish-lover.'

A murmur ran through the crowd of onlookers. Hector realised that many of them must have seen him in quiet conversation with Peralta. Others would have known that he was responsible for saving the Spaniard from the sea.

'He would betray us if it suits him,' Coxon continued. His tone had dropped to a low snarl now. Hector was open-mouthed, taken completely by surprise and so stunned by the accusation that he did not know how to respond. The captain pressed home his advantage.

'Someone among us warned the Spaniards at Santa Maria of our coming. That is why we found so little plunder there.' His words dropped into the awkward silence as the general buzz and chatter ceased. 'I have often wondered who it was, and how the garrison was alerted. It was easy enough for someone to send a warning by the hand of his friend the striker.'

Belatedly Hector remembered that in the last day before the assault on Santa Maria, he had seen little of Dan. The Miskito had been away on a hunting trip to obtain fresh food.

Coxon was icily certain of himself. 'I will not include a traitor in my company. He stays here.'

Hector had a quick glimpse of the vindictive expression on the buccaneer's face as the man began to make his way to join the group who had chosen him as their leader.

'If he stays here, then I do too,' said Jezreel. He stepped out of the crowd and began to make his way back towards Hector. His great height made his departure very obvious.

There was another movement among the men who had voted to follow Coxon. This time it was Jacques. He too was abandoning the group.

Hector remained where he was, numbed by the turn of events as his two friends came back across the deck. 'Looks like we're staying in the South Sea,' announced Jezreel loud enough for all to hear. 'Captain Sawkins was always a better bet than Coxon.'

They moved across to the port side where Sawkins' company was assembled and as they did so, Hector became conscious of more movement behind him. Glancing back over his shoulder he saw that at least a dozen men who had previously decided to follow Coxon, had now changed their minds. They too were switching sides. One by one they were deserting Coxon's group in full view of the man they had chosen to follow only minutes earlier.

Suddenly a hand gripped Hector by the shoulder, and he was swung round. He found himself staring into Coxon's livid face. It was contorted with rage. 'No man crosses me twice,' he snarled. The buccaneer captain was shaking with anger. His hand dropped towards his waistband, and a moment later Coxon had pulled out a pistol and had rammed the barrel hard into the young man's stomach. Hector felt the muzzle quivering with the force of Coxon's anger. 'This is what I should have done when I first laid eyes on you,' Coxon hissed.

Hector tensed, already feeling the bullet in his guts, when an arm seemed to come from nowhere, sweeping down towards the pistol and knocking it aside just as Coxon pulled the trigger. The pistol ball buried itself in the wooden deck, and at the same moment someone kicked the buccaneer captain's feet from under him so that he fell heavily to the deck. Looking up, Hector saw that it was Jezreel who had deflected the pistol's aim while Jacques had tripped the buccaneer. Both men were looking grim.

No one made any move to help Coxon though Dan collected the empty pistol which had been dropped, and handed it to Coxon once he was back on his feet.

Aware that the entire company was watching him, the captain brushed himself down without saying a word. Then he stepped up close to Hector, and said in a voice so low that no one else could hear but thick with menace, 'You would be well advised to leave your bones here in the South Seas, Lynch. Should you ever return to a place where I can reach you, I will make sure that you pay for what you have done today.'

ELEVEN

Next morning Captain Coxon and his company were gone. They left before sunrise in one of the captured vessels, eighty men in all. 'Bastards, bastards, utter bastards!' announced one of the surgeons who had decided to stay on. He had just discovered that Coxon's company had taken with them most of the expedition medicines. 'How are we expected to do our job when we lack the remedies. They scamper off, tails between their legs, while we're the ones who can expect to see action.' To show his disgust, he spat over the side of the galleon.

She was now to be their flagship, and at 400 tons made an impressive show with a wealth of gilding to show off her high stern in the typical Spanish style. She lacked cannon, but with luck their victims would not even know that she was in foreign hands until she was within musket range. The men had been debating what to call her. *La Santissima Trinidad* sounded too much like popery. Yet every sailor knew that it was bad luck to change a vessel's name. So at Hector's suggestion they had decided to keep the name but change the language, calling her *Trinity*, and even the most superstitious of their company had been content.

'I've still got a few medicines stowed in my knapsack,' Hector told the disgruntled surgeon. Basil Ringrose was originally from Kent, and Hector had taken an instant liking to him. Ringrose had a friendly manner which matched his open, freckled face topped by a mass of chestnut curls.

'We must put together a common stock of all the medicines that remain.' Ringrose said. 'It's fortunate that I always carry my surgical instruments with me in their own roll of oil cloth.'

It was Ringrose who had amputated one of Captain Harris's legs, trying unsuccessfully to save his life. But the stump had begun to rot, and with gangrene had come death.

'I'm only a surgeon's assistant,' Hector confessed. 'I came to help Surgeon Smeeton of Captain Harris's company, and he's turned back. But I have been keeping notes of how to prepare various medicines using local ingredients.'

'I saw you writing things down and thought that you were helping Dampier over there,' explained Ringrose. He nodded towards a saturnine, lantern-jawed man who was leaning perilously far out over the side of the anchored galleon and staring down into the sea. The man was dropping small chips of wood into the water and watching them float away. Propped against the bulwark was a bamboo tube similar to the one that Hector carried.

'What's he doing?' Hector asked.

'I have no idea. You had better go and ask him for yourself. Dampier seems to take an interest in nearly everything that we come across.'

Hector approached the stranger, who was now writing down something on a scrap of paper.

The man looked up from his quill. Brown melancholy eyes framed a narrow nose above a long upper lip. He looked too scholarly to be a sea thief.

'Tides,' said the man pensively, even before Hector could pose his question. 'I'm trying to work out the source of the tides. You may have noticed that here in the South Sea the tides run much stronger than those we left behind in the Caribbean.'

'I had remarked on that,' said Hector. Dampier shot him a quizzical glance from the sad-looking eyes.

'Then how do you explain it? Surely if the ocean is all one body of water, the tides should be similar everywhere. Some people claim that the fierce tides in the South Sea are made by water rushing through tunnels under the land, flooding here from the Caribbean. But I do not believe it.'

'Then what do you think is the reason?'

Dampier bent his head to blow gently on the wet ink. 'That I have not yet understood. But I believe it is to do with the wind patterns, the shape of the ocean floor, and phases of the moon of course. What is important at this time is to make observations. Interpretation can come later.'

'I was told that you make observations of everything.'

Dampier had a habit of rubbing his finger along his long upper lip. 'Nearly everything. I'm interested in fish and fowl, people and plants, the weather and the seasons. It is my chief reason for travelling.'

'Surgeon Smeeton, for whom I was an assistant, was of a like mind. Though he was mainly interested in the medical practices of native peoples.'

'Surgeon Smeeton, I hear that he has left the expedition. A pity. I knew him in Jamaica.'

Hector felt a quick surge of interest at the mention of Jamaica. 'Do you know Jamaica well?' he asked.

'I was there for a few months, training to be an overseer on a sugar plantation,' Dampier replied. 'But I disagreed with my employer, and the opportunity to go on the account – as these buccaneers call their adventuring – was too tempting. It was a chance to see new places.'

'When you were in Jamaica did you hear anything of the Lynch family?'

'Difficult not to. He was the governor, and his family possess as much, if not more acreage, than any other landowners on the island.'

'What about the son, Robert Lynch, and his sister Susanna? Did you meet them by any chance?'

'Far too grand for me,' said Dampier shaking his head. 'Though I did encounter young Robert briefly. He wanted information about the best conditions for planting indigo. I told him that he was better to consult an established indigo grower.'

'What about his sister Susanna?'

'I never met her in person though I saw her at a distance. A very pretty creature. Destined for a grand marriage, I would say. One day her parents will be taking her to London to find a suitable match.'

Hector felt a stab of disappointment. It was exactly what the surveyor Snead had said. 'So you don't think she would stay on in Jamaica?'

'There's nothing for her there. Why all the questions? Do you know her?'

'I met her just once,' Hector confessed.

Dampier treated him to a shrewd look. 'Sweet on her, are you? Well, that's as strange and curious as anything I've observed in the South Sea, a humble adventurer pining after a grandee's daughter.' He gave a lugubrious sniff, and began to roll up the piece of paper ready to slide it into the bamboo tube with his other notes. Then a thought must have occurred to him, for he looked up and said, 'If Surgeon Smeeton no longer requires your services, perhaps you would lend me a hand in making my observations.'

'I would be pleased to,' Hector assured him, 'though my chief duty must still be to assist the surgeons.'

'Yes, you were talking with Ringrose. You'll discover that he's got clever hands and is as much interested in navigation as he is in medicine. Enjoys making instruments to read the angle of the sun and devising sighting tables, that sort of thing.'

'I had noticed that all morning he's been making a sketch map of the bay and its islands.'

'A very sensible precaution. We have no charts of this area.

We are utterly ignorant of the ports and anchorages, currents, reefs and islands. Such details are known only to the Spaniards. In case we come back here, Ringrose is making notes so that we know just where to anchor, find water and shelter.'

'I worked for a Turkish sea captain once, assisting him with sea charts. But apart from a single ocean crossing, I lack practical experience of navigation.'

'Stick close to Ringrose and you'll learn a lot, though I expect it will be mostly coastal pilotage rather than deep-sea navigation,' Dampier assured him.

❋

SO IT TURNED OUT. For the next two months *Trinity* stayed near the coast, a hungry predator looking for scraps of plunder. News of her presence had yet to spread to the Spanish settlements and in the first ten days she loitered off Panama she snapped up several unwary prizes, which sailed straight into her jaws and gave up without a fight. One was an advice ship loaded with pay for the Panama garrison, fifty-one thousand pieces of eight, and – equally welcome – fifty great earthen jars of gunpowder which replenished stocks that had run low. Other hapless victims provided rations – flour, beans, cages of live chickens, sacks of chocolate beans which the buccaneers ground to powder and drank mixed with hot water. The captured vessels were small barks and of little value. Anything useful by way of rigging or sails was taken off, then the boarding party smashed holes in their planking and sank them on the spot.

But the weather was against them. Not a day passed without frequent downpours of heavy rain which soaked the men and their clothing. The sails grew great patches of stinking mildew in the muggy tropical heat, and a miasma of damp hung over the sodden vessel. The run-off dripped through cracks in the deck spoiling everything below. Guns and equipment rusted overnight. Bread and biscuits in the cook's stores went mouldy. In search of fresh supplies of food, Sawkins the fire-eater led a raid ashore. The local inhabitants hastily threw up breastworks at the entrance to their little town, and Sawkins was tugging at one of the wooden posts trying to uproot it when he was killed outright by a Spanish shot. His death only added to the general sense of disappointment that *Trinity* was wasting too much time. When the wind failed she was gripped by unknown currents which one day brought her close to the shore, and the next night pushed her almost out of sight of land. In June the rainfall eased, but the sky remained overcast and sullen, leaving the men frustrated and discontent. They grumbled and bickered, knowing they needed to progress east and south along the coast before the alarm was raised. Instead the wind, when it did blow, was fitful, and almost always from ahead. *Trinity* was obliged to tack back and forth. The crew found themselves staring at the same landmarks – a headland, a small island, a rock with a particular profile – from dawn until dusk, and then again at the next sunrise. They did not need a chart to tell them that they were almost standing still.

'What else did your people expect? Did they know nothing of our equatorial weather?' commented Capitan Peralta to Hector. The Spaniard was one of the growing number of prisoners, and the two of them were in the habit of meeting in the bows of the ship where they could not be overheard.

'Are the rains finally over?' Hector asked.

Peralta shrugged. 'There can be heavy downpours at this time of year, even into August. I wonder if your comrades will still want to follow their captain by then?'

Peralta gave Hector a sideways look. The buccaneer council had elected Bartholomew Sharpe as their new general, the grand title they now gave to their overall commander.

Hector hesitated before replying, and Peralta was quick to pick up on the delay. 'There's something a little devious about him, isn't there? Something not quite right.'

Hector felt it would be disloyal to agree, so said nothing. But Peralta had a point. There was an unsettling quality about

Sharpe. It was something that Hector had noted at Golden Island. Even then he had thought that Sharpe was a natural mischief maker. Behind the amiable smile on the fleshy, pouting lips was an evasiveness which made one reluctant to trust him entirely. Now that Sharpe had been made general, Hector was even more apprehensive. He sensed the man was self-serving and devious.

'Don't be surprised if some of your colleagues decide to break away on their own when conditions get more difficult,' Peralta continued. 'Your shipmates are easily swayed and can be pitiless.'

To change the subject Hector showed the Spaniard a new backstaff that Ringrose had fashioned.

Peralta watched him slide the vanes of the backstaff along its wooden shaft.

'It seems a more complicated instrument than usual, more movable parts,' observed the Spaniard.

'Ringrose assures me that it will allow us to calculate our latitude position even where the sun is so high in the sky at noon that a normal backstaff is inaccurate. See here . . .' Hector handed Peralta the instrument so he could inspect the extra vanes. 'They allow readings even when the sun is at ninety degrees overhead.'

'Fortunately I don't depend on such a device for finding my position. I know the coast from here to Lima and beyond,' the Spaniard answered dryly. 'And if I am in doubt I turn to the pages in my derotero, my pilot book, and then I know where I am.' He allowed himself a sardonic smile. 'That's your new commander's real dilemma. He doesn't know where he is or what he's up against, and sooner or later his men will realise it too. They are a wolf pack, ready to show their fangs, and their leader may turn out to be equally ruthless.'

*

HECTOR RECALLED Peralta's warning in the third week of August when *Trinity* overhauled another small coaster. Unusually, her crew put up a fight. They draped waistcloths along the bulwarks in order to conceal their numbers, and men fired old-fashioned arquebuses at the approaching galleon. The battle lasted only half an hour and the outcome was never in doubt. *Trinity* was by far the larger vessel and mustered three or four times as many marksmen. Yet two buccaneers were badly wounded by enemy bullets before the bark dropped her topsail in a sign of surrender and her survivors cried for quarter.

'Search and sink her, and be quick about it!' Sharpe shouted angrily as he watched the canoe which served as *Trinity*'s cockboat being lowered into the water. He was in an evil humour. The enemy's fire had cut up *Trinity*'s newly over-hauled rigging which would have to be spliced and mended, resulting in further delay, and it was three weeks since they had last taken any plunder.

The canoe made a dozen trips between the two vessels to ferry back the captive crew, who would now be held for ransom or obliged to work as forced labour aboard the galleon. On the final trip the buccaneers were crowing with delight and holding up leather bags and glass bottles. The bark was carrying five thousand pieces of eight as well as a generous stock of wine and spirits. *Trinity*'s quartermaster, Samuel Gifford, lost no time in distributing the loot at the foot of the mainmast, and each man came away carrying his share of the coins in his hat. Every fourth man, drawn by lot, also received a bottle.

'Here you!' said Sharpe beckoning to Hector. 'Find out from the prisoners why they resisted when they had no chance against us. '

'Who is your captain?' Hector asked. Only a handful of the captives wore the clothes of working sailors. He guessed they were the bark's sailing crew. The majority – some thirty men –

were too well dressed to be mariners and looked more like minor gentry. There was a priest among them, an elderly red-faced friar who was clutching his gown close around him as though he feared some sort of profane contagion.

A small man in a brown doublet and a stained but costly shirt stepped out of the group.

'My name is Tomas de Argandona. I am the mestre de campo from the town of Guayaqil over there.' He gestured vaguely towards the horizon.

'I need a list of everyone's names and where they come from,' explained Hector.

'I assure you that will not be necessary,' said the little man, a touch pompously. 'We are aware that you pirates are accustomed to asking ransom for your prisoners, and we have agreed among ourselves not to participate in that sordid practice.'

'What's he talking about?' demanded Sharpe. There was a nasty edge to his voice.

Argandona was speaking again. 'We were looking for you.'

'Looking for us . . . ?' said Hector, startled.

'The entire coast is aware that you are sailing in these waters aboard the *Santissima Trinidad* which you have stolen. My colleagues and I offered our services to His Excellency the Viceroy of Peru. We intended to seek you out, and then inform his Excellency exactly where you might be found so that he could direct the armadilla to seek and destroy you.'

'But surely you must have known that your vessel was no match for us.'

'We never expected to confront you,' answered Argandona condescendingly. 'Only to observe and report. But once we were challenged, we as gentlemen, ' – and he emphasised the word gentlemen – 'could not decline the battle. Our honour was involved.'

Hector translated this defiant reply to Captain Sharpe who gave a dangerously mirthless laugh. 'Ask the coxcomb if his honour will allow him to tell us exactly what the Viceroy and his armadilla are proposing.'

To Hector's increasing amazement, the mestre de campo's response was utterly frank. 'His Excellency the Viceroy disposes three great warships in the Armada del Sur but, sadly, all of them are unfit for sea at this time. So he has ordered an equal number of merchant ships to be armed with their brass cannon and placed seven hundred and fifty soldiers aboard them. He has also sent extra guns to defend the ports. In our town of Guayagil we have mustered more than eight hundred soldiers to defend our property and constructed two new forts to guard the harbour.'

'He's trying to scare us off,' grated Sharpe when Hector relayed the information to him. 'I don't think so,' said Hector quietly. 'I think he is being truthful. It's a matter of his honour.'

'We'll see about that,' said Sharpe. Looking round, he saw Jezreel standing nearby. Taking a pistol from his sash, Sharpe handed it to the giant. 'Point this at the belly of that sneering priest over there, and make it look threatening,' he ordered. In a lower voice he added, 'It's charged with powder but not ball. I want to scare the pompous little shit.'

Turning back to Hector the buccaneer captain said, 'Now inform the puffed-up runt that I don't believe him, and I'm calling his bluff. If he doesn't change his story I'll send his priest to the hell he deserves.'

The Spaniard was quivering with a combination of fright and indignation. 'Your captain is a savage. I have already told him the truth.'

'Pull the trigger,' snarled Sharpe.

A moment later there was a loud explosion and, to Hector's horror, the friar was thrown backward and fell to the deck. A great stain of blood spread across his gown. Jezreel, standing with the smoking pistol in his hand, looked down at the weapon in disbelief. He was too shocked to speak.

'A genuine mistake,' said Sharpe smoothly. Stepping forward quickly he took back the pistol. 'I thought the weapon was charged but not fully loaded.'

Hector had gone forward to where the priest lay. A dark red rivulet, glinting in the sun, was trickling from under the body and seeping its way to the scuppers. He knelt down and placed his hand on the man's chest. Through the thick brown cloth he could detect a faint heart beat. 'He's still alive!' he called out, looking around frantically for a surgeon. A moment later Ringrose was at his side, his fingers gently probing for the entry wound. 'Gut shot,' he muttered under his breath. 'He'll not live.'

'Get out of my way!' ordered a hoarse voice. Hector was aware of a shadow falling over him. He looked up. It was a crew man by the name of Duill who had always seemed to him to be particularly uncouth and brutish. He had enormously wide shoulders, a short body and a neck that seemed too long to support a small round head. It was as if he had been put together from the body parts of strangers. 'Bugger off!' growled Duill. His speech was slightly slurred, and Hector smelled the reek of brandy on his breath. 'This is what we do to Papists.' He leaned down and, pushing Hector aside, took the priest by the shoulders and began to drag the dying man towards the ship's rail.

'Here, give me a hand,' he called out. A second crew man, obviously one of Duill's cronies, ran forward. He stumbled momentarily, and gave a whooping laugh. The two drunks took the priest by the shoulders and feet and began to swing him back and forth between them like a heavy sack. 'One, two and away,' they chanted, and with a drunken cheer heaved the body over the rail and into the sea. Then they toppled against one another and broke into boozy laughter.

'Savages!' murmured Ringrose. He had risen to his feet and had gone pale.

'The priest was still alive,' groaned Hector. He felt that he was going to vomit.

Ringrose gripped his arm. 'Steady, Lynch. Remember where we are. Look at the men.'

The crew of the *Trinity* were staring at the patch of blood on the deck. Many of them were silent and thoughtful. But at least a score of them were grinning broadly. Suddenly Hector remembered Peralta's warning. They were like a wolf pack gloating over a kill. They had enjoyed the spectacle.

✳

'OF COURSE he knew his pistol was loaded,' said Jacques. It was just after sunset on the evening of the murder, and the four friends were gathered by the lee rail to discuss the atrocity. 'In the toughest Paris gangs the leader would select one of his men at random and order him to slit a throat or break an innocent head. If the man refused or delayed, then he was likely to suffer that same fate himself. That was the gang leader's way to gain respect and impose his authority.'

'But I was tricked,' said Jezreel.

'Sharpe's more cunning. He has shown the crew that he's ruthless, and at the same time made sure that he does not have blood on his own hands.'

'So why did he pick on me?' added Jezreel. His face set hard. 'Why was I the one selected to do the job?'

'Because he wants to bind us to him,' said Dan quietly. The others looked at the Miskito in surprise. It was rare for him to make any comment. Immediately, he had their complete attention. 'Remember when Coxon refused to include Hector in his group returning to Golden Island? We stuck together, Coxon was made to look a fool, and several of the other men came over to our side. Sharpe doesn't want that happening to him when he is in charge.'

Hector was beginning to understand the point that Dan was

making. 'So you think Sharpe was making sure we stay on *Trinity*?'

Dan nodded. 'Several men have already approached me to ask if I was satisfied with Sharpe as general. They are plotting to depose him by vote. If that fails, they are planning to leave the expedition.'

'You mean that if we went with them back to the Caribbean, word of the priest's death is sure to get out and Jezreel could finish up on the gallows in Port Royal.'

'Sharpe knows that we stay together as a group, and he needs us,' Dan said, and his unhurried manner of speaking gave his words all the more weight. 'Consider who we arc. When it comes to hand-to-hand fighting, no one aboard this vessel is more skilled than Jezreel. The men look up to him. They like him to be on their side when we send out a boarding party. Hector is the best interpreter. Plenty of others can speak some Spanish, but Hector has a knack of getting along well with the Spaniards, men like Peralta. They confide in him.'

'What about Jacques, surely there's nothing special about him?' said Jezreel showing a glimmer of his usual banter.

Dan gave a faint smile. 'Surely you know that on a ship a good cook is more valuable than a good captain.' The smile vanished, to be replaced by a solemn expression. 'As for myself, there are only two Miskito strikers left with the expedition. Without us the company would be even hungrier than they are now. And starving men are discontents.'

That was true enough, thought Hector. Finding enough food to satisfy *Trinity*'s large crew was a constant problem.

'Capitan Peralta said to me as far back as Panama that the expedition would disintegrate,' he said.

'This is worse than when I killed a man in a prize fight,' said Jezreel glumly, looking down at his hands. 'At least that was in a fit of rage. This time I have been made a dupe.'

'The situation is not hopeless,' Hector comforted him. 'Given enough time, the death of the priest will be forgotten or perhaps Sharpe's double-dealing will be exposed. But for the moment our general holds the advantage. However unwilling we may be, he has bound us to him, just as Dan says, and we must wait until matters right themselves.'

TWELVE

HECTOR WATCHED Bartholomew Sharpe throw himself a double four. Passage was a brutally simple game of dice but well suited to the gamblers aboard *Trinity*. They wanted to wager their loot with the least effort and the quickest results. The rules were straightforward: three dice and two players. The first player to get a double using only two of the dice, then threw the third. If the total on all three dice was more than ten, that man won. Ten or under and he lost.

The captain threw again, a five, and reached out to sweep up the coins wagered by his opponent. As he transferred his winnings into a purse, he became aware of Hector standing behind him. 'What do you want?' Sharpe asked brusquely, turning to glare at the young man. Hector detected a moment of unease in his captain's eyes and the briefest flicker of dislike. It was enough to make him wonder if his new captain might become just as much a threat as Captain Coxon, as dangerous but more subtle.

'A word in private, please.'

Sharpe treated his gambling victim to a shrug of false sympathy. 'That's enough for today. I've won back all the money I lent you, and you'll need more plunder before we play again.'

He deliberately left his dice on the capstan head. It was not something he would have risked with more sophisticated gamblers in London or professional players though the three dice were masterpieces of the counterfeiter's art. Two were paired delicately so they tended to come up with doubles. The other, of course, was adjusted so it gave a high number. It was that last dice which had a very slight discolouration of one of the pips, just enough for Captain Sharpe to recognise. Naturally he always took care that he lost several throws before he began to use the three dice in the correct sequence, and now after two months of gambling he judged that he personally held fully ten per cent of all the plunder taken on the cruise.

'Well, what is it?' he asked gruffly as he and Hector moved out of earshot of the gamblers.

'There's a risk of a prisoner uprising,' Hector told him.

'Why so?'

'Because we don't have enough men to supervise the prisoners properly.'

The captain looked hard at Hector. 'Anything else?'

'Yes. It's not just the numbers of prisoners. We've been keeping back those who are wealthy or were officers on the ships we captured.'

'Of course. They were the only ones worth holding.'

'They are the ones most likely to organise an uprising.'

Sharpe made no reply, but looked out across the sea. The sinking sun had coloured the underbellies of the clouds a deep and angry red. It was as though a great fire had been lit beyond the horizon. It reminded Bartholomew Sharpe of the unsatisfactory outcome to the raid on the mainland a fortnight earlier. The Spaniards had already retreated into the hills, taking their valuables with them. He had threatened to burn down their houses and farms unless protection money was paid, but the Spaniards were astute. They dragged out the negotiations until they had gathered enough soldiers to chase the buccaneers back to the beach. In their frustration the raiders torched the farms anyhow.

A few days later forty members of his crew, dissatisfied with the poor progress of the venture, had left *Trinity*. They had sailed away on a captured bark, heading north on the return journey to the Caribbean. Barely a hundred members of the original expedition remained, and that was not enough to deter a revolt among the prisoners.

'What do you propose we do?' he asked Hector.

'Set the prisoners free.'

Sharpe gave Hector a calculating glance. Here was an opportunity to gain the young man's trust. The captain was aware that he and his friends were suspicious and resentful of him. But the trick with the loaded pistol had been a necessity. It had impressed the crew and cowed the Spaniards.

'Are you suggesting this because you are friendly with Captain Peralta?'

'No. I think it would be a prudent action.'

Sharpe thought for a moment. 'Very well. Next time we come to land, you will see that I can be generous, even with my enemies.' In fact he had already decided several days earlier to rid himself of the captives. No one seemed willing to pay a ransom for them, and they had become so many useless mouths to feed.

'Rocks! Rocks! Dead Ahead!' the lookout suddenly bellowed. Sharpe looked up in surprise. The note of alarm in the man's voice indicated that he had been dozing at his post and suddenly seen the danger. 'Reefs! Breaking water! No more than a quarter mile away.'

'Ringrose!' Sharpe shouted. 'What do you make of it?'

'Impossible! We're thirty miles off the coast,' exclaimed Ringrose who had taken a sun sight earlier in the day. He jumped up on the rail and shaded his eyes as he peered forward. 'I wish to God we had a decent chart. This groping about in the unknown is madness. One night we'll run ourselves full tilt onto a reef in the dark and never know what happened.'

'Rocks to starboard as well!' The lookout's voice was shrill with panic. This time his shout caused a surge of activity aboard *Trinity*. There was the noise of running feet as men appeared on the deck and rushed into the bows and gazed forward trying to identify the danger. 'Bear away to port,' Sharpe called out to the helmsman, 'and reduce sail.' The order was unnecessary. Men were already easing out the main sheets and bracing round the yards. Others were standing by the reefing tackles.

'White water to port!' roared a sailor. He was pointing, open-mouthed with alarm. There was a foaming patch on the surface of the sea no more than a hundred paces beside *Trinity*. The galleon had sailed herself into a trap. There were reefs on each side and ahead, and little room to manoeuvre. 'Bring her head to wind!' snapped Sharpe to the steersman.

'Lucky she's so nimble,' said Ringrose beside Hector as *Trinity*'s bow turned into the wind, the sails came aback against the mast in an untidy tangle of ropes and sails, and the galleon came to a halt, gathered sternway and began to fall off on the opposite tack.

'Merde! Look there behind us! We sailed right over those rocks and never saw them.' Jacques had arrived on the quarter-deck and was gazing back towards the expanse of sea which the galleon had just negotiated. That too was boiling up in a white froth.

Beside him, Dan began to chuckle. Jacques looked at him in astonishment. 'What's so funny? We're boxed in by rocks!'

Dan shook his head. He was smiling. 'Not rocks . . . fish!'

Jacques scowled at him and then turned back to stare again at the sea. One of the foaming reefs had disappeared, abruptly sunk beneath the waves. But another had taken its place, fifty paces from the spot. There too the water was boiling upward.

'What do you mean . . . fish?'

Dan held up his hand, finger and thumb no more than three inches apart. 'Fish, small fish. More than you can count.'

Hector was concentrating on a nearby white patch. It was definitely on the move and coming closer to the ship. A moment later he saw that it was formed of myriads of tiny fish, millions upon millions of them, weaving and flashing and churning in a dense mass which occasionally broke the surface of the sea in a white spuming flurry.

'Anchovies!' cried Jacques.

There was relieved laughter from all around *Trinity* as the crew realised their error. 'Resume course!' ordered Sharpe. He, as much as anyone else, had been misled, but he had noted how the crew had taken matters into their hands in the imagined crisis. They had not consulted him, nor waited for orders. It was time that he found something to distract them.

He sent for the gentleman prisoner, Tomas de Argandona. The Spaniard was much less self-assured now that he had witnessed the shooting of the priest, and Sharpe was waiting in his cabin with a pistol lying on his desk. One glance and Argandona told Sharpe what he wanted to know: the nearest town on the mainland was La Serena and wealthy enough to have five churches and two convents. It lay two miles inland and had neither a garrison nor a defensive wall. A watchtower overlooked the closest anchorage but there was an unguarded landing beach some distance away. Small boats could put men ashore there and it was no more than a three-hour march to reach the town.

The general council held on the open deck the following morning went just as smoothly. The men voted overwhelmingly in favour of a raid.

'I propose John Watling to lead the attack,' Sharpe announced after Gifford, the quartermaster, had counted the show of hands. 'He lands with fifty men and takes the town by surprise. I then bring *Trinity* into the main anchorage and we ferry the plunder aboard.'

Looking on, Hector knew that Sharpe was being as wily as ever. Hector had seen little of Watling since the day they had been in the same canoe during the attack on Panama, but he knew Watling was popular with the men. He had sailed with

Morgan and they would follow him without question. He was one of those rigid, grim, old-fashioned Puritans who detested Catholics and observed the Sabbath scrupulously. Also, as Hector had noted, Sharpe had never been able to cheat Watling at dice, because he never gambled.

*

'LOOKS AS THOUGH we were expected,' Dan said under his breath. He, Jezreel and Hector had come ashore with Watling's raiders as soon as there was enough daylight to approach the landing beach safely. Now they were trudging along the dusty coastal track that would lead them to La Serena. Jacques had been left behind with a dozen men to guard the boats.

Hector followed the Miskito's glance. From a spur of high ground overlooking the track a horseman was watching them. He made no attempt to conceal himself.

'There goes our chance of surprise,' Jezreel commented.

Hector scanned the countryside. The day was promising to be overcast and very humid, and the raiders were advancing across rolling scrubland. Occasionally the path dipped into small gullies washed out by rainstorms. It was ideal terrain for an ambush, and there was a faint whiff of smoke in the air. He wondered if the Spaniards who farmed the area were burning their crops to prevent them falling into the hands of the raiders.

Suddenly there were shouts from the head of the column, and someone came running back, urging everyone to close up and look to their weapons. Hector brought his musket off his shoulder, checked that it was loaded and primed and that the ball had not been dislodged from the barrel, then placed the hammer at half-cock. Holding the gun in both hands he walked cautiously forward, Hector and Dan at his side.

The track had been no more than the width of a cart but now it broadened out as it entered a clearing in the scrub. The bushes had been cut back for a distance of some fifty paces, and at the edge of the clearing were several clumps of low trees.

'Lancers over there, hiding in the woods!' warned someone.

'How many?' called a buccaneer.

'Don't know. At least a couple of dozen. Form up in a square and look lively.'

At that moment came the sound of muskets, no more than a dozen shots. There were puffs of smoke from the bushes farthest from the column and Hector heard bullets flying overhead. But the shots went wide and no one was hurt. He dropped on one knee and aimed his gun towards a bush where he could see the haze of musket smoke still hanging above the leaves. He could not make out the man who had fired, and waited for him to show himself. Away to his right he heard several shots as the buccaneers saw their targets.

Hector's arm was beginning to ache as he tried to keep his gun trained on the suspect bush. The muzzle was wavering, but he was reluctant to waste a shot. It would take a long time to reload, and in that interval the cavalry might show themselves.

Seconds later, the Spanish cavalry burst from the thickets. They crashed out in a wild charge and rode straight for the formation of buccaneers. There must have been about sixty or seventy of the riders mounted on small, light-boned horses. A few riders held pistols which they discharged as they came careering forward, and Hector glimpsed one man brandishing a blunderbuss. But the majority were armed only with twelve-foot lances. Whooping and cheering they galloped forward in a confused mass, hoping to skewer their enemy. Hector swung the muzzle of his gun to aim into the charging body of riders. None of the Spaniards wore uniform or armour. These were not professional troopers, but farmers and cattlemen seeking to protect their property.

He selected his target – a stout, red-faced cavalier astride a dun horse with a white blaze – and pulled the trigger. In the confusion and through the gun smoke he could not see whether his shot went home.

He rose to his feet, placed the butt of his musket on the

ground, and plucked a new powder charge from the cartouche box on his belt. Beside him Jezreel was doing the same. Vaguely Hector sensed that the Spaniards' attack had come to nothing. A scatter of horsemen was galloping back towards the shelter of the woods. One or two bodies had been left lying on the ground, and a riderless horse came tearing past, reins hanging loose, the bucket-shaped saddle empty. Hector charged and primed his gun, selected a musket ball from the bag hanging from his waist and dropped it down the barrel. He was about to tamp the bullet home with his ramrod when, beside him, Jezreel said, 'No time for that!' Hector watched his companion lift his musket a few inches off the ground and slam the butt down sharply so the bullet came up hard against the wadding. 'Saves a few seconds,' grinned Jezreel, as he dropped back on one knee and brought the weapon to his shoulder. 'Now let them come at us again.'

But the skirmish was over. The Spaniards had withdrawn. They had lost four men, while not one of Watling's group had been wounded. 'Honour satisfied, I think,' said Jezreel. 'I feel sorry for them. One of their lancers was carrying nothing more than a sharpened cattle prod.'

The column moved forward, more cautiously now, and two miles farther on arrived at the outskirts of La Serena. It was the first Spanish colonial town that Hector had ever entered, and he was struck by the mathematical precision of the place. Compared to the haphazard jumble of Port Royal with its narrow lanes and dogleg streets, La Serena was a model of careful planning. Broad straight avenues were laid out in an exact grid, every intersection was a precise right angle, each house stood at the same distance from its neighbour, and their frontages matched as if in mirrors. Even the town fountain was located at the geometrical centre of the market square. The two-storey houses were of pale yellow sandstone and most of them had carved wooden balconies, studded double doors and heavy shutters. Occasionally there was a glimpse of a garden or small orchard behind a boundary wall, or the ornate bell tower of a church rising above the red-tiled roofs. Everything was solid, neat and substantial. But what made La Serena seem to be an architect's concept rather than a living township was that the town was empty. There was not a single living creature in its streets.

At first Watling's force hesitated at each crossroads, making sure that a street was safe before they ventured across it, and they kept a watch on the balconies and roofs expecting the sudden appearance of an enemy. But there was no movement, no response, no sound. La Serena was totally abandoned by its people, and gradually the buccaneers became more confident. They divided into small groups and dispersed throughout the town, looking for valuables to carry away.

'Why didn't they lock up behind them when they left?' asked Hector wonderingly as he pushed open the heavy front door of the third house he and Jezreel had decided to investigate.

'Probably thought we would do less damage if we could just walk in,' guessed his friend. He had a trickle of juice running down his chin from a half-eaten peach he had plucked in the garden of the house next door.

'They must have had plenty of warning,' said Hector. 'They've removed everything that could be carried away easily.'

It was the same in every house they entered: a central hallway off which were large, high-ceilinged rooms with thick, whitewashed walls and deeply recessed windows. The floors were invariably of tile, and the furniture dark and heavy, too cumbersome to be moved easily. Halfway down this hallway stood a massive cupboard made from some dark tropical wood. Hector swung open the double doors. As he had expected, the shelves were bare. He wandered into the kitchen at the back of the house. He found a large stove against one wall, a place to wash the dishes, a huge earthenware jar used for keeping water cool, more empty cupboards, a tub for laundry. But there were no pots and pans, no dishes. The place had been stripped bare.

They crossed the entry hall and tried a door on the other side. This time it was locked. 'At last, somewhere we are not meant to be,' said Jezreel. Putting his shoulder to a panel, he barged it open, and went inside with Hector at his heels.

'Now we know what the owners looked like,' commented the big man.

They were standing in a large reception room which the owners of the house had failed to strip entirely. They had left behind a large table, several heavily carved chairs with uncomfortable velvet seats, a massive dresser that must have been fully nine feet wide, and a row of family portraits hanging along one wall. Hector presumed that the paintings in their ornate gilded frames were too big to be carried away.

He walked along the line of pictures. Dignitaries, dressed in old-fashioned doublets and hose, stood or sat gazing solemnly out at him, their serious expressions set off by wide lace collars. The men were uniformly sombre in their dress, and all wore narrow pointed beards except one man who was clean-shaven and had a priest's cape and skull cap. The women were posed even more stiffly and looked self-conscious. They held themselves carefully so as not to disturb the folds of their formal gowns whose fabrics were very costly, silks, brocade and lace. All the women wore jewellery, and Hector wondered how many of the pearl necklaces, diamond pendants and gemstone bracelets were now safely in the hills or buried in secret hiding places.

He reached the end of the row of pictures and came to a dead stop. He was gazing into the grey eyes of a young woman. Only her face and shoulders were shown in the portrait, and she was regarding him with a slightly mischievous expression, her lips parted in the hint of a smile. Compared to the other portraits the young woman's complexion was pale. Her chestnut hair had been carefully arranged in ringlets to show off the delicate sweep of her neck and the creamy skin, and she wore a simple gold locket on blue silk ribbon. Her bare shoulders were covered with a light soft scarf.

Hector felt a rush of dizziness. For an instant he thought he was seeing a portrait of Susanna Lynch. Then the moment passed. It was ridiculous to think of finding Susanna's picture in the home of a prosperous Spaniard living in Peru.

For several minutes he just stood without moving, trying to puzzle out why he had mistaken the portrait. Perhaps it was the smile which had reminded him of Susanna. He looked more closely. Or maybe it was the locket that the young woman in the picture was wearing. He was almost sure that Susanna had a locket just like it. He searched the details of the picture, lingering over them as he sought to identify the likeness between this young woman and Susanna. The more he tried, the less certain he became. He believed he could recall exactly how Susanna walked, the way she held her body, the whiteness of her arms, the slope of her shoulders. But when he tried to visualise the precise details of her face, the picture in front of him kept intruding. He became muddled and anxious. The beauty of the girl in the picture began to overlap and merge with his memory of Susanna. He felt uncomfortable, as if he was somehow betraying her.

His reverie was interrupted by a shout from outside. Someone in the street was calling his name. He was wanted in the plaza mayor.

Leaving Jezreel to continue searching, he found Watling and several buccaneers on the steps of the town hall. To judge by the small pile of silver plate and a few candlesticks on the ground before him, the ransack of La Serena was going very badly. Watling was glowering at a trio of Spaniards.

'They rode into town under a white flag,' Watling said. 'Find out who they are and what they want.'

Quickly Hector established that the Spaniards were an embassy from the citizens and wished to discuss terms.

'Tell them that we want a hundred thousand pesos in coin, or we burn the town to the ground,' growled Watling. He was wearing a greasy and threadbare military coat that must have done service in Cromwell's time.

The leader of the Spanish delegation flinched at the mention of so much money. The man was in his late fifties and had a long, narrow face with bushy eyebrows over deep-set brown eyes. Hector wondered if he was related to the family in the portraits, and the young girl.

'It is a huge sum. More than we can afford,' the man said, exchanging glances with his companions.

'A hundred thousand pesos,' repeated Watling brutally.

The Spaniard spread out his hands in a gesture of helplessness. 'It will take days to raise so much money.'

'You have until tomorrow noon. The money is to be delivered here by midday. Until then my men will stay in possession of your town,' retorted Watling.

'Very well,' answered the Spaniard. 'My companions and I will do what we can.' The delegation remounted and slowly rode their horses away.

Watching them leave, one of the buccaneers beside Watling asked, 'Do you think they will keep their word?'

'I doubt it,' answered Watling bluntly, 'but we need time to search the town thoroughly. I want those churches ransacked down to the gilded statue and side altar, and don't forget to pull up the paving stones. It's under them that the priests usually bury their treasures. Tonight we post double sentries in case the Spaniards try to retake the town in the dark.'

*

FORTY-EIGHT hours later Hector was wondering if he and Dan would be accused of cowardice or desertion. They had slipped quietly out of La Serena without informing Watling and made their way back to the landing beach. There, with Jacques's help, they had persuaded the boat guards to let them use a small canoe to get back aboard *Trinity*. As had been planned, their ship was now moored a few miles down the coast in La Serena's anchorage and waiting to pick up the raiders and their booty.

'Where's Watling?' Sharpe called out to them as the canoe came alongside.

'Still in La Serena,' Hector answered.

'What about plunder?' enquired the captain. He had seen that the canoe was empty.

'Not much, at least by the time we left,' said Hector as he and Dan clambered up the swell of the galleon's tumblehome and onto her main deck.

'But surely Watling and his men took the town?'

'Yes, and with little resistance. The citizens agreed to a ransom of one hundred thousand pesos if our men would leave.'

'Then what are they waiting for?' Sharpe asked.

'Neither side kept the bargain. That same night the quartermaster led out a raiding party of forty men, hoping to catch the Spaniards by surprise and rob them. The following day the citizens of La Serena opened the sluice gates of the town reservoir. We woke to find the streets a foot deep in water.'

Sharpe frowned. 'I suppose they thought it would make it much more difficult to set fire to the town.'

'Watling flew into a rage. When I left, the men were in the churches, scraping off any gold or silver leaf, smashing windows, overturning statues.'

'You should be there with them.'

'It was more important to come to warn you that a trap is closing about them. I tried to tell Watling, but he was too angry to listen.'

'What sort of a trap?'

'Dan went out to scout. He counted at least four hundred militiamen moving into position on either side of the road leading here. They'll wait for our men to come to the anchorage loaded with the plunder. Then they'll cut them to pieces.'

Captain Sharpe stared thoughtfully towards the shore. There was no sign of life. He could make out the flagpole on the tall stone watchtower the Spaniards had built to survey the anchorage. If the tower was manned its occupants would long ago have hoisted signals to alert their forces farther inland. But the flag staff was bare. Nor was there any movement among the cluster of warehouses, or on the broad gravel-and-sand road which led up from the shingle beach and inland towards the town. But anything could be happening out of sight behind the swell of the ground. That is where the Spanish troops could be massing. He took Hector by the arm. 'Let me show you something.' He led the young man to the stern of the ship. 'Look over the rail,' he said. 'What do you see?'

Hector stared down towards the galleon's rudder. There were black scorch marks on the timber and the rudder's fastenings, traces of a fire.

'Someone tried to burn away our steering,' he said.

'If they had succeeded, this ship would have been crippled. Luckily we spotted the fire before it had spread and managed to put it out. Someone came quietly out from shore in the darkness, stuffed pitch and rags between the rudder and the stern, and set it alight.'

Hector thought back to how Dan had disabled the Spanish patrol ship off the Campeachy coast.

'It was a brave thing to do.'

'We found the float the arsonist must have used, an inflated horse hide lying on the beach.'

Sharpe wheeled to face Hector and said fiercely, 'Make no mistake about it. The Spaniards are willing to fight for what is theirs, and fight hard. I want you to return to La Serena. If Watling won't listen to you, persuade the others. Tell them to abandon the place and get back here as fast as possible.'

Hector shook his head. 'Half the men are drunk. They

won't leave the town until they've looted it to their satisfaction, probably by mid afternoon. Then they'll stumble back in no fit condition to fight their way through.'

Sharpe regarded the young man with interest. There was something about his quiet manner which suggested that he had a plan in mind.

'Now is the time to use our prisoners,' said Hector. 'Put them ashore where they will be visible to the Spanish, but keep them under guard. I will go to the Spaniards and tell them that we will release the prisoners unharmed if they allow our men to return safely to the ship.'

Sharpe gave Hector a long, calculating look. 'You're learning this trade,' he said softly. 'One day you could be elected general yourself.'

'I've no wish for that,' said Hector. 'Just let me talk to Captain Peralta and his comrades.'

Sharpe gave a grunt. 'This scheme is your responsibility. If something goes wrong, and I have to leave you on shore, I will do so.'

Hector was about to answer that he expected nothing less, but instead began arrangements with Jacques and the crew of the canoe to ferry Peralta and the prisoners ashore.

✳

'SHARPE IS NOT to be trusted,' was Peralta's immediate response when he and Hector had landed on the beach and the young man told him what was intended. 'The moment your captain sees that his men are safe, he'll decide to take his prisoners back on board and sail away.'

'That is why you – not I – will be the one who goes to find the commander of the Spanish forces and arrange the safe conduct.'

Peralta pursed his lips and looked doubtful. 'Are you telling me that you will stay with the prisoners and personally see that they are released unharmed?'

'Yes.'

'All right then. I am known in these parts and my word will carry weight.' The Spaniard's voice grew very serious. 'But if the sack of La Serena has been barbarous, then I cannot guarantee to hold back its citizens from seeking revenge. My countrymen think of your people as bloodthirsty vermin to be exterminated.'

'I intend to place half a dozen of the prisoners on the top of the watchtower. They'll be standing on the parapet, with a rope around each man's neck. Tell whoever is in charge of the ambush that if there is any treachery, the captives will be hanged in public view.'

Peralta raised his eyebrows. 'You are beginning to think like a pirate.'

'Captain Sharpe said something very similar to me earlier today.'

The Spaniard gave a slow, reluctant nod. 'Let us both hope that your plan works. If there is falsehood on either side, each of us will live in shame for the rest of our lives.' He turned on his heel and began to walk up towards the road leading inland.

The watchtower was some forty feet high and a series of ladders led to its flat roof, passing through small square openings in the building's three floors. With Jacques's help, Hector bound the hands of six of the prisoners, placed nooses around their necks, and ordered them to climb the ladders. They made awkward progress, fumbling their way up the rungs, hampered by their bonds. Hector followed and when he reached the top of the first ladder, he pulled it up after him, and laid it on the floor. The remaining prisoners would be locked into the ground floor of the tower. He did not want them climbing up and interfering. Arriving on the flat roof of the tower, Hector fastened the free ends of the nooses to the base of the flagpole. 'Up on the parapet and face inland,' he told his prisoners. Then he sat down to wait.

*

HECTOR WAITED for half a day. Peralta was nowhere to be seen and there was nothing to do but be patient. The wind gradually eased until it was no more than the slightest whisper of a breeze, and from a cloudless sky the sun beat down on the flat roof of the tower. There was no shade, either for Hector or his prisoners, and after a while he allowed them to be seated. They took it in turns one man at a time to stand on the parapet with a rope around his neck. Hector thought the threat was sufficient.

Twice Jacques sent up one of his captives with a flask of water. No one spoke as the drink was handed round, and then the waiting continued. The parched countryside lay silent and still. There was no sign of any activity apart from a bird of prey riding the air currents and circling over the bush. The only sound was the low incessant rumble of the surf on the beach. Half a mile away *Trinity* rode at anchor on a sparkling sea.

Finally, far into the afternoon, there was movement along the road, tiny figures in the distance, putting up a small cloud of dust. Slowly they came nearer and resolved themselves in an untidy straggle of men. They were Watling's company. Someone had found half a dozen mules and these were laden high with untidy loads of boxes and sacks. But most of the men were their own porters. They were trudging along, hung about with bundles, satchels and bags. One or two had rigged up wicker baskets on their backs to serve as panniers, while a group of four men were pushing a handcart piled with various items they must have looted. Oddest of all was a man with a wheelbarrow. He was wheeling along a companion, who must have been so drunk that he was incapable of walking. At the rear was the unmistakable figure of Jezreel. He and half a dozen other men had muskets on their shoulders and formed a semblance of a rearguard.

Anxiously Hector checked the countryside. Still there was no hint of movement among the scrubland and trees on each side of the road. He could see nothing but tangles of grey-brown bushes, stunted trees, and the open patches where wild grass and reeds grew waist high. Then, suddenly, he saw a glint of light reflected from metal. He concentrated his gaze on the spot, and gradually he was able to make out the figures of soldiers, half a company at least, crouching motionless in one of the washed-out gullies which bordered the road. They were visible from his vantage point high on the tower, but from the road they would have been hidden. Concealed in the broken ground must be the remainder of the Spanish force.

'On your feet! All of you!' he snapped at his prisoners. 'Move to the parapet and show yourselves!'

The Spaniards shuffled forward and stood in line. Several were trembling with fear. One man had wet himself and the flies were settling on the damp patch on his breeches. Another cast a nervous glance behind him, and Hector snarled at him to face the front. He felt demeaned by the whole charade. Hector knew that he lacked the nerve to push any man to his death dangling at the end of a rope, but the barbarity had to continue. Without it, Jezreel and the other raiders would have no chance of reaching the beach alive.

He looked away to his left, along the coast, and to his relief saw two canoes and a ship's launch sailing parallel to the shore, coming closer. They were *Trinity*'s remaining boats. Now it would be possible to evacuate the entire raiding party at one time.

His attention returned to the road. Watling's company were closer now, still straggling along in disorder. To his dismay he saw there were several women in the party. If the buccaneers had kidnapped La Serena's women, then he doubted that the Spaniards would hold back their ambush even at the risk of the public hanging of the prisoners on the parapet. A second glance revealed his mistake. He was seeing not La Serena's womenfolk, but buccaneers who must have found women's clothes in the town, and stolen them. Now they were wearing them as the easiest way to carry them. They made a strange sight, their skirts and shawls worn over smocks and breeches. One man had a mantilla draped over the top of his head to keep off the sun.

Watling's rabble slowly advanced. Occasionally a man would halt and double over, vomiting in the road. Others stumbled and tripped. One fell flat on his face in the dust before he was pulled back to his feet by a comrade. Soon the gaggle of drunken looters were level with the gully where the Spaniards waited in ambush, and for one alarming moment Hector saw a buccaneer break away from the group and run to the side of the road. If he stumbled into the ambush, a massacre would follow. The man was clawing at his breeches as he ran, and he must have been caught short, for before he reached the roadside, he suddenly squatted and defecated in the dust. Gorged on too much fresh fruit from the gardens of La Serena, Hector thought grimly, as the man pulled up his breeches and broke into a weaving run to rejoin the column.

'Canoes ready on the beach,' Jacques called up from the foot of the tower. At last some of Watling's men had noticed the row of figures standing on the parapet. Faces turned up as the returning buccaneers began to wonder what was happening. Others were pointing, and Jezreel and the rearguard could be seen bringing their muskets to the ready. Hector stepped forward, hoping that he would be recognised, and waved at them, urging them to hurry down the final slope to the waiting canoes.

'Don't move!' Hector snapped at his hostages. 'We stay here until everyone is safe back to the ship.'

One of the Spaniards shifted on his feet and asked mockingly, 'And what about you, how will you leave?'

Hector did not answer. Watling's party were sliding and stumbling down the slope towards the beach. He could hear the crunch and clatter of the shingle beneath their feet and, amazingly, a snatch of drunken song. Some of the buccaneers still did not understand the danger they were in. From his vantage point Hector saw Jacques emerge from the base of the tower below him and run forward and speak urgently to Jezreel. Watling was beside him. A sense of urgency finally spread through the entire group. Some of them turned to face inland, reaching for their muskets.

Hector looked towards the ridge at the top of the beach. Now it was lined with dozens of Spanish soldiers. More and more armed men were appearing out of ravines and dips in the ground, or pushing out from the bushes. There must have been at least four companies of soldiers, and they were well disciplined and trained for they took up their positions in orderly formation, looking down on the buccaneers as they splashed out into the shallows and began loading their booty into the canoes. If anything went wrong now, the beach would become a killing ground.

A sudden flurry of movement, and Hector saw Jezreel reach out and wrest a gun away from a drunken buccaneer. He must have been preparing to fire a shot in bravado.

The loaded canoes began leaving the beach, heading towards *Trinity*. Only the smallest one was left, and Jezreel was standing up to his knees in the water holding the bow steady, waiting for him.

From below, a group of men came into view. They were the Spaniards whom Jacques had been holding captive. They were running towards the militiamen at the top of the slope. As they ran they were gesticulating and shouting out that they were Spanish, calling on the soldiers not to shoot. Now the only remaining prisoners were the half dozen men with Hector on the roof of the tower.

He went over the row of hostages, and raised the nooses from their necks. He crossed to the ladder which led down from the roof and began to climb down the rungs. As his head came level with the flat roof, he took out his knife and cut the cords which bound the ladder in place. Reaching the foot of the ladder, he pulled it clear. It would take several minutes for the prisoners to free themselves and still they would be trapped in the tower.

Continuing down the ladders, Hector removed each one as he descended. Reaching the ground, he walked out of the door and onto the beach. He was alone. To his right Jezreel waited with the canoe. To his left, no more than fifty paces away, stood the line of Spanish soldiers. They had advanced down the slope in open formation, muskets ready. Hector remembered how he had gone forward under the white flag of truce to the palisade of Santa Maria. But this time he had no white flag, only his faith in Peralta.

Someone stepped out from the Spanish line. It was Peralta himself. He came down the slope of beach, unarmed, his face sad.

'Your people have gutted La Serena,' he said. 'But I am grateful to you for making sure that my colleagues and I were released unharmed.' Behind him, Hector heard Jacques shouting that *Trinity* was weighing anchor and they must leave now if they were to reach the ship in time. Peralta stared into his eyes and his gaze was unflinching.

'You may tell your captain that the next time he tries to raid us, he and his men will not be so lucky. Now go.'

Hector did not know how to answer. For a moment he stood where he was, conscious of the hostility of the Spanish soldiers fingering their guns and Peralta's flinty tone. Then he turned, walked down the beach and climbed into the waiting canoe.

THIRTEEN

HECTOR HAD grown accustomed to the constant moaning and braying, barking and hissing, bubbling and trumpeting. The clamour had been in the background from the day *Trinity* arrived at the island exactly two weeks after the withdrawal from La Serena. The hubbub came from hundreds upon hundreds of large furry seals which lounged and fought and squabbled on the rocks. There were so many of the creatures and they were so sure of their possession that when the sailors first landed, the men had to force their way through the ranks of fishy-smelling beasts, clubbing them aside. The largest of the bull seals, gross lords and terrors of their harems, had resented the intrusion. They rushed furiously at the strangers, silver manes swollen, long yellow fangs bared, grunting and roaring hoarsely until the seamen fired pistols down their angry pink throats. The dark, almost black seal meat had been welcome at first, but the men soon tired of the taste. Now, if a seal was killed, the carcass was left to rot.

Sharpe had brought *Trinity* to Juan Fernandez at the crew's angry insistence. After the disappointment of La Serena the men had voted to spend Christmas there, far from the constant threat of vengeful Spanish cruisers. Hector wondered how sailors had known about the remote, mountainous island. Juan Fernandez

lay 400 miles from the South American coast, and the South
Sea was an uncharted mystery to all but the Spaniards. Yet
there were men aboard *Trinity* who were aware that this bleak,
unfrequented place offered a refuge. He supposed that somehow
in the taverns of European ports and Caribbean harbours where
sailors gathered, men talked of the island and how they had
been able to recruit their strength there, repair their vessels, and
relax.

When *Trinity* arrived on a grey, windswept day in early
December the island was uninhabited. But it was obvious that
people had visited Juan Fernandez because someone had stocked
the place with goats. The animals had thrived and wild herds
of them roamed the broken scrub-covered uplands. Their flesh
was much to be preferred to seal meat, so Dan and the other
remaining striker, another Miskito named Will, went off daily
with their muskets and came back with goat carcasses draped
over their shoulders. However, it was Jacques who had provided the most certain proof that other sailors had used the
island as a resting place. Shortly after landing, he had come
hurrying back, beaming with pleasure and brandishing a handful
of various leaves and plants. 'Herbs and vegetables!' he crowed.
'Someone planted a garden here and left it behind to grow!
Look! Turnips, salads, green stuff!'

The crew of *Trinity* had quickly made themselves comfortable. They draped spare sails over the branches of trees to make
tents, set up frames on which they barbecued goat meat and
fish, filled their water jars at the stream which emptied across a
beach of small boulders and into the bay. On Christmas Day
itself Jacques had cooked the entire company a great dish of
lobsters, broiling them over the fire. He insisted on calling them
langoustes, and they crawled in the shallows of the bay in such
numbers that one had only to wade out into the chilly water
and gather them by hand, dozens at a time. For their vegetable
the company had eaten finely sliced strips of tree cabbage cut
from the tender head of sprouting palms.

Yet the atmosphere continued to be very sour and unhappy. The crew grumbled about the lack of plunder. The sack of La Serena had yielded barely 500 pounds' weight of silver to be divided between nearly 140 men. They felt this was a paltry sum for all the risks they had taken, and it made matters worse that many of the malcontents had gambled away their booty in the long, dull sea days that followed. By the time they reached Juan Fernandez, a majority of the dice and card players were virtually penniless, and they muttered darkly that they had been swindled. When they did so, they looked towards Captain Sharpe. Unable to prove it, they were sure that he had somehow gulled them.

To leave behind the bickering and the acrimony of the camp, Hector had got into the habit of going for a long walk each day. From the pleasant glen where the sailors had set up their shelters, a narrow goat track climbed steeply inland, leaving behind the groves of sandalwood and stands of pimento trees and passing up through dense thickets of brush. The path doubled back and forth, and after the long weeks spent on board ship he found that his legs were quickly tired by the demands of the steep ascent. Now his leg muscles were aching, and it would take him another hour of hard climbing to reach the crest of the narrow ridge where he liked to spend a few moments looking out over the ocean, quietly contemplating. This morning he needed to hurry because there was to be a general council of the expedition at noon, and he wanted to be back in time to attend. The men were to vote whether Bartholomew Sharpe was to continue as their general and – equally important – what was to happen when *Trinity* left the island.

Hector took deep breaths as he scrambled upward. In places the bushes grew so close together that he had to force his way through, the branches snagging at his clothes. Occasionally he caught the distinctive acrid smell of goat hanging in the air, and once he startled a small herd, three billies and as many she-goats, which ran up the path ahead of him with their odd mincing stride, before plunging aside into the thickets and disappearing. As he ascended, the sounds of the seal colonies grew fainter and fainter from below, and whenever he stopped to turn and look down into the bay, *Trinity* looked increasingly small and insignificant until finally a turn in the path meant that he could no longer see the ship at all. From now on he might as well have been alone in the entire world. To his left rose a mist-shrouded mountain, a gloomy square mass with the shape of a gigantic anvil. On his right the island was a densely forested jumble of ravines and cliffs and spurs and ridges which were impenetrable to anyone except an expert hunter.

Eventually he reached his destination, the narrow saddle of the ridge joining the anvil mountain to the wilderness, and sat down to rest. The crest of the ridge was no more than a yard or two in breadth and the view to either side was magnificent. Ahead of him the ground dropped away in sheer scree and he was looking out over a wave-flecked ocean which spread out to a horizon of cobalt blue. When he turned in the opposite direction, he was facing into the sun and the surface of the sea became an enormous glittering silver sheet across which drifted dark shadows cast by the clouds. Everything seemed far, far away, and the high ridge was exposed to a wind which rushed past, swirling over the crest of land.

He sat in the lee of a great flat rock, clasped his arms around his knees, and gazed out to sea, trying to think of nothing, losing himself in the vastness of the great panorama before him.

He must have been sitting silently for five or ten minutes when he became aware of an occasional small black speck which sped past him, flitting through the air. To begin with, he thought the specks were a trick of his vision, and he blinked, then rubbed his eyes. But the phenomenon continued, momentary glimpses of some tiny flying object which came up from the scree slope behind him, moving so fast that it was impossible to identify, then vanished ahead, dipping down the slope in front of him. He concentrated his gaze on a clump of bushes a few paces below where he sat. That's where the flying specks seemed to disappear. Cautiously he eased himself off the ridge and, still seated, slid down towards the bush. There was a slight brushing sensation on his cheek as another of the little specks flew past, so close that he distinctly felt the wind of its passage. It vanished so quickly that he still could not identify what it was. He suspected it was some sort of flying insect, perhaps a grasshopper or a locust. He came to within an arm's length of the bush, and waited motionless. Sure enough, there was a quick darting movement as another of the flying specks came up from behind him, slowed in mid-air for an instant, then plunged in among the branches. Now he knew what it was: a tiny bird, no bigger than his thumb.

Another few moments passed, and then one of the diminutive creatures rose from within the bush. It ascended vertically and began to hover in the air, its wings moving in a blur. The bird was no more substantial than a large bumblebee and astonishingly beautiful. The feathers were green, white and brilliant blue. A moment later it was joined by a companion rising from the foliage. This time the plumage was a glossy dark maroon, the colour of drying blood, which glowed in the sunshine. A few heartbeats later and the two tiny creatures began to dance together in the air, circling and dipping, hovering to face one another for a few moments, then suddenly diving and turning and making short arcs and loops until they came together again and stayed hovering. Spellbound, Hector watched. He was sure that the two birds were male and female and they were performing a mating dance.

With a sudden pang of memory he recalled the last time he had seen a hummingbird. It had been just over a year ago with Susanna when they were travelling towards Port Royal and she had said he possessed the soul of an artist because he had compared the whirring sound made by the wings to the noise of a miniature spinning wheel. Now he listened carefully to the two birds dancing in the air before him. But he could hear nothing above the sound of the wind sighing over the ridge. An image of Susanna came to mind with painful clarity. He saw her dressed in a long, resplendent gown and attending a grand occasion in London where she had been taken by her father. She was dancing with her partner before a crowd of onlookers, all of them wealthy and sophisticated and of her own social standing. With an effort Hector tried to push the apparition out of his mind. He told himself that he was seated on a mountain-side on the far side of the world, and this image of Susanna was entirely make-believe. He scarcely knew her. It did not matter what happened in the next months or years, whether he stayed with *Trinity* and her crew, whether he returned with riches or in poverty. Susanna was always going to be unattainable. His encounter with her would never be more than a chance meeting, however much it had affected him. He should learn from his moment of confusion when he had stood before the portrait of a young lady in La Serena and found himself uncertain of what exactly reminded him of Susanna. As more time passed, he would remember less and less of the true Susanna and what had happened during those few hours he had spent in her company. Instead he would substitute fantasy until everything about Susanna was make-believe. It was an irreversible process and his best course was to free himself of false hope. It was time he acknowledged that he was keeping alive an illusion that had no place in the true circumstances of his own life.

He shivered. A cloud had passed across the sun and the wind brought a momentary chill in the shadow. Robbed of sunlight, the plumage of the two dancing hummingbirds abruptly lost its irridescence and, as if sensing the change in his mood, they darted back into the foliage. Hector got to his feet and began to descend the path back to camp.

✳

He arrived to find the general council already in session. The entire crew of *Trinity* was gathered in the glade where they had set up their tents. Watling was standing on a makeshift platform of water barrels and planks and haranguing them in his gruff soldierly voice.

'What's going on?' Hector asked quietly as he joined Jezreel and Jacques at the back of the crowd.

'Watling has just been elected our new general by a majority of twenty votes. They've turned Sharpe out and chosen Watling to replace him,' answered the big man. Hector peered over the shoulders of the men. Bartholomew Sharpe was in the front rank of the assembly, over to one side. He appeared relaxed and unconcerned, his head tilted back as he listened to Watling's announcements, his soft round face inscrutable. Hector remembered how he had thought when he had first laid eyes on Sharpe that his fleshy lips reminded him of a fish, a carp, and there was still that same faint air of guile. Seemingly, Sharpe was unaffected by his abrupt dismissal from overall command but Hector wondered what was going on behind that bland exterior.

'We return to the ways of our gallant Captain Sawkins before his death,' Watling was saying loudly. 'Courage and comradeship will be our watchwords!'

There was a murmur of approval from one section of his audience. Among them Hector recognised several of the more brutish members of the crew.

'There will be no more blasphemy!' grated Watling. 'From now on we observe the Sabbath, and unnatural vice will be punished!' His tone had turned harsh and he was staring directly at someone in the crowd. Hector craned his neck to see who it was. Watling had singled out Edmund Cook, the fastidiously dressed leader of one of the companies that set out from Golden Island. Hector had heard a rumour that Cook had been found in bed one day with another man, but had dismissed the tale as mere gossip.

Watling was speaking again, barking out his words.

'Gambling is forbidden. Anyone who plays at cards or dice will have his share of plunder reduced . . .' Watling stopped abruptly, and suddenly his arm shot out as he pointed at Sharpe. 'Hand your dice to the quartermaster,' he ordered.

Hector watched Bartholomew Sharpe reach into his pocket and produce his dice. They were taken from him by Duill, one of the men who had tossed the shot priest overboard while he was still alive.

'What's happened to Samuel Gifford? I thought he was our quartermaster,' Hector asked Jezreel.

'Watling insisted on having a second quartermaster appointed. John Duill is one of his cronies.'

Duill had handed the dice on to Watling who held them up over his head for all to see and called out, 'These are not fit to be aboard a ship.' Then he drew back his arm and flung them far into the bushes. From several onlookers came catcalls and scornful whistles, clearly directed at Sharpe. The demoted captain still showed no emotion.

'Where would you lead us?' yelled someone from the crowd.

Watling paused before answering. His eyes swept across his audience. He looked very sure of himself. When he did finally speak, his voice rang out as though he was a drill sergeant.

'I propose we attack Arica.'

There was a moment's lull, then an excited noisy chatter broke out in the crowd. Hector heard one scarred buccaneer give a subdued snort of approval.

'What's so special about Arica?' he whispered to Jezreel.

'Arica is where the treasure from the Potosi silver mines is brought to be loaded on the galleons for shipment. It's said that bars of bullion are left stacked on the quays.'

'Surely a place like that would be powerfully defended,' said Hector.

Someone in the crowd must have thought the same, for he called out to Watling, 'How can we take such a stronghold?'

'If we attack boldly, we can overrun the town in less than an hour. We'll use grenades in the assault.'

Hector caught sight of Ringrose in the crowd. He was standing beside Dampier, and both men looked unconvinced by Watling's confident assertion. Duill, the new second quartermaster, was already calling for a show of hands to vote on his commander's proposal.

The vote was two-thirds in favour of an assault on Arica, and Watling's supporters cheered loudly, slapping one another on the back and promising their comrades that soon they would all be rich beyond their dreams. The council over, Samuel Gifford was calling for volunteers to help prepare the grenades to be used in the assault.

'Why don't we join the grenade makers,' suggested Jacques. 'I'm growing bored on this island, and it will give us something to do.'

As the three of them walked over to where Gifford was assembling his work crew, Hector found himself agreeing with Jacques. Life on Juan Fernandez had grown wearisome and dull. Five weeks spent on the island was enough. He had no wish to go raiding the Spaniards but he was looking forward to getting to sea again. He wondered if the reason for his restlessness was wanderlust or had more to do with his decision to leave aside his dream about Susanna.

'I need someone to cut up musket bullets in half,' said Gifford. His glance fell on Jezreel. 'That's a job for you.'

He sent Hector to search *Trinity*'s stores for lengths of condemned rope while Jacques was to bring back a large iron cooking pot and a quantity of the pitch normally used to treat the vessel's hull.

When the materials arrived, the quartermaster set Jacques to melting the pitch over a fire while the others unpicked the rope into long strands of cord.

'Now follow closely what I do,' Gifford said as he took a length of the unravelled cord and began to wind it around his fist. 'Make a ball of the twine but do it carefully, from the outside in and leaving the coils loose so they run out freely.'

When he had the ball of twine completed, he showed the loose end of the string which emerged from the centre like the stalk on a large apple.

'Now for the coating,' he announced. He took a sharp straight stick and carefully pushed it through the completed ball. Going across to Jacques's iron pot he dipped the ball into the melted pitch and held it up in the air for the pitch to harden. Then he repeated the process. 'Two or three coatings should be right. Enough to hold a shape.'

He beckoned to Jezreel. 'Hand me some of those half musket balls,' and he began to stick the lead bullets into the soft tar.

'Now comes the tricky part,' Gifford said. Carefully he removed the stick, then felt for the free end of the string. Gently he began to tease the string out of the globe. It reminded Hector of the day that Surgeon Smeeton had showed him how to extract the Fiery Serpent from an invalid's leg.

When all the string had been pulled from the ball of pitch, leaving it hollow, the quartermaster turned it over in his hand.

'I want at least twenty of these,' he said. 'Later we fill them with gunpowder and fit a fuse. When we get to Arica . . .' He hefted the empty grenade in his hand and pretended to lob it towards the enemy, 'Pouf! It'll clear our way to the bullion.'

Watling's promotion had brought a sense of energy to the expedition. In the two days it took for Hector and his companions to prepare the grenades, the buccaneers shifted all *Trinity*'s equipment back onto the vessel, set up her rigging, filled her water casks, replenished the firewood for the cook's galley, struck camp and moved themselves back aboard. All that remained was to take on fresh food. Jacques went ashore on a mission to gather a supply of herbs and greens, and the ship's launch was despatched in the opposite direction with half a dozen armed men. They were to wait at the foot of the cliffs while Dan and Will, the other remaining striker, went inland and drove a herd of wild goats towards them. After shooting as many goats as possible for *Trinity*'s larder, the launch's crew was to collect Dan and Will and return to the ship.

'We'll have to fight our way into Arica so I might as well give you a few tips on hand-to-hand combat while we are waiting for Dan to get back,' Jezreel said to Hector. He handed him a cutlass and stood back, raising his short sword. 'Now strike at me!'

The two of them sparred, Jezreel easily deflecting Hector's blows before making his counterstrokes which usually slipped past his opponent's defence. Occasionally Jezreel stopped and adjusted the position of Hector's sword arm. 'It's all in the wrist action,' Jezreel explained. 'Keep your guard up high, flex the wrist as you parry, then strike back. It must all be one swift movement. Like this.' He knocked aside Hector's weapon and tapped him on the shoulder with the flat of his own blade.

'I don't have your height advantage,' Hector complained.

'Just stick to the basics and stay light on your feet,' the ex-prizefighter advised. 'In battle there's no time for fancy sword play, and you can expect your opponent to fight dirty like so!'

This time he distracted Hector by aiming a high blow at his head, and at the same time moved close enough to pretend to knee him in the groin. 'And always remember that in a close scuffle, the hilt of your sword is more effective than the edge. More men have been clubbed down in a brawl than were ever run through or cut.'

Hector lowered his cutlass to rest his arm. Just then there was the sound of a musket shot, closely followed by two more in quick succession. They came from *Trinity*'s launch which had gone to meet Dan and Will and shoot wild goats. The crew were rowing frantically back to the ship. Clearly something had gone wrong.

'Loose the topsail to show we've heard their signal!' Watling bellowed. Half a dozen men ran to obey his command, and

Hector found himself with the rest of the crew, waiting anxiously at the rail for the launch to come within shouting distance.

'I can see Dan in the boat, but not Will,' muttered Jezreel.

Just then Watling stepped up beside him, cupping his hands around his mouth and using his drill sergeant's voice to call out. 'What's the trouble?'

'Spaniards! Three ships hull-down to the east,' came back a shout. 'They're heading this way.'

'Shit!' Watling swore and turned on his heel, looking out to sea. 'We can't see anything from here. The headland blocks our view.'

He hurried back to the rail and bellowed again at the approaching launch. 'What sort of vessels?'

'They have the look of men of war, but it's difficult to be sure.'

Watling glanced up at the sky, gauging the direction and strength of the wind. 'Quartermasters! Call all hands and prepare to raise anchor. We have to get out of this bay. It's a trap if the Spaniards find us here.' He caught a seaman by the shoulder and barked, 'You! Get two of your fellows and bring up all the weapons we have. I want them loaded and ready on deck in case we have to fight our way clear.'

There was a rush of activity as men began to bring the galleon back to life after weeks of idleness. They cleared away the deck clutter, braced round the yards ready to catch the wind, and hoisted a foresail and the mizzen so that *Trinity* hung on her anchor, ready to break free and sail out of the bay at a moment's notice. Quartermaster Gifford himself took the helm and stood waiting.

Watling was back at the rail, bawling at the men in the launch. 'Get a move on! Tie the launch off the stern and lend a hand.'

'What about the men still on shore? We cannot abandon them!' Hector blurted.

Watling swung round, face hard set, his eyes furious. 'They shift for themselves,' he snapped.

'But Jacques is not back yet, and Will was with Dan. He must still be on the island.'

An angry scowl spread across Watling's face. He was about to lose his temper.

'Do you question my orders?'

'Look over there,' said Hector, pointing towards the beach. 'You can see Jacques now. He's standing there, waiting to be picked up by a boat.'

'Let him swim,' snarled Watling. He turned back and shouted at the men to get to the capstan and begin retrieving the anchor.

Hector was about to say that Jacques did not know how to swim when Jezreel, short sword in hand, strode across the deck and stood beside the capstan.

'The first person who slots in a capstan bar loses his fingers,' he announced. Then he casually whipped his sword through the air, the blade making a figure of eight and a low swishing sound as he turned his wrist.

The approaching sailors stopped short. They looked warily at the ex-prizefighter.

'The anchor stays down until Jacques is safely aboard,' Jezreel warned them.

'We'll see about that,' growled one of the sailors. It was Duill, the second quartermaster. He made his way to the quarterdeck. 'General, may I have the loan of one of your pistols so I can put a bullet in that bugger's guts.'

Hector forestalled him. Stepping across to where the ship's armament was being made ready, he picked up a loaded blunderbuss, and pointed it at Duill's stomach. 'This time it's your corpse that will have to go over the side,' he said grimly.

Everyone stood still, waiting to see what would happen. Watling looked as if he was about to spring at Hector. Duill was eyeing the gap between himself and the muzzle of the gun.

Into this tense lull came a languid voice. 'No need for so much fuss. I'll take the launch, if someone will care to accompany me, and collect our French friend. '

It was Bartholomew Sharpe. He sauntered across the deck casually.

'What about Will the Miskito,' Hector asked, his voice harsh with strain.

'I'm sure he'll be able to look after himself,' said Sharpe soothingly. 'He's got a gun and ammunition, and will make himself comfortable until we can get back to collect him or another ship comes along.' He attempted a lighter touch. 'Your friend Jacques is another matter. What would we do without his pimento sauce?'

'Then get on with it,' snapped Watling. Hector could see that the new captain was keen to re-establish his authority and show that he, not Sharpe, was in command. 'The launch picks up the Frenchman, and we waste no more time getting ready for action.'

Twenty minutes later, a relieved Jacques was scrambling aboard clutching a sack of salad leaves, and *Trinity*'s anchor was emerging dripping from the sea as the ship began to gather way.

'Don't fret about Will. A Miskito will be able to look after himself on the island,' Dan quietly reassured Hector. 'There's more to worry about close at hand.'

He nodded towards the foredeck where a sullen-looking Duill was standing by to oversee the catting of the anchor. 'The crew don't like what happened. They think we were prepared to sacrifice them in favour of our friends. From now we'll have to watch our backs.'

FOURTEEN

*

'EACH GRENADIER will receive a bonus of ten pieces of eight,'
declared Watling from the rail of the quarterdeck, his gaze
sweeping across the assembled crew. It was a fortnight since
Trinity had run from Juan Fernandez, easily slipping past the
Spanish squadron. Now she lay hove-to off the mainland coast
and in sight of the long, dark line of hills which loomed behind
Arica.

'If he still has both his hands to count the money,' mocked
a voice at the back of the crowd.

Watling ignored the gibe. 'The success of our assault may
depend on our grenadiers. Who will volunteer?'

His plea was met with silence. The men were nervous about
touching the home-made bombs now they had been filled with
gunpowder and fitted with their stubby fuses.

'If you handle grenades properly, they are safe,' Watling
insisted. 'I myself will show how it's done.'

'How about giving them out to the bastards who made
them,' suggested the same anonymous voice. 'If they get it
wrong, they'll know who's to blame.'

The sally caused a ripple of laughter, and Duill was smirking
as he stepped forward and beckoned to Hector and his friends.
'You heard what the general said. He'll tell you what to do.'

Hector watched as Watling picked up one of the grenades from a wooden box at his feet. The young man had to admit that Watling, though bull-headed and short-tempered, was prepared to lead by example.

'Each grenadier will carry three of these in a pouch on his right side, and a length of slow match wrapped around his left wrist. When the time comes, he turns his left shoulder towards the enemy, takes up a grenade in his right hand like so, blows on the slow match to make it glow, and brings the lighted match to the fuse.'

Watling mimed the action.

'He then steps forward with his left foot and bends his right knee so he is in a crouching position. After checking that the fuse is burning steadily, he stands up and hurls the grenade, keeping his right arm straight.'

'Let's hope that none of those buggers is left-handed,' shouted the wag, and Watling had to wait until the ensuing guffaws had subsided.

'I propose that *Trinity* stays out of sight over the horizon so as not to alert the defenders to our presence, and under cover of darkness our boats land our force some five leagues to the south of the town. We spend our first day ashore in hiding. At nightfall we leave behind our boats under guard and advance across country to a point close to Arica from which we can launch a dawn assault. We capture the town before the citizens are awake.'

'How many men in the attack?' Jezreel asked.

'Everyone who is fit enough. It must be a forced march if we are to take the town by surprise. Then, as soon as we have seized Arica, we signal to our boats. They come to pick us up and we begin loading our plunder.'

'What happens if the raid runs into trouble? How do we get back to the ship safely?'

'There will be two different signals: a single fire with white smoke tells our boat crews to come halfway to meet us and evacuate the force; two white smokes is the sign that we have captured the town and they enter into harbour to collect us and our plunder.'

Watling gestured towards the distant hills. 'You have all heard the rumour of a mountain which is made of solid silver, and how the Spaniards of Peru keep the native people in chains, toiling away like ants to dig out the bullion. In the next forty eight hours, we will relieve them of their riches.'

*

'I FEEL LIKE a worker ant myself,' said Jacques at noon the next day. He was burdened down with a musket and cartridge box, a pistol and a cutlass as well as a satchel containing three grenades. He was gasping from the heat. 'This place is a furnace.'

Jezreel had persuaded his friends that they should take on the role of grenadiers. The ex-prizefighter had argued that by volunteering for such dangerous work they might improve their standing with the rest of *Trinity*'s crew. Until there was a chance of breaking away on their own, it was safer if the four of them showed willing to cooperate with their shipmates.

Watling's column had spent an uncomfortable night on the rocky foreshore, shivering in a cold clammy mist that had oozed in from the sea. At daybreak they had set out across country, leaving a handful of men under Basil Ringrose to guard the boats and wait for the signal fires. Within half an hour the sun had sucked up the mist and the day had turned blisteringly hot. The men, ninety-two of them, had marched for hours and had not seen a single house or field or sign of human occupation. The landscape was utterly barren, a sun-blasted expanse of scoured rock and sand with an occasional steep-sided ravine. The only vegetation was a few spiny plants or stunted bushes with dry, brittle branches, and they had not found a single stream or pond where they could refill their water canteens.

Jacques gave a yelp of pain, took a half stride, and sat

down, clutching at his foot. He had stepped on one of the needle-like spines of a desert plant and it had pierced right through the thick leather sole of his boot. 'Surely Arica can't be much farther now,' he said through dry, cracked lips as he began to remove his boot.

'Beyond that next rise of ground, perhaps,' Hector answered. In the distance the low hills shimmered in the heat.

'Why would anyone want to live in such a desperate place,' muttered Jacques as he searched for the broken end of the offending spine.

'To be near the source of so much silver,' said Hector. The weight of his three grenades was pressing uncomfortably on his right hip and he eased the satchel strap across his chest. He had decided against carrying a musket, but wore the cutlass that Jezreel had provided him with.

'I would rather be marooned on a desert island than live in such a hellish place,' Jacques grumbled.

A slight movement on the gravel caught Hector's attention. A scorpion was edging away in the shade of a low shrub whose small white flowers were the only colour in the landscape of drab grey and brown.

'Here comes Dan now,' said Jacques, grimacing as he plucked out the broken spine. 'I wonder what he's found.'

The Miskito had gone forward to scout, leaving his satchel of grenades with Jezreel. Now Dan was returning, musket balanced on his shoulder and loping along as if the blazing heat was nothing. As usual, it was difficult to read anything into his expression.

'Arica's a mile beyond that ridge, and the town is expecting us,' he announced.

Watling came striding up. 'What do you mean, expecting us?' he demanded.

'The Spaniards have built a barricade of timber and earth across the main approach leading into the town. It's manned by soldiers, a lot of them. There's also a fort over to one side, and that seems to have a large garrison on the alert.'

'How many defenders?'

'It's impossible to say. But several hundred.'

Watling took off his broad-brimmed hat, wiped his brow with a large orange handkerchief, and beckoned to Duill, his second in command. 'The Miskito says that Arica is expecting an attack. The place may have been reinforced.'

Duill showed his teeth in a wolfish smile. 'That only goes to prove they have something worth defending.'

Watling brushed the fine desert dust off his sleeve. He turned to Dan. 'Do you think that we've been seen?' he asked.

'Certainly,' the Miskito replied. 'Three horsemen over on our right flank. They have been shadowing us for the past two hours. They know our strength, and purpose.'

'Then that decides it,' said Watling firmly. 'There's no going back. If we are seen in retreat, Arica's garrison will come out in pursuit and things will go badly for us. We stick to the original plan. When we reach the high ground ahead of us, we camp for the night. In the morning we advance on the town and rush the barricade.'

*

HECTOR WAS surprised that Arica was such an ordinary, rundown place. He lay on the ridge above the town as the sky began to lighten and the streets of Arica emerged from the shadows. They had been laid out in the grid pattern familiar from La Serena. But he saw nothing to match La Serena's fine stone buildings. Arica's houses were unpainted single-storey dwellings made of what looked like humble mud brick. The single church tower was modest in size, and the perimeter wall of the fort that Dan had mentioned was no higher than the flat roofs of the nearby houses which surrounded it. From his vantage point Hector could see down into the parade ground where soldiers were emerging from their barracks and assembling for dawn muster. What held his attention was the makeshift outwork of rubble and earth which blocked the main approach to the town. It was at least fifty paces in length and built to a height so that a defender could rest his musket on it and take steady aim. There were sentinels posted at regular intervals and an officer was walking behind the line, checking that his lookouts were alert. Hector could see no sign of artillery, and for this he breathed a sigh of relief. To attack into the mouths of cannon would have been suicidal.

'On your feet! First rank make ready!' It was Watling, his army training evident. This was to be a disciplined assault, unlike previous campaigns against towns which had often been little more than an unruly rush against the defence. This time the buccaneers were to advance in three waves. The first and second were to alternate, one moving forward as the other gave covering fire, leapfrogging forward until they were close enough to reach the breastwork in a concerted charge. The four grenadiers and a dozen of the older, less active men were being held back in reserve. Under Bartholomew Sharpe they would stay fifty yards in the rear of the attack, ready to be called on wherever the need arose.

'Advance!' Watling was moving forward. Behind him the first wave of buccaneers began to make their way down the slope at a fast walk. Each man had an orange ribbon tied to his left shoulder to identify him in the coming engagement. Hector tried to judge the distance they would have to cover. It was perhaps half a mile. Several outhouses and barns would provide some cover, and there was an occasional fold in the ground where a man could crouch down in safety and reload his musket. Below him the officer in charge of the barricade had already turned towards the town and was gesticulating urgently. He must have seen the movement on the hill. Moments later a squad of armed men came running out from the town and took up their positions at the outwork. Counting them, Hector calculated that there must be at least forty musketeers facing the buccaneer attack. Allowing for the fact that a great many more Spanish soldiers were being held in reserve in the fort, Watling's force was heavily outnumbered. If the buccaneers were to take Arica, they would have to rely on their superior musketry and the professional ferocity of their assault.

The second wave had left its position and was also advancing down the slope. The men spread out in a skirmishing line, wide gaps between them to reduce the target. A scatter of shots came from the barricade, but the range was too great and the firing quickly died away. Hector supposed that a Spanish officer had restrained his men.

'I suppose we should get moving too!' said Sharpe in a relaxed voice. He got casually to his feet as though about to go for a stroll in the country and puffed on a clay pipe. He took the pipe stem from his mouth, blew out a thin plume of smoke, and watched the smoke hang in the air before slowly dissipating. 'Perfect day for a grenadier,' he observed. 'No chance of the match blowing out in the wind.' He glanced up at the cloudless sky and gave a sardonic smile, 'And of course no likelihood of a rain shower to extinguish it.'

Hector held out the length of match cord that had been issued to him. Sharpe sucked vigorously on the pipe, then thrust the end of the cord into the glowing tobacco. 'You've got enough match there for about five hours. Let's hope the battle is over by that time,' he said as he handed it back. Hector blew gently on the glowing end of the cord, wound the extra length around his wrist, then held the burning end between his fingers. He waited for Sharpe to light the match held out by his companions, and they began to make their way cautiously down the hill towards Arica.

The front rank of buccaneers were now within range of the barricade. One by one they paused, took aim and fired towards the defenders behind their earthwork. Hector thought he saw splinters and spurts of dust fly up. There was a scatter of answering musketry from the Spanish defenders, but they were outranged by the buccaneers' better weapons and their response did no damage. The second wave of attackers was passing through the front line of skirmishers, and had taken up their positions. There was no cheering. The only sounds were the flat detonations of their flintlocks, and the shouted insults and defiance from the Spaniards.

Moments later Hector saw the first of the buccaneers fall. The man was on his feet, taking aim, and the next instant he spun round and dropped to the ground. There was a whoop of triumph from the barricade.

Watling shouted an order and waved his orange handkerchief. His signal was followed by a ragged volley and all of a sudden the buccaneers were running forward in a concerted rush. Now they were shouting and hallooing, muskets and cutlasses in hand. A crackle of musketry from the barricade, and this time Hector saw at least three of the assailants knocked down before the first of them reached the earthwork and began to scramble over. There was a glimpse of a single buccaneer – he was almost sure it was Duill – balancing on top of the barricade and swinging his musket by the barrel, using it as a club to strike downward. A dozen of his men had gone wide, intending to get around the end of the barricade, even as their comrades swarmed over the obstacle. For several minutes the outcome of the pitched battle was in the balance. Men were shouting and yelling, hacking and stabbing. There was the clash of metal in the dust and smoke, cries of pain, and several times Hector heard the lighter crack of pistol shots.

The furore began to ease, and Watling was climbing up back on the barricade and beckoning urgently to the reserve. 'Close up, close up,' he was yelling. 'Hold our ground.'

He jumped back down out of sight as Hector and his comrades ran the last few paces to the barricade and clambered over. On the far side was a scene of devastation. Corpses lying in the dust, the ground was torn and tramped and stained with blood. A buccaneer with a terrible gash on the side of his face was stumbling around in a daze, and at least thirty or forty Spaniards were standing or sitting on the ground in a state of shock, their faces black with powder smoke and several of them wounded. 'Guard the prisoners while we move forward,' Watling bawled. There was the sound of more musket fire. From within the town the defenders of Arica were sniping at the attackers.

'Put your hands behind your heads!' Hector screamed in Spanish at the prisoners. They looked at him in disbelief. Hector realised that, without a firearm, he must have looked a harmless figure, with only a cutlass at his waist and the slow match coiled around his wrist. 'Do as he says,' growled Jezreel. He spoke in English but his giant size and fierce scowl made it clear what he wanted. The prisoners hurriedly obeyed.

From within the gateway came the sound of more gunfire, a lot of it. Watling's advance guard was encountering furious resistance. A man came scurrying out from the town, bent low to dodge stray bullets. 'There are more barricades inside,' he gasped. 'The Spaniards have built them at every street corner. Watling says we need grenades to clear them.'

'I'll go,' said Jezreel. He unfastened the flap to his satchel and hurried off behind the messenger. Hector turned back to face the prisoners. 'No one move!' he ordered. Looking around, he saw a musket lying on the ground where it had been dropped by one of the defenders. He picked it up and took a quick glance at the lock. It appeared to be primed and loaded. He pointed it at the captives.

Minutes passed and there was a muffled explosion from inside the town, not far away. Hector presumed the grenade had done its work, for there was a lull in the sounds of fighting. Then almost at once the crackle of musket fire resumed.

'We need reinforcements! Come on ahead!' Duill had

appeared in the entrance to the town. He was dishevelled and streaked with grime. There was a look of urgency in his movements.

'On whose orders?' Sharpe snapped.

'The general! Watling orders the rearguard to enter the town!'

'And what about the prisoners?'

Duill swore at him and for a moment Hector thought that the second quartermaster would strike Sharpe in the face. 'Leave a couple of men in charge of them,' he snarled. 'There's no time to argue.'

Sharpe turned to Hector. 'You and Jacques stay to guard the prisoners,' he ordered. 'Dan, leave your grenades here and go back up the hill. Your task is to keep a lookout for any extra Spanish troop reinforcements arriving. Let us know if you see anything that poses a risk. The rest of you follow me.' At an unhurried walk he set off towards the sound of the musketry.

A groan came from Hector's right. It was the buccaneer with the wounded face. He had slumped against the barricade and, with his forearm, was trying to staunch the flow of blood from his ravaged face. Hector set down his musket and hurried across to him. 'Here, let me bandage that,' he said and reached for his satchel before he realised that it did not contain medicines and bandages, but grenades. The corpse of a Spanish soldier was lying on the ground nearby. The dead man had worn a cotton scarf around his throat. Hector reached down and removed the neck cloth, then began to knot the bandage around the wounded man's head. Behind him, he heard Jacques let out a curse. Hector spun round in time to see at least twenty of the Spanish prisoners running away. 'Halt!' he shouted. 'Halt or I fire.' But he knew it was a bluff. There was no way that he and Jacques could restrain them.

'Not much point in hanging about here,' said Jacques. 'We should see if we can help Jezreel and the others.'

The two of them cautiously made their way into the town.

At the first crossroads they came upon the wreckage of another barricade. It had been made of upturned carts, planks and old furniture. There was a gap where Watling's men must have forced their way through. On the far side lay more dead men, both Spanish and buccaneer. A second crossroads and another barricade, and this time the buccaneers were using it as a breastwork themselves, taking shelter behind it, then standing up and taking shots at the enemy.

Hector spotted Jezreel. He was aiming his flintlock towards a nearby roof top, and a second later he pulled the trigger. A Spanish arquebusier ducked back out of sight. 'Missed him,' grunted Jezreel. He extracted the ramrod from under the barrel, spat on a rag to moisten it and began to clean out the gun. 'We can't keep up this rate of fire. Our weapons are getting fouled.'

Watling was in a doorway, conferring with Duill. The two men beckoned to Sharpe and spoke with him for a few moments before Sharpe came running back, tapped Hector on the shoulder, and shouted to him, 'Collect together the rearguard, and as many men as you can. We must take the fort. Until we secure our flank, we are exposed. The others will deal with the town itself.'

Hector passed the word to Jacques and soon they and some thirty men, including Jezreel, were fighting their way down a narrow street. Ahead of them, Spanish militiamen could be seen falling back, retreating to the safety of the fort. As the last of them passed through the wooden gate, it was heaved shut, and a fusillade from loopholes in the wall forced the attackers to take cover.

Bartholomew Sharpe ducked back into an alleyway and leaned against a mud wall, catching his breath. 'Time for another of our famous grenades,' he said. Hector realised that to this moment he had not fired a single shot but had been swept along in the general confusion. He looked down at his left wrist, and was surprised to see red burn marks on his skin where the lit end of the match had scorched him. In the chaos of battle he had never noticed the pain. He opened the flap of his satchel and took out a grenade. The little bomb looked very ill-made. The covering of hardened pitch had softened in the heat and lost its shape. Several of the half musket bullets had fallen loose. The fuse, a short length of slow match an inch long, was pressed over to one side and stuck into the pitch like the bent wick of a candle. Carefully he prised the fuse straight.

'Try to throw it over the gate! And good luck!' muttered Sharpe as he backed away. Hector brought the glowing end of the slow match across to the fuse and touched the two ends together. He saw the grenade's fuse begin to burn and, forcing himself to stay calm, started to count to ten very slowly. He stepped out from cover and as Watling had instructed, tossed the grenade, keeping his arm straight. The bomb flew through the air and, to his chagrin, thudded against the wall of the fort at least a foot beneath the top, dropped down, and lay on the road.

'Beware bomb!' he shouted and leaped back into shelter, pressing himself into a doorway. Several moments passed and nothing happened. Cautiously he peered out, and saw the grenade lying in the dust. He could not see any smoke rising from it. The device had failed to work. He fumbled in his satchel for a second grenade.

'Don't be in a hurry. Let's use our heads about this,' said Sharpe, who had reappeared beside him. 'You and Jacques follow me.'

He pushed open the door to the house and led the two of them inside. A buccaneer was already in the room, kneeling by the window and aiming his musket towards the fort. Sharpe looked up. The ceiling was made of narrow poles laid horizontally, above them a layer of palm fronds.

'There must be a way onto the roof,' Sharpe said. He crossed the room and pulled open the back door. 'Just as I thought, there's a ladder.' He began to climb its rungs with Hector and Jacques at his heels.

Emerging on the flat roof Hector found that he was level with the top of the wall of the fort just across the street. The roof itself was made of clay and tamped earth. Sharpe gripped his arm, holding him back. 'We don't want to be seen before we are ready, and we've got to get this right,' he said quietly.

Jacques had scrambled up beside them and was already selecting a grenade from his satchel.

'Compare your fuses, and make sure that both are the same length,' Sharpe advised. 'I'll light both the fuses so that the two of you can concentrate on the throw. When I give the word, step across the roof, it's no more than five paces, and hurl the bombs. Don't worry about hitting a precise target, just make sure they fall inside the fort. As soon as you've thrown your grenades, get back here and crouch down.'

Hector unwound the slow match from his wrist, gave it to Sharpe, and then picked out the better of his two remaining grenades. 'Are you ready?' Sharpe asked. Both men nodded, and their commander pressed the slow match to the fuses. They began to burn, the dull red glow steadily eating its way towards the gunpowder. But Sharpe appeared to ignore them. He was gazing out across the roof tops. As the seconds dragged past, Hector found himself sweating with apprehension. He could smell the acrid stench of the burning match.

Finally, and very softly, Sharpe said, 'Now!' With Jacques by his side, Hector started out across the flat roof. For one heart-stopping moment he felt the surface crumble beneath his weight, and thought he would fall through with the lit grenade still in his grasp. Then he was at the edge of the roof, overlooking the street. The top of the fort wall was no more than thirty feet away. Hector swung back his arm and threw the little bomb. It went in an arc over the fort wall, cleared it easily, and dropped out of sight. Out of the corner of his eye he saw Jacques's grenade follow.

There was a musket shot and Hector felt a tug at his sleeve. A defender must have seen them and opened fire. Bending double, the two men scurried back to where Sharpe was waiting. 'Now we wait,' he said.

For what seemed like an age nothing happened. Then abruptly there was the sound of a detonation, followed by shouts of fear, then silence.

They waited another minute, but there was no further explosion. 'One bomb seems to have been enough,' said Sharpe. He cocked his head to one side, listening. 'We've given them something to think about.'

✳

THERE WAS an anxious shout from below. Someone was calling 'Captain Sharpe! Captain Sharpe!' and a worried-looking buccaneer appeared at the rear of the building. He had a bloody rag wrapped around one hand.

'Who are you calling "Captain"? I'm just one of the company now!' exclaimed Sharpe, looking down.

'The general's dead!' cried out the newcomer. 'He was shot at the barricades. We need someone to lead us.'

'Really?' said Sharpe. 'I thought quartermaster Duill was second in command. Let him take over.'

'Duill has disappeared,' answered the man. 'No one can find him, and we're in a bad way in the town.' He was begging now. 'Captain, come back down to assist us.'

Sharpe descended the final rungs slowly and deliberately. 'Do all the men want me back in charge?'

'Yes, yes. The situation is very bad.'

Sharpe turned towards Hector and there was a gleam of satisfaction in his pale blue eyes. 'Hector, tell the men to abandon the attack on the fort and fall back.'

'We are too few,' the exhausted-looking buccaneer was saying. 'Every time we overrun one of their barricades and move forward, the Spaniards come in behind us and reoccupy the position they just lost. We can't spare anyone to look after all our prisoners. Many of them make their escape and rejoin the fight.'

They had reached the main square, and the extent of the raiders' difficulties was all too evident. The main force had fought its way into the heart of the town but the Spaniards had sealed off all the streets leading from the far side of the central square with piles of stone and rubble. They had placed sharpshooters where they could fire on anyone who tried to advance any further, and several buccaneers had been shot down as they tried to cross the open ground. Their bodies lay where they had fallen. Some two dozen of their comrades were now taking shelter in side alleys or crouching in doorways. Occasionally they fired towards the Spanish positions. A group of about twenty Spanish prisoners, clearly terrified, were lying face down on the ground watched over by a couple of wounded buccaneers. It was obvious that the attack had come to a standstill.

'Our wounded are in that church over there,' said their guide, pointing. 'Our surgeons are with them. They broke into an apothecary shop and took some medical supplies. But the longer we stay here, the bolder the Spaniards are becoming. They're moving up closer. It's becoming dangerous even to venture out into the open.'

He ducked as a musket ball struck the wall above his head. Somewhere in the distance a trumpet sounded.

Sharpe took stock of the situation. 'The Spaniards are bringing up reinforcements, and we can expect a sortie from the garrison in the fort when they are in position. Then we'll be caught in a pincer movement, and crushed. We've no choice but to make an orderly retreat while we are still able to do so.'

'What about our wounded in the church? We can't leave them!' said Hector.

Sharpe treated him to a sour smile. 'You're always worried about leaving someone behind, aren't you? As you are so concerned, I suggest you dash off and check on the situation in the church. See if any of the men can be evacuated. Then report back to me. Hurry!'

Hector swallowed hard. His throat was dry and he had a raging thirst. It occurred to him that no one had drunk anything that day. Nor had they eaten. 'Jezreel and Jacques, give me some covering fire!'

He removed his grenade satchel and laid it on the ground. He would have to cross thirty yards of open ground before he reached the portico of the church, and he could be halfway there before the Spanish musketeers realised what he was doing. He took a deep breath and burst out from cover.

As he sprinted across the plaza's flagstones, he expected a musket ball to strike him at any moment. But there was not a single shot and he crashed full tilt into the great wooden door. The heavy black iron handle was in his hand. He tugged the door open and threw himself inside.

After the blinding sunshine of the plaza, the interior of the church was so dark that he had to pause and let his eyes adjust to the gloom. In front of him the nave was a nightmare scene. All the church furniture – benches, carved wooden screens, a confessional, even the lectern – had either been roughly pushed to one side or overturned and smashed. At the far end the altar stood bare, stripped of its cross. Wall hangings had been torn down and were now spread out on the floor to serve as bedding on which lay wounded men. The place smelled of vomit and excrement. From outside still came the crack of musket shots but here in the half-darkness the sounds were moans, coughs and an occasional whimper of pain. Somewhere a man was cursing, softly and steadily, as if to distract himself from his suffering.

Hector looked around, trying to locate the surgeons. Some-one was wearing a loose white cloak trimmed with gold and sitting on the step in front of the altar. He seemed to be unhurt. Hector went forward to speak with him. 'Are there any walking wounded?' he asked even as he realised that the seated figure was wrapped in the altar cloth. The man looked up. He was glassy-eyed and his breath stank of alcohol. 'Go look for yourself,' he mumbled. Appalled, Hector seized him by the shoulder and shook him. 'Where are the surgeons!' he shouted. Under his grip, Hector felt the limp and sagging movements of someone who was completely drunk. The man's head flopped back and forward loosely. 'The surgeons! Where are the surgeons?' Hector repeated angrily. The man hiccuped. 'Over there, waiting for a sermon,' he replied. He gave a tipsy laugh and waved vaguely towards the pulpit steps.

Lolling there was another man. He had a bottle in his hand and was clearly as intoxicated as his colleague. Hector recognised one of the surgeons who had worked alongside Smeeton and stayed on with the expedition. He was waving the bottle at Hector. 'Come and join us, young man!' he called out, slurring his words. 'Come and enjoy the finest fruits of the apothecary's skill. The medicine to cure every ailment.' He raised the bottle to his mouth, drained the last of its contents, and tossed it on the floor where it broke with a loud crash. 'That fool Watling is all piss and wind. A hotbrain who led us all into a death trap.' He wiped drool from his mouth with the back of his hand. 'We are the only ones who will get out of this alive,' he announced solemnly. 'We, the honoured gentlemen of the medical profession, are always welcome guests. The Spaniards will look after us. They need our skills. You were Smeeton's assistant, weren't you? So why don't you join us?' His knees gave way, and he sat back heavily on the pulpit steps.

Hector felt nausea rising within him, and a sense of betrayal. 'Won't you at least help the wounded get out of here?' he asked.

'Let them take their chances. Why should we risk our lives?' the surgeon retorted.

Hector made his way among the rows of wounded men.

The injuries inflicted by musket bullets were brutal. Several of the men on the floor appeared to be dead already, others were delirious or lying with their eyes closed.

Sick to his stomach, Hector found his way back to the door of the church. There was nothing he could do to help the wounded, and the longer he delayed, the more dangerous and difficult it would be for Sharpe to extricate the remainder of the buccaneers.

He eased the church door open and peered out through a narrow crack. Little seemed to have changed. His comrades were still pinned down, facing across the barricade, occasionally firing at the Spaniards on the far side of the plaza.

He darted out from the portico and set off at a dead run for the barricade. This time he jinked from side to side to distract the aim of the Spanish marksmen, and once again his luck held. He heard several musket shots, the smack of something which must have been a bullet striking the ground ahead of him. Then he was vaulting onto the barricade, and Jezreel was standing up to grasp him by the arm and drag him into cover.

'There's nothing to be done about the wounded. And the surgeons are too drunk to join us,' Hector blurted.

'Then we delay no longer!' said Sharpe briskly. 'Get the prisoners on their feet and bring them forward to the barricade. We fall back by the same route by which we entered the town. You, you and you . . .' He selected a dozen men. 'Stay here at the barricade. Each of you get behind one of the Spanish prisoners and use him as a shield. Put a gun muzzle to his spine, if necessary. As soon as the rest of us get back to the next barricade, we will give you covering fire. Then it's your turn to retreat, keeping the Spaniard between you and the enemy.'

There was a scramble to abandon the forward position. It was now well past noon, and the day was at its hottest.

As they retreated to the second abandoned barricade, Hector noticed a corpse with an orange handkerchief clenched in its fist. John Watling had been hit in the throat by a Spanish bullet and his shirt front was drenched with his blood. Duill, his second in command, was nowhere to be seen, and Hector presumed that the quartermaster had either also been killed or had fallen into the hands of the Spanish. Sharpe, who seemed to relish his renewed command, set the men to searching the corpses for spare cartridge pouches and bullet bags.

There was no respite from the Spanish counter-attack. As the buccaneers fell back street by street, their opponents kept pressing on, shooting down from the roof tops or suddenly appearing from lanes and passageways to fire and then slip away. The citizens of Arica knew the layout of their town and used that knowledge to their advantage. They paid no heed to their countrymen being used as human shields, and kept up their fire, killing or injuring several of their own people. If Sharpe had not been on hand to steady the buccaneers, their retreat could have become a panic-stricken flight.

Eventually the raiders were at the place where they had started – the barricade where they had first attacked the town in the light of dawn. Here Sharpe took a brief head count. Nearly one-third of the raiding force, some twenty-eight men, were missing. They were either dead or had been captured. Among those who now crouched exhausted in the shelter of the earthwork, eighteen had serious wounds. Everyone was dispirited, drooping with thirst and hunger.

'We'll be shot down like rabbits as we ascend the slope,' said Jacques despondently. 'The moment the Spaniards reoccupy this earthwork, it'll be like target practice for them.'

'Has anyone still got any grenades left?' Jezreel asked. Hector shook his head. He had left his satchel behind after his run to the church.

'I'm afraid I got rid of mine when we began the retreat,' said Jacques.

'What about Dan's grenades? They should be here somewhere,' suggested Hector. He remembered that the Miskito had left his satchel by the breastwork when he went up the hill to act as lookout. After a few moments of searching Hector spotted the bag tucked away in a corner.

He handed the satchel to Jezreel who brought out three grenades, then called out to Sharpe, 'Captain! Get going with the others. My friends and I will cover your retreat.'

Sharpe looked at the grenades and frowned. 'They're unreliable.'

'No matter. They will do the job.'

Sharpe did not need to be asked a second time. 'Come on!' he shouted to his men. 'Turn loose any prisoners. Back up the hill!' He turned to Jezreel. 'Is there nothing we can do?'

'Half a dozen men. Good shots. Place them half way up the slope where they have the range of the Spaniards. That might help.'

The buccaneers began their flight, stumbling wearily up the hill, some using their muskets as crutches, others helped along by comrades.

Jezreel started work on the grenades. He adjusted their fuses until he was satisfied, then buried them in the barricade a few paces apart. Looking over his shoulder to check that Sharpe and the main body of buccaneers were well on their way up the hill, he lit the three fuses and then shouted at his friends to turn and run.

The three friends scrambled back across the rough ground. Behind them came a flurry of shots, and Jacques stumbled and fell. Hector ran across to him while Jacques was struggling to stand up. He seemed dazed and blood was gushing from his head. He clapped a hand to his ear and brought it away. 'The bullet clipped my ear!' he exclaimed with a relieved grin. 'It's nothing.' There was an explosion from the barricade. The first of the grenades had detonated, throwing up a spurt of smoke and dirt. Several Spanish militiamen who had ventured into the gateway, dived back into shelter.

'Two more to go,' said Jezreel with a satisfied grunt.

Holding out a hand, he helped Jacques to stand upright, then put an arm around him and began to assist him up the hill. 'When I was in the fight game, there was a troupe of actors who used our ring as a stage between-times. When they needed to bring on or take off an actor, they had a hidden assistant who set off an explosion with lots of smoke and noise. It worked every time.'

FIFTEEN

✳

'IT WAS A SHAMBLES!' Basil Ringrose was still fuming, his anger fuelled by the fact that he and his comrades had also very nearly fallen victim to the Spaniards. 'Two white smokes! I nearly took the boats right into Arica harbour. We would have been blown out of the water.'

He glared angrily at Sharpe who was standing by the lee rail.

Hector watched the two men bicker. It was two months since the defeat at Arica, yet the panicked desperation of the withdrawal still provoked recriminations. He, Jacques and Jezreel had reached the ridge behind the town to find Sharpe and the others uprooting dry weeds and brushwood to make a signal fire. 'One white smoke,' someone was saying. 'Let's hope that the boat crews are quick about it. We have to get out of here before the Spaniards catch up with us.' The words were scarcely spoken when Dan, who had rejoined them, had said quietly, 'That's not our worry now.' He was looking back towards Arica. From the town were rising two thick columns of white smoke, reaching into the sky on that windless, scorching day and hanging there in false welcome. Dan had gone running to the shore to intercept Ringrose and the small boats before they were lured into the Spanish trap. Sharpe and the rest of the survivors had hobbled and limped behind him, half-dead of thirst and utterly spent. Troops of Spanish horsemen had harassed them all the way, then rolled rocks down the cliffs at them as they scrambled into the boats.

Back aboard *Trinity*, the men had divided into two camps, bitterly opposed: those who blamed Watling for the debacle and those who still detested Sharpe enough to resent serving under him again. After weeks of squabbling, a council had been held to decide the expedition's future. There was to be a simple vote: the majority would get to keep *Trinity* while the minority would receive the ship's launch and the canoes to do with them what they wanted. At the show of hands, seventy had chosen to keep on Sharpe as leader and forty-eight had been against. The losers had taken their share of the accumulated plunder and set out on the hazardous return voyage to Golden Island, intending to make the final leg of their journey back over the isthmus of Panama. Hector was sorry that William Dampier had gone with them, though he himself was in no hurry to return to the Caribbean now that he had given up his hopes of finding Susanna again. The longer he stayed away, the less likely he was to run across Captain Coxon. Hector had no doubt that Coxon remained a dangerous foe and would have his revenge if he ever had the chance.

Ringrose was speaking once more, a frown replacing his normally cheerful expression. 'I say that it was Duill who betrayed our signals to the Spanish. They must have taken him prisoner and tortured him.'

Sharpe shrugged. 'There's no way of knowing. What happened at Arica is in the past. Under my command we'll make no more shore landings against well-defended targets. We stick to what we do best – taking prizes at sea, and we cruise wherever there's the best chance to do so.'

Hector found himself wondering if he and his three friends had been wise to vote for Sharpe. Life aboard *Trinity* had quickly reverted to its former easy-going ways. Dice and cards had reappeared, shipboard discipline had grown slack, the men were irritable and slovenly. Only their care for their ship and their weapons was irreproachable. The men's clothing was falling into rags and they were often short of food, but they kept the tools of their trade – their muskets and blunderbusses – clean and smeared with seal fat against the salt air. Their cutlasses, swords and daggers were regularly sharpened and oiled. Their diligence for the ship was no less impressive. They experimented endlessly with improvements to their galleon's performance by adjusting the rake of the masts or the angle of the spars, and crewmen spent hour after hour seated on deck with needles and thread, working to shape new sails under the direction of the ship's sailmaker, or using marlin spikes and fids to mend and splice and tune the rigging.

Hector felt the deck tilt slightly beneath his bare feet. The warm breeze was strengthening. Beneath an overcast sky *Trinity* was running on a course parallel to the Peruvian coast, which was no more than a faint line on the horizon. As her captain had implied, her hunting ground was the broad strip of sea along which the coasting vessels travelled back and forth between the Peruvian ports. Here, only a week ago, the buccaneers had already taken one ship with 37,000 pieces of eight in chests and bags. Equally encouraging they had captured a government advice boat on its way to Panama with despatches. Hector had translated the official letters and it appeared that the Spanish authorities believed that all the buccaneers had left the South Sea. It meant that the coastal shipping might again be venturing out from their well-defended ports.

He sauntered forward to the bows where Jacques was taking his turn as lookout.

'Has the chase made any move to get away from us?' he asked. Since first light *Trinity* had been tracking a distant sail, and the gap between the two vessels had narrowed to less than a mile. The Spaniard had proved to be a merchant vessel of medium size and, judging from her smart paintwork, a ship that was making money for her owners.

'She's still plodding along. I doubt she suspects anything yet,' replied the Frenchman. He gave one of his sardonic grins. 'Bartholomew Sharpe is a past master in fakery. If we set too much canvas, they would be suspicious.'

Hector glanced up at the spars. *Trinity* was proceeding under plain sail as if she was an ordinary merchant ship going about her business, not a predator closing in on her victim.

'How long before they realise their mistake?'

'Perhaps another hour. *Trinity* has the lines of a locally built ship. That must reassure them more than our Spanish colours.'

'You're beginning to sound like a right sailor.'

'I've grown to appreciate this roving life,' Jacques answered, rubbing his cheek where his ex-galerien brand was now barely visible beneath his deep tan. 'It's better than scrabbling for an existence in the Paris stews.'

'Then it's lucky that our dice fell that way.'

Before the vote in the general council, the four friends had been undecided whether or not to support Bartholomew Sharpe. Jacques had suggested that they leave it to chance by throwing dice. If the number was high, they would vote in Sharpe's favour, a low number and they would side with Dampier and the other malcontents. The dice had shown a six and a four.

'That wasn't luck, as Jezreel and Dan already know,' Jacques confessed.

'What are you trying to say?'

'I didn't waste my time when I was nearly left behind on shore on Juan Fernandez. Do you remember those two dice that Watling flung into the bushes, the ones he took from Sharpe?'

'Were they the dice you used?'

'Yes, I searched for them because I thought they might come in handy one day. I knew they were loaded.'

'I don't remember you gambling against Sharpe.'

Jacques treated Hector to a look which told him that in many ways he was still very naive. 'I didn't. But I watched the pattern of his play. Did you ever wonder why the game the crew is so fond of is called Passage?'

'I think you're going to tell me.'

Jacques allowed himself a crafty smile. 'That's how the English pronounce passe dix – "more than ten", its French name. The game was invented in France and there's little that I don't know about how to cheat at it.'

'So our captain is not the only one who knows all about fakery and deception,' Hector rejoined.

A movement aboard the Spanish vessel caught his eye. The crew were reducing sail in response to the strengthening of the wind. From the quarterdeck behind him came a low command. Sharpe was issuing orders.

'Do as they do, but take your time about it! The slower you are, the more ground we will gain,' he called.

No more than a dozen of *Trinity*'s crew went to obey him. The rest of the buccaneers were hidden, either crouching behind the bulwarks or waiting below deck. A glimpse of so many men would instantly warn their prey that *Trinity* was not an innocent merchant vessel.

'Lynch! Come back here to the quarterdeck,' called Sharpe. 'I'll want you to address the Spaniards when we are within speaking distance. '

Hector made his way back to the helm but his assistance was not needed. Half an hour later when the gap between the two ships was less than three hundred paces, the Spanish ship suddenly veered aside, there was the sound of a cannon shot, and a neat round hole was punched in *Trinity*'s forecourse.

'All hands now!' shouted Sharpe. There was a surge of activity as the full complement of sail handlers sprang into action. Extra sails blossomed along the yards and *Trinity* accelerated forward, showing her true pace. Within moments she was ranging up to windward, rapidly overhauling her prey. Her best marksmen took their positions, some in the rigging, the others along the rail, and they moved unhurriedly, confident in their skill. By contrast there was a panicked flurry of action on the deck of the Spanish vessel. Men were hastily clearing away loose deck clutter and erecting makeshift firing positions. It was evident that *Trinity*'s victim was utterly unused to violent confrontation.

Another bang from the chase's cannon, and again the shot was wasted. It threw up a spout of water as it plunged into the sea well short of its mark. The wind had raised a short rolling sea, making it difficult for the Spanish gun crew to aim their weapon accurately.

'Seems they have only a single cannon aboard,' commented Sharpe calmly, 'and their gunners need some practice.'

Trinity's musketeers had not yet fired a single shot, but were waiting patiently for their target to come within easy range. Samuel Gifford, the quartermaster, had warned them that they were not to waste ammunition. The ship's supply of lead for making bullets had been badly depleted by the raid on Arica.

There was a ragged scatter of firing from the Spanish ship, and a spent musket ball struck *Trinity*'s mainsail, dropped onto the deck, and rolled towards the scuppers. Jezreel reached down and picked it up. The bullet was still warm. 'Here, Jacques, you might return the compliment,' he said, tossing the bullet to his friend.

Bartholomew Sharpe was watching the gap between the two ships carefully, gauging the distance and the speed of the two vessels. 'Hold her just there,' he told the helmsman when *Trinity* was level with the Spanish ship, a hundred yards away and upwind, close enough for the buccaneers to pick their individual targets. The figure of the Spanish captain was clearly visible. He was darting back and forth among his men, obviously encouraging them to stand firm. 'You would have thought they would see sense and surrender,' Sharpe muttered to himself. Hector remembered how Sharpe had tricked Jezreel into shooting an innocent priest, and was surprised by the captain's reluctance to press home the attack. The captain, it seemed, was capable of compassion as well as savagery.

The Spanish had once again reloaded their single cannon and this time the shot struck *Trinity* amidships. Hector felt the hull quiver, but a moment later the carpenter came up on deck to report that no damage had been done. The cannonball had been too light to penetrate the heavy planking.

'Open fire! Clear their decks!' ordered Sharpe after a pause, and the musketry began. Almost immediately the figures on the deck of the Spanish ship began to fall. Their captain was among the first to be hit. He was making his way towards the entrance to his cabin at the break of the poop deck when a musket ball struck him for he suddenly pitched sideways and lay still. Seeing their commander go down, the two steersmen abandoned the helm and ducked into cover. The Spanish vessel, no longer under control, slowly began to turn up into the wind and lose speed.

'Close to fifty paces,' Sharpe told his steersman, and *Trinity* moved into even easier range for her musketeers. *Trinity* possessed the advantage in height, and her marksmen were shooting downwards on their targets now. In a short time not a single Spanish seaman was visible. They had all fled below hatches, leaving only their dead and badly wounded on the deck. Their vessel slowed to a halt, the wind spilling from her sails, the canvas flapping uselessly.

'Call on them to surrender,' Sharpe ordered Hector, handing him a speaking trumpet. 'Say we will do them no harm.'

Hector took the speaking trumpet and had to repeat his shouted instructions three or four times before a small group of sailors emerged warily from the hatches and made their way to the sheets and halyards. Minutes later they had brailed up the sails and the Spanish ship lay rolling on the swell, waiting submissively for her captors to take possession.

'The sea's too rough for us to go alongside. We risk damaging our ship,' observed Ringrose.

'Then lower the pinnace,' Sharpe told him, 'and go across with half a dozen men and see what we've caught. Take Lynch with you as interpreter.' Sharpe was looking satisfied with himself for he had not had a single one of his own men killed or injured, and the Spanish ship appeared to be a juicy prize.

As Hector helped ease the pinnace into the water, Jezreel appeared beside him, carrying his smallsword. 'I think I'll go with you in case it is a trick. The Spaniards gave up all too easily. I'm suspicious that they've merely retreated below deck and are waiting to ambush us.'

Hector murmured his thanks, and the two friends helped to row the boat across to the waiting prize. As he approached the Spanish ship, Hector looked up at its wooden side and, as always, was struck by the fact that the vessel which had seemed so low in the water from a distance, was much higher and more awkward to board when seen from close at hand. Timing his leap, Hector jumped for the rail of the ship, caught hold and swung himself aboard. Jezreel, Ringrose and three of *Trinity*'s men armed with muskets and cutlasses followed him.

The body of the dead Spanish captain was the first sight that met Hector's eyes. It lay where it had fallen, close to the break of the poop deck. The captain had dressed in a faded blue uniform jacket which was now soaked with blood. His hat had rolled off, revealing wisps of grey hair surrounding a bald patch of scalp. One hand was flung out as if still reaching out to open the door to his cabin. Standing beside the corpse was a thin-faced young man, no more than Hector's own age, and he was pale with shock. Hovering in the background half a dozen sailors were casting nervous glances at the boarding party.

'Who is in charge?' asked Hector quietly.

There was a pause before the young man answered shakily, 'I suppose I am. You killed my father.'

Hector glanced down at the corpse. The face was turned to

one side, and the profile was enough for him to see the resemblance.

'I'm very sorry. If you had not opened fire on us, this would not have happened.'

The young man said nothing.

'What is the name of your vessel?' Hector enquired as gently as possible.

'*Santo Rosario*. We sailed from Callao yesterday morning.' The young man's voice was thick with misery.

'With what cargo?'

Again the captain's son did not reply. Hector recognised the symptoms of deep distress and realised that there was little point in asking any more questions. 'There will be no more bloodshed if you and your men cooperate peacefully. We'll search the ship, and after that my captain will decide what is to be done.'

Behind him he heard Jezreel warning the other members of the boarding party to watch out for hidden surprises. Then came the sounds of the men opening up the hatches to the cargo hold.

Searching a captured ship was always a tense time. No one knew what might be found in the darkness of the hold, a desperate sailor lurking with a knife or cudgel, or someone holding a lighted match near the gunpowder store and threatening to blow up the ship unless the boarders withdrew. Ringrose kept a pistol pointing at the crew of *Santo Rosario* while he and Hector waited to learn what the ship had been carrying.

There was disappointment on the faces of the buccaneers as they re-emerged from the hatchways. 'Just some sacks of coconuts and a few bales of cloth which might be useful for sail-making,' one of them exclaimed. 'The ship's in ballast. There are several hundred ingots of lead in the bilges.'

'If it's lead, then that will make the quartermaster happy,' commented Ringrose. 'Bring up a sample so we can take a closer look.'

When the buccaneer returned, he was cradling a misshapen lump of some dull grey metal in his arms. Ringrose took out his knife and scratched the surface of the ingot. 'Not lead, more like unrefined tin,' he announced. 'Gifford will be disappointed. But at a pinch it just might do for making bullets. We'll take one of them back to *Trinity* to try it out.'

Hector turned to the young man. 'My captain will want to see the ship's papers,' he said. 'And any other documents such as bills of lading, letters, maps, charts. Also I need to speak with the pilot.'

The captain's son looked back at him with grief-stricken eyes. 'My father took charge of everything. This was his own ship, held in partnership with friends. He had sailed these waters all his life, he didn't need a pilot or charts. Everything was in his head.'

'Nevertheless I must examine the ship's papers.' said Hector.

The young man seemed to accept the inevitable. 'You'll find them in his cabin.' He turned and walked to the stern rail, where he stood, staring down into the sea, lost in his private wretchedness.

As Hector made his way towards the captain's cabin, Jezreel, who had reappeared on deck, fell in step beside him. 'There's still something not quite right here,' the big man muttered. 'If the ship was sailing empty why did they put up a fight? They had nothing worth defending. And why would such a fine ship as this one be on a purposeless voyage?'

'Perhaps the ship's papers will tell us,' answered Hector. They skirted round the body of the captain and had reached the door to his cabin. Hector attempted to open it. To his surprise the door was locked.

'That's odd,' he said. 'Jezreel, see if you can find a key in the dead man's pocket.'

Jezreel searched the corpse but found nothing. 'We'll have to break it open,' he said and, stepping back, delivered a hefty kick at the woodwork. The door shook in its frame and, just as Jezreel was about to deliver a second blow, Hector heard the sound of the lock clicking back. Suddenly he wished that he was carrying a weapon to defend himself. Fearing that whoever was inside might fire a shot through the wooden panel, he quickly edged to one side, out of the line of fire.

The door swung back, and out stepped a woman.

Hector was so surprised that his mouth fell open in astonishment. The woman was perhaps twenty years old, yet she held herself with the assurance of someone accustomed to being treated with respect, even deference. She was immaculately dressed in a long, dark green travelling mantle trimmed at the shoulders and sleeves with lines of black braid. A broad collar of fine lace emphasised her pale ivory skin. Her hair was so dark as to be almost black and had been dressed in long, loose curls, now partly covered by a light shawl. Her oval face was perfectly symmetrical with a high forehead and large, dark eyes. These now regarded Hector with defiance mingled with disdain.

'I wish to speak with whoever is in charge,' she said calmly. She spoke slowly and clearly as if addressing a dull-witted servant.

Hector stood in stunned silence, feeling foolish. He swallowed nervously and words failed him.

'I am Dona Juana de Costana, wife of the Alcalde of the Real Sala del Crimen of Paita,' she said. 'It would be wise of your captain to make arrangements for my safe return to my family with as little delay as possible. I presume that, as pirates, you are more interested in what you can steal.' She gestured towards the open doorway behind her, and said, 'Please bring out the purse, Maria.' To Hector's increasing amazement a second woman emerged from the cabin. She was of much the same age, but more plainly dressed in a long-sleeved, brown gown with a light collar of white linen. Her head of nut-brown hair was uncovered. She was clearly a companion to Dona Juana. In her hand she carried a small bag of soft leather.

Dona Juana took the bag and held it out to Hector. 'Here, you may have this,' she said with a trace of condescension in her voice. 'It will save you searching the cabin for other valuables. It contains all our jewellery.'

Hector accepted the bag and, through the soft leather, felt the irregular shapes of brooches and the smoother sensation of what he guessed were pearl necklaces. Maria, the companion, had taken up her position half a pace behind her mistress, and was regarding him with similar distaste. She had a darker complexion, lightly freckled, and Hector noticed that her hands which she clasped in front of her in a gesture of exasperation were small and very neat. Neither woman showed the least trace of fear.

He cleared his throat, still struggling to overcome his surprise, and said, 'We wish you no harm, but it is my duty to search the cabin. I need to retrieve the ship's documents.'

'Then do your duty,' said Dona Juana crisply. 'You will find that poor Captain Lopez,' and she cast a glance towards the captain's corpse, 'kept his papers in a chest under the stern window. But I would be obliged if you and your men refrained from touching any of the clothes or personal effects belonging to myself or my companion. You already have all our valuables.'

'I will respect your private possessions,' said Hector finally. 'In the meantime I am sure that my ship's navigator Mr Basil Ringrose would like to make your acquaintance.' Ringrose was standing goggle-eyed at the imperious young lady's beauty. She gave him a glance which clearly sent the young navigator reeling.

'If you'll excuse me,' said Hector and he ducked in through the low door of the cabin to begin his search. Behind him the doorway darkened and glancing back over his shoulder he saw that the companion, Maria, had followed him and was standing, arms folded, watching him. Evidently she was not taking his word that he would not touch the women's possessions. Self-consciously he began to rummage the low-ceilinged cabin. The two women were travelling in some style. A folding dressing table was covered with expensive brushes and toiletries. There was a fine silk shawl draped over a cushioned stool, and two elegant cloaks hung from pegs. A silk rug was spread on the floor of the small, ill lit cabin, and over against a bulkhead stood a large trunk, obviously containing a full wardrobe. He smelled costly perfume.

He lifted the lid of the sea chest that Dona Juana had mentioned. It contained a log book and several scrolls and parchments as well as a thin leather case with several documents inside. They were various letters and bills of lading. Looking through them rapidly, Hector saw that the *Santo Rosario* had been bound for Panama. A letter addressed to the governor from Dona Juana's husband, the Alcalde, recommended Captain Lopez to him in the most civil terms, and there were several notes of credit in favour of the captain and drawn on leading merchants. The notes were for substantial sums of money. It was clear that Captain Lopez had been a wealthy man in his own right and well known throughout the colonial trading community.

He selected the more significant of the documents and tied them together with a length of silk ribbon he picked off the dressing table. He sensed Maria's disapproval behind him. Adding the captain's journal to the bundle, he straightened up and looked around him wondering if there was anything else that he should check. It was common practice for a ship's captain to have a secret hiding place where he kept his most valuable possessions and sensitive papers. 'To save you doing any damage, you will find there's a hidden compartment behind that trunk of clothes,' Maria said. 'It's where Captain Lopez kept the crew's wages and his own money he used in trade.' Her tone was scornful.

Hector pushed the trunk aside and soon found what he was

looking for. The hiding place contained a substantial quantity of coin in bags and a collection of domestic silverware. There were salvers, jugs, silver gilt cups, and four very fine candlesticks. It was evident that Captain Lopez kept an elegant table. There was also a large folder, wrapped in a loose oilskin slip and evidently much handled. Opening it, Hector saw that he was holding a collection of sea charts. The first was a very detailed map of the approaches to Panama, showing rocks and reefs and shoals, and how to bring a ship safely into the anchorage. The remainder of the maps were much less precise. They showed the general outline of the entire South Sea coast, all the way from California to the South Cape.

Summoning one of the buccaneers to help, Hector carried the money and valuables out on deck and put them in a sack, ready to be transported across to *Trinity*. The oilskin folder he kept separately.

Sharpe had already brought his vessel close enough for a shouted conversation across the water, and when Hector explained what he had found, the captain told him to return to *Trinity*, bringing the documents, valuables and the female prisoners.

But when the young man explained these instructions to Dona Juana, he was met with a flat refusal.

'I have not the slightest intention of going aboard your ship,' she announced imperiously. 'If your captain wishes to speak with me, he can come across here.'

Hector wondered for a moment whether he should get Jezreel to pick up the woman and carry her into the cockboat, but Ringrose came to his rescue. Stepping across to the rail he bawled out to Sharpe, 'It would be easier if you would come across with a prize crew.'

To Hector's relief Sharpe agreed to this suggestion and before long the buccaneer captain was standing on the deck of the *Santo Rosario* and Hector was introducing him to the wife of the senior magistrate of the Criminal Court of Paita.

'I am most honoured to make your acquaintance,' Sharpe said, making a bow. His Spanish was slow and clumsy, and from the way he was looking at the young woman, it seemed that he was very much taken with her beauty as Ringrose had been.

'You are the leader of these people?' Juana asked. She managed to put her question as if she and Sharpe were superior to everyone else, should he prove to be in command.

Sharpe preened himself. 'Indeed I am the captain of that ship over there, señora, and at your service,' he confirmed.

'No doubt your own vessel is well appointed but it is hardly likely to offer the same quality of accommodation as this one. My companion and I have managed to make ourselves as comfortable as possible in such trying and cramped conditions. I have informed your assistant here that I have no intention of leaving the *Santo Rosario.*'

Sharpe was positively fawning. 'I would not wish you to be put to any inconvenience, señora. By all means you may stay here. I will instruct my men not to disturb you.' Hector wondered if Bartholomew Sharpe knew what a spectacle he was making of himself.

'Come, Maria, it is time we withdrew,' said Dona Juana and without another word she swept back into her cabin in a swirl of green silk, followed by her companion.

'She should fetch a choice ransom,' observed one of the buccaneers.

Sharpe rounded on him in a fury. 'Keep a civil tongue in your head,' he snapped. 'What happens to the lady will be decided by the council, and in the meantime you have work to do. For a start you can help dispose of the dead bodies, and clean this deck.'

Then Sharpe turned to Hector, who was still holding the bundle of ship's documents, and asked, 'What did you find out?'

'The vessel was bound for Panama. This folder contains a

chart for the final approach. There are also general maps for all the entire coast. Her captain was an important man, a friend of the governor there, and Dona Juana was on her way to stay with him.'

'Lucky fellow,' commented Sharpe.

'There's also a considerable quantity of cash on board, and Ringrose believes that the ship's ballast could be turned into musket bullets.' Hector would have continued but the captain was scarcely listening to him.

'We must show her that we are not barbarians,' was all Sharpe said. 'Confine the ship's officers to the forepeak, and have them give their word that they'll not make trouble, and this evening we will entertain the señora and her companion. On this ship of course. Perhaps your friend the Frenchman can prepare a special meal.'

'What about the captain's son? He's over there.' Hector nodded towards the young man still standing miserably at the stern rail.

'Put him in the forepeak with the last of them.'

'His father possessed some fine tableware; solid silver.'

'Good. We'll use that. Later we can have it broken up and divided among the men.'

*

'SHARPE SEEMS utterly smitten,' Hector commented to Jacques in the galley of the *Santo Rosario* that evening. The wind had died away and the two ships lay becalmed on a quiet sea. The Frenchman had been rowed across to the prize, bringing his preferred cooking utensils and dried herbs and a large tuna which he had been marinading in a mixture of sugar and salt. Jacques lifted the lid of a chafing dish, dipped a tasting spoon in the sauce, and said, 'Never underestimate the power of a beautiful woman. Particularly on men who have been so long at sea. Their heads can be set spinning until they are dizzy.'

Jezreel, who was listening in, was sceptical. 'I still think that there's something not quite right about this ship. Maybe her crew put up a fight because they had a brave captain and he did not want to surrender a judge's wife. But there's more to it. I watched how she twisted Sharpe around that elegant little finger of hers. Our captain rolled over on his back and wagged his tail.'

Hector had to agree with him. He was full of admiration for the resolute poise of the two women, but he sensed a hidden reason for the women's attitude, and he was puzzled what it might be. 'If I hadn't read those despatches, I'd have said that Dona Juana was deliberately delaying us because she knows that the Spaniards are assembling a squadron of warships and will soon be here to rescue her,' he said.

Jacques blew on a spoonful of broth to cool it. 'Maybe she didn't know what was in those despatches.'

'Her husband would never have allowed her to set sail if he thought that *Trinity* was still operating in the South Sea.'

'Then you have to ask yourself exactly what Dona Juana wants.' Jacques took a sip from the spoon, then added a pinch of pimento powder to the broth.

'To be allowed to stay on this ship.'

'Anything else?'

'That we weren't to interfere with their private possessions.'

'Then that's where you need to look.'

'But they have been promised that we would do no such thing,' Hector objected.

Jacques shrugged. 'Then make sure that neither they nor Sharpe get to know. Dinner is to be served in the open air, out on the quarterdeck. I suggest while the two ladies and our gallant captain are enjoying my cuisine, someone searches their cabin. Dan climbs like a goat. He can get in through the stern window, examine the cabin and get out again before they finish my dessert – it will be a syllabub of coconut, worth lingering over.'

'I have a better idea,' said Jezreel. 'There's a small hatch in the floor of the stern accommodation. I found it when we were checking the cargo hold. It's normally used by the ship's carpenter when he inspects the tiller trunking. Someone small – either Dan or Hector – should be able to get into the cabin that way.'

In the end it was decided that it would be quicker if both Dan and Hector carried out the search together, and they managed to squeeze their way into the cabin without much difficulty. There they found nothing suspicious except that the large clothing trunk was firmly locked.

'I can't imagine that the ladies feared the crew would steal their dresses,' said Dan. He felt in his pocket and produced the priming wire he used for cleaning the vent of his musket. Slipping the end of the wire into the lock, he gave a twist and a moment later was easing back the lid.

'Jacques would be proud of you. I doubt he was quicker in his time as a Paris burglar,' whispered Hector.

The trunk was stuffed with gowns, skirts, petticoats, mantuas, capes, chemises, gloves and stockings, all so tightly packed together that Hector wondered if it would ever be possible to shut the lid again. He plunged his arms into the mass of taffeta and silk and lace, and began to feel down through the layers. Two-thirds of the way through the excavation his fingers met a solid object. It felt like a large book. Carefully easing it out of the hiding place, he saw that it was another folder, very similar to the one in which Captain Lopez had kept his charts. Hector stepped across to the stern window where the light was better, and turned back the cover. He knew at once that he was holding in his hands the dead captain's private book of navigation. It was filled with his daily drawings and observations. There were diagrams of anchorages marked with their soundings, drafts of harbour approaches, dozens of coastal profiles, sketches of islands, observations of tides and currents. The folder contained a lifetime of Captain Lopez's experience as a navigator. Quickly Hector riffled through the pages. There must have been almost a hundred of them, covered with drawings and notes. Some were many years old. They were sea-stained and frayed, the ink fading, and probably drawn when Lopez first went to sea. Other pages were drafted by a different hand and appeared to have been copied from official books of sailing instructions. 'So it was not all in his head,' Hector muttered to himself as he replaced the folder, burying it deep within the scented garments. Then Dan relocked the trunk, and Hector followed the Miskito down through the little hatchway.

'That's why the captain risked our musket fire. He was trying to get to the cabin to reach the folder,' said Hector when he and Dan got back to the galley and found Jezreel running a large thumb round the salver on which Jacques had served the coconut syllabub. 'He must have known that his ship was likely to be captured and he was determined not to let his navigation notes fall into our hands. He would have dumped the folder into the sea the moment he decided to surrender.'

'But what about those other charts, the ones in the oilskin folder?'

'Those were much less detailed. They provide only the general outline of the coast. To use them properly, Lopez would be relying on his detailed navigation notes.'

'Ringrose is going to be happy. It's going to save him a lot of paper and ink. He's been scribbling away at that sort of stuff ever since we came into the South Sea,' commented Jezreel, licking his thumb.

'Ringrose has been mapping only a small portion of the coast,' Hector corrected him. 'I didn't have time to check just how far Captain Lopez's navigation notes extend, but he was exceptionally well travelled. He may have had precise sailing and pilotage directions all the way from California to the Cape.'

'Is that important?' asked Dan.

'I worked for a land surveyor in Port Royal for a few days, copying maps for him. One day when he was drunk he said to me that really good charts of the South Sea would be priceless. They would be the key to enormous riches. I remember him saying that the Spaniards would murder to prevent such information falling into the wrong hands.'

'Sounds as though they are as dangerous as they are valuable,' joined in Jezreel doubtfully. 'Captain Lopez's charts would be handy for us now, but we've been managing pretty well without them, thanks to you and Ringrose as our navigators. If Dona Juana and her companion are released back to their own people, what happens then? The Spaniards will know we have the folder, and they will redouble their efforts to hunt us down.'

'And anyone they caught would be tortured to learn just how much was known, who else had the same information, and then strangled to silence them.' Jacques added.

Hector thought for a moment before replying. 'Then we'll keep quiet about our discovery . . . At least for now.'

'What about Sharpe? Do we tell him what we've found?' Jezreel asked.

Again, Hector paused before replying. His mistrust of Sharpe made him cautious. 'No. He'll be outraged if he learns that Dona Juana has made a fool of him. We'll do what Jacques did with those dice he retrieved from the bushes. He guessed they would come in useful at some time. These maps could be the same for us when it comes to dealing with Sharpe.'

'And how do we prevent the two women from knowing that we have the charts?'

'We copy them,' said Hector firmly. 'Dan can help me. There was a time when we both drew maps and charts for a Turkish sea captain. Dan's a quick and accurate draughtsman.'

'Even so, it will take time,' Jezreel objected.

'Captain Sharpe seems in no hurry to part company with the beautiful Juana,' said Hector. 'He will be cosying up to her for the next few days. I already have a supply of paper and ink for helping Ringrose. Every time we have the chance, we remove a few sheets from the folder, copy them, and return them. I doubt that Dona Juana or Maria do more than check that the folder is still safe in their trunk. They won't have time to count the pages.'

'How long will all this take?' asked Jezreel.

'Dan and I should be able to complete the job in less than a week. We don't have to make fair copies, only quick sketches and notes. I'll keep the results safe in that bamboo tube I've been carrying so no one will even suspect what we are doing.' He looked at his friends. 'Are we all agreed?'

Dan and Jacques nodded, and Jezreel with a glance at the Frenchman added, 'Jacques, here's your chance to shine. Let's hope you can come up with seven days of dinner dishes and never repeat the same menu.'

In the end it took a full ten days to copy the contents of the folder. Hector had failed to anticipate how often he would be needed to act as interpreter for Sharpe. In his infatuation for the delectable Dona Juana, Sharpe took every excuse to visit the *Santo Rosario*, and Hector had to be on hand to untangle the buccaneer's clumsy gallantry. So it was left to Dan to burgle the cabin while Hector remained outside on deck, deliberately prolonging his captain's flowery compliments to the Alcalde's wife. By the time all the pages had been copied, the crew of *Trinity* were at breaking point with their captain's dalliance. They demanded a general council and insisted that the two women be sent on their way. Reluctantly Sharpe agreed.

'We will sail to Paita, contact Dona Juana's family and arrange an exchange,' he told the crew assembled on *Trinity*'s maindeck.

'What sort of an exchange?' someone had called out.

'The lady in return for a pilot who can guide us in these waters. In addition we'll demand a ransom to be paid in ship's supplies. We are running short of sail cloth and rope.'

'But we can take the sails and rigging from the *Santo Rosario*,' objected one of the older men.

'That is not sufficient for what I have in mind,' said Sharpe. He paused for effect, then called out, 'We need that material if *Trinity* is to make a long voyage. I am proposing that we return back to the Caribbean by sailing around the Cape!'

There was a widespread murmur of approval. Many of the crew were heartily tired of the South Sea. Sharpe looked towards where Hector was standing with his friends.

'I am appointing Lynch as our go-between. Off Paita we will intercept a local fishing boat, and put Lynch aboard so that he can go ashore. He will conduct negotiations on our behalf.'

'What am I to say?' asked Hector. Sharpe was manipulating the situation, and might even be seeking to get rid of him.

'Tell the Spaniards that once we have the pilot safely aboard and received the supplies, we will hand back the *Santo Rosario* and the lady, unharmed. We'll leave the vessel at a suitable rendezvous which we decide.'

Hector voiced his misgivings. 'Why should the Spaniards believe me? They might just execute me out of hand.'

Sharpe smiled cynically. 'The Spaniards will do anything to speed us on our way, and we still have Dona Juana.'

'And how can they be sure that Dona Juana has not been harmed?'

'Because you will go to Paita with her companion Maria. She will tell them that Dona Juana has been very well treated. Maria will serve as your security.'

Again there was a murmur of approval from the crew clustered around Hector, and before he could raise another objection, Sharpe treated him to one of his sly looks and added in a voice loud enough for all to hear, 'I was very impressed with how you dealt with the Spaniards at La Serena. I'm sure you will do just as well on this occasion.'

SIXTEEN

✳

A WEEK LATER, Hector was uncomfortably aware of how thoroughly he had been out-manoeuvred. Sharpe had disembarked him and Maria, Dona Juana's companion, onto a small fishing smack out of Paita, and already *Trinity* had dwindled to a tiny dark shape on the horizon. The galleon, which had been his home for the last fifteen months, would soon be lost from view in the gathering darkness, and Maria was taking pleasure in baiting him.

'Your new shipmates don't seem to like you,' she said mockingly. She was seated facing him on the centre thwart and had noted the surly looks of the smack's crew. They were understandably sullen. *Trinity* had robbed them of their catch of mackerel and anchovies and, to make matters worse, the wind had turned foul. It was going to be a long hard slog for them to sail back into Paita.

'One word from me when we land in Paita and the governor could have you garotted,' Maria added maliciously.

Hector said nothing. A burst of spray struck the back of his neck and he pulled his cloak around him.

'It's no more than you and your companions deserve. They are nothing but arrogant brigands of the sea. Blood-soaked murderers.'

The young woman had a low, musical voice, and the harsh words sounded strange coming from her.

'If the *Santo Rosario* had not opened fire on us, we would not have been obliged to take the vessel by force,' Hector replied.

Maria wrinkled her nose in disbelief. 'You would have pillaged the ship, and not touched us?'

'You call us brigands. So think of us as highwaymen who stop and rob travellers on the road. If the travellers are sensible they offer no resistance and are merely relieved of their valuables and allowed to go on their way. But if there is opposition, and someone fires a pistol, there is bloodshed. The travellers seldom come out best.'

'And why do you choose to make your living by such theft and piracy rather than by honest toil? You don't look or talk like a cut-throat.' Her tone was a little softer, and there was a hint of curiosity in her voice.

'There were special circumstances . . .' Hector began, and was about to explain how he came to be in the South Sea when he thought better of it and instead looked out towards the horizon. *Trinity* was no longer visible. The daylight was almost gone, and the first stars were appearing through rents in the rapidly moving clouds. It was threatening to be a wild night. The little boat was beginning to pitch and lurch on the blackness of the waves. The swirl of bilgewater beneath his feet released the smell of rotten fish. He wondered about Dan and the others.

Maria seemed to read his thoughts for suddenly she asked, 'What about your friends? There's one very big man, I think his name is Jezreel. I saw you often talking with him, and there was the Frenchman who was our cook, and a man who looked like an Indian.'

'They are my comrades, and we have come through many difficult times together.'

'Then why aren't they here with you now?'

Hector decided that the astute young woman deserved an

honest answer. 'All three of them offered to accompany me. But I told them that their presence would only increase the danger. In Paita your people might decide to hold back one or more of them as hostages until your mistress is released, and even then there was no guarantee of their safety.'

'And what about you? Aren't you afraid of being held?'

Hector shook his head. 'No, if your people want the safe return of Dona Juana, they will have to let me go. I am the only one who can arrange her exchange.'

'And what if "my people", as you describe them, decide that it would be easier to torture you?'

Hector tried to meet her eyes, but it was now too dark to see her expression. 'That is a risk I am prepared to take. If you help me and the mission goes well, it means that my friends will be able to return to their homes.'

Maria paused before answering, and Hector detected that her antipathy was waning.

'And what about you? Do you have a family who are expecting you to return?'

'No, my father died some years ago, and I have lost touch with my mother. She is the one from whom I learned to speak Spanish.'

'From Galicia, to judge by your accent. It is surprising that you do not speak Galego.'

'My mother insisted that we learn Castilian. She said it would be of more use.'

'We?'

'My sister and I. But I will never see my sister again.'

He had expected Maria to question him further, but she fell silent, doubtless understanding that he did not wish to talk about his loss.

When she did speak again, it was in a much more friendly tone, almost confiding. 'I understand your feeling of being alone. But not because I have lost my parents. They are still alive as far as I know, small farmers in Andalucia. Life is hard in that part of Spain, and they were enthusiastic when the opportunity came for me to go abroad as Dona Juana's companion. So I was happy to accede to their wishes.'

'And you like the post?'

There was a short pause before Maria replied. 'Yes. I am fortunate. Dona Juana is a kind employer. She treats me as a friend, not as a servant which is what I could be.'

'But you still miss your family?'

'Spain seems so far away. Sometimes I think I will never see my homeland again.'

For a long time they both sat quietly, hearing the run of water along the sides of the little fishing boat as it grew more urgent, and the rising note of the wind in the rigging.

'Tell me about Dona Juana's husband, the Alcalde,' Hector said.

'He's older than her. Perhaps by twenty years, and he has the reputation of being a harsh man. He believes in the stern application of the law.'

'Would he put the law ahead of the well-being of his wife?'

Maria thought for a moment before replying. 'I believe so, but it is always hard to tell with him. He is a man of very strict principle.'

The moan of the wind and the noise of the waves were making their conversation difficult. Occasionally the little boat thrust her bow into the waves, and water came sluicing onboard. Hector had noticed a small cuddy under the foredeck where the fishermen stowed their nets, and he suggested to Maria that she might take shelter there. She stood up from the thwart, reached out to steady herself as the boat lurched, and placed her hand on his shoulder. He was aware of her grip, light but firm, a woman's touch. Then she was clambering past him, her hip brushed his shoulder, and all of a sudden he was swept by the knowledge that she was very attractive. He found himself wishing that she had stayed much closer to him, where he could relish her nearness and learn more about her.

※

NEXT MORNING the last of the gale was still whipping up a lively sea, the waves sending tremors through the hull planking of the little boat as she battled her way towards the watch-tower at the entrance to Paita's harbour. Hector sat on a pile of damp sacking and rope, his back pressed against the mast step. He was bleary-eyed, for he had slept only fitfully, his mind returning again and again to thoughts of the young woman curled up in the dark cave of the cuddy. He rehearsed every word of their conversation, still wondering how Maria had seemed to be able to read his thoughts. From time to time he glanced towards the place where she lay asleep, and waited for her to awake. When Maria did emerge half an hour later and crawled out from the cuddy, Hector had a glimpse of a neat ankle and a small bare foot. Sensibly she had removed her shoes before going to sleep. Maria stood up and turned her face into the wind and her long, loose hair streamed out behind her. In that moment Hector was confronted by a young woman very different from the person he had known aboard the *Santo Rosario*. In the shadow of her mistress Maria had been quietly dutiful and unassuming, easily overlooked, and probably this had been her intention. Now he saw that Maria had the gift of a natural, healthy beauty. As she closed her eyes and took a deep breath, relishing the fresh morning breeze after the stuffy confines of the cuddy, Hector noted the small heart-shaped face with a short straight nose, a soft mouth perhaps a trifle too wide for the delicacy of her features, a skin lightly freckled. Every-thing about Maria was neat and pleasing in a way that was simple and tempting. Then she turned and looked at him and the dark brown eyes under the perfectly arched eyebrows held an almost conspiratorial expression.

'Did you manage to get any rest?' he asked, aware that he felt light-headed, off balance.

She nodded, and all of a sudden Hector was overwhelmed by her presence. She was wearing the fine cloak which he had seen hanging in her cabin, but now it was bedraggled and crumpled, the hem sodden with bilgewater. Awkwardly he started to get to his feet, hoping to find an excuse to extend a hand, to touch her again and help her to climb over the thwart, when, without warning, he was rudely elbowed aside. One of the fishermen pushed passed him. The man was holding a chunk of dry bread and an earthenware flagon of water which he held out to Maria. He offered nothing to Hector. Instead he turned to face towards the land, placed two fingers into his mouth and let out a piercing whistle. In response a watchman appeared on the top of the watchtower. The fisherman waved, making what must have been an agreed code of signals, for the watchman disappeared, and soon a squad of soldiers was running to take position by a gun platform, and a horseman was galloping inland clearly carrying a message to the town.

'What was all that about?' Hector enquired.

The fisherman gave him a black look. 'Ever since you and your rabble attacked Arica we've been asked to keep a special lookout. Told to report any sightings of unknown vessels and report back immediately. Never thought I would be bringing in one of the scum who was responsible. I'll enjoy watching your punishment. I lost a younger brother at Arica.'

The motion of the boat eased as the fishing smack passed into the shelter of the headland protecting Paita's anchorage, and soon the fishermen were changing course to lay their vessel alongside the jetty where a file of Spanish soldiers already stood waiting. Their grey-haired sergeant wore on his tunic the faded red saltire which marked him as a veteran of the European wars.

'Here's one of the pirates! And you're welcome to him,'

called out the fisherman. The boat bumped against the landing place, Hector lost his balance, and he was pushed hard in the back so that he sprawled forward ignominiously onto the weed-covered stone steps. A hand seized him by the collar of his cloak, and he was hauled upright roughly.

'Treat him gently. He's an envoy, not a prisoner!' Maria said sharply. She was being helped out of the boat by one of the fishermen and was glaring angrily at the sergeant. He looked back at her in disbelief. 'He's come here to speak with the Alcalde,' she snapped. 'Escort us to his office at once.'

The sergeant's expression of disgust made his feelings clear as he ordered his men to form up on either side of Hector and march with him into the town. Maria kept pace, walking beside the little group as it made its way past the customs house and harbour offices and the warehouses where the merchants of Paita stored their goods. Looking about him, Hector saw that the town exceeded Arica for prosperity. Besides the usual piles of fishing gear, there were stacks of timber for boatbuilding, ranks of wine barrels awaiting shipment, huge jars which he guessed contained olives for export, and in open-sided sheds he glimpsed wooden crates and bales painted with strange markings. Maria noted his interest and remarked, 'Those have come from China. They arrive in Acapulco with the Manila galleon, and are on their way farther south to customers in Peru. The consulado of Paita arranges the distribution.' She saw his puzzlement and explained, 'The consulado is the guild of merchants. They have the money and the influence if a ransom is demanded for Dona Juana.' But Hector was not thinking of a ransom. Maria's comment had reminded him of the maps and sailing directions he had been copying from Captain Lopez's navigation notes. If the captain had been trading as far north as Mexico to meet the incoming Manila galleon, his knowledge of the northern shores was likely to be very accurate.

By now word had spread that the fishermen were bringing in a pirate. As the little group walked farther into Paita, more and more people appeared on the streets, and they were in an ugly mood. Women as well as men began to shout insults and make threatening gestures. There were cries of 'Hang him but disembowel him first!', 'Hand him over to us. Let us deal with him', and soon the onlookers were throwing lumps of dung and dirt and the occasional stone. Their aim was poor and, as often as not, the missiles hit the escorting soldiers. But occasionally Hector had to duck. He was shocked by the hostility of the crowd. Their hatred was like a physical force.

To her credit, Maria did not falter. She walked beside him, level with the crowd, and did not flinch when she too was hit by mis-thrown projectiles.

Eventually they arrived at the Plaza Mayor. Here a number of sentries were guarding the municipal buildings which stood across from the church, and they joined the escort guards in holding back the angry crowd. Hector, Maria and the sergeant hurried up a flight of steps and into the town hall, the angry jeers of the mob following them. After the gauntlet of their arrival it was a relief to be away from the hysteria of the crowd, waiting in an antechamber while a minor official went to find Dona Juana's husband. He returned to say that the judge was at a meeting with the cabildo, the city council, and could not be disturbed. But the Alcalde was expected to preside over a session of the Criminal Court later that day, and it might be possible for him to interview Hector while the Court was in recess. In the meantime, the official suggested, Maria should go to her lodgings at the Alcalde's house where she might like to rest. The official himself would take responsibility for looking after Hector until the judge was free to speak with him.

The moment that Maria was gone, the sergeant seized Hector roughly by the shoulder and bundled him along a corridor and down a short flight of steps. The official, who had been scurrying along behind making approving noises, produced a key to a heavy iron-bound door, unlocked it, and Hector was flung inside. He found himself in a small stone cell furnished with nothing but mouldy straw and a bench. The only light came through a small window, little more than a slit, high in the opposite wall. Behind him the door slammed shut, and he was left in half-darkness.

He made his way to the bench and sat down, gagging at the stench of urine from the damp straw. Evidently he had been confined in the holding cell for the Criminal Court, and he doubted that anyone would take the trouble to bring him anything to eat or drink. The malice and loathing shown towards him was so intense and venomous that he wondered if Bartholomew Sharpe had made a miscalculation. There would be no exchange of Dona Juana and the *Santo Rosario* because the Alcalde would never negotiate. Instead Hector would be taken out of the cell, tried and executed for piracy. If the mob did not get to him first.

＊

HIS INTERVIEW with Dona Juana's husband in mid afternoon got off to a disastrous start. He was led to what appeared to be a private chamber behind the courtroom. There the Alcalde sat waiting behind a massive desk. Clearly he had interrupted his court session for he was wearing his red and gold sash of office over a doublet of charcoal velvet. Hector, dishevelled and unwashed, was made to stand before him while the sergeant who had brought him up from the cell stood so close behind his right shoulder that Hector could hear his breathing. For several moments the Alcalde sat scowling at his visitor and not saying a word. Dona Juana's husband was a hulking, heavy-set man who affected an old-fashioned appearance. His beard was carefully shaped to join thick dark mustaches extending across his cheeks in a downsweep that accentuated the fleshy, peevish mouth and bushy, scowling eyebrows. Hector wondered if such an intimidating appearance was genuine or merely an artificial pose to frighten those who appeared in court before him. But the Alcalde's opening remark left little doubt that his bad temper was real.

'Who do you represent?' he asked rudely. 'Your last captain's head was paraded around Arica on a pole.' Hector supposed that he was referring to Watling whose body they'd had to leave behind.

'I am here on behalf of Captain Bartholomew Sharpe and his company,' Hector began. 'I have been sent to arrange terms for the release of the *Santo Rosario* and Dona Juana who is, I believe, your wife.'

Immediately the Alcalde bridled. 'The identity of the passengers is of no immediate concern. What is evident is that you are guilty of piracy in seizing the vessel.'

'With respect, your excellency. I have come here in good faith to arrange the return of the vessel, her passengers and crew, unharmed.'

'Unharmed!' The Alcalde thrust his head forward angrily. 'I am told that Captain Lopez was shot down, killed in cold blood.'

'He mistook our vessel's approach as aggressive,' said Hector. Maria must have already been interviewed.

'He was callously murdered, and the crime will be punished,' the Alcalde retorted.

'If it pleases your honour,' Hector said carefully, 'I should like to state the message that I was charged to deliver.'

'Then do so!' The Alcalde leaned back in his chair and began to drum thick stubby fingers on the desk.

'Captain Sharpe is willing to deliver up the *Santo Rosario*, her illustrious passenger and crew in exchange for the services of a pilot competent to navigate his vessel southward, and a store of seagoing supplies.'

Hector paused, allowing the Alcalde a moment in which to appreciate that he was being offered a way of ridding himself of the pirate menace.

'If His Excellency agrees to these terms, I have been instructed to guide the pilot to the place where the exchange will take place. Captain Sharpe gives his word that the lady, Dona Juana, will be released unharmed. Afterwards he and his vessel will depart the South Sea.'

The Alcalde looked at Hector with pure scorn. 'What happens to your bandit comrades is not for me to decide. Were that so, I would see to it that Captain Sharpe and all his crew hang from the mastheads of our Armada del Sur. Unfortunately there has to be a due process.' He looked towards the sergeant. 'Take him away, and keep him locked up until further notice.'

The sergeant grasped Hector by the arm and was about to wheel him about. There was just enough time for the young man to add, 'With respect, Your Excellency. Captain Sharpe instructed me to say that if I do not return within a week, he will steer south, without a pilot, and take Señora Juana with him.'

The Alcalde slammed his hand down on the desk. 'Not another word!' he barked.

*

BACK IN his cell, Hector watched the daylight fade through the small window in the wall, and thought of how much he depended on Maria. Only her evidence would persuade the Alcalde and his fellow officials that Dona Juana had not been harmed. Also, they were sure to question her about everything she had seen while a prisoner. They would want to know about *Trinity*, her condition and armament, the morale and number of her crew, and whether Bartholomew Sharpe was capable of carrying out his threat and sailing off if his seven-day deadline was not met, and if he could be trusted to honour an exchange. For a second time in twenty-four hours Hector found himself reassessing Maria's qualities. On the fishing boat she had shown herself to be thoughtful and level-headed, and in the presence of the angry crowd she had kept cool. He told himself that she would not allow herself to be browbeaten by the Alcalde into giving false evidence or understating her case. And knowing her affection for Dona Juana, he was sure that Maria would do everything in her power to convince the Alcalde that he should agree to an exchange.

With that reassuring thought Hector stretched himself out on the narrow bench and closed his eyes. The image that once again floated into his mind just before he fell asleep was of Maria on the fishing boat earlier that morning as she stood up and faced into the wind. She had looked so composed and at ease. He allowed himself a moment's optimism which had nothing to do with his mission to the Alcalde: he speculated that perhaps Maria had been pleased to be starting the day in his company.

A voice speaking English woke him. For a moment he thought he was back on *Trinity*. Then the rancid smell of mouldering straw rather than Stockholm tar reminded him that he was in a cell. 'Well, Lynch, haven't seen you since Arica,' said the voice again. Hector swung his legs off the bench and sat up, conscious that he was very hungry, also that he was sore and stiff from sleeping on the hard surface of the bench.

The door to the cell stood open. Leaning against the jamb was a figure that stirred a hazy, vaguely disagreeable memory. Even seen against the light it was evident that the man in the doorway was well turned out. He was dressed in knee breeches and good stockings and a well-tailored dark blue vest with gilt buttons over a fresh white shirt. He wore expensive-looking buckled shoes and had tied his hair back in a neat queue. Everything about him spoke of prosperity and the contentment of a man of means. It took Hector, still slightly groggy, a moment to identify his visitor. He was one of *Trinity*'s surgeons whom he had last seen blind drunk in the squalor of the desecrated church in Arica. Then the man had scarcely been able to stand, his speech slurred with alcohol, and he had been wearing soiled and sea-stained rags. Now it was as if he had just emerged freshly washed and shaved from a barber shop, ready to take a stroll through a fashionable part of town.

The surgeon's name, Hector now remembered, was James Fawcett.

'I hear that conniving swindler Sharpe is back in command, and that he intends to run for home with his tail between his legs. But I doubt he'll make it with his skin intact,' Fawcett observed. His tone was casual, almost smug.

Hector's mind was in a whirl. He looked searchingly at his visitor. Fawcett was in his late thirties, a lantern-jawed raw-boned man whom Hector remembered from as far back as Golden Island when Fawcett had gone ashore with Cook's company. On the march through the jungle Fawcett had struck up a friendship with Hector's own mentor, Basil Smeeton. The two had often compared medical notes and talked together of the new techniques in surgery. When Smeeton turned back after the disappointment of Santa Maria and its phantom gold mine, Fawcett had borrowed some scalpels from Smeeton and had continued on with the expedition. Later Hector had seen him firing a musket against the Spanish flotilla in the sea battle before Panama. So it was all the more extraordinary that Fawcett should now be loafing about a Spanish courthouse looking like a respectable member of Paita's professional community. It would have been more understandable if he had been half-naked, shackled in chains and awaiting the garotte.

'Don't look so surprised, Lynch. The last time we met I seem to remember telling you that people like ourselves are too valuable to be slaughtered uselessly.'

Hector swallowed. His throat was dry. 'Could you ask someone to bring me some water to drink, and perhaps a little food. I haven't eaten for the past thirty-six hours,' he said.

'Of course.' Fawcett spoke over his shoulder to someone in the corridor behind him. His Spanish was slow but accurate. Then he turned back to face the young man.

'There's no need for you to continue to be cooped up in this disgusting hole. The Alcalde can arrange for you to be transferred to more comfortable accommodation. I've persuaded him that you are halfway to having a full medical qualification. Smeeton always said that you showed great promise, and there's such a shortage of surgeons here that you'll be able to set up your own practice almost anywhere in Peru even without formal credentials.'

Hector was scarcely listening, his attention distracted by his recollection of what had happened in the church at Arica, the charnel house of the makeshift hospital, the wounded men lying groaning on the flagstones of the church floor.

'What about the other surgeon? The other man who was meant to be taking care of the wounded? What's happened to him?'

Fawcett gave a wolfish smile. 'Same as me. He's got a very lucrative medical practice. Not here in Paita but farther along the coast in Callao. Doing very well I'm told. Even found himself a wife, the handsome widow of a peninsular as they call those who were born in Spain. I doubt that he'll ever go back to life at sea.'

'What about the others? The wounded men in the church in Arica? What happened to them?'

Fawcett gave a casual shrug. 'The Spaniards knocked them all on the head. Saved a lot of trouble. Not many of them would have survived their wounds, and those who did would have been tried and executed.'

Hector felt sick to the stomach. Fawcett appeared utterly indifferent to the massacre of the wounded.

'The Alcalde said something about Watling's head being carried around the town on a pole.'

'The worthy citizens of Arica made a real fiesta of the affair. Dancing in the streets, bonfires, self-congratulatory letters to the Viceroy and the Court in Madrid saying how they had vanquished the pirates. Of course they exaggerated the number of the attacking force. Said it was four times more numerous than it really was.'

The mention of bonfires had jogged Hector's memory. 'After we evacuated Arica, the Spaniards sent up two columns of white smoke, the agreed signal to our boats. We thought someone, maybe the quartermaster Duill, was tortured to reveal the signal. It nearly brought our boats into harbour and they would have been annihilated. What really happened?'

There was a slight hesitation before Fawcett replied, and Hector noted that the surgeon did not look at him directly as he gave his answer. 'I don't know how the Spaniards obtained the signal. I have no idea of Duill's fate. I didn't even see his corpse. He simply disappeared.'

At that moment a court usher appeared, carrying a large pitcher of water and some bread, dried fish and olives. Hector gratefully drank, then leaned forward and poured the rest of the flagon over his head, neck and shoulders. He felt better, though he wished he could find a water trough and wash himself properly. He sat up, stared at Fawcett and waited for him to broach the subject which, Hector had already guessed, was the real reason for his visit.

'Lynch, don't be in a hurry to judge me harshly. I came to the South Sea to get rich, to have my share of the wealth of this land. I have not altered that ambition. Instead I've decided to earn it honestly rather than take it at pistol point. I'm using my skills as a healer. I look after people who are ill with fever or have sickly children or need assistance in childbirth. Surely that's something to approve of?'

'So you are proposing that I do the same?'

'Why not? You could settle down here and have a very pleasant life. You speak the language fluently, and in a year or so you too could find a wife and maybe go on to raise a family in ease and comfort.'

For a moment the thought of Maria flashed into Hector's

mind, but he put it to one side. 'And to do this I have to betray Sharpe and the company?' He did not add that he thought this was what Fawcett had done at Arica.

'You owe Sharpe nothing. He would do the same in your position. He always looks after himself, first and last.'

'And the rest of the men on *Trinity*, what about them?'

'I realise you have friends on board. The striker Dan, and Jacques the Frenchman and big Jezreel. It's quite possible that Don Fernando, the Alcalde, will agree to their freedom in exchange for your cooperation.'

'My cooperation in what . . .' Hector prompted him.

'. . . in arranging some sort of ambush where *Trinity* might be lured into a trap and overwhelmed by Spanish cruisers.'

Hector stared down at the floor. Already he had made up his mind. It was the mention of Jezreel which had decided the matter for him. He recalled the day that Sharpe had tricked Jezreel into pistolling the innocent Spanish priest. Spanish prisoners had been exchanged or released from *Trinity* since then, and they would have carried the story of the atrocity back to the authorities. If Jezreel ever appeared before a Spanish tribunal, he would certainly be condemned to a painful death, even if Hector had pleaded on his behalf.

The young man raised his head and looked back at Fawcett still standing in the doorway. 'I prefer to carry out my mission,' he said quietly.

Fawcett looked unsurprised. 'I thought you would say that,' he said. 'I once said to Smeeton that you had the manner of someone who always took his own line even if it meant being out of step with everyone else. I'll tell Don Fernando of your decision. It's up to him and the council to decide what is to be done with you. And I'll ask the guards here to let you have a proper wash. You're beginning to get that prison stink.'

*

THE VETERAN sergeant and two soldiers came to fetch Hector in mid afternoon. Fawcett had kept his word for they took Hector out to a pump at the rear of the courthouse and stood by while he washed himself. Feeling cleaner but still very dishevelled, he was then brought into the same interview room as before. This time the Alcalde, Don Fernando, was not alone. An extra table had been set at right angles to his desk. Seated behind it was a thin-faced man with heavily lidded eyes and an austerely intellectual appearance emphasised by his high forehead and receding hairline. He wore a lawyer's black robes. A few sheets of blank paper and a pen lay on the table before him. Hector, looking around, saw no sign of any secretary or official clerk and this gave him a moment's hope. Whatever was going to be decided at this meeting was to be known to only a few. Even the sergeant and his escort had been told to leave the room.

One other man was present, someone whose weatherbeaten features Hector recognised at once. Seated beside the lawyer was Captain Francisco de Peralta whom he had last seen on the beach at La Serena.

'I believe you already know the Capitan del Navio. He is attending in an expert capacity,' began the Alcalde. His eyes flicked towards the black-robed lawyer. 'Don Ramiro is His Majesty's fiscal. As an attorney, he is here to represent the audiencia, the council.'

The man in the lawyer's robes acknowledged his introduction with the briefest of nods.

Already Hector had detected a subtle change in the Alcalde's manner. Don Fernando was not as openly aggressive as before. His hostility was still there, seething below the surface, but it was being kept in check.

The Alcalde addressed his opening remarks to the fiscal. 'This young man has brought a proposal from the leader of a pirate band operating in this area. You will already be familiar with some of the atrocities they have committed. Recently they captured the merchant ship *Santo Rosario*. The leader of the pirates offers to return the vessel, her passengers and surviving crew in exchange for naval stores and the services of a pilot who can assist the pirates in leaving our waters.'

The Alcalde lifted a sheet of parchment from the desk in front of him. 'This is a deposition made by a passenger on the *Santo Rosario*. It describes an unprovoked attack on the vessel, the butchery of her captain, and the capture and pillaging of the ship. It also states that the survivors of the assault are unhurt.'

'Can we be sure of the accuracy of the deposition?' asked the fiscal.

'I have arranged for the deponent to be available for questioning.' Raising his voice, the Alcalde called, 'Send in Dona Juana's companion.'

The door opened, and Maria stepped into the room. In that moment Hector's eager anticipation of seeing her again turned to disappointment. Maria had reverted to the person he remembered from the *Santo Rosario*. She was wearing a long, plain brown skirt with a matching bodice, and her hair was covered with a simple cotton kerchief. She was deferential and subdued, and she did not even look in his direction. Her face showed no expression as she walked forward and stopped a few paces in front of the Alcalde. The anticlimax was so great that Hector felt as if a chasm had suddenly opened beneath his feet and he had dropped into it.

'Señorita Maria,' the Alcalde began, 'Don Ramiro is an attorney for the audiencia. He wishes to question you about your statement concerning the seizure of the *Santo Rosario*.' He handed the sheet of paper across to the lawyer who took it and began to read aloud. Occasionally he looked up at Maria to make sure that she was paying attention.

Maria listened with her eyes fixed on the floor and her hands demurely clasped in front of her. Hector recalled that this was exactly how she had stood and looked when he saw her on the day he had gone onto the *Santo Rosario* with the boarding party. He even recollected how he had noticed on that day how small and neat her hands were. With a pang, he also remembered exactly how it had felt when she placed her hand on his shoulder and steadied herself as she climbed across the thwart of the little fishing boat.

The attorney continued with his dry, punctilious reading, pausing between the sentences. Despite his inner turmoil, Hector had to admire Maria's memory for detail and the accuracy of her testimony. She described *Trinity*'s slow, innocent-seeming approach in the wake of *Santo Rosario*, and the moment that Captain Lopez had become suspicious. She made no mention of the death of Lopez because, by the time he was shot, she and her mistress had been sent away to the safety of the locked cabin. Her description resumed at the point that she had heard the boarding party attempting to open the door of the cabin and she and Dona Juana had stepped out to confront Hector, Ringrose and the others.

The fiscal reached the end of his narration and looked up at Maria. 'You provided this deposition?' he asked.

'I did,' Maria answered. Her voice so low as to be barely audible.

'Is it accurate?'

'Yes.'

'And no violence was shown to your mistress or yourself, then or at any other time?'

'No.'

'Nothing was stolen or pillaged from you?'

'Dona Juana handed her jewellery and other valuables to the pirates before they made any demands. She wished to forestall any excuse for violence.'

'And that was all that was taken from you and your mistress during this piracy?'

'That is correct.'

The attorney placed the deposition on the table, picked up his pen, and made a note at the foot of the page.

'Señorita,' he said. 'You have heard your statement read out to this gathering and agreed to its authenticity. I would be grateful if you would sign it.'

Maria crossed to the table and, taking the pen held out to her by the fiscal, she signed the deposition. The lawyer set the document neatly on top of the other sheets of paper before him, squaring up the pile with his fingertips. There was something about that little gesture, its air of finality, that alerted Hector. It appeared that the attorney had made up his mind about something significant.

'I have no further questions,' said the lawyer.

'Maria, you may now leave,' said the Alcalde, his voice formal.

Hector watched the young woman walk to the door, and he tried to memorise the moment for he had a premonition that he might never see Maria again. Until she passed from view, he still hoped that Maria might perhaps glance in his direction. But she left the room without a backward glance.

'Capitan, do you have any observations to make?' The Alcalde's truculent voice broke into Hector's thoughts. The judge was looking towards Peralta.

The Spanish captain leaned back in his chair and surveyed Hector for several seconds before he spoke.

'Young man, when we met on the beach at La Serena I gave you a warning. I said that you and your piratical band would not be so lucky next time they came ashore. The events at Arica proved me correct. Only one thing drives your people – insatiable greed. Can you give me any reason why they can be trusted to honour any agreement we might make?'

'Captain Peralta,' Hector answered, standing a little straighter. 'I can give no guarantee. The decisions of our company are made by general vote. But I can say this – and with your seagoing experience you will know that I speak the truth – we have been in the South Sea now for well over a year. Many of the men are looking forward to returning to their homes. I believe that they are in a majority.'

'And what about Dona Juana? We have been told that she is unharmed and that she cooperated in the matter of handing over her valuables. If we agree to the exchange, we expect her to continue to be treated with the respect due to a lady of her quality.'

'Captain Sharpe has already made her welfare a priority,' Hector assured him.

Peralta looked towards the Alcalde, and Hector had the feeling that an unspoken message had passed between them when Peralta continued.

'Your Excellency, I recommend that we agree to an exchange but make sure of Dona Juana's well-being.'

'How can that be done?'

'Send this young man back to his ship. Let him take the pilot with him. That will be the first part of our bargain. The second part will be honoured only after the pirates have brought the *Santo Rosario* within range of our shore cannon. We will send out an inspection party and if they find the lady onboard and unharmed, we will despatch a supply boat with the stores they require.'

'Isn't that taking a risk? Surely the pirates will sail away the moment they have a pilot, and not wait for the stores.'

'Speaking as a seaman, I would say that the intruders' vessel needs a thorough refit. The ship has been operating in hostile waters for so long that her rig will be worn out. There will be an acute shortage of rope and canvas. If her crew are contemplating a voyage out of the South Sea, those stores could mean the difference between foundering and survival.'

'Thank you for your contribution, Capitan,' said the Alcalde, and once again Hector had the feeling that something was left unsaid. 'I would be obliged if you could select a suitable pilot and also draw up a list of appropriate ship's stores. Enough to encourage the pirates to leave our waters, but no more. If the fiscal has no objection, I will make an order for the material to be released from the royal dockyard without delay. I wish to be rid of these bandits, and I am sure that Dona Juana does not want to spend a moment longer in their company.'

＊

THE PILOT provided by Captain Peralta turned out to be a small, wiry man whose expression of distaste on meeting Hector made his feelings obvious.

'I hope your ship handles well in bad weather?' he grumbled as he stepped aboard the fishing boat waiting at the quay. It was the same vessel that had brought Hector and Maria ashore.

'*Trinity*'s crew know their business,' Hector replied. He had been half-hoping that Maria would be sent to rejoin her mistress. But the pilot had arrived alone.

'They'll need to,' retorted the little man waspishly. 'Where we're going the weather turns nasty very quickly.'

'You must be very familiar with that part of the coast,' said Hector, anxious to please.

'Enough to know that I wouldn't chose to go there if I had a choice in the matter.'

'I imagine the Alcalde can be persuasive.'

'Someone tipped him off that my last ship had a slimy waterline when we came into harbour.'

'What's a slimy waterline got to do with it?'

'It meant that she was riding higher than when we left our last official port of call. I was accused of stopping on the way to Paita and offloading cargo without paying import duty.'

'And had you?'

The pilot shot Hector a venomous glance. 'What do you think? The captain and the owner were both peninsulares, good Spaniards, so no one is ever going to charge them with smuggling, nor accuse the local consulado who sell on the contraband. On the other hand I am a foreigner. So I am disposable.'

'I thought I detected a foreign accent,' said Hector.

'I'm originally from Greece. In the merchant service hereabouts you'll find Portuguese, Corsicans, Genoese, Venetians, men from all over. Local-born lads prefer to stay ashore and run plantations with Indian labourers. It's an easier life than tramping up and down the coast in merchant tubs.'

'But at least everyone respects a pilot.'

The Greek gave a cynical laugh. 'I'm only half a pilot. The Alcalde and his sort fear that we'll gang up and run for home and take our knowledge with us. So the rules say that I can never serve aboard a ship whose captain is also a foreigner.'

'But now you'll be aboard *Trinity* and that's a foreign ship.'

'Even then my knowledge won't be of much use. I only know the coast south of here, and most of that is a barren, godforsaken land. That's about as much as this addled head can hold at any one time.' The Greek smiled sourly and tapped his brow.

'So you don't have any charts?'

The Greek bared his teeth at Hector in astonishment. 'Charts! If the Alcalde got to learn that I was making charts, or even possessed one, I would prefer to take my punishment as a smuggler. No one except a handful of the most trusted captains are allowed to keep a derotero and they must be Spaniards, like Captain Lopez of the *Santo Rosario*, God rest his soul.'

His remark reminded Hector of the glance that had passed between the Alcalde and Captain Peralta. It dawned on him now that the real reason why they had agreed to an exchange was the need to recover Captain Lopez's folder of navigation notes and sketches. All their talk about Dona Juana's well-being had been a sham. They had insisted that she was treated with respect because then no one would search her belongings and find the derotero.

Hector groaned inwardly. If he had not been so distracted by Maria, he would have worked this out for himself. Then an even more dispiriting thought occurred: the only person who could have told the Alcalde about the hidden derotero was Maria.

Looking back towards Paita's church tower, Hector cursed himself for being a fool. He had allowed himself to be misled. But what made his chagrin even more painful was that he still could not stop thinking about Maria.

SEVENTEEN

'YOU WEREN'T exactly honest with her either,' Dan bluntly pointed out when Hector told him of Maria's deception. 'Neither she nor Dona Juana know that we've made a copy of the derotero. That was done behind their backs.'

It was a breezy afternoon with a scattering of high cloud and *Trinity* was beating out to sea under plain sail. Hector had come back aboard three days earlier and, as arranged with the Alcalde, Dona Juana and the *Santo Rosario* had been left behind at Paita in exchange for the stores from Paita's royal dockyard. The supply of rope, canvas, tallow and tar meant that *Trinity* could be made fit for a long voyage, and as none of the crew relished the prospect of sailing back to Panama and returning through the jungle to the Caribbean, it had been decided to leave the Pacific by sailing south, all the way around the tip of South America.

'Do you think our pilot knows what he's doing? He seems more interested in gambling than in making sure we are heading the right way,' asked Dan dubiously. He was watching the Greek, whose name was Sidias. After telling the helmsman his course, he had produced a tavil board and started a game of backgammon against the quartermaster. Now they were quarrelling as to how the game should be played. Sidias was insisting that they follow the Greek rules, as they were more ancient.

'No harm in following his advice, at least for now,' Hector assured the Miskito. 'He says there's a strong adverse current along the coast and we need to be at least a hundred miles offshore before we turn south. Sidias claims that, by staying well out to sea, we'll trim weeks off our passage.'

'Is he proposing to take us through the Passage or around the Cape?'

'He hasn't said,' Hector answered.

'Not much use as a pilot then,' sniffed Jacques who had walked over to join them. He lowered his voice. 'Will those navigation notes you copied be of any use when we are trying to find the Passage?'

'I can't be sure. We've never put any of them to the test.'

'If Captain Lopez's navigation notes were so precious, I don't understand why Dona Juana did not simply get rid of them overboard. She could have dropped the folder out of the stern window at any time,' said Dan.

'You don't know how those aristocratic women think,' Jacques told him. 'Dona Juana might have known the value of the folder and wanted to make sure it got back into Spanish hands. But more likely she took a delight in believing that she was making fools of a group of slow-witted mariners. It was a game for her, to demonstrate her superiority.'

He fell silent as someone behind them coughed. It was Basil Ringrose who had just appeared on deck, carrying a backstaff and notebook. He looked ill, his skin waxy and pale, eyes bloodshot, and he had difficulty in breathing. Many of the crew believed that he was still suffering from taking shelter under a manzanilla tree on a night he had spent ashore. There had been a shower of rain in the night and he had woken up with his skin covered in red spots from the poisonous drips which had sprinkled on him while he slept. The spots and their burning sensation had long since faded, but Ringrose remained sickly. He suffered from frequent headaches and bouts of near-blindness.

Ringrose reached out and grasped a weather shroud for support as another fit of violent coughing racked him.

Dan spoke up. 'I was just asking Hector if we would be better going around the Cape or through the Passage.'

'The Passage would be my choice,' Ringrose answered huskily. 'Provided we can find the entrance. The coast is likely to be scattered with islands and reefs. We could finish up smashed to pieces.'

'Then why not try for the Cape?'

'Because no English vessel has ever gone that way. That's something our captain failed to mention when he suggested we should sail our way out of the South Sea. The Spaniards and the Dutch have gone round the Cape, but no other nation as far as is known. Even Drake himself preferred the Passage. There are ice islands down there.' He hawked, turned his head and spat a gob of phlegm over the rail. 'Anyway, that's a much longer way. I doubt we'd be back in home waters before Christmas. And who knows what sort of reception we will receive.'

'Couldn't be worse than what the Spaniards will do to us if we stay around here,' said Jacques.

Ringrose treated him to a sardonic smile. 'You forget that we are the rump of an irregular expedition. Captain Sharpe and his friends left Jamaica without so much as by-your-leave to the governor. Not one of our leaders carried a commission to go raiding the Main. That makes us all pirates, if the authorities choose to think so.'

'But Sir Henry Morgan never obtained prior permission when he attacked Panama, and he finished up with a knighthood,' Hector objected.

'He brought back so much plunder that he was too wealthy to be prosecuted. By contrast, what have we got to show for our efforts? A few hundred pieces of eight for every man? That's not enough to buy our way out of trouble. Besides, we don't have Morgan's connections with the rich and powerful.'

There was a short silence, then Ringrose was speaking again. 'In the time we've been gone from Jamaica, anything can have happened. A new king on the throne, a different governor, wars declared and peace treaties signed. We've no idea of what might have changed, and how that will affect our return. We'll not find out until we get there.' He glanced up at the sky. 'Sun's close to its zenith, Hector.'

Hector walked aft with him to where Sidias was sitting cross-legged on the deck, still absorbed in his game of backgammon. He did not even glance up as their shadows passed over him. Ringrose took the noon sight and wrote down the reading. Hector noticed that his hand was shaking.

'How long do you think it is before we reach the mouth of the Passage?' Ringrose said, speaking loudly so that Sidias could no longer ignore him.

The Greek looked up grudgingly. He wrinkled his brow as if in deep thought before announcing, 'Five or six weeks.' Then he turned his attention back to the tavil board and ostentatiously moved one of the counters, making it clear that he had no interest in further conversation.

*

SIX WEEKS out from Paita, Sidias declared it was time to steer back towards the land and Sharpe followed his advice. As if to endorse the decision, the wind shifted into the ideal quarter, south-west, and with a fresh gale on the beam *Trinity* fairly tore along. The mood on the ship quickly became light-hearted and expectant. For some time past there had been a drop in the temperature of the air, and the men guessed that they were now far enough south to be in the region of the Passage. They acted with a careless exuberance as if to celebrate the final leg of their voyage. Hidden stocks of brandy and rum were broached, and several of the crew were fuddled, staggering and tripping as they made their way about the deck. Hector, however, was increasingly uneasy. He and Ringrose had been using dead reckoning to fix the ship's position. From time to time the two of them had disagreed on progress, the number of miles sailed, and whether or not there had been an ocean current taking them off track. On each occasion Hector had deferred to the more experienced man, partly because Ringrose's illness had made him argumentative and tetchy. Only the readings from the backstaff could be relied on, and they placed the vessel at 50 degrees south. But that was no indication of how close they were to land, and Hector had long ago decided that Sidias was worse than useless. The Greek was a gambler by nature, and would trust to luck that they would make a safe arrival on the coast. Whenever asked how soon they would raise the land, Sidias was evasive. His job, he always answered, was to identify the landfall, then indicate which way the ship should go. The Greek was so aloof that Hector felt obliged to seek him out that evening and ask if he was not concerned about how he would get back to Paita. In reply the Greek gave a dismissive shrug. 'What makes you think I want to leave this ship? There's no reason for me to return to Paita.'

'But you told me that the Alcalde forced you to become our pilot.'

'And he will make my life miserable once again if ever I return there. So I prefer to stay with this company.'

Taken aback by the Greek's self-regard, Hector went to join his friends. It was too chilly at night to sleep on deck, and they had slung hammocks in the aft end of the hold. Groping his way through the semi-darkness, he found Jezreel and Jacques already sound asleep. Only Dan was awake and when Hector told him of his concerns about Sidias' competence, Dan advised him not to fret. Perhaps in the morning they would have a chance to look through the notes copied from Lopez's derotero and see if they would be useful when they eventually made a landfall. In the meantime there was nothing to be done, and Hector should get some rest. But Hector was unable to sleep. He lay in his hammock, listening to the swirl of water along the hull and the creaking and working of the ship as *Trinity* forced her way through the sea.

Hector must have dozed off, for he came sharply awake to the sound of roars of panic. They came from directly above him, from the quarterdeck, and were loud enough to be heard above the sound of the waves crashing against the wooden hull. *Trinity* was heaving and pitching awkwardly, and water was surging back and forth across the bilge. The wind had increased in strength. In the pitch dark Hector rolled out of his hammock and felt for his sea coat. All around him were the noises of men scrambling out of their hammocks, asking questions, wondering what was happening. The shouts came again, more urgent now. He heard the words 'Cliffs! Land ahead!'

Clambering up the companion ladder and onto the quarter-deck, he came upon a scene of confusion. A sliver of moon rode a sky streaked with skeins of high, thin cloud. There was just enough light to show men frantically hauling on ropes, scrambling to reduce sail, and when he looked aft, the figure of Bartholomew Sharpe beside the helm.

'White water close on the port bow!' came a terror-stricken shout from the bows.

'Get the topsails off! Quick now!' bellowed Sharpe. He was half-dressed and must have run out from his cabin. A high-pitched squealing, frenzied and unearthly, set Hector's teeth on edge. For a moment he froze. Then he remembered that among the stores loaded at Paita had been a half-grown sow. The animal was being kept as a Christmas feast. She had sensed the mood of terror on board and was squealing in fright.

Sharpe caught sight of Hector and beckoned him over with furious gestures. 'That cursed numbskull of a pilot!' he shouted above the roar of the wind. 'We're entangled among rocks!'

Looking forward over the bowsprit, Hector caught a glimpse of something which showed white for a brief moment. Perhaps a hundred paces ahead, it was low down and above it loomed what seemed to be a darker shape though he could not be sure. Even with his limited experience he half-recognised waves beating against the foot of a cliff. *Trinity* answered the helm and began to turn away from the danger directly ahead, but almost immediately there was another cry of alarm, this time from his right. A sailor was pointing out into the darkness and there, not more than fifty yards away, was another eruption of white foam. This time he was sure. It was water breaking over a reef.

Sharpe was shouting again, even more angry. 'We've been driven into a skerry. I need sober lookouts, not tosspots. Lynch! Get up there into the foretop and sing out if you see a danger. Take your friend, the striker, with you. He sees things when others can't.'

Hector ran to find Dan and together they scrambled up the shrouds and onto the small platform of the foretop. The wind was strengthening still further, and on their exposed perch they peered forward, trying to see into the darkness. Below their legs the forecourse still bellied out, providing steerage way for the helmsmen. From farther aft came the shouts of men taking in the mainsail, urgently reducing the speed of the ship.

'How much longer until first light?' Hector yelled, trying to keep the alarm out of his voice. He could see almost nothing in the murk, only vague and indistinct shapes, some darker than others. It was impossible to judge how far away they were.

'Maybe an hour,' Dan answered. 'There! A reef or a small island. We're coming too close.'

Hector turned and shouted out the information. Someone down on deck must have heard him for he saw the foreshortened figure of a man running to the helm and relaying the message, then a group of men hastily sheeting in the triangular mizzen sail to assist the action of the rudder in turning the ship. *Trinity* changed direction, clawing up into the wind.

'More rocks, by that patch of foam,' announced Dan. This time he was pointing to starboard.

Hector cried out another warning and, standing up on the platform, wrapped one arm around the foretopmast. With the other arm he pointed which way *Trinity* should go. At that instant a cloud passed across the moon, and there was complete darkness. All of a sudden he was completely disoriented, the ship swayed beneath his feet, the motion magnified by his height above the deck, and he felt dizzy. For one heart-stopping moment his grip on the mast slipped, and he tottered, feeling that he was about to fall. He had a sudden, awful vision of smashing down onto the deck or, worse, landing in the sea unnoticed and being left behind in the wake of the vessel. Hurriedly he clamped his other arm around the mast, clutching it to his chest in a fierce grip, and slithered down to a sitting position. Within a minute the cloud had passed, and there was enough moonlight to see his surroundings. Dan seemed not to have noticed his brief horror, but Hector could feel his clothes clammy with cold sweat.

For an hour or more the two of them conned the ship from the foremast as *Trinity* swerved and sidled her way past one danger and then the next. Gradually the sky began to lighten and, very slowly, the extent of their predicament became clear.

Ahead stretched an iron-bound coast, a vista of grey and black cliffs and headlands which extended in both directions far into the distance. Behind the cliffs rose ridges of bare rock which became the slopes and screes of a coastal mountain range whose jagged crest was lightly dusted with snow. Nowhere was there anything to relieve the impression of monotonous desolation except an occasional clump of dark trees growing in sheltered folds of the austere landscape. Closer to hand were the small offshore islands and reefs which had so nearly destroyed the ship in the darkness and still menaced her. Here the surface of the sea sporadically exploded in warning spouts of spray or heaved and sank in sudden upwellings which warned of submerged rocks and shoals. Even the channels between the islands were forbidding. In them the water moved strangely, sometimes streaked with foam, at other times with the deep, blue-black slickness of a powerful current.

'Hang on!' said Dan. He had seen the telltale white flurry of a squall which had suddenly ripped up the surface of the sea and was now racing towards them. Hector braced himself. *Trinity* abruptly heeled under the force of the wind. From below them came the creaking sound of the foresail spar as it took the strain and then the sudden crack of something breaking. The squall was strong enough to lift a vaporous whirl of fine spray and send it over the ship, darkening her timbers and leaving a slick on the deck. Hector felt the moisture settle on his face and trickle down inside his collar.

A hail from the deck made him look down. Sharpe was beckoning to him, ordering him to return to near the helm. He made his way carefully down the shrouds, gripping tightly in case another squall struck, and reached the poop deck. Sharpe was no longer in a towering rage but seething with subdued anger. Beside him Sidias looked shamefaced, clearly ill at ease.

'Lynch, this idiot seems to have lost his command of English,' snarled Sharpe. 'Tell him that I want some sensible advice, not pretence and falsehood. Ask him in a language he understands what he recommends, which way we go.'

Speaking in Spanish, Hector repeated the question. But he knew already that the pilot had been feigning incomprehension.

'I don't know,' the Greek confessed, avoiding Hector's gaze. 'I have no knowledge of this part of the coast. It is strange to me. I have never been here before.'

'Is there nothing you recognise?'

'Nothing,' Sidias shook his head.

'What about the tides?'

Sidias nodded towards a nearby island. 'Judge for yourself. That line of the weeds indicates a rise and fall of at least ten or twelve feet and that would be normal for the parts of the coast I am familiar with.'

Hector relayed the information to Sharpe who glowered at the pilot. 'What about an anchorage or a harbour? Ask him that.'

Again the pilot could only speculate. He supposed there would be bays or inlets where a ship might find shelter, but anchoring was sure to be difficult. The drop-off from the land was usually so abrupt that an anchor seldom reached to the seabed before its cable ran out.

'We follow along the coast until we find shelter,' Sharpe decided. He had to raise his voice above the moan of the wind. 'God grant that we can scrape through.'

It was a wild, intimidating ride. Every member of *Trinity*'s crew was now up on deck, either spread along the rails or in the shrouds. Even the drunkards had sobered up. They knew the danger, the strain showing on their faces as they watched the reefs slide by. Sometimes their vessel came so close to disaster that her hull brushed fronds of seaweed writhing in the backwash of the swells. Only the skill of the helmsmen, responding to every shift of the current or change in the strength and direction of the wind, kept their ship from being driven into the turmoil of waves which broke and thundered against the cliffs. Finally, after nearly an hour of this unnerving progress, they came level with an entrance to a narrow bay. 'Turn in! And stand by to lower the pinnace,' Sharpe ordered. He had noted the area of calm water behind a low promontory. Here a skilfully handled ship might find shelter and lie at rest. More crucially, a great solitary tree stood on the point of land, only a few paces from the water's edge. *Trinity* sidled in and the crew began to clew up the foresail. As the vessel slowed, the pinnace splashed down in the water, and a dozen men rowed furiously for the land, towing the main cable behind their boat. They scrambled up the beach, made fast the cable around the tree, and *Trinity* gathered sternway. She fell back until the heavy rope came taut, and the ship slowed to a halt, tethered to the land and safe.

A sense of relief spread throughout the ship. Men thumped one another on the back in celebration. Some climbed into the rigging and out along the foremast yard and began to furl the sails. Sharpe was halfway back to his cabin when a last great gust of wind came raging over the promontory and struck the ship. Under the impact *Trinity* reared back like a startled mare against her bridle. The main cable sprang from the surface, water spraying from the strands of rope as they took the strain, and when the full force of the wind drove upon her, there was a loud, rending crack. The great tree holding the ship came toppling down, the ancient roots giving up their hold. *Trinity*, her sails furled, was helpless. The gust drove her backwards across the small bay and, with an impact that shuddered the length of her keel, she struck stern first upon the shingle beach. Above the shriek of the wind, every man aboard heard the sound as her rudder sheered. The vessel was crippled.

✳

FOR THREE WEEKS the wounded *Trinity* lay in the bay. A web of ropes fastened to boulders and posts driven into the shingle held her steady against the rise and fall of the tides while the carpenters worked to fashion and fit a new rudder. The great gust had been the gale's final stroke, and the wind was never again so fierce. Instead the weather was continually cold, damp and oppressive. Thick cloud clamped down, obscuring the mountains, so that the leaden sky blended with the slate-grey landscape. Those men who were not working on the repairs reverted to their endless games of cards and dice or prowled the beach and prised mussels off the rocks. They shot penguins to boil and roast. The flesh was quite palatable, being as dark as venison though oily. Dan volunteered to explore inland and came back to report no sign whatever of human life. The interior was too harsh and craggy to support settlement. He claimed to have come across unknown wild plants which might prove useful additions to the near-empty medicine chest, but this was only an excuse so that he and Hector could go ashore. They took with them the bamboo tube containing their copies of Captain Lopez's navigation notes.

Safely out of sight of the ship, they tried to make some sense of their notes, smoothing out the pages and putting them in order.

'I think this sheet shows the coast and the approaches to the Passage,' said Hector. He placed a page on the flat surface of a boulder and weighed the corners down with pebbles. 'But it has very little detail. The mountain range is shown as extending all along the coast, and there are at least two dozen islands marked. But they all look much the same. We could be anywhere.'

Dan ran his finger down the page. 'See here, the entrance to the Passage is clearly shown.'

Hector brightened. 'If our notes are accurate – and Captain Lopez's original is right – I'm confident that I could find the Passage. All we need to know is our latitude.'

Dan rubbed his chin. 'What if there's an overcast sky like these past few days and you cannot take a backstaff reading? I doubt very much that the crew will want to risk this coast again. They've had a bad fright already.'

Hector was about to reassure his friend that even a glimpse of the sun would be enough, when Dan added, 'And if we suddenly announce to the crew that we have these navigation notes, we'll bring further trouble on ourselves. They will want to know why we did not say so before.'

'Then we go around the Cape and not through the Passage, and say not a word to anyone about Captain Lopez's notes,' Hector answered. 'Those more general maps we took out of the *Santo Rosario* are good enough to get us around the Cape if we go to fifty-eight degrees and then turn east. After that, we should come into the Atlantic.'

He rolled up the papers and slid them back into the tube.

'Come on, Dan. No one wants to stay a moment longer in this dreary place.'

✳

So it turned out. *Trinity*, with her rudder repaired and rerigged with the cordage from Paita, took advantage of an offshore breeze and threaded her way through the skerries until she reached the open ocean. Shortly after, she turned south and sailed into waters known to her crew only from hearsay. There they came upon sights that confirmed the stories they had heard – immense blocks of blue-white ice, the size of small islands and drifting on the current, whales of monstrous size, and birds who followed the ship day after day, gliding on wings whose span exceeded the width of even Jezreel's outstretched arms. All this time the weather remained kind, and *Trinity* entered the Atlantic without enduring a single storm. Northwards next, the sea miles rolling by, the sun higher each day, and the temperature increasing. With no sight of land or other ship, *Trinity* might have been the only vessel on the ocean. To pass the time, the men reverted yet again to their favourite pastime – gambling. It was as if nothing had changed since the South Sea. Those who gambled lost most of their plunder to Captain Sharpe who, fearful of their resentment, took to sleeping with a loaded pistol beside him. Only Sidias was his rival for winnings. The Greek's cunning at backgammon meant he swept up most of what the captain missed.

Christmas came and Paita's sow was slaughtered and eaten under a clear blue sky while waiting for the fickle doldrum winds. By that time the men were so anxious for the voyage to end that they clustered around Hector and Ringrose as they took each midday sight, demanding to know how much progress had been made. Ringrose's health had improved with the warmer weather, and he had regained his usual cheerful manner. It was he who finally declared that they must make their landfall very soon. The following dawn a low, green island on the horizon was recognisable as Barbados, though the unwelcome sight of an English man-of-war in the offing led to a hastily called general council. It was decided to find a more discreet place in which to dispose their booty, and on the last day of January *Trinity* dropped anchor in a deep and deserted inlet on the rocky coast of Antigua. They had completed eighty days at sea.

'No one is to go ashore until I've had a chance to learn our situation,' warned Sharpe for perhaps the twentieth time. The crew were gazing impatiently at a small stone jetty and a handful of whitewashed houses nestled in the farthest curve of the bay. 'If the governor receives us, there'll be time enough for every man to enjoy his rewards. If he's hostile, then we go elsewhere.' He turned towards Hector. 'Lynch, you come with me. You look more presentable than most.'

Together the two men clambered down into the cockboat and were rowed towards the jetty. Seated beside Sharpe on the after thwart, Hector found himself recalling the last time he had gone ashore with a buccaneer captain so warily. That had been with Captain Coxon more than two years earlier and so much had happened since then: his own flight from Port Royal, the hurricane among the logwood cutters of Campeachy, the steamy march across the isthmus and the near-fatal charge on the stockade at Santa Maria, then the long plundering South Sea cruise that followed. He wondered what had happened to Coxon, whom he had last seen after the frustrated attack on Panama. Perhaps the buccaneer captain had given up seafaring and retired with whatever plunder he had amassed. But Hector rather doubted it. Coxon was the sort of person who would always be seeking to make one last lucrative coup.

The cockboat scraped against the rough stones of the jetty and Hector followed Sharpe up the steps. No one greeted them or paid the least attention. Indeed the few people on hand, a couple of fishermen mending nets and a man who might have been a minor government official, deliberately looked the other way.

'That's encouraging,' grunted Sharpe. 'It seems we don't exist. So no questions asked.'

Without even a nod to the onlookers, he began walking up the unpaved road that led past the little houses and over the brow of a low hill. At the point where the road began to descend they had a fine view over a larger, busier anchorage than the one they had just left. Sharpe paused for a moment to check what vessels lay at anchor.

'No sign of a king's ship,' he observed. Spreading across the slope below them was a modest-sized town of stone-built houses. A single, rather ugly church tower rose above their roofs. To Hector's eye the place looked haphazard and chaotic compared to the orderly Spanish towns he had become used to.

'Are we going to meet someone you know?' he asked.

Sharpe shot him a sideways look, full of cunning. 'Depends who is in charge. Antigua's not as prosperous as Jamaica, or even Barbados for that matter. Only a few plantations as yet, though doubtless they will come. The place is happy to make a bit of money with whoever comes to trade, if the price is right.'

He started down the hill and evidently knew his way for he went briskly along the main street and halted before the front door of a two-storey building more substantial than the others. A black servant answered his knock and when Sharpe asked if Lieutenant Governor Vaughan was at home, the black man at first looked puzzled, then beckoned them inside before retreating down a hallway. A few moments later a loud voice called, 'Who's looking for James Vaughan?' and a stout, red-faced man appeared. He was in undress, had removed his wig to reveal a scalp covered with a crop of short, sparse bristles. Draped around him was a loose dressing gown of patterned calico, and he was sweating heavily.

'My name is Captain Bartholomew Sharpe,' the buccaneer captain said. 'I'm looking for Lieutenant Governor Vaughan.'

The red-faced man took out a large handkerchief and wiped his forehead. 'Jim Vaughan is no longer the lieutenant governor,' he said. 'He's retired to his estate. Cane is the thing now.'

'Then perhaps I can speak with the governor, Sir William Stapleton,' Sharpe suggested.

'Sir William is not on the island. He's visiting Nevis in the course of his official duties.'

All this time the man's shrewd eyes had been sizing up his visitor.

'Captain, I did not see your vessel enter harbour. What did you say is the name of your ship?' he asked.

'We arrived only this morning, and are anchored in the next inlet.' It was clear that Sharpe did not wish to give further details. 'I had hoped to engage in a little discreet commerce during the visit.'

The man in the calico gown needed no further prompting. 'If you would step this way into my study, we can discuss matters in private,' he said.

He led them into a side room which had the bare look and slightly musty smell of a little used administrative office. On the shelves were several ledgers and minute books whose spines were mottled with mildew. The furniture was a plain wooden table and a cupboard, several chairs, and two large chests, one of which was securely padlocked and marked with a government crest.

'My name is Valentine Russell,' said their host, closing the door firmly behind them. 'I have replaced James Vaughan as lieutenant governor.' He crossed to the cupboard and took out three glasses and a squat dark green bottle. 'Perhaps I can offer you some refreshment. My rumbullion is prepared with a dash of lime, some tea and red wine. I find that it relieves the heat.'

The two men both accepted a glass of the liquid which Hector discovered left a metallic aftertaste in his throat. Valentine Russell drank off the contents of his glass in a single gulp and then poured himself a second helping from the bottle.

Sharpe came straight to the point. 'I have some merchandise aboard whose sale could be of mutual benefit.'

'What sort of goods?' enquired the lieutenant governor.

'Some silks, a quantity of plate, curiosities, lace . . .'

Russell held up his hand to stop him. 'Can you supply documents to say where the goods originate?'

'No, I'm afraid not.'

The lieutenant governor took another sip of his drink, his small, covetous eyes watching Sharpe over the rim of his glass. Hector thought that the lieutenant governor had a slight resemblance to *Trinity*'s Christmas pig. Then Russell set down his glass with a rueful sigh.

'I'm afraid, Captain Sharpe, things have changed entirely since the time of my predecessor. More rules, more questions. The authorities in London are very keen to encourage trade with our neighbours, especially those in the Spanish possessions. There have been a number of complaints from Madrid. They refer to hostile acts by foreign ships and their commanders. Much of it is nonsense, of course.'

Sharpe said nothing, but stood gently twirling the stem of his glass between finger and thumb, waiting for the lieutenant governor to continue.

'His majesty's representatives throughout the colonies have been instructed to put a stop to these alleged unfriendly deeds,' said Russell.

'Very laudable,' commented Sharpe dryly.

Russell treated him to a conspiratorial smile which, however, contained an undercurrent of warning. 'The commanders of the king's ships, both here in the Windward Caribees and in Jamaica, have lists of those who are suspected of harrying our new Spanish friends. I myself have not seen such a list, but I understand that they are remarkably accurate. The same commanders have instructions to seize any vessels which may have been implicated in lawless activities, arrest their crews, and hand them over for justice. All goods found on board are to be confiscated.'

'And you say that these strictures apply throughout his majesty's possessions?'

'Indeed.'

'Even in Jamaica?'

As Sharpe put the question, Hector wondered if the buccaneer captain was implying that he would dispose of his plunder in Jamaica if Russell was uncooperative. If so, Russell's response must have come as a shock.

'Above all in Jamaica,' said the lieutenant governor firmly. 'Sir Henry applies the law most strictly. Last month he presided at the trial of two most notorious villains found guilty of taking part in the late raid into Darien. One of the accused saved his life by turning state's evidence. The other, a most bloody and obdurate rogue, was found guilty. Sir Henry ordered that he be hanged from the masthead of a ship in harbour. Later his corpse was transferred to the public gibbet in Port Royal. It dangles there still, so I'm told.'

Hector had rarely seen Sharpe taken aback. But the mention that Morgan was executing his former accomplices made the wily buccaneer pause, though only for a moment. He reached into his pocket and pulled out a double-stranded bracelet of pearls, holding it up just long enough for Russell to appreciate the lustre of the pearls.

'Please give my compliments to James Vaughan when you next meet him,' he said. 'I brought with me this little trinket as a gift for Mrs Vaughan, but as I shall not have the opportunity of seeing them on this visit, perhaps you would be kind enough to hand it on with my respect and compliments.'

He passed the necklace over to the lieutenant governor who admired it for a moment before slipping it into the pocket of his dressing gown. Watching the charade, Hector was sure that the necklace would never reach Mrs Vaughan. Russell gave a small bow and said, 'Captain Sharpe, your generosity is to be commended. I feel that I should await further instructions from my superior before deciding whether or not you may do business on this island. Governor Stapleton is not expected to return to Antigua for another ten days. Should you wish to remain at anchor during that interval, you would be most welcome.'

'You are very kind,' replied Sharpe, 'and as there is much to be done aboard my ship, I wish you good day.' As Hector followed his captain out of the room, the young man was still puzzling where Sharpe had obtained the pearl bracelet which he had used as his bribe. Then he remembered the velvet purse of jewels which Donna Juana had handed over after the capture of the *Santo Rosario*. The jewels were general plunder and should have been distributed equally among the crew. But it seemed that Sharpe had helped himself.

✳

'THE ADVENTURE is over and finished!' announced Sharpe on *Trinity*'s main deck in the cool of the same evening. His audience was the general council of the crew, and a long silence greeted his declaration. Looking around, Hector counted less than sixty men. They were all that were left of more than three hundred raiders who had marched inland from Golden Island with such jaunty hopes of winning riches. The survivors were gaunt and shabby, their clothes a mass of patches and mends. Their vessel was equally care-worn, ropes knotted and frayed, sails threadbare, woodwork bleached to a dingy grey by months of sun and scouring spray.

'The lieutenant governor has granted us leave to stay at anchor here for ten days, no more. After that we must depart or face the consequences.'

'Where will we go?' demanded an elderly sailor. Hector

remembered him, a cooper by trade. He had made the barrels that had held their water supply for the long voyage around the Cape, a vital role. Now he was at a loss what to do. For him, like many of his shipmates, *Trinity* had become home.

'It must be each man for himself,' announced Sharpe. 'We go our separate ways. The authorities have lists of some of those who went to the South Seas. Any person on those lists is a wanted man.'

'Who made those lists and who is on them?' The question came from Gifford, the quartermaster. His bald scalp had turned the colour of mahogany, and his skin hung loose on his frame. He looked to have aged by at least ten years in the last few months.

Sharpe shrugged. 'I was not told. But some have already danced the Tyburn jig. Henry Morgan strung up one of our comrades recently.'

Gifford turned to address the entire crew. 'Does anyone wish to elect a new captain and continue with the cruise?'

His question was met with a silence. There was resignation in the expressions of the men. They were weary of voyaging. Those who had kept their plunder were eager to spend it.

'Very well,' announced Gifford. 'As quartermaster my duty is to supervise the final distribution of our prize. As soon as that is done, the company is dissolved.'

There followed an extraordinary ransacking of the ship. Men brought up on deck, piece by piece, all the items that *Trinity* had captured during her cruise and had not as yet been turned into cash – bolts of cloth for sail repairs, kegs of dried fruit, a firkin of wine, some painted church statues looted in La Serena, a spare ship's compass robbed from the *Santo Rosario*, even the lump of lead from her bilge which they had thought to melt down for musket balls. Everything was carried to the capstan and stacked in an untidy heap.

Abruptly, Sidias spoke up. Until now, the Greek had been standing to one side. He was not a member of the company and had no vote in the council. Nor was he entitled to a share in plunder though he had amassed considerable winnings from backgammon.

He walked over and stood by the pile of ship's goods. 'My name does not appear on any of the lists. Therefore I propose that I go ashore and find a broker to purchase these items.'

'How do we know you will not cheat us?' The question came from one of the men who had lost heavily to Sidias.

The Greek threw out his hands in a gesture of resignation. 'I will put down a deposit of fifty pounds in coin for this material. If I sell the stock for more, then I get to keep the profit as reward for my troubles. If I cannot find a buyer, then I would accept the loss. Surely that is fair.'

There was some murmuring among the men, and it was clear that Sidias was not entirely trusted. But when Gifford put the matter to the vote, it was agreed that £50 would cover the value and that the ship's launch would ferry Sidias and his goods to the jetty. After that, he was on his own.

The quartermaster moved on to other matters. 'It will be too dangerous to land as a single group. To do so would draw the attention of the authorities. Instead we go ashore in small groups, over the next few days, no more than ten or twelve at a time and disperse.'

'How do we do that?' asked the cooper.

Sharpe intervened. 'Buy passage on local ships and quietly leave. Your silver will open many doors.'

'And what about those who have no silver?' Hector searched the faces of the crowd, to see who had asked the question. The tone had been bitter. He saw it was one of a dozen or so men who were inveterate gamblers. During the return voyage they had wagered away all their plunder, mostly to Sharpe himself.

There was an awkward silence and for a moment Hector thought that there might be violence. He sensed a wave of sympathy wash through the assembled crew. A couple of the malcontents were armed. They could set upon Sharpe and give him a beating.

Sharpe must have spotted the danger for he turned to Gifford. 'Quartermaster, I propose that *Trinity* is given to all those who have no money. They can use the vessel in whatever manner they wish, though I suggest they sail her to a port where she will not be recognised as a Spanish built. Thus they get away from Antigua and may have a chance to earn some capital.'

There was a murmur of approval from the crew, and the moment of tension passed.

'Neatly done,' murmured Jacques beside Hector. 'Our captain is as slippery as ever. He's got rid of *Trinity* and saved his own skin.'

Gifford was already drawing lots to decide the order of disembarkation. Hector and his friends were among the earliest to be set ashore, and they had barely time to collect their share of plunder which amounted to some three thousand pieces of eight each, mostly in coin but also in broken pieces of plate before they were on their way to the jetty.

As they climbed up the steps they found Sidias already there, seated on a roll of sailcloth and looking very satisfied with himself.

'How will you get all this stuff to the town for sale?' asked Hector.

'I won't bother,' the Greek replied. 'It can stay here and rot.'

'But you just paid fifty English pounds for it,' Hector said.

'And I'll pay your giant friend another five shillings if he carries this into town.' With his foot Sidias nudged the heavy ingot brought up from *Santo Rosario*'s bilge.

'Lead's not that valuable,' said Hector.

'It's not lead,' answered the Greek with a crafty grin. 'Those nincompoops wouldn't recognise raw silver if they shat it out of their posteriors. This "lead" as you call it is a half-smelted silver from the Potosi mines. Fifty per cent pure. On its way for further smelting in Panama. I'd say it's worth seventy or eighty English pounds. Enough to set me up here as a shop-keeper.'

Jacques let out a groan, 'Hector, do you remember how many more of those ingots were in the *Santo Rosario*'s bilge? Seven or eight hundred wasn't it? So many that we thought it was nothing more than ballast and paid no attention. We gave away a fortune. The Spaniards in Paita must still be laughing themselves sick at our stupidity.'

EIGHTEEN

THE SUNNY Caribbean had been left far behind. A small group of port officials, dressed in long cloaks and broad-brimmed hats, stood waiting patiently on the wharf for the ship to make fast. A cold penetrating drizzle was drifting down, soaking everything it touched. The fronts of the warehouses which lined the dockside were streaked with rainwater dripping from slate roofs. The air smelled of damp, fish refuse and wet sacking. This was Dartmouth in Devon on a blustery March day, and the four friends were sheltering under the awning rigged to protect the cargo hatch of the merchant ship that had brought them from Antigua. It had been a plodding six weeks' voyage across the Atlantic, and the ship's agent had insisted on being paid in English coin, grossly overcharging them. But they had been glad to accept his price, knowing that every mile would put them at a greater distance from the South Seas raid. Their only concern had been to discover that a dozen others of *Trinity*'s former crew, including Basil Ringrose, were among their fellow passengers.

The mooring ropes were made fast, and the little covey of officials on the dockside moved forward as a gangplank was manhandled into place.

Without warning Jacques put out an arm, holding back his companions.

'What's the matter?' asked Hector.

'I'd recognise a police agent anywhere,' the Frenchman said softly.

'We don't have police in England,' Jezreel corrected him. 'That's only for uncivilised foreigners like you.'

'Call him what you want. But the tall fellow with the satchel is something to do with the law. And those other two close behind are the same. I spent too many months on the run in Paris not to recognise legal jackals when I see them.'

The tall man with the satchel was making his way onto the ship. Behind him, his two assistants took up position on either side of the gangplank, blocking it.

The ship's master, a rotund and genial Welshman with a beerswiller's belly, waddled forward from where he had been standing to supervise the process of docking. Hector was near enough to hear him demand of the stranger, 'From the customs office, are you?'

The tall man did not reply directly but opened his satchel and took out some sort of document which he showed to the captain. Hector watched the captain read through the paper, then glance nervously towards the place where Ringrose and the others from *Trinity* were gathered, waiting to disembark.

'Gentlemen!' he called out. 'Would you be kind enough to step this way? There's something which may require your attention.'

Ringrose and the others sauntered over though Hector could tell from their watchful manner that they were on their guard.

'This is Mr Bradley,' said the captain. 'He comes with a warrant from the High Court of Admiralty and has a watch list of persons whom he has been instructed to escort to London.'

The law officer consulted his hand bill. 'Which one of you is Bartholomew Sharpe?'

When there was no reply, he looked around the little group and read out Samuel Gifford's name. Again he received no acknowledgement, and this time he stared straight at Ringrose and said, 'I presume that you are Mr Ringrose. You fit the description I have here.' He consulted the paper again. 'About thirty years of age though may look younger, average height and well set up, curly chestnut hair and fair complexion.'

Ringrose nodded. 'I am Basil Ringrose.'

'You are to accompany me to London.'

'By whose authority?'

'I am a marshal of the court.'

'This is preposterous.' Ringrose's eyes flicked towards the gangway but he could see that there was no escape in that direction.

'He's taking only those who held some sort of rank on our expedition,' Jacques whispered to Hector.

Bradley folded up his paper and replaced it in the satchel. Turning towards Ringrose he announced, 'We leave for London in an hour's time by coach. Bring only essential personal possessions with you.'

'Am I under arrest?' demanded Ringrose.

'Detained for questioning.'

'And what am I to be questioned about?'

'His Excellency the Spanish ambassador has brought several complaints to the attention of the Court and demands redress. The charges include murder on the high seas, robbery and assault on Spanish possessions in contravention of existing treaties of friendship.'

'His Excellency the ambassador,' mimicked Jacques in the marshal's tight voice, but speaking softly, 'wields a broad brush. Where's that bastard going now? I doubt he's just getting himself out of the rain.' Bradley was following the captain towards his cabin.

'Probably off to inspect the ship's manifest,' said Dan, and was proved right when some minutes later, the captain's steward came over to where Hector was still standing with his friends. 'The marshal's asking for you by name,' the steward said, then added in a lower voice, 'He's a right puritan, that one.'

'I'll be there in just a moment,' Hector assured him, and as soon as the steward was out of earshot he turned to his friends. 'Get off the ship as soon as you can, and disappear! Take my sea chest and my prize money. Anything that may connect me with the *Trinity*.'

'You'll need to keep some money by you if they're taking you to prison, to sweeten the gaolers,' Jacques said.

'I've a few coins in my purse. Enough to see me through. I'll contact you when I know what's happening. Where will I find you?'

'In Clerkenwell,' said Jezreel at once. 'I'll take Dan and Jacques there and find lodgings for us. Ask for "Nat Hall" or the "Sussex Gladiator" in Brewer's Yard behind Hockley in the Hole. That's the name they would know me by from the days when I used to perform the stage fights. It's a rough part of town where few questions are asked. Also it's full of foreign mountebanks who perform in the sideshows when there's bull and bear baiting.'

As Hector turned to go, Jacques clapped him on the shoulder and said, 'Keep your wits about you, Hector, and rejoin us soon. Otherwise Jezreel will have me performing conjuring tricks, and Dan put up on display as a painted Indian.'

Ducking in through the low door to the captain's cabin, Hector came face to face with the marshal.

'Your name is Hector Lynch?' Bradley asked. He had taken off his hat, revealing that he wore his straggly grey hair long and tied back in a queue.

There was no point in denying it. That was the name Hector had used when buying his passage, and it was entered on the ship's passenger roster.

'You speak Spanish?'

The question took Hector by surprise. 'My mother was Spanish. Why do you ask?'

'My instructions are to detain one Hector Lynch, but the name appears on a separate warrant and no physical description is given. Only that he speaks good Spanish. It is important that I make the correct identification.' The marshal had the list of wanted men in his hand. 'His Excellency the Spanish ambassador has particularly requested that you be brought to justice promptly.'

Hector was thunderstruck. 'Why have I been singled out in this way?'

'That I am not at liberty to say,' replied the marshal stiffly. He gave a small, brittle cough. 'Please be ready to leave within the hour.'

*

DURING THE LONG, slow and muddy journey to London in the coach provided for their transport, Hector and Ringrose talked much about the marshal's watch list. When Hector told his companion about the interview with the lieutenant governor of Antigua, Ringrose gave a snort of disgust.

'The greedy swine! He didn't have enough men to seize *Trinity* so he took his bribe. Then the moment we were gone, he informed on us. There was plenty of time for his message to get here ahead of us in that tub of a merchantman, and have the marshal waiting on the quayside.'

'Do you think that Sharpe, Gifford and the others have been picked up as well?' Hector asked.

Ringrose looked thoughtful. 'Probably not Sharpe. He's astute. He told me he was going to Nevis before finding a ship bound for England. He must have suspected that vessels arriving direct from Antigua would be watched.'

The coach gave a sudden jolt on its unsprung axle as a wheel dropped into a rut. Both men had to hold on to their wooden seats or be thrown to the floor.

'Lynch, how is it that marshal's list is so accurate? He even had my physical description.'

'Maybe Henry Morgan had a hand in it. A poacher turned gamekeeper never relents.'

'But I've never met Sir Henry so he could not know what I look like.'

Hector watched the drenched countryside drag by and did not answer. He had his own suspicions of the informer's identity, but he was far more perplexed that the Spanish ambassador should be showing such a special interest in him. He could think of no reason why the ambassador was so anxious to arrange his prosecution.

Finally, after six days of sluggish progress, the coach deposited him and Ringrose at the destination that Mr Bradley had arranged – the Marshalsea Prison in Southwark. Despite brick walls topped by revolving iron spikes and a massive entry gate plated with iron, the Marshalsea proved much more comfortable than *Trinity*'s dank and rat-infested accommodation. They were shown to a set of well-appointed rooms and told that their meals would be brought in from the outside.

'Tomorrow morning, Mr Lynch, you are required to attend a preliminary assessment of your case,' Bradley told him in his punctilious manner. 'Customarily the High Court of Admiralty deals with matters of prizes taken by sea. It decides their legitimacy and value and awards portions. But there are new procedures to adjudicate on matters which might normally be dealt within a criminal court . . . that is to say, you will be appearing before a Court of Instance not a Court of Prize. Mr Brice, an attorney to the court, has been appointed to determine how your case should be dealt with.'

*

MR BRICE proved to be a man so unassuming and nondescript that for a moment Hector mistook him to be an under-clerk. The attorney was waiting to interview Hector in the prison governor's office next morning. Of middling height and indeterminate age, Brice's pallid features were so bland that Hector would later have difficulty in recalling exactly what Brice looked like. His clothing gave no clue to his status for he was dressed in a suit of plain drab whose only effect was to make him even less obtrusive. Had it not been for the gleam of penetrating intelligence when he caught Hector's eye, Brice would have seemed a very ordinary person of little consequence.

'My apologies for disturbing you, Lynch,' Brice began in an affable tone. Various legal-looking documents and scrolls were spread on the governor's desk and Brice was leafing through them casually. 'I need to ask you a few more questions in relation to a charge arising from information provided by our lieutenant governor in Jamaica. Namely, that you were an originator of an illegal scheme to despoil the territories of a ruler in treaty and friendship with our king.

'What is the evidence for this charge?'

Brice frowned. 'We will come to that. First, would you be kind enough to write a few words on this sheet of paper for me?'

'What should I write?'

'Some of those exotic Caribee names that we hear from time to time – Campeachy, Panama, Boca del Toro, half a dozen will do.'

Hector, bewildered by the request, wrote down the names and handed the sheet back. Brice sprinkled sand on the wet ink, fastidiously poured the excess sand away, then laid the sheet on the desk. Selecting a large scroll from the pile of documents beside him, he undid the ribbon which held it. Hector had presumed the scroll was some sort of legal document but now he recognised it as a map. His mind leapt back to the days in Port Royal. It was one of the sheets that he had copied for the surveyor Snead in Jamaica.

Brice compared Hector's writing with the names written on the map and gave a small cluck of recognition. 'The same hand,' he announced. 'The deposition placed before the Court states you provided maps and charts, knowing they were to be used in the planning and execution of an expedition contrary to the interests of His Majesty.'

'Who accuses me of this?'

Brice glanced down at his notes. 'The witness has signed his statement and sworn to its truth. He sent this map as his evidence. His name is John Coxon, and he styles himself "Captain". Do you know him?'

'I do.'

'There is also a letter from Sir Henry Morgan, the lieutenant governor in Jamaica. Sir Henry affirms that Captain Coxon's testimony is credible.'

Hector felt a twinge of satisfaction mixed with outrage. He had guessed correctly. It was Coxon who had provided Morgan with the names of those who had been on the South Seas raid. Coxon was the turncoat and informer. He was still seeking to curry favour with Morgan just as he had done when he had tried to hand Hector over, believing him to be related to Governor Lynch.

The attorney was speaking again. 'Did you provide maps to assist the planning and execution of this illegal raid?'

'I was destitute and without employment. I had no idea that the charts would be used in that manner.'

'Can anyone vouch for the truth of this or provide you with character?'

Desperately Hector tried to think of someone who might speak up on his behalf. Snead was far away and would never admit to copying. There was no one else who might speak up for him. Then he remembered the carriage ride from Morgan's plantation in company with Susanna and her brother and the friendship that seemed to blossom between them.

'There is someone,' he said, 'Mr Robert Lynch, the nephew of Governor Lynch, would speak up for me. He was in Jamaica when all this took place.'

Brice looked disappointed. His lips set in a thin line. 'Sir Thomas Lynch is unavailable as he left London only recently to return to his duties as governor. Unfortunately Robert Lynch also cannot be here.'

Hector detected the sombre note in the reply. 'Has something happened to Robert Lynch?'

'Six months ago he died of the flux and, it is said, of chagrin. He had lost a great deal of money in indigo plantation.'

'I'm sorry to hear it. He was kind-hearted and generous.'

'Indeed. Have you no one else to substantiate your story?' Brice was looking at him as if genuinely interested in helping him.

Taking a deep breath, Hector said, 'Perhaps Mr Lynch's sister, Susanna, would be able to give evidence on my behalf in place of her brother.'

The attorney raised his eyebrows in shock. 'Mr Lynch, if I were you I would think carefully before approaching that person. Sir Thomas Exton would not take it kindly that his daughter-in-law is called as a character witness in a criminal case.'

Hector tried to make sense of the reply. 'I'm sorry, I don't know what you mean.'

'Sir Thomas Exton is the Advocate General. He is also the senior member of the Admiralty Court. This means that he will be president of the Court if your case comes to trial. Last month his oldest son John – whom I may say has the reputation as an up-and-coming attorney in his own right – married Miss Susanna Lynch. That is why Sir Thomas delayed his departure for Jamaica. To celebrate the wedding.'

Hector's spirits sagged. The news of Susanna's wedding was not unexpected. He had always imagined that she would one day marry someone of her own background. But the knowledge that she was now the wife of a lawyer somehow made the announcement more hurtful.

'I admit that I copied the maps but I was merely using my experience in cartography in the same way that I assisted Mr Ringrose in making drawings and plans of all the anchorages and places we visited in the South Seas.'

For the first time in the interview Hector sensed that he had said something to assist his case. Brice said softly, 'You made maps in the South Seas? Tell me about them.'

'Mr Ringrose always took sketches of the places where we anchored, and he drew profiles of the coast whenever we were near land. I helped him. Occasionally we took soundings with lead and line. Much as the Spaniards do when they prepared their own deroteros and pilot books.'

'You have seen a pilot book for the Peruvian coast?' Belatedly Hector realised that Brice knew exactly what a derotero was.

'There was one aboard a vessel we captured – the *Santo Rosario*.'

'What happened to it?'

'It was returned to the Spaniards.'

A flicker of disappointment crossed the attorney's face.

'But we made notes and sketches before it was handed back,' Hector hastened to add.

'We?'

'My colleague Dan and I.'

Brice looked at Hector with narrowed eyes.

'If you still have this material, I would like to see a sample.'

'If you allow me to contact my friend, that can be arranged.'

Brice began rolling up the Caribbean chart. 'We will continue our discussion just as soon as you can produce some of those notes. Do you think you could have them available next week, perhaps on Thursday?'

'I'm sure that can be arranged.'

'I'll ask Mr Bradley to bring you to somewhere more congenial than these rather depressing surroundings.' He glanced around the prison governor's austere office as he wound the ribbon neatly around the rolled-up chart, pausing only to say in a quiet, confidential voice, 'Mr Lynch, I would be grateful if you talked to no one about my visit here today.'

'As you wish,' Hector assured him, though he was wondering why a lawyer like Brice knew such a complicated way to tie the ribbon. Either Brice was a fly-fisherman or he had sea-going experience.

✳

BY THURSDAY, when Bradley came to collect him, Hector had assembled the material Brice had requested. Dan had brought the bamboo tube containing the notes and sketches, and Ringrose had lent his journals from the South Sea. After Hector introduced Dan to the marshal, the three of them set off on foot into Southwark's tangle of alleyways. An overcast grey sky threatened yet another day of blustery showers as they joined the slow-moving mass of pedestrians, carts and carriages using London Bridge to cross the river. On the far side they turned right into a street lined with tall commercial buildings. After about a quarter mile they came to a shop front over which hung a trade sign showing an outline map of Britain and Ireland. Here Bradley led them down a narrow passageway and then up a flight of outside stairs to a large first-floor room at the rear of the building. Several windows looked out across London Pool and its constant activity of wherries and lighters attending to the needs of the anchored shipping. Beside a broad table littered with drawing instruments, Brice was waiting. With him was a stooped, rather bookish individual wearing a pair of spectacles.

The lawyer came quickly to the point. 'Mr Lynch, please show to Mr Hack your material from the South Sea.'

From his bamboo tube Hector slid the page copied from Captain Lopez's notes which he and Dan had consulted as they tried to decide where *Trinity* had so nearly been wrecked. The paper was creased and stained, and there were scuff marks where they had laid it out on the rock many months ago. Hack walked over to the window to examine their handiwork in the light. Beyond him the surface of the Thames suddenly flecked with white as a gust of wind riffled the water. A moment later came the sound of raindrops spattering against the window glass.

'What do you make of it, Mr Hack?' Brice was asking.

There was a long pause. 'Very interesting. The entrance to the Fretum Magellanicum agrees with Mr Jansson's depiction in his atlas, but here it is in greater detail.'

'Would such information help a navigator attempting the Strait?'

'Most certainly.'

'This provides extra detail,' said Hector holding out Ringrose's journal.

Hack took it from him and began to turn the pages slowly and deliberately until he came to Ringrose's sketch of the anchorage where they had mended *Trinity*'s rudder. Several moments passed before he looked up and said, 'If I had time to correlate the details in this journal with the page of navigation notes, I would be hopeful of providing a chart for this section of the coast.'

Earlier Hector had thought that Hack might be a sea captain. Now he knew that Hack was a professional cartographer.

Brice glanced at the bamboo tube Hector was holding. 'Mr Lynch, you say that you have other pages of navigation notes. Who made them?'

'The captain of the *Santo Rosario*. He was a very experienced mariner, and conscientious. Besides making his own observations, he compiled information from other captains, going back many years. There are details of anchorages and navigation dangers and port facilities.'

Brice picked up a pair of compasses from the mapmaker's table and began fiddling with them, opening and closing them as he considered Hector's statement. 'Mr Lynch, the Spanish ambassador, Señor Ronquillo, is pressing to have your case decided by the Court. He has personally intervened with His

Majesty who has agreed to his demand. I have an offer to make to you.'

'What do you have in mind?' Hector asked.

'If you agree to work with Mr Hack, correlating your notes with the general maps of the South Sea coast, I am willing to represent you in any action brought against you by the ambassador. I will ensure that you receive a fair hearing.'

Hector looked Brice in the eye. He was reassured by that same gleam of penetrating intelligence that he had noted on their first encounter. He decided that he had nothing to lose by trusting the attorney.

'If I'm to work on the maps, I'll need Dan to help me.'

'Of course. That will be easy. There is no mention of him or your other companions on the watch list we received from the Caribees.'

Brice spoke to the mapmaker. 'Mr Hack, I suggest that Mr Lynch and his colleague Dan spend some time with your staff. Not here at your official premises, but somewhere in the close vicinity.'

Brice gazed out of the window, thinking aloud. 'Of course the Spaniards are aware that we must have acquired some knowledge of the Peruvian coast. But as yet they don't know how much.'

'We also found a folder of more general charts aboard the *Santo Rosario*. They cover the coast all the way from California to the Cape and the Land of Fire,' Hector said.

'And where is this folder now?'

'It was given to Captain Sharpe.'

'Then we will find Captain Sharpe and get it. Our sources tell us that Captain Sharpe has reached London and is staying in lodgings in Stepney,' said Brice. He seemed remarkably well informed. The lawyer looked across at the marshal who had been standing patiently near the door. 'Mr Bradley, do you have with you the watch list?'

Bradley handed him the document, and Brice took a pen and struck out a name.

'It would seem sensible that I remove Mr Ringrose's name from the list of Gaol Delivery.'

'Why's that?' Hector dared to ask.

'Because Mr Ringrose will be your unwitting ally. With his help I'm sure that Mr Hack here can produce a South Sea atlas which will satisfy and distract the king. The basis of that atlas will be the folder of maps now in the possession of Captain Sharpe. The new atlas will be a work of art. It will be beautiful but of little practical use to navigators, and serve the dual purpose of reassuring the Spanish ambassador that we have learned little of real value. Meanwhile the more detailed version – your prime derotero as we may call it – will be lodged with the Admiralty against the time when it might come in useful.'

Brice's expression became very serious. 'Lynch, the Spanish ambassador remains most insistent that you are put on trial for piracy. I gather his people have been working hard to prepare evidence to place before the Court.'

Hector was taken aback. 'But I thought the Court of Admiralty was to oversee the gathering of evidence?'

Brice allowed himself a weary grimace. 'The ambassador has friends in high places, and permission has been granted for his legal counsellor to question you and prepare witness statements.'

'When is this to happen?'

'In three days' time marshal Bradley must bring you to the ambassador's residence where you will be interviewed. I have arranged that I will be present at the meeting and, as promised, I will do my best for you. But please bear in mind that officially we have never met, and that the outcome of the questioning will decide your future.'

✳

WILD HOUSE, the Spanish ambassador's mansion near Lincoln's Inn Fields, was a building designed to impress the visitor. Hector was intimidated by the imposing facade, its array of glittering windows separated by tall ornamental pilasters, and set off with a balustraded parapet which ran the full width of the building. Wild House was screened from public view by a tall brick wall and Hector had the sense of entering a secluded, private world as marshal Bradley escorted him across the broad gravel forecourt. A major domo opened the ornate double front doors and escorted the two visitors across a tiled entrance hall under a cupola decorated with scenes from classical mythology. Beyond it a long corridor, hung with tapestries, led to the rear of the house. There, without a word, the major domo indicated that Bradley was to wait in the corridor while he ushered Hector into what was evidently a private library. Most of the wall space was taken up with shelves of books, and the only light came in through a leaded window looking out on a small garden. A log fire was burning in a large grate to keep out the chill.

Involuntarily, Hector was reminded of his examination by the Alcalde of Paita. The furniture had been arranged in much the same manner. At a table, seated with his back to the window, was Brice, now wearing a lawyer's sombre black suit with a white tab collar. He glanced briefly at Hector, as if he had never seen him before, and then looked down and began to arrange the papers on the table before him with the same neat gestures that Hector recognised from the fiscal in Paita. It set him wondering if all lawyers were alike, with identical mannerisms and the same circumspect outward show. Next to Brice a secretary was ready to take notes, and at a separate desk a few paces away sat a man dressed with great elegance in a sleeveless jacket embroidered with silver thread over a white satin shirt. A glimpse of his feet beneath the table revealed that he was wearing fine chamois leather shoes. Hector supposed that he was an embassy counsellor who was to conduct the cross-examination.

'The purpose of this meeting is to establish whether you should face a charge of murder and piracy,' began Brice. 'Señor Adrian,' the counsellor gave a slight inclination of his head, 'is to present the evidence. The proceedings will be conducted in English as far as practicable.'

Hector was not invited to sit so he remained standing, feeling the thick carpet beneath his feet. Brice turned towards the Spaniard. 'Perhaps we may begin?'

The counsellor picked up a paper from his desk, cleared his throat and in strongly accented English began to read aloud. After a few sentences it was clear that he intended to deliver a lengthy preamble to the case. Brice held up his hand to stop him.

'Señor Adrian, from what I have already seen of the documents, the crux of what we have to decide today concerns the capture of the ship named *Santo Rosario* off the coast of Peru. Perhaps we can proceed directly to that event.'

With an exasperated look the counsellor searched through his pile of documents until he found the one he wanted, then once again he began to read aloud. He described the events of that day: the slow approach of *Trinity*, the moment when Captain Lopez had grown suspicious, the firing of the first cannon shot, the musketry that followed. As he listened, Hector slowly became aware that he had heard the contents before. It was, word for word, the same deposition that Hector had heard at Paita, read out to Maria. Grudgingly he had to admire the thoroughness of Spanish bureaucracy. Somehow the colonial officials in Peru had managed to supply the document from half a world away.

Señor Adrian came to the end of his recitation, and Brice turned his attention to Hector.

'Were you present during these events?'

Hector felt trapped. Faced with such a precise and accurate

account of what had happened, he could see no way of saving himself except to tell an outright lie and pit his word against Maria's testimony. Yet he knew that to contradict her sworn statement was a betrayal of what he felt about her, her honesty and her courage. He hesitated before answering, and when the words finally came out, there was a catch in his voice as he uttered the falsehood.

'I know nothing of the events you describe. I was aboard *Trinity* early in her voyage and only for a few weeks.'

The Spanish counsellor looked at him with open disbelief. 'All the accounts we have from Peru speak of a young man, of your age and description, who acted as interpreter and negotiator. You – alone of all the pirates – were seen face to face by our officials.'

'You'll have to prove that,' intervened Brice.

'I will, beyond all doubt,' snapped the counsellor. Turning to the secretary he said, 'Summon our first witness.'

The secretary rose from his chair and, crossing the library, left by a far door. He returned a few moments later. Behind him walked Coxon.

Hector suppressed a gasp of surprise. The last time he had seen Coxon had been at Panama on the evening before the buccaneer captain departed to return to the Caribbean. Then Coxon had been carrying plunder looted from the Spanish. Now he was serving them. Hector wondered how the buccaneer had managed to convince the Spaniards of his new allegiance, and at the same time maintain his links as an informant for Morgan. Whatever Coxon had arranged, he was clearly prospering. He was expensively dressed in a dark blue coat worn over a fashionably long waistcoat whose sleeves had been turned back to show his ruffled lace shirt-cuffs. Coxon had also put on weight. He was chubbier than before, there was even more grey in his reddish hair, and he was beginning to go bald. Hector enjoyed an instant of satisfaction from observing that Coxon had powdered his face and neck thickly in an unsuccessful attempt to hide the blotches and sores on his skin. Hector hoped that the damage to Coxon's complexion was permanent and owed something to the Kuna salve. Coxon gave him a malicious glance, full of quiet triumph, before turning to face the Spanish counsellor.

'Your name is Captain John Coxon?'

'Yes.'

'And you took part in the assault on His Catholic Majesty's possessions in the Americas two years ago?'

'Only briefly. I had been led to believe that we were campaigning against the heathen savages of the area, and they had been troubling the civilised settlers. As soon as I realised the truth, I withdrew my men.'

Hector was stunned. Involuntarily he thought of the phrase his shipmates used to describe a turncoat. He 'turned cat in the pan'. Hector stole a glance towards Brice. The lawyer's face was expressionless. Hector had a worrying feeling that Coxon's presence had also taken Brice by surprise.

'Do you recognise this person standing here?' asked the embassy counsellor.

Coxon's face was hard-set. He looked Hector up and down as if identifying an item of lost property. Hector was reminded of the pitiless reptilian look he had seen when Coxon seized the *L'Arc-de-Ciel*.

'He was one of the worst on the expedition. A number of your countrymen lost their lives when he promised them safe conduct, knowing that the savages were waiting in ambush to murder them.'

'Where did this happen?'

'At Santa Maria, in the Darien.'

Brice interrupted. 'Señor Adrian, this line of questioning is irrelevant. The charge we are here to substantiate is one of piracy on the high seas. The event your witness has described took place on land and within the overseas territory of Spain, and is therefore outside the jurisdiction of the Court of Admiralty. It will not be admissible.'

The Spaniard looked exasperated. He made a gesture of impatience. 'Captain Coxon, please wait outside. I will need you to give evidence in support of my next witness.'

As Coxon left the room, the smug expression on his face left no doubt that the buccaneer would take pleasure in doing Hector as much harm as possible.

'Please call the second witness,' said the counsellor. He was looking towards the door with an air of triumphant expectation.

Maria walked in.

Hector felt as if all the air had suddenly been emptied from his lungs. Maria was dressed in a plain russet gown with a lace collar, and her head was uncovered. She wore no jewellery and she looked the same as he remembered her, perhaps a little more mature, but just as composed. Hector was reminded of the moment when he had seen her standing in the little fishing boat early on the morning they had landed at Paita. Then, as now, she had seemed so self-contained, so sure of herself, and just as beautiful.

'You are Maria da Silva, and you are companion to Dona Juana, the wife of the Alcalde of Paita?' asked the counsellor.

'That is correct.' Maria's response was strong and clear.

'And you were aboard the *Santo Rosario* when the vessel was attacked by pirates, and witnessed the murder of her captain, Juan Lopez?'

'I did not witness his death but I saw his body later.'

'And you spent the next three weeks aboard the *Santo Rosario*, in company with your mistress, while the vessel was in the hands of the pirates.'

'That too is correct.'

Hector could not take his eyes off Maria. The initial shock of seeing her had given way to an urge to attract her attention, to re-establish contact with her and somehow not let it slip away. But she did not look towards him. Her gaze seemed to be fixed on the papers lying on the counsellor's polished desk.

Her questioner ground on. 'During that time or at any other time, did this man offer you violence or rob your possessions?'

Only then did Maria turn her head and look directly at Hector and their eyes met. He could read nothing in her expression, however hard he tried. To his dismay he saw a disinterest, a blankness as if he was a stranger.

'He did not.'

'As far as you know was he responsible for the death of Captain Lopez?'

'As I said, I did not see Captain Lopez die. I have no knowledge of the matter.'

The counsellor was becoming irritated. Hector detected that he wanted to clinch the matter.

'Maria da Silva, was this man a member of the crew of pirates?'

Maria looked again towards Hector. There was a pause of a few heartbeats and then she said quietly, 'He may have been aboard the other ship, but he never set foot on the *Santo Rosario*.'

Hector thought that he had misheard.

The counsellor was looking utterly taken aback. 'Do you say that he was *not* aboard the *Santo Rosario*?'

'Yes.'

The counsellor picked up the written deposition, and held the paper out for Maria to inspect.

'Do you recognise your signature at the bottom of this document?'

'Of course. That is my signature.'

'And was this statement not prepared in the presence of this young man and the Alcalde of Paita?'

'It was prepared in the office of the Alcalde. But I have never set eyes on the young man before.'

The counsellor took a sharp breath, expressing utter disbelief. 'Maria da Silva, this is a serious matter. You have been brought from Peru to serve as a witness to the piracy of the *Santo Rosario* and the murder of Captain Lopez. Yet you claim not to know one of the gang of brigands who was involved.'

'I repeat, I do not know this man. There has been some mistake.'

Angrily, the counsellor tossed the sheet on the table before him. Maria looked down at the floor and clasped her hands in front of her in a gesture that Hector recognised. It was a sign that Maria was stubborn and unshakeable.

Brice intervened smoothly. 'Señor Adrian, perhaps you have other witnesses?'

The Spanish counsellor was finding it difficult to conceal his exasperation. 'Not now,' he snapped.

'Then we should ask the young lady to withdraw.'

Hector watched Maria leave the room, his mind racing. He wanted desperately to believe that Maria had denied knowing him in order to protect him, but her repudiation of him had been absolute. It appeared that she had no difficulty at all in wiping out any recollection of him. Her rejection had been definitive and credible, and he felt as though a vast, icy space had opened between them. He no longer understood her.

'That will be all, Mr Lynch,' 'Brice was saying. 'You may leave this inquiry.'

Bradley was waiting outside, seated on a bench in the passageway. He got up with a look of concern on his face as Hector emerged from the library, and took him by the arm. 'Are you all right?' he asked anxiously. 'You seem pale. Mr Brice wanted to meet us after the interview, to discuss its outcome. His chambers are not far, in Lincoln's Inn. We should make our way there slowly and wait for him to conclude his business here.'

They had to wait for almost an hour. Brice's offices were what Hector had come to expect of him — two small rooms discreetly tucked away down a side street. Brice's clerk, a taciturn figure with the bony frame and frequent cough of a consumptive, brought them a small tray with two glasses and a bottle of canary wine and then left them alone. By the time Hector had drunk his second glass, he was beginning to feel less numb from the shock of his encounter with Maria. Gathering himself, he forced the recent image of her to the back of his mind, and tried to concentrate on his immediate difficulties: the likelihood of being tried at the Admiralty Court presided over by Susanna's potentially hostile father-in-law and Coxon's perjured claim that he had been involved in the planning for the South Sea Adventure. The future seemed very bleak.

To his surprise Brice, when he arrived, was looking as pleased with himself as his habitual reticence would allow.

'The Spanish ambassador is dropping his complaint against you, Hector,' he said. 'I discussed the matter with his counsellor, Señor Adrian, and we agreed that in the absence of his star witness, that attractive young lady, there is little prospect of his case succeeding.'

Hector took a moment to digest the unexpected news. 'The counsellor seems to have given up very easily.'

'It all goes back to those missing navigation notes. I managed to plant the idea in Señor Adrian's mind that if anyone had possession of them, it would be your captain, Bartholomew Sharpe. Doubtless the Embassy will now concentrate their enquiries in his direction.'

'What about Captain Coxon's accusation that I provided maps and charts for an illegal venture? Will I still have to answer for that?'

Brice allowed himself the glimmer of a smile. 'I am recommending to the Court that Captain Coxon's charge is dropped for lack of evidence. Should he continue to make such allegations, based on the map he sent us, I shall enquire how he acquired it in the first place. I will use the same threat if I hear he is again offering his services to Señor Ronquillo.'

He reached into his pocket and drew out a letter. 'This was

handed to me as I was leaving Wild House after my discussions with Counsellor Adrian.' From his guarded look, Hector guessed Brice had read the contents. He took the page and, unfolding it, read:

Dearest Hector,

Denying you was the hardest thing that I ever had to do in my life. Not until I entered the room did I realise why I had been brought to London and what the consequences might be. I hope you will understand my response. By the time this note reaches you, I expect I will be on my way back to Peru. There I rejoin Dona Juana whose husband has been promoted to the audiencia. I cherish every hour that we spent together. You will always be in my thoughts.

Maria.

Brice had been watching his reaction. 'I would suggest that as soon as your work with Mr Hack is done, it would be prudent if you quietly disappeared. This would avoid any difficult questions which might arise later. If you were thinking of a sea career, a position as a ship's navigator could be arranged for you. Clearly your talents lie in that direction.'

✳

HECTOR'S MIND was in a whirl. His circumstances seemed to be changing by the minute. New opportunities were opening up. Yet all he could think of was Maria and what she had been feeling as she stood opposite him in the interview. Above all, that he had mattered to her ever since the days in the South Sea. Belatedly he became aware of Brice waiting for a response.

'What about my friends? Two of them, Jezreel and Jacques, are already lying low. They were with me in the South Sea. They too might be picked up and questioned. And I'll have to ask Dan what his plans are after we've completed our work on the South Sea charts.'

'Berths could also be found for all your friends, if they care to join you,' Brice assured him.

Hector's thoughts were racing ahead. 'If I am to go to sea again, it is on one condition.'

'What is that?'

'That I have a choice of the ship on which we sail.'

Already he was thinking that he would try to persuade his three friends to join a vessel on a westward voyage. That was the direction in which – if he persevered and fortune was with him – he might eventually find his way to Maria again.

HISTORICAL NOTE

On Saturday 10 June 1682 Captain Bartholomew Sharpe and two of *Trinity*'s crew appeared on a charge of piracy and murder before the High Court of Admiralty in Southwark. The advocate general, Sir Thomas Exton, presided. The jury found all three men not guilty, though gave no reason for their decision. The Spanish ambassador to London, who had pressed for their trial, was outraged. Four months later William Hack produced a lavishly illustrated book of Pacific charts, with a dedication to King Charles II from Bartholomew Sharpe. This atlas was of limited practical use to mariners, but other, much more detailed versions of this South Sea atlas entered private circulation.

Basil Ringrose, who had played a major role in navigating the *Trinity*, was never brought before the court. His journal, illustrated with coastal views and harbour plans along the South American coast, was published three years later, also with Hack's cooperation.

Captain John Coxon continued to operate in the Caribbean and turned 'cat in the pan' several more times. Governor Lynch even hired him to hunt down pirates, but Coxon could not resist reverting to his former trade as a buccaneer. He attacked Spanish settlements and looted foreign ships. Several warrants were issued for his arrest. He was never captured.

*The story of Hector Lynch continues in
the next book in the Pirate series*

PIRATE

VOLUME THREE
SEA ROBBER

Ambushed by a gang of hardened sea robbers headed for the South Sea, Hector Lynch, pirate and fugitive, must navigate their vessel on a nightmarish journey through the stormy seas off Cape Horn. There Hector uncovers the macabre and eerie remains of a small warship entombed on an ice float. Her only crew are two skeletons – the unfortunate captain and his dog, both frozen to death.

When his ruthless shipmates abandon him in Peru, Hector learns from the dead captain's brother that Maria, the young Spanish woman who stole his heart and whose false testimony saved him from the gallows, is now living on the remote Ladrones, the Thief Islands, on the far side of the Pacific.

Hector's epic voyage to reach Maria will bring him face to face with a Japanese warlord who submits trespassers to his island to a deadly duel and a naked Stone Age tribe who file their teeth to sharp points and sail boats that outpace the fastest galleon.

The first chapter follows here.

ONE

IT WAS NUMBINGLY HOT, even in the shadow of the fort. Hector Lynch felt his shirt sticking to his back despite the afternoon sea breeze which stirred the shrivelled tips of the palm thatch over his head. The lean-to was built against the fort's seaward wall, and the wind carried the sound of the surf, a constant rumble as waves crested and broke on the long expanse of sandy beach. At a distance the regular lines of crashing foam were hypnotically beautiful. Their brilliant whiteness contrasted with the translucent jade green of the sea behind them. But, up close, he knew from experience that the surf was a menace. The curving walls of water churned and tumbled and threatened to overset any small boat that risked a landing. He had a fine view of the anchorage from where he sat. Five ships were waiting to take on cargo half a mile out to sea. They were moored safely in ten fathoms of water, anchors firmly lodged in good holding ground. Yesterday a longboat from one of them had attempted a landing through the surf and been thrown upside down. A man had drowned, his corpse eventually pulled from the water by one of the local fishermen, whose canoes were better able to deal with the breakers.

Hector looked down at the ledger book open on the rough plank table before him. It was hard to concentrate in the stifling heat. 'Cutlasses, carbines, musketoons, amber beads, cristal beads, rough coral, small shells called cowries,' he read. These were what the slave dealers expected. This was the Guinea coast, and the *Carlsborg* which had brought him and his three friends to west Africa, was among the ships waiting to complete her human lading. Her supercargo normally kept the accounts, but he had died of smallpox the previous week, and Hector had been charged with drawing up an inventory of goods remaining for barter.

A movement out to sea caught his attention. A launch was putting out from one of the anchored ships and heading towards the beach. Either the oarsmen were very confident or the surf had abated a little. He watched the boat approach the area where the waves began to heap up, and there it paused. He could see the coxswain standing in the stern, scanning the backs of the waves, waiting for the right moment. Faintly over the roar of the surf, Hector heard a shouted command. A moment later the rowers were digging their blades into the water, urging their boat forward to catch the sloping back of a wave, then riding just behind the crest as it rolled towards the beach. The final twenty yards were covered in a frothing welter of foam. Then the launch, still on even keel, was cast surging up the beach. Two men leaped out and grabbed hold to prevent their boat being sucked away in the backwash. A small crowd of natives came running to help manhandle her further up the beach. The landing had been neatly done. The half-dozen men who had landed began walking across the sand, heading towards the fort.

Hector turned back to his ledger. What on earth, he wondered, were the 'perputtianes and sayes, and paintradoes'? Maybe these were Danish words. The supercargo had written his other entries in English, though both *Carlsborg* and the fort belonged to the Det Vestindisk–Guineiske kompagni, the Danish West India–Guinea Company. Perhaps someone in the fort would be able to translate.

An eddy of the breeze along the foot of the fortress wall brought a whiff of some foul smell. It was the stench of stale sweat and human waste combined with the sickly sweet odour of rotting fruit. The smell came from iron grilles set low in the wall, almost at the level of the sandy ground. Behind the metal bars lay the 'storerooms' as the dour Danish commandant called them. Hector tried not to think about the misery being suffered by the inmates crammed in the heat and semi-darkness, awaiting their fate. Hector, still barely into his twenties, had spent time as a slave in North Africa. Kidnapped from his Irish village by Barbary corsairs, he had been sold in the slave market of Algiers. Yet he had never been exposed to such vile conditions. His owner, a Turkish sea captain, had valued his purchase and treated Hector generously. The young man shifted uncomfortably on his bench at the memory. To please his master, Hector had agreed to convert to Islam and be circumcised. He had since abandoned all religious faith, but he still recalled the shocking pain of the circumcision.

The recollection of his days in Algiers made him look across at his friend, Dan. The two of them had met in the slave barracks of Barbary and eventually gained their freedom. Now Dan was seated across the table, his mahogany-coloured face bent over a sheet of parchment and concentrating as he drew a picture. He had tied his long black hair in a queue so that it did not interfere with his pen and coloured inks. Dan did not appear much affected by the heat. Maybe that was because he was a Miskito Indian from the Caribbean coast, where the summers could be almost as hot and humid.

'What's that you're drawing?' Hector asked.

'A bug,' answered Dan. He lifted an upturned wooden bowl on the table by his elbow, and Hector had a glimpse of a huge beetle. It was half the size of his fist, its shell yellow-orange with black stripes.

'I've never seen anything like it before,' Dan said. 'In the jungles back at home we have plenty of bright shiny beetles but nothing nearly so big, nor quite this colour.' He clapped the cup back over his captive before the insect could escape.

'I hope the captain is quick in filling his quota,' observed Hector. In his pocket was a letter written by a young Spanish woman, Maria. He read it at least a dozen times each day and by now the paper was falling to pieces along the folds. Maria had spoken up for him the previous year when he was on trial for piracy in London. The prosecution had been relying on Maria's statement for his conviction, and when she had retracted her evidence at the last moment, the case against Hector collapsed. He had been allowed to go free on condition that he left the country. Maria had returned to South America, and Hector had set himself the task of finding her again. The voyage from West Africa to the Caribbean would be the first leg on that quest, though he loathed being involved in the slave trade.

'Let's hope there's been a local war upcountry. That'll mean plenty of prisoners for sale,' answered Dan. A week ago the *Carlsborg*'s commander had set off inland with a party of sailors. He intended to negotiate directly with the local chiefs because the stock of slaves held in the fort had already been promised to other ships.

Hector thought Dan's remark was very callous. Then he remembered that the Miskito were notorious slavers, who raided the neighbouring tribes and took men, women and children.

He was about to change the subject when a mocking voice behind him announced loudly, 'If it isn't young Lynch, and poring over a book as usual.'

Hector turned in his seat and found himself looking into the cynical gaze of a man of middle age who, despite the heat, was wearing a smart coat of bottle-green serge with a lace jabot tied at his neck. It took Hector a moment to recognise his former shipmate John Cook, whom he had last seen off the coast of South America. That had been during the buccaneering raid that had nearly led to Hector's execution. Judging by the motley collection of rough-looking seamen behind him, John Cook still kept the same raffish company.

'Still with your Indian friend, I see,' commented Cook smoothly. Hector remembered Cook as someone ruthless yet astute, quick to seize an opportunity or to save his own skin. He and a number of the other buccaneers had deserted the South American expedition when they judged the risks of being caught and executed by the Spanish colonists were getting too great.

'How did you manage to escape the thief takers in London? I had heard you were on the wanted list,' said Cook.

Hector did not answer. His visitor was referring to the trial at which Maria had changed her evidence.

'And that other friend of yours, the big man? I would have expected him to be here.'

'If you mean Jezreel,' Hector replied, 'he's out on our ship as he's a watch keeper for the day.'

'Which ship is that?' enquired Cook, squinting against the glare as he looked out to sea.

Belatedly Hector realised that Cook and his companions were the party of sailors he had just seen come ashore in the launch. 'The big merchantman, flying the Danish flag.'

'A fine vessel. She looks well armed.'

'Thirty-two guns.'

'Hmm . . .' Cook looked impressed. He turned to face Hector. 'But a ship is only as good as her crew. I didn't know that Jezreel was a sailor. I thought he was more a swordsman, a professional pugilist.'

'*Carlsborg* is short-handed. Her captain has gone inland with half the crew to see if he can find a source of prime slaves. There are few to be had at the fort.'

'I wouldn't know about that,' said Cook. 'We haven't had time to pay our respects to the governor. Not that we will be staying very long.'

'What brings you here?' Hector asked cautiously. Something

about Cook and his ruffianly companions made him wary. They didn't look like merchants interested in trade. 'What happened after you and the others left us off Peru?'

Cook looked vague. 'It's a long story. Back in the Caribbean some of us found regular employment. A few gave up the sea altogether. But recently myself and my colleagues here got an offer. A group of investors asked if we might try a roving commission . . .'

His voice trailed off. He was gazing out at the anchored ships, a thoughtful look on his face. He glanced down again at Hector and said, 'So you've become a bookkeeper.'

'We buried our supercargo a week ago. I've been asked to take over temporarily.'

'It's good to meet a former shipmate. If you've got a spare moment, perhaps you can show me around.'

Grateful for an excuse to put aside the ledger, Hector got to his feet and led Cook around the side of the fort, heading towards the main gate. The rest of the shore party stayed behind in the shade of the lean-to. As Hector left he heard one of them ask Dan if he knew where they could find some palm toddy as their throats were dry.

'I'm elected captain for the venture,' said Cook casually. His remark confirmed what Hector had begun to suspect. Only buccaneer crews chose their captains by popular vote. Merchant crews obeyed officers appointed by the owners. Cook was tactfully letting it be known that he and his men had returned to buccaneering. They had gone back to a life as sea robbers.

'You wouldn't care to join us, would you?' said Cook softly. 'I seem to remember that you've some medical knowledge which could come in handy, and your friend is an excellent striker.' The skill of the Miskito Indians at harpooning fish and turtles was greatly valued among buccaneers. It fed hungry crews.

Hector muttered something about having to consult with his companions, but his reply seemed only to encourage Cook.

'I'm sure that Jezreel would be more than welcome. And also the Frenchman who was usually in your company – what's his name?'

'Jacques.'

'Yes, Jacques. I can still taste the pimento sauce he made for us when we were off Panama.'

Cook was pressing his point very strongly, Hector thought. He decided to pry a little further. 'You're not planning to return to the South Sea, are you?'

'We called in here to wood and water. It'll be a long voyage, south and west across the Atlantic, then through the Magellan Strait and along the coast of Peru. But it's the route that will bring us there undetected.'

Hector's mind raced. Here, unforeseen and very tempting, was the perfect chance for him to reach Peru directly and find Maria. If he stayed with the *Carlsborg*, the best he could hope for was to arrive in the West Indies. From there he still had to make his way overland across Panama and onward to Peru. If his identity was discovered by the Spanish during this journey, nothing would save him a second time.

'Which is your ship?' he asked.

They had passed along the length of the fort's wall and were about to turn the corner below the eastern bastion, losing sight of the anchorage. Cook paused for a moment and pointed. 'There, anchored just astern of your Danish ship. That's our vessel. We've decided to call her the *Revenge*.'

He gave Hector a meaningful glance. It occurred to the young man that Cook and his colleagues were seeking retribution for the defeats inflicted on them during their incursion into the Pacific. Hector's mood of excitement subsided abruptly. Maria, who had saved his life, was Spanish, and he had no desire to go fighting the Spaniards again.

Also, the *Revenge* looked ill suited for such an ambitious enterprise. Cook's ship was shabby and sea worn, and much smaller than the *Carlsborg*. She looked as if she carried eight cannon at most, and he wondered how much success the *Revenge* would have against colonial shipping in the South Sea. The Spanish vessels would be much better armed after their earlier experience with a buccaneering raid. He decided that, on the whole, he would be wiser to stay with the *Carlsborg*.

They resumed their walk along the foot of the fortress wall. The massive grey and white stones reflected the heat. Glancing up, Hector saw a Danish sentry watching them incuriously from the battlements. The man had draped a chequered cloth over his head to keep off the sun and looked bored. Standing guard on a slaving fort was grindingly dull work. There was little risk of attack from the outside, so the job was more like being a prison warder. What mattered was to prevent a rebellion and escape by the slave inmates.

The main gate stood open, and they turned in. Ahead, the main compound was an open expanse paved with brick and shimmering in the heat. On their right were the slave holes, dreaded for good reason. Hector had been shown them briefly and the sight had left him sickened. The slave holes were used as punishment. The size and shape of large bread ovens, they were just large enough for one man to be thrust inside. Then the door was locked. Once incarcerated, the victim was left to broil until the captors decided that he risked dying of suffocation. Often they preferred to pull out a corpse.

An African was standing at the foot of the flight of steps leading up to the commandant's office. His billowing robe of yellow and orange served to emphasise his muscular bulk, and he must have stood at least six feet six inches tall. A three-cornered cocked hat, edged with silver braid and decorated with a cluster of drooping ostrich plumes, was placed squarely on his head. In one hand he held his badge of office, a long, elaborately carved staff. With the other he was fanning himself with a delicate Chinese fan. As the two white men approached, he looked them up and down in a calculating manner. His fleshy face was marked with tribal scars and the whites of his eyes were discoloured and bloodshot. Judging the visitors to be unimportant, the chief deliberately turned away.

'Vicious-looking bastard,' commented Cook under his breath.

'He's probably from the Akwamu tribe. One of their chiefs. They control the immediate area around the fort and drive a very hard bargain when it comes to selling slaves.' Hector explained.

'That's not all they have to sell. Look at those teeth!' Cook had spotted a pile of elephant tusks piled in one corner. His covetous tone of voice made Hector wonder for one moment whether the buccaneer captain was daring to think of plundering the fort. But the young man dismissed the idea. Cook had too few men to risk an attack.

They walked on across the compound. There were very few people about apart from the native chief and his attendant, who held a parasol over his master, and a trio of Danish soldiers. Tunics unbuttoned, they were lounging in the shade of the arches that led to the dormitory for the garrison.

'It would be interesting to see where the slaves are kept,' said Cook. The slave pens lay directly ahead, behind a row of stout iron-bound doors on the far side of the compound. Hector had never visited the holding pens before, but *Carlsborg*'s quartermaster, a man experienced in the slave trade, had told him that the fort was designed for smooth handling of the human contents. A brick-lined passageway pierced the outer wall and led directly from the pens to a gate overlooking the beach. When the time came to load the *Carlsborg*, the slaves would be chained together in batches, led down the passageway, then marched directly across the strand to where boats were waiting to run a shuttle service out to the ship. Hector had asked whether *Carlsborg* had enough boats for the task, only to be told that the local fishermen made a handsome living by hiring out themselves and their canoes as transport.

The iron-bound doors were locked. With no one to give

them any directions, the two men climbed a wooden stairway that led to an upper floor. Here they came to a small wooden door, which was ajar. Entering, they found themselves in a long corridor that ran almost the full width of the building. After the blinding glare of the compound, it took a moment for Hector's eyes to adjust to the deep gloom inside. The rank stench which he had smelled earlier was now so strong that he had to swallow hard to prevent himself gagging. In the opposite wall of the corridor he could make out the outline of a small, heavily barred window. Dimly he was aware of more windows on either side where the gallery stretched away into the darkness. He stepped up to the window and peered in.

*

HE WAS LOOKING DOWN into a dungeon. From a height of a dozen feet it was difficult to see much of what was immediately below him, but the dungeon appeared to be about fifteen paces square. The only source of light and air were three small square windows on the far wall. They were set close to ceiling height and showed that the roof of the cell was a curved vault of dressed stone. Nearly all the light fell on the far end of the dungeon so it was there that he could see most. The floor was thickly covered with humans. They were seated on the flagstones, their heads bowed, arms clasped around their knees. A few had somehow managed to find space to lie down. Hector wondered if some of them might be dead or very sick. His nose told him that they had no latrine, and he tried to work out how such a dense mass of humanity could be fed and given water. Right beneath where he stood the light was so poor that it was difficult to distinguish individuals. They all seemed to coalesce into one shadowy, intertwined mass. Uncannily, there was no sound except when someone coughed or gave a low moan. A sense of hopeless resignation seemed to press down on this thick carpet of humanity. Hector was appalled.

Cook's face was just beside him, only inches away. The

captain was also peering into the dungeon. Hector smelled some
sort of perfume the captain was using. 'A bachelor's delight!'
Cook breathed wonderingly. Hector puzzled for an instant, and
then understood. Several of the captives in the dungeon had
sensed that they were being observed. They had raised their
heads and were looking up towards the spy hole. Hector could
just make out their faces and the occasional gleam of an eye.
He saw that every person in the dungeon was a woman. This
was a dungeon exclusively for female slaves awaiting shipment.

'*Al solgt*,' said a husky voice. A Danish gaoler was standing
in the corridor, a few paces away. He was tapping his shoulder
with one hand.

Hector stepped back from the window. He remembered
from the supercargo's ledger that *solgt* meant 'sold'. The Dane
had presumed that they were potential slave buyers examining
the sale stock.

'How do you feed the prisoners?' Hector asked. He mimed
his question by pointing to his mouth and pretending to eat
and drink, then gesturing towards the dungeon. The gaoler
imitated picking up a long-handled shovel, loading the blade,
then thrusting it between bars.

'Like feeding animals,' muttered Cook.

'*Kom!*' The Dane made it clear that the visitors should
leave. He escorted the two men back to the door at the head of
the stairway, ushered them out, and then closed the door behind
them.

'I've seen enough,' said Cook as they walked back across
the compound. They were passing a blacksmith's workplace.
Instead of horseshoes there were heaps of chains and ankle
rings. Cook stopped. Hanging from a row of hooks were
several long thin metal rods.

'That's what the gaoler meant when he touched his shoulder. Those rods are branding irons. When the slaves are sold,
they're branded on the chest to show who their new owner is.'

He paused, as if a thought had occurred to him. 'That

Frenchman, your friend, has a brand on his cheek as I remember?'

'Yes,' answered Hector. 'The letter G. It stands for "galerien". It was burned on him when he was convicted in France and sent to the royal galleys. But the mark hardly shows when he is suntanned.'

'Then perhaps you would ask him if he could come across to the *Revenge* later this evening and meet one of my crew. He's another Frenchman, also an ex-convict, and speaks very little English. He's very sick, and likely to die. Another case of Guinea fever. Perhaps your Jacques can have a few last words with him.'

'Jacques is out on the *Carlsborg*, with Jezreel. They're on the same watch.'

'Then why don't I bring you and your Indian friend out to your ship on *Revenge*'s launch. You can ask Jacques if he'll do this favour. I would appreciate it.'

'We'll have to wait until the surf eases. That's usually once the sea breeze drops after dusk.'

'And when does Jacques have to go back on watch?'

'Tomorrow morning. Dan and I will be joining them.'

'Sounds as though you all stick together. Just like the old days.'

'That's true.'

'Then it's settled. I'll see you and Dan on the beach around sunset and bring you back out to the *Carlsborg*.'

Cook straightened the lace at his neck and brushed a speck of dust off the sleeve of his coat.

'Lynch, think over my offer about joining the crew of the *Revenge*. Meanwhile I had better pay my respects to the commandant.'

He turned away and went towards the governor's office, leaving Hector with the distinct feeling that something was not quite right, that John Cook had been hiding the real reason for their conversation.

extracts reading groups
competitions books new
discounts extracts
competitions
books new
events books
extracts
new reading groups
interviews
events extracts
discounts
new books events
events new events
discounts extracts discounts
www.panmacmillan.com
extracts events reading groups
competitions books extracts new